PENGUIN BOOKS

THE GOLD BAT
AND OTHER STORIES

P. G. Wodehouse was born in Guildford in 1881 and educated at Dulwich College. After working for the Hong Kong and Shanghai Bank for two years, he left to earn his living as a journalist and storywriter, writing the 'By the Way' column in the old *Globe*. He also contributed a series of school stories to a magazine for boys, the *Captain*, in one of which Psmith made his first appearance. Going to America before the First World War, he sold a serial to the *Saturday Evening Post* and for the next twenty-five years almost all his books appeared first in this magazine. He was part author and writer of the lyrics of eighteen musical comedies including *Kissing Time*; he married in 1914 and in 1955 took American citizenship. He wrote over ninety books and his work has won world-wide acclaim, being translated into many languages. *The Times* hailed him as 'a comic genius recognized in his lifetime as a classic and an old master of farce'.

P. G. Wodehouse said, 'I believe there are two ways of writing novels. One is mine, making a sort of musical comedy without music and ignoring real life altogether; the other is going right deep down into life and not caring a damn . . .' He was created a Knight of the British Empire in the New Year's Honours List in 1975. In a BBC interview he said that he had no ambitions left now that he had been knighted and there was a waxwork of him in Madame Tussaud's. He died on St Valentine's Day in 1975 at the age of ninety-three.

P. G. WODEHOUSE

THE GOLD BAT
AND OTHER STORIES

PENGUIN BOOKS

Penguin Books Ltd, Harmondsworth, Middlesex, England
Viking Penguin Inc., 40 West 23rd Street, New York, New York 10010, U.S.A.
Penguin Books Australia Ltd, Ringwood, Victoria, Australia
Penguin Books Canada Limited, 2801 John Street, Markham, Ontario, Canada L3R 1B4
Penguin Books (N.Z.) Ltd, 182–190 Wairau Road, Auckland 10, New Zealand

The Gold Bat first published by A. & C. Black 1904
The Head of Kay's first published by A. & C. Black 1905
The White Feather first published by A. & C. Black 1907

Published in Penguin Books 1986
Reprinted 1986

Made and printed in Great Britain by
Richard Clay (The Chaucer Press) Ltd,
Bungay, Suffolk

To
THAT PRINCE OF SLACKERS,
HERBERT WESTBROOK

CONTENTS

I

The Fifteenth Place

"Outside!"

"Don't be an idiot, man. I bagged it first."

"My dear chap, I've been waiting here a month."

"When you fellows have *quite* finished rotting about in front of that bath don't let *me* detain you."

"Anybody seen that sponge?"

"Well, look here"—this in a tone of compromise—"let's toss for it."

"All right. Odd man out."

All of which, being interpreted, meant that the first match of the Easter term had just come to an end, and that those of the team who, being day boys, changed over at the pavilion, instead of performing the operation at leisure and in comfort, as did the members of houses, were discussing the vital question—who was to have first bath?

The Field Sports Committee at Wrykyn—that is, at the school which stood some half-mile outside that town and took its name from it—were not lavish in their expenditure as regarded the changing accommodation in the pavilion. Letters appeared in every second number of the *Wrykinian*, some short, others long, some from members of the school, others from Old Boys, all protesting against the condition of the first, second, and third fifteen dressing-rooms. "Indignant" would inquire acidly, in half a page of small type, if the editor happened to be aware that there was no hair-brush in the second room, and only half a comb. "Disgusted O. W." would remark that when he came down with the Wandering Zephyrs to play against the third fifteen, the water supply had suddenly and mysteriously failed, and the W.Z.'s had been obliged to go home as they were, in a state of primeval grime, and he thought that this was "a very bad thing in a school of over six hundred boys", though what the number of boys had to do with the fact that there was no water he omitted to explain. The editor would express his regret in brackets, and things would go on as before.

There was only one bath in the first fifteen room, and there were on the present occasion six claimants to it. And each claimant was of the fixed opinion that, whatever happened subsequently, he was going to have it first. Finally, on the suggestion of Otway, who had reduced tossing to a fine art, a mystic game of Tommy Dodd was played. Otway having triumphantly obtained first innings, the conversation reverted to the subject of the match.

The Easter term always opened with a scratch game against a mixed team of masters and old boys, and the school usually won without any great exertion. On this occasion the match had been rather more even than the average, and the team had only just pulled the thing off by a couple of tries to a goal. Otway expressed an opinion that the school had played badly.

"Why on earth don't you forwards let the ball out occasionally?" he asked. Otway was one of the first fifteen halves.

"They were so jolly heavy in the scrum," said Maurice, one of the forwards. "And when we did let it out, the outsides nearly always mucked it."

"Well, it wasn't the halves' fault. We always got it out to the centres."

"It wasn't the centres," put in Robinson. "They played awfully well. Trevor was ripping."

"Trevor always is," said Otway; "I should think he's about the best captain we've had here for a long time. He's certainly one of the best centres."

"Best there's been since Rivers-Jones," said Clephane.

Rivers-Jones was one of those players who mark an epoch. He had been in the team fifteen years ago, and had left Wrykyn to captain Cambridge and play three years in succession for Wales. The school regarded the standard set by him as one that did not admit of comparison. However good a Wrykyn centre three-quarter might be, the most he could hope to be considered was "the best *since* Rivers-Jones". "Since" Rivers-Jones, however, covered fifteen years, and to be looked on as the best centre the school could boast of during that time, meant something. For Wrykyn knew how to play football.

Since it had been decided thus that the faults in the school attack did not lie with the halves, forwards, or centres, it was more or less evident that they must be attributable to the wings. And the search for the weak spot was even further narrowed down by the general verdict that Clowes, on the left wing, had played well. With a beautiful unanimity the six occupants of the first fifteen room came to the conclusion that the man who had let the team down that day had been the man on the right— Rand-Brown, to wit, of Seymour's.

"I'll bet he doesn't stay in the first long," said Clephane, who was now in the bath, *vice* Otway, retired. "I suppose they had to try him, as he was the senior wing three-quarter of the second, but he's no earthly good."

"He only got into the second because he's big," was Robinson's opinion. "A man who's big and strong can always get his second colours."

"Even if he's a funk, like Rand-Brown," said Clephane. "Did any of you chaps notice the way he let Paget through that time he scored for them? He simply didn't attempt to tackle him. He could have brought him down like a shot if he'd only gone for him. Paget was running straight along the touch-line, and hadn't any room to dodge. I know Trevor was jolly sick about it. And then he let him through once before in just the same way in the first half, only Trevor got round and stopped him. He was rank."

"Missed every other pass, too," said Otway.

Clephane summed up.

"He was rank," he said again. "Trevor won't keep him in the team long."

"I wish Paget hadn't left," said Otway, referring to the wing three-quarter who, by leaving unexpectedly at the end of the Christmas term, had let Rand-Brown into the team. His loss was likely to be felt. Up till Christmas Wrykyn had done well, and Paget had been their scoring man. Rand-Brown had occupied a similar position in the second fifteen. He was big and speedy, and in second fifteen matches these qualities make up for a great deal. If a man scores one or two tries in nearly every match, people are inclined to overlook in him such failings as timidity and clumsiness. It is only when he comes to be tried in football of a higher class that he is seen through. In the second fifteen the fact that Rand-Brown was afraid to tackle his man had almost escaped notice. But the habit would not do in first fifteen circles.

"All the same," said Clephane, pursuing his subject, "if they don't play him, I don't see who they're going to get. He's the best of the second three-quarters, as far as I can see."

It was this very problem that was puzzling Trevor, as he walked off the field with Paget and Clowes, when they had got into their blazers after the match. Clowes was in the same house as Trevor—Donaldson's—and Paget was staying there, too. He had been head of Donaldson's up to Christmas.

"It strikes me," said Paget, "the school haven't got over the holidays yet. I never saw such a lot of slackers. You ought to have taken thirty points off the sort of team you had against you today."

"Have you ever known the school play well on the

second day of term?" asked Clowes. "The forwards always play as if the whole thing bored them to death."

"It wasn't the forwards that mattered so much," said Trevor. "They'll shake down all right after a few matches. A little running and passing will put them right."

"Let's hope so," Paget observed, "or we might as well scratch to Ripton at once. There's a jolly sight too much of the mince-pie and Christmas pudding about their play at present." There was a pause. Then Paget brought out the question towards which he had been moving all the time.

"What do you think of Rand-Brown?" he asked.

It was pretty clear by the way he spoke what he thought of that player himself, but in discussing with a football captain the capabilities of the various members of his team, it is best to avoid a too positive statement one way or the other before one has heard his views on the subject. And Paget was one of those people who like to know the opinions of others before committing themselves.

Clowes, on the other hand, was in the habit of forming his views on his own account, and expressing them. If people agreed with them, well and good: it afforded strong presumptive evidence of their sanity. If they disagreed, it was unfortunate, but he was not going to alter his opinions for that, unless convinced at great length that they were unsound. He summed things up, and gave you the result. You could take it or leave it, as you preferred.

"I thought he was bad," said Clowes.

"Bad!" exclaimed Trevor, "he was a disgrace. One can understand a chap having his off-days at any game, but one doesn't expect a man in the Wrykyn first to funk. He mucked five out of every six passes I gave him, too, and the ball wasn't a bit slippery. Still, I shouldn't mind that so much if he had only gone for his man properly. It isn't being out of practice that makes you funk. And even when he did have a try at you, Paget, he always went high."

"That," said Clowes thoughtfully, "would seem to show that he was game."

Nobody so much as smiled. Nobody ever did smile at Clowes' essays in wit, perhaps because of the solemn, almost sad, tone of voice in which he delivered them. He was tall and dark and thin, and had a pensive eye, which encouraged the more soulful of his female relatives to entertain hopes that he would some day take orders.

"Well," said Paget, relieved at finding that he did not stand alone in his views on Rand-Brown's performance, "I must say I thought he was awfully bad myself."

"I shall try somebody else next match," said Trevor. "It'll be rather hard, though. The man one would naturally put in, Bryce, left at Christmas, worse luck."

Bryce was the other wing three-quarter of the second fifteen.

"Isn't there anybody in the third?" asked Paget.

"Barry," said Clowes briefly.

"Clowes thinks Barry's good," explained Trevor.

"He *is* good," said Clowes. "I admit he's small, but he can tackle."

"The question is, would he be any good in the first? A chap might do jolly well for the third, and still not be worth trying for the first."

"I don't remember much about Barry," said Paget, "except being collared by him when we played Seymour's last year in the final. I certainly came away with a sort of impression that he could tackle. I thought he marked me jolly well."

"There you are, then," said Clowes. "A year ago Barry could tackle Paget. There's no reason for supposing that he's fallen off since then. We've seen that Rand-Brown *can't* tackle Paget. Ergo, Barry is better worth playing for the team than Rand-Brown. Q.E.D."

"All right, then," replied Trevor. "There can't be any

harm in trying him. We'll have another scratch game on Thursday. Will you be here then, Paget?"

"Oh, yes. I'm stopping till Saturday."

"Good man. Then we shall be able to see how he does against you. I wish you hadn't left, though, by Jove. We should have had Ripton on toast, the same as last term."

Wrykyn played five schools, but six school matches. The school that they played twice in the season was Ripton. To win one Ripton match meant that, however many losses it might have sustained in the other matches, the school had had, at any rate, a passable season. To win two Ripton matches in the same year was almost unheard of. This year there had seemed every likelihood of it. The match before Christmas on the Ripton ground had resulted in a win for Wrykyn by two goals and a try to a try. But the calculations of the school had been upset by the sudden departure of Paget at the end of term, and also of Bryce, who had hitherto been regarded as his understudy. And in the first Ripton match the two goals had both been scored by Paget, and both had been brilliant bits of individual play, which a lesser man could not have carried through.

The conclusion, therefore, at which the school reluctantly arrived, was that their chances of winning the second match could not be judged by their previous success. They would have to approach the Easter term fixture from another—a non-Paget—standpoint. In these circumstances it became a serious problem : who was to get the fifteenth place? Whoever played in Paget's stead against Ripton would be certain, if the match were won, to receive his colours. Who, then, would fill the vacancy?

"Rand-Brown, of course," said the crowd.

But the experts, as we have shown, were of a different opinion.

II

The Gold Bat

Trevor did not take long to resume a garb of civilisation.
He never wasted much time over anything. He was gifted
with a boundless energy, which might possibly have made
him unpopular had he not justified it by results. The football of the school had never been in such a flourishing
condition as it had attained to on his succeeding to the
captaincy. It was not only that the first fifteen was good.
The excellence of a first fifteen does not always depend on
the captain. But the games, even down to the very humblest
junior game, had woken up one morning—at the beginning
of the previous term—to find themselves, much to their
surprise, organised going concerns. Like the immortal
Captain Pott, Trevor was "a terror to the shirker and the
lubber". And the resemblance was further increased by the
fact that he was "a toughish lot", who was "little, but steel
and india-rubber". At first sight his appearance was not
imposing. Paterfamilias, who had heard his son's eulogies
on Trevor's performances during the holidays, and came
down to watch the school play a match, was generally
rather disappointed on seeing five feet six where he had
looked for at least six foot one, and ten stone where he had
expected thirteen. But then, what there was of Trevor was,
as previously remarked, steel and india-rubber, and he
certainly played football like a miniature Stoddart. It was
characteristic of him that, though this was the first match
of the term, his condition seemed to be as good as possible.
He had done all his own work on the field and most of
Rand-Brown's, and apparently had not turned a hair. He

was one of those conscientious people who train in the holidays.

When he had changed, he went down the passage to Clowes' study. Clowes was in the position he frequently took up when the weather was good—wedged into his window in a sitting position, one leg in the study, the other hanging outside over space. The indoor leg lacked a boot, so that it was evident that its owner had at least had the energy to begin to change. That he had given the thing up after that, exhausted with the effort, was what one naturally expected from Clowes. He would have made a splendid actor : he was so good at resting.

"Hurry up and dress," said Trevor; "I want you to come over to the baths."

"What on earth do you want over at the baths?"

"I want to see O'Hara."

"Oh, yes, I remember. Dexter's are camping out there, aren't they? I heard they were. Why is it?"

"One of the Dexter kids got measles in the last week of the holidays, so they shunted all the beds and things across, and the chaps went back there instead of to the house."

In the winter term the baths were always boarded over and converted into a sort of extra gymnasium where you could go and box or fence when there was no room to do it in the real gymnasium. Socker and stump-cricket were also largely played there, the floor being admirably suited to such games, though the light was always rather tricky, and prevented heavy scoring.

"I should think," said Clowes, "from what I've seen of Dexter's beauties, that Dexter would like them to camp out at the bottom of the baths all the year round. It would be a happy release for him if they were all drowned. And I suppose if he had to choose any one of them for a violent death, he'd pick O'Hara. O'Hara must be a boon to a house-master. I've known chaps break rules when the spirit moved them, but he's the only one I've met who breaks them all day long and well into the night simply for amusement. I've often thought of writing to the S.P.C.A. about it. I suppose you could call Dexter an animal all right?"

"O'Hara's right enough, really. A man like Dexter would make any fellow run amuck. And then O'Hara's an Irishman to start with, which makes a difference."

There is usually one house in every school of the black sheep sort, and, if you go to the root of the matter, you will generally find that the fault is with the master of that house. A house-master who enters into the life of his house, coaches them in games—if an athlete—or, if not an athlete, watches the games, umpiring at cricket and refereeing at football, never finds much difficulty in keeping order. It may be accepted as fact that the juniors of a house will never be orderly of their own free will, but disturbances in the junior day-room do not make the house undisciplined. The prefects are the criterion. If you find them joining in the general "rags", and even starting private ones on their own account, then you may safely say that it is time the master of that house retired from the business, and took to chicken-farming. And that was the state of things in Dexter's. It was the most lawless of the houses. Mr Dexter belonged to a type of master almost unknown at a public school—the usher type. In a private school he might have passed. At Wrykyn he was out of place. To him the whole duty of a house-master appeared to be to wage war against his house.

When Dexter's won the final for the cricket cup in the summer term of two years back, the match lasted four afternoons—four solid afternoons of glorious, up-and-down cricket. Mr Dexter did not see a single ball of that match bowled. He was prowling in sequestered lanes and broken-down barns out of bounds on the off-chance that he might catch some member of his house smoking there. As if the whole of the house, from the head to the smallest fag, were

not on the field watching Day's best bats collapse before
Henderson's bowling, and Moriarty hit up that marvellous
and unexpected fifty-three at the end of the second
innings!

That sort of thing definitely stamps a master.

"What do you want to see O'Hara about?" asked
Clowes.

"He's got my little gold bat. I lent it him in the holidays."

A remark which needs a footnote. The bat referred to
was made of gold, and was about an inch long by an
eighth broad. It had come into existence some ten years
previously, in the following manner. The inter-house
cricket cup at Wrykyn had originally been a rather tar-
nished and unimpressive vessel, whose only merit consisted
in the fact that it was of silver. Ten years ago an Old
Wrykinian, suddenly reflecting that it would not be a bad
idea to do something for the school in a small way, hied
him to the nearest jeweller's and purchased another silver
cup, vast withal and cunningly decorated with filigree work,
and standing on a massive ebony plinth, round which were
little silver lozenges just big enough to hold the name of the
winning house and the year of grace. This he presented with
his blessing to be competed for by the dozen houses that
made up the school of Wrykyn, and it was formally established as the house cricket cup. The question now arose:
what was to be done with the other cup? The School
House, who happened to be the holders at the time,
suggested disinterestedly that it should become the property of the house which had won it last. "Not so," replied
the Field Sports Committee, "but far otherwise. We will
have it melted down in a fiery furnace, and thereafter
fashioned into eleven little silver bats. And these little silver
bats shall be the guerdon of the eleven members of the
winning team, to have and to hold for the space of one
year, unless, by winning the cup twice in succession, they

gain the right of keeping the bat for yet another year. How is that, umpire?" And the authorities replied, "O men of infinite resource and sagacity, verily is it a cold day when *you* get left behind. Forge ahead." But, when they had forged ahead, behold! it would not run to eleven little silver bats, but only to ten little silver bats. Thereupon the headmaster, a man liberal with his cash, caused an eleventh little bat to be fashioned—for the captain of the winning team to have and to hold in the manner aforesaid. And, to single it out from the others, it was wrought, not of silver, but of gold. And so it came to pass that at the time of our story Trevor was in possession of the little gold bat, because Donaldson's had won the cup in the previous summer, and he had captained them—and, incidentally, had scored seventy-five without a mistake.

"Well, I'm hanged if I would trust O'Hara with my bat," said Clowes, referring to the silver ornament on his own watch-chain; "he's probably pawned yours in the holidays. Why did you lend it to him?"

"His people wanted to see it. I know him at home, you know. They asked me to lunch the last day but one of the holidays, and we got talking about the bat, because, of course, if we hadn't beaten Dexter's in the final, O'Hara would have had it himself. So I sent it over next day with a note asking O'Hara to bring it back with him here."

"Oh, well, there's a chance, then, seeing he's only had it so little time, that he hasn't pawned it yet. You'd better rush off and get it back as soon as possible. It's no good waiting for me. I shan't be ready for weeks."

"Where's Paget?"

"Teaing with Donaldson. At least, he said he was going to."

"Then I suppose I shall have to go alone. I hate walking alone."

"If you hurry," said Clowes, scanning the road from

his post of vantage, "you'll be able to go with your fascinating pal Ruthven. He's just gone out."

Trevor dashed downstairs in his energetic way, and overtook the youth referred to.

Clowes brooded over them from above like a sorrowful and rather disgusted Providence. Trevor's liking for Ruthven, who was a Donaldsonite like himself, was one of the few points on which the two had any real disagreement. Clowes could not understand how any person in his senses could of his own free will make an intimate friend of Ruthven.

"Hullo, Trevor," said Ruthven.

"Come over to the baths," said Trevor, "I want to see O'Hara about something. Or were you going somewhere else."

"I wasn't going anywhere in particular. I never know what to do in term-time. It's deadly dull."

Trevor could never understand how any one could find term-time dull. For his own part, there always seemed too much to do in the time.

"You aren't allowed to play games?" he said, remembering something about a doctor's certificate in the past.

"No," said Ruthven. "Thank goodness," he added.

Which remark silenced Trevor. To a person who thanked goodness that he was not allowed to play games he could find nothing to say. But he ceased to wonder how it was that Ruthven was dull.

They proceeded to the baths together in silence. O'Hara, they were informed by a Dexter's fag who met them outside the door, was not about.

"When he comes back," said Trevor, "tell him I want him to come to tea tomorrow directly after school, and bring my bat. Don't forget."

The fag promised to make a point of it.

III

The Mayor's Statue

One of the rules that governed the life of Donough O'Hara, the light-hearted descendant of the O'Haras of Castle Taterfields, Co. Clare, Ireland, was "Never refuse the offer of a free tea". So, on receipt—per the Dexter's fag referred to—of Trevor's invitation, he scratched one engagement (with his mathematical master—not wholly unconnected with the working-out of Examples 200 to 206 in Hall and Knight's Algebra), postponed another (with his friend and ally Moriarty, of Dexter's, who wished to box with him in the gymnasium), and made his way at a leisurely pace towards Donaldson's. He was feeling particularly pleased with himself today, for several reasons. He had begun the day well by scoring brilliantly off Mr Dexter across the matutinal rasher and coffee. In morning school he had been put on to translate the one passage which he happened to have prepared—the first ten lines, in fact, of the hundred which formed the morning's lesson. And in the final hour of afternoon school, which was devoted to French, he had discovered and exploited with great success an entirely new and original form of ragging. This, he felt, was the strenuous life; this was living one's life as one's life should be lived.

He met Trevor at the gate. As they were going in, a carriage and pair dashed past. Its cargo consisted of two people, the headmaster, looking bored, and a small, dapper man, with a very red face, who looked excited, and was talking volubly. Trevor and O'Hara raised their caps as the chariot swept by, but the salute passed unnoticed. The Head appeared to be wrapped in thought.

"What's the Old Man doing in a carriage, I wonder," said Trevor, looking after them. "Who's that with him?"

"That," said O'Hara, "is Sir Eustace Briggs."

"Who's Sir Eustace Briggs?"

O'Hara explained, in a rich brogue, that Sir Eustace was Mayor of Wrykyn, a keen politician, and a hater of the Irish nation, judging by his letters and speeches.

They went into Trevor's study. Clowes was occupying the window in his usual manner.

"Hullo, O'Hara," he said, "there is an air of quiet satisfaction about you that seems to show that you've been ragging Dexter. Have you?"

"Oh, that was only this morning at breakfast. The best rag was in French," replied O'Hara, who then proceeded to explain in detail the methods he had employed to embitter the existence of the hapless Gallic exile with whom he had come in contact. It was that gentleman's custom to sit on a certain desk while conducting the lesson. This desk chanced to be O'Hara's. On the principle that a man may do what he likes with his own, he had entered the room privily in the dinner-hour, and removed the screws from his desk, with the result that for the first half-hour of the lesson the class had been occupied in excavating M. Gandinois from the ruins. That gentleman's first act on regaining his equilibrium had been to send O'Hara out of the room, and O'Hara, who had foreseen this emergency, had spent a very pleasant half-hour in the passage with some mixed chocolates and a copy of Mr Hornung's *Amateur Cracksman.* It was his notion of a cheerful and instructive French lesson.

"What were you talking about when you came in?" asked Clowes. "Who's been slanging Ireland, O'Hara?"

"The man Briggs."

"What are you going to do about it? Aren't you going to take any steps?"

"Is it steps?" said O'Hara, warmly, "and haven't we——"

He stopped.

"Well?"

"Ye know," he said, seriously, "ye mustn't let it go any further. I shall get sacked if it's found out. An' so will Moriarty, too."

"Why?" asked Trevor, looking up from the tea-pot he was filling, "what on earth have you been doing?"

"Wouldn't it be rather a cheery idea," suggested Clowes, "if you began at the beginning."

"Well, ye see," O'Hara began, "it was this way. The first I heard of it was from Dexter. He was trying to score off me as usual, an' he said, 'Have ye seen the paper this morning, O'Hara?' I said, no, I had not. Then he said, 'Ah,' he said, 'ye should look at it. There's something there that ye'll find interesting.' I said, 'Yes, sir?' in me respectful way. 'Yes,' said he, 'the Irish members have been making their customary disturbances in the House. Why is it, O'Hara,' he said, 'that Irishmen are always thrusting themselves forward and making disturbances for purposes of self-advertisement?' 'Why, indeed, sir?' said I, not knowing what else to say, and after that the conversation ceased."

"Go on," said Clowes.

"After breakfast Moriarty came to me with a paper, and showed me what they had been saying about the Irish. There was a letter from the man Briggs on the subject. 'A very sensible and temperate letter from Sir Eustace Briggs', they called it, but bedad! if that was a temperate letter, I should like to know what an intemperate one is. Well, we read it through, and Moriarty said to me, 'Can we let this stay as it is?' And I said, 'No. We can't.' 'Well,' said Moriarty to me, 'what are we to do about it? I should like to tar and feather the man,' he said. 'We can't do that,' I said, 'but why not tar and feather his statue?' I said. So we thought we would. Ye know where the statue is, I suppose? It's in the recreation ground just across the river."

"I know the place," said Clowes. "Go on. This is ripping. I always knew you were pretty mad, but this sounds as if it were going to beat all previous records."

"Have ye seen the baths this term," continued O'Hara, "since they shifted Dexter's house into them? The beds are in two long rows along each wall. Moriarty's and mine are the last two at the end farthest from the door."

"Just under the gallery," said Trevor. "I see."

"That's it. Well, at half-past ten sharp every night Dexter sees that we're all in, locks the door, and goes off to sleep at the Old Man's, and we don't see him again till breakfast. He turns the gas off from outside. At half-past seven the next morning, Smith"—Smith was one of the school porters—"unlocks the door and calls us, and we go over to the Hall to breakfast."

"Well?"

"Well, directly everybody was asleep last night—it wasn't till after one, as there was a rag on—Moriarty and I got up, dressed, and climbed up into the gallery. Ye know the gallery windows? They open at the top, an' it's rather hard to get out of them. But we managed it, and dropped on to the gravel outside."

"Long drop," said Clowes.

"Yes. I hurt myself rather. But it was in a good cause. I dropped first, and while I was on the ground, Moriarty came on top of me. That's how I got hurt. But it wasn't much, and we cut across the grounds, and over the fence, and down to the river. It was a fine night, and not very dark, and everything smelt ripping down by the river."

"Don't get poetical," said Clowes. "Stick to the point."

"We got into the boat-house—"

"How?" asked the practical Trevor, for the boat-house was wont to be locked at one in the morning.

"Moriarty had a key that fitted," explained O'Hara, briefly. "We got in, and launched a boat—a big tub—put in the tar and a couple of brushes—there's always tar in the boat-house—and rowed across."

"Wait a bit," interrupted Trevor, "you said tar and feathers. Where did you get the feathers?"

"We used leaves. They do just as well, and there were heaps on the bank. Well, when we landed, we tied up the boat, and bucked across to the Recreation Ground. We got over the railings—beastly, spiky railings—and went over to the statue. Ye know where the statue stands? It's right in the middle of the place, where everybody can see it. Moriarty got up first, and I handed him the tar and a brush. Then I went up with the other brush, and we began. We did his face first. It was too dark to see really well, but I think we made a good job of it. When we had put about as much tar on as we thought would do, we took out the leaves—which we were carrying in our pockets—and spread them on. Then we did the rest of him, and after about half an hour, when we thought we'd done about enough, we got into our boat again, and came back."

"And what did you do till half-past seven?"

"We couldn't get back the way we'd come, so we slept in the boat-house."

"Well—I'm—hanged," was Trevor's comment on the story.

Clowes roared with laughter. O'Hara was a perpetual joy to him.

As O'Hara was going, Trevor asked him for his gold bat.

"You haven't lost it, I hope?" he said.

O'Hara felt in his pocket, but brought his hand out at once and transferred it to another pocket. A look of anxiety came over his face, and was reflected in Trevor's.

"I could have sworn it was in that pocket," he said.

"You *haven't* lost it?" queried Trevor again.

"He has," said Clowes, confidently. "If you want to

know where that bat is, I should say you'd find it somewhere between the baths and the statue. At the foot of the statue, for choice. It seems to me—correct me if I am wrong —that you have been and gone and done it, me broth av a bhoy."

O'Hara gave up the search.

"It's gone," he said. "Man, I'm most awfully sorry. I'd sooner have lost a ten-pound note."

"I don't see why you should lose either," snapped Trevor. "Why the blazes can't you be more careful."

O'Hara was too penitent for words. Clowes took it on himself to point out the bright side.

"There's nothing to get sick about, really," he said. "If the thing doesn't turn up, though it probably will, you'll simply have to tell the Old Man that it's lost. He'll have another made. You won't be asked for it till just before Sports Day either, so you will have plenty of time to find it."

The challenge cups, and also the bats, had to be given to the authorities before the sports, to be formally presented on Sports Day.

"Oh, I suppose it'll be all right," said Trevor, "but I hope it won't be found anywhere near the statue."

O'Hara said he hoped so too.

IV

THE LEAGUE'S WARNING

The team to play in any match was always put upon the notice-board at the foot of the stairs in the senior block a day before the date of the fixture. Both first and second fifteens had matches on the Thursday of this week. The second were playing a team brought down by an old Wrykinian. The first had a scratch game.

When Barry, accompanied by M'Todd, who shared his study at Seymour's and rarely left him for two minutes on end, passed by the notice-board at the quarter to eleven interval, it was to the second fifteen list that he turned his attention. Now that Bryce had left, he thought he might have a chance of getting into the second. His only real rival, he considered, was Crawford, of the School House, who was the other wing three-quarter of the third fifteen. The first name he saw on the list was Crawford's. It seemed to be written twice as large as any of the others, and his own was nowhere to be seen. The fact that he had half expected the calamity made things no better. He had set his heart on playing for the second this term.

Then suddenly he noticed a remarkable phenomenon. The other wing three-quarter was Rand-Brown. If Rand-Brown was playing for the second, who was playing for the first?

He looked at the list.

"*Come* on," he said hastily to M'Todd. He wanted to get away somewhere where his agitated condition would not be noticed. He felt quite faint at the shock of seeing his name on the list of the first fifteen. There it was, however,

as large as life. "M. Barry." Separated from the rest by a
thin red line, but still there. In his most optimistic moments
he had never dreamed of this. M'Todd was reading slowly
through the list of the second. He did everything slowly,
except eating.

"Come on," said Barry again.

M'Todd had, after much deliberation, arrived at a
profound truth. He turned to Barry, and imparted his
discovery to him in the weighty manner of one who
realises the importance of his words.

"Look here," he said, "your name's not down here."

"I know. *Come* on."

"But that means you're not playing for the second."

"Of course it does. Well, if you aren't coming, I'm off."

"But, look here——"

Barry disappeared through the door. After a moment's
pause, M'Todd followed him. He came up with him on
the senior gravel.

"What's up?" he inquired.

"Nothing," said Barry.

"Are you sick about not playing for the second?"

"No."

"You are, really. Come and have a bun."

In the philosophy of M'Todd it was indeed a deep-
rooted sorrow that could not be cured by the internal
application of a new, hot bun. It had never failed in his
own case.

"Bun!" Barry was quite shocked at the suggestion. "I
can't afford to get myself out of condition with beastly
buns."

"But if you aren't playing——"

"You ass. I'm playing for the first. Now, do you see?"

M'Todd gaped. His mind never worked very rapidly.

"What about Rand-Brown, then?" he said.

"Rand-Brown's been chucked out. Can't you understand? You *are* an idiot. Rand-Brown's playing for the second, and I'm playing for the first."

"But you're——"

He stopped. He had been going to point out that Barry's tender years—he was only sixteen—and smallness would make it impossible for him to play with success for the first fifteen. He refrained owing to a conviction that the remark would not be wholly judicious. Barry was touchy on the subject of his size, and M'Todd had suffered before now for commenting on it in a disparaging spirit.

"I tell you what we'll do after school," said Barry, "we'll have some running and passing. It'll do you a lot of good, and I want to practise taking passes at full speed. You can trot along at your ordinary pace, and I'll sprint up from behind."

M'Todd saw no objection to that. Trotting along at his ordinary pace—five miles an hour—would just suit him.

"Then after that," continued Barry, with a look of enthusiasm, "I want to practise passing back to my centre. Paget used to do it awfully well last term, and I know Trevor expects his wing to. So I'll buck along, and you race up to take my pass. See?"

This was not in M'Todd's line at all. He proposed a slight alteration in the scheme.

"Hadn't you better get somebody else——?" he began.

"Don't be a slack beast," said Barry. "You want exercise awfully badly."

And, as M'Todd always did exactly as Barry wished, he gave in, and spent from four-thirty to five that afternoon in the prescribed manner. A suggestion on his part at five sharp that it wouldn't be a bad idea to go and have some tea was not favourably received by the enthusiastic three-quarter, who proposed to devote what time remained before lock-up to practising drop-kicking. It was a painful alternative that faced M'Todd. His allegiance to Barry demanded that he should consent to the scheme. On the

other hand, his allegiance to afternoon tea—equally strong
—called him back to the house, where there was cake, and
also muffins. In the end the question was solved by the
appearance of Drummond, of Seymour's, garbed in football
things, and also anxious to practise drop-kicking. So
M'Todd was dismissed to his tea with opprobrious epithets,
and Barry and Drummond settled down to a little serious
and scientific work.

Making allowances for the inevitable attack of nerves
that attends a first appearance in higher football circles
than one is accustomed to, Barry did well against the
scratch team—certainly far better than Rand-Brown had
done. His smallness was, of course, against him, and, on the
only occasion on which he really got away, Paget overtook
him and brought him down. But then Paget was exceptionally fast. In the two most important branches of the
game, the taking of passes and tackling, Barry did well.
As far as pluck went he had enough for two, and when the
whistle blew for no-side he had not let Paget through once,
and Trevor felt that his inclusion in the team had been
justified. There was another scratch game on the Saturday.
Barry played in it, and did much better. Paget had gone
away by an early train, and the man he had to mark now
was one of the masters, who had been good in his time,
but was getting a trifle old for football. Barry scored twice,
and on one occasion, by passing back to Trevor after the
manner of Paget, enabled the captain to run in. And
Trevor, like the captain in *Billy Taylor*, "werry much
approved of what he'd done." Barry began to be regarded
in the school as a regular member of the fifteen. The first
of the fixture-card matches, versus the Town, was due on
the following Saturday, and it was generally expected that
he would play. M'Todd's devotion increased every day.
He even went to the length of taking long runs with him.
And if there was one thing in the world that M'Todd
loathed, it was a long run.

On the Thursday before the match against the Town, Clowes came chuckling to Trevor's study after preparation, and asked him if he had heard the latest.

"Have you ever heard of the League?" he said.

Trevor pondered.

"I don't think so," he replied.

"How long have you been at the school?"

"Let's see. It'll be five years at the end of the summer term."

"Ah, then you wouldn't remember. I've been here a couple of terms longer than you, and the row about the League was in my first term."

"What was the row?"

"Oh, only some chaps formed a sort of secret society in the place. Kind of Vehmgericht, you know. If they got their knife into any one, he usually got beans, and could never find out where they came from. At first, as a matter of fact, the thing was quite a philanthropical concern. There used to be a good deal of bullying in the place then —at least, in some of the houses—and, as the prefects couldn't or wouldn't stop it, some fellows started this League."

"Did it work?"

"Work! By Jove, I should think it did. Chaps who previously couldn't get through the day without making some wretched kid's life not worth living used to go about as nervous as cats, looking over their shoulders every other second. There was one man in particular, a chap called Leigh. He was hauled out of bed one night, blindfolded, and ducked in a cold bath. He was in the School House."

"Why did the League bust up?"

"Well, partly because the fellows left, but chiefly because they didn't stick to the philanthropist idea. If anybody did anything they didn't like, they used to go for him. At last they put their foot into it badly. A chap called Robinson— in this house by the way—offended them in some way, and

one morning he was found tied up in the bath, up to his
neck in cold water. Apparently he'd been there about an
hour. He got pneumonia, and almost died, and then the
authorities began to get going. Robinson thought he had
recognised the voice of one of the chaps—I forget his name.
The chap was had up by the Old Man, and gave the show
away entirely. About a dozen fellows were sacked, clean
off the reel. Since then the thing has been dropped."

"But what about it? What were you going to say when
you came in?"

"Why, it's been revived!"

"Rot!"

"It's a fact. Do you know Mill, a prefect, in Seymour's?"

"Only by sight."

"I met him just now. He's in a raving condition. His
study's been wrecked. You never saw such a sight. Everything upside down or smashed. He has been showing me
the ruins."

"I believe Mill is awfully barred in Seymour's," said
Trevor. "Anybody might have ragged his study."

"That's just what I thought. He's just the sort of man
the League used to go for."

"That doesn't prove that it's been revived, all the same,"
objected Trevor.

"No, friend; but this does. Mill found it tied to a chair."

It was a small card. It looked like an ordinary visiting
card. On it, in neat print, were the words, "*With the
compliments of the League*".

"That's exactly the same sort of card as they used to
use," said Clowes. "I've seen some of them. What do
you think of that?"

"I think whoever has started the thing is a pretty
average-sized idiot. He's bound to get caught some time or
other, and then out he goes. The Old Man wouldn't think
twice about sacking a chap of that sort."

"A chap of that sort," said Clowes, "will take jolly good care he isn't caught. But it's rather sport, isn't it?"

And he went off to his study.

Next day there was further evidence that the League was an actual going concern. When Trevor came down to breakfast, he found a letter by his plate. It was printed, as the card had been. It was signed "The President of the League." And the purport of it was that the League did not wish Barry to continue to play for the first fifteen.

V

Mill Receives Visitors

Trevor's first idea was that somebody had sent the letter for a joke,—Clowes for choice.

He sounded him on the subject after breakfast.

"Did you send me that letter?" he inquired, when Clowes came into his study to borrow a *Sportsman*.

"What letter? Did you send the team for tomorrow up to the sporter? I wonder what sort of a lot the Town are bringing."

"About not giving Barry his footer colours?"

Clowes was reading the paper.

"Giving whom?" he asked.

"Barry. Can't you listen?"

"Giving him what?"

"Footer colours."

"What about them?"

Trevor sprang at the paper, and tore it away from him. After which he sat on the fragments.

"Did you send me a letter about not giving Barry his footer colours?"

Clowes surveyed him with the air of a nurse to whom the family baby has just said some more than usually good thing.

"Don't stop," he said, "I could listen all day."

Trevor felt in his pocket for the note, and flung it at him. Clowes picked it up, and read it gravely.

"What *are* footer colours?" he asked.

"Well," said Trevor, "it's a pretty rotten sort of joke,

whoever sent it. You haven't said yet whether you did or not."

"What earthly reason should I have for sending it? And I think you're making a mistake if you think this is meant as a joke."

"You don't really believe this League rot?"

"You didn't see Mill's study 'after treatment'. I did. Anyhow, how do you account for the card I showed you?"

"But that sort of thing doesn't happen at school."

"Well, it *has* happened, you see."

"Who do you think did send the letter, then?"

"The President of the League."

"And who the dickens is the President of the League when he's at home?"

"If I knew that, I should tell Mill, and earn his blessing. Not that I want it."

"Then, I suppose," snorted Trevor, "you'd suggest that on the strength of this letter I'd better leave Barry out of the team?"

"Satirically in brackets," commented Clowes.

"It's no good your jumping on *me*," he added. "I've done nothing. All I suggest is that you'd better keep more or less of a look-out. If this League's anything like the old one, you'll find they've all sorts of ways of getting at people they don't love. I shouldn't like to come down for a bath some morning, and find you already in possession, tied up like Robinson. When they found Robinson, he was quite blue both as to the face and speech. He didn't speak very clearly, but what one could catch was well worth hearing. I should advise you to sleep with a loaded revolver under your pillow."

"The first thing I shall do is find out who wrote this letter."

"I should," said Clowes, encouragingly. "Keep moving."

In Seymour's house the Mill's study incident formed the only theme of conversation that morning. Previously the sudden elevation to the first fifteen of Barry, who was popular in the house, at the expense of Rand-Brown, who was unpopular, had given Seymour's something to talk about. But the ragging of the study put this topic entirely in the shade. The study was still on view in almost its original condition of disorder, and all day comparative strangers flocked to see Mill in his den, in order to inspect things. Mill was a youth with few friends, and it is probable that more of his fellow-Seymourites crossed the threshold of his study on the day after the occurrence than had visited him in the entire course of his school career. Brown would come in to borrow a knife, would sweep the room with one comprehensive glance, and depart, to be followed at brief intervals by Smith, Robinson, and Jones, who came respectively to learn the right time, to borrow a book, and to ask him if he had seen a pencil anywhere. Towards the end of the day, Mill would seem to have wearied somewhat of the proceedings, as was proved when Master Thomas Renford, aged fourteen (who fagged for Milton, the head of the house), burst in on the thin pretence that he had mistaken the study for that of his rightful master, and gave vent to a prolonged whistle of surprise and satisfaction at the sight of the ruins. On that occasion, the incensed owner of the dismantled study, taking a mean advantage of the fact that he was a prefect, and so entitled to wield the rod, produced a handy swagger-stick from an adjacent corner, and, inviting Master Renford to bend over, gave him six of the best to remember him by. Which ceremony being concluded, he kicked him out into the passage, and Renford went down to the junior day-room to tell his friend Harvey about it.

"Gave me six, the cad," said he, "just because I had a look at his beastly study. Why shouldn't I look at his study if I like? I've a jolly good mind to go up and have another squint."

Harvey warmly approved the scheme.

"No, I don't think I will," said Renford with a yawn. "It's such a fag going upstairs."

"Yes, isn't it?" said Harvey.

"And he's such a beast, too."

"Yes, isn't he?" said Harvey.

"I'm jolly glad his study *has* been ragged," continued the vindictive Renford.

"It's jolly exciting, isn't it?" added Harvey. "And I thought this term was going to be slow. The Easter term generally is."

This remark seemed to suggest a train of thought to Renford, who made the following cryptic observation. "Have you seen them today?"

To the ordinary person the words would have conveyed little meaning. To Harvey they appeared to teem with import.

"Yes," he said, "I saw them early this morning."

"Were they all right?"

"Yes. Splendid."

"Good," said Renford.

Barry's friend Drummond was one of those who had visited the scene of the disaster early, before Mill's energetic hand had repaired the damage done, and his narrative was consequently in some demand.

"The place was in a frightful muck," he said. "Everything smashed except the table; and ink all over the place. Whoever did it must have been fairly sick with him, or he'd never have taken the trouble to do it so thoroughly. Made a fair old hash of things, didn't he, Bertie?"

"Bertie" was the form in which the school elected to serve up the name of De Bertini. Raoul de Bertini was a French boy who had come to Wrykyn in the previous term. Drummond's father had met his father in Paris, and Drummond was supposed to be looking after Bertie. They shared a study together. Bertie could not speak much

English, and what he did speak was, like Mill's furniture,
badly broken.

"Pardon?" he said.

"Doesn't matter," said Drummond, "it wasn't anything
important. I was only appealing to you for corroborative
detail to give artistic verisimilitude to a bald and uncon-
vincing narrative."

Bertie grinned politely. He always grinned when he was
not quite equal to the intellectual pressure of the conversation. As a consequence of which, he was generally, like
Mrs Fezziwig, one vast, substantial smile.

"I never liked Mill much," said Barry, "but I think it's
rather bad luck on the man."

"Once," announced M'Todd, solemnly, "he kicked me
—for making a row in the passage." It was plain that the
recollection rankled.

Barry would probably have pointed out what an excellent and praiseworthy act on Mill's part that had been,
when Rand-Brown came in.

"Prefects' meeting?" he inquired. "Or haven't they
made you a prefect yet, M'Todd?"

M'Todd said they had not.

Nobody present liked Rand-Brown, and they looked at
him rather inquiringly, as if to ask what he had come for.
A friend may drop in for a chat. An acquaintance must
justify his intrusion.

Rand-Brown ignored the silent inquiry. He seated himself on the table, and dragged up a chair to rest his legs on.

"Talking about Mill, of course?" he said.

"Yes," said Drummond. "Have you seen his study since
it happened?"

"Yes."

Rand-Brown smiled, as if the recollection amused him.
He was one of those people who do not look their best
when they smile.

"Playing for the first tomorrow, Barry?"

"I don't know," said Barry, shortly. "I haven't seen the list."

He objected to the introduction of the topic. It is never pleasant to have to discuss games with the very man one has ousted from the team.

Drummond, too, seemed to feel that the situation was an embarrassing one, for a few minutes later he got up to go over to the gymnasium.

"Any of you chaps coming?" he asked.

Barry and M'Todd thought they would, and the three left the room.

"Nothing like showing a man you don't want him, eh, Bertie? What do you think?" said Rand-Brown.

Bertie grinned politely.

VI

Trevor Remains Firm

The most immediate effect of telling anybody not to do a thing is to make him do it, in order to assert his independence. Trevor's first act on receipt of the letter was to include Barry in the team against the Town. It was what he would have done in any case, but, under the circumstances, he felt a peculiar pleasure in doing it. The incident also had the effect of recalling to his mind the fact that he had tried Barry in the first instance on his own responsibility, without consulting the committee. The committee of the first fifteen consisted of the two old colours who came immediately after the captain on the list. The powers of a committee varied according to the determination and truculence of the members of it. On any definite and important step, affecting the welfare of the fifteen, the captain theoretically could not move without their approval. But if the captain happened to be strong-minded and the committee weak, they were apt to be slightly out of it, and the captain would develop a habit of consulting them a day or so after he had done a thing. He would give a man his colours, and inform the committee of it on the following afternoon, when the thing was done and could not be repealed.

Trevor was accustomed to ask the advice of his lieutenants fairly frequently. He never gave colours, for instance, off his own bat. It seemed to him that it might be as well to learn what views Milton and Allardyce had on the subject of Barry, and, after the Town team had gone back across the river, defeated by a goal and a try to nil, he changed and went over to Seymour's to interview Milton.

Milton was in an arm-chair, watching Renford brew tea. His was one of the few studies in the school in which there was an arm-chair. With the majority of his contemporaries, it would only run to the portable kind that fold up.

"Come and have some tea, Trevor," said Milton.

"Thanks. If there's any going."

"Heaps. Is there anything to eat, Renford?"

The fag, appealed to on this important point, pondered darkly for a moment.

"There *was* some cake," he said.

"That's all right," interrupted Milton, cheerfully. "Scratch the cake. I ate it before the match. Isn't there anything else?"

Milton had a healthy appetite.

"Then there used to be some biscuits."

"Biscuits are off. I finished 'em yesterday. Look here, young Renford, what you'd better do is cut across to the shop and get some more cake and some more biscuits, and tell 'em to put it down to me. And don't be long."

"A miles better idea would be to send him over to Donaldson's to fetch something from my study," suggested Trevor. "It isn't nearly so far, and I've got heaps of stuff."

"Ripping. Cut over to Donaldson's, young Renford. As a matter of fact," he added, confidentially, when the emissary had vanished, "I'm not half sure that the other dodge would have worked. They seem to think at the shop that I've had about enough things on tick lately. I haven't settled up for last term yet. I've spent all I've got on this study. What do you think of those photographs?"

Trevor got up and inspected them. They filled the mantelpiece and most of the wall above it. They were exclusively theatrical photographs, and of a variety to suit all tastes. For the earnest student of the drama there was Sir Henry Irving in *The Bells*, and Mr Martin Harvey in

The Only Way. For the admirers of the merely beautiful
there were Messrs Dan Leno and Herbert Campbell.

"Not bad," said Trevor. "Beastly waste of money."

"Waste of money!" Milton was surprised and pained
at the criticism. "Why, you must spend your money on
something."

"Rot, I call it," said Trevor. "If you want to collect
something, why don't you collect something worth
having?"

Just then Renford came back with the supplies.

"Thanks," said Milton, "put 'em down. Does the billy
boil, young Renford?"

Renford asked for explanatory notes.

"You're a bit of an ass at times, aren't you?" said
Milton, kindly. "What I meant was, is the tea ready? If
it is, you can scoot. If it isn't, buck up with it."

A sound of bubbling and a rush of steam from the
spout of the kettle proclaimed that the billy did boil. Renford
extinguished the Etna, and left the room, while Milton,
murmuring vague formulae about "one spoonful for each
person and one for the pot", got out of his chair with a
groan—for the Town match had been an energetic one—
and began to prepare tea.

"What I really came round about—" began Trevor.

"Half a second. I can't find the milk."

He went to the door, and shouted for Renford. On that
overworked youth's appearance, the following dialogue
took place.

"Where's the milk?"

"What milk?"

"My milk."

"There isn't any." This in a tone not untinged with
triumph, as if the speaker realised that here was a distinct
score to him.

"No milk?"

"No."

"Why not?"

"You never had any."

"Well, just cut across—no, half a second. What are you doing downstairs?"

"Having tea."

"Then you've got milk."

"Only a little." This apprehensively.

"Bring it up. You can have what we leave."

Disgusted retirement of Master Renford.

"What I really came about," said Trevor again, "was business."

"Colours?" inquired Milton, rummaging in the tin for biscuits with sugar on them. "Good brand of biscuit you keep, Trevor."

"Yes. I think we might give Alexander and Parker their third."

"All right. Any others?"

"Barry his second, do you think?"

"Rather. He played a good game today. He's an improvement on Rand-Brown."

"Glad you think so. I was wondering whether it was the right thing to do, chucking Rand-Brown out after one trial like that. But still, if you think Barry's better—"

"Streets better. I've had heaps of chances of watching them and comparing them, when they've been playing for the house. It isn't only that Rand-Brown can't tackle, and Barry can. Barry takes his passes much better, and doesn't lose his head when he's pressed."

"Just what I thought," said Trevor. "Then you'd go on playing him for the first?"

"Rather. He'll get better every game, you'll see, as he gets more used to playing in the first three-quarter line. And he's as keen as anything on getting into the team. Practises taking passes and that sort of thing every day."

"Well, he'll get his colours if we lick Ripton."

"We ought to lick them. They've lost one of their for-

wards, Clifford, a red-haired chap, who was good out of
touch. I don't know if you remember him."

"I suppose I ought to go and see Allardyce about these
colours, now. Good-bye."

There was running and passing on the Monday for every
one in the three teams. Trevor and Clowes met Mr
Seymour as they were returning. Mr Seymour was the
football master at Wrykyn.

"I see you've given Barry his second, Trevor."

"Yes, sir."

"I think you're wise to play him for the first. He knows
the game, which is the great thing, and he will improve
with practice," said Mr Seymour, thus corroborating
Milton's words of the previous Saturday.

"I'm glad Seymour thinks Barry good," said Trevor,
as they walked on. "I shall go on playing him now."

"Found out who wrote that letter yet?"

Trevor laughed.

"Not yet," he said.

"Probably Rand-Brown," suggested Clowes. "He's the
man who would gain most by Barry's not playing. I hear he
had a row with Mill just before his study was ragged."

"Everybody in Seymour's has had rows with Mill some
time or other," said Trevor.

Clowes stopped at the door of the junior day-room to
find his fag. Trevor went on upstairs. In the passage he
met Ruthven.

Ruthven seemed excited.

"I say, Trevor," he exclaimed, "have you seen your
study?"

"Why, what's the matter with it?"

"You'd better go and look."

VII

"With the Compliments of the League"

Trevor went and looked.

It was rather an interesting sight. An earthquake or a cyclone might have made it a little more picturesque, but not much more. The general effect was not unlike that of an American saloon, after a visit from Mrs Carrie Nation (with hatchet). As in the case of Mill's study, the only thing that did not seem to have suffered any great damage was the table. Everything else looked rather off colour. The mantelpiece had been swept as bare as a bone, and its contents littered the floor. Trevor dived among the débris and retrieved the latest addition to his art gallery, the photograph of this year's first fifteen. It was a wreck. The glass was broken and the photograph itself slashed with a knife till most of the faces were unrecognisable. He picked up another treasure, last year's first eleven. Smashed glass again. Faces cut about with knife as before. His collection of snapshots was torn into a thousand fragments, though, as Mr Jerome said of the papier-maché trout, there may only have been nine hundred. He did not count them. His bookshelf was empty. The books had gone to swell the contents of the floor. There was a Shakespeare with its cover off. Pages twenty-two to thirty-one of *Vice Versâ* had parted from the parent establishment, and were lying by themselves near the door. *The Rogues' March* lay just beyond them, and the look of the cover suggested that somebody had either been biting it or jumping on it with heavy boots.

There was other damage. Over the mantelpiece in

happier days had hung a dozen sea gulls' eggs, threaded on
a string. The string was still there, as good as new, but of
the eggs nothing was to be seen, save a fine parti-coloured
powder—on the floor, like everything else in the study.
And a good deal of ink had been upset in one place and
another.

Trevor had been staring at the ruins for some time, when
he looked up to see Clowes standing in the doorway.

"Hullo," said Clowes, "been tidying up?"

Trevor made a few hasty comments on the situation.
Clowes listened approvingly.

"Don't you think," he went on, eyeing the study with
a critical air, "that you've got too many things on the floor,
and too few anywhere else? And I should move some of
those books on to the shelf, if I were you."

Trevor breathed very hard.

"I should like to find the chap who did this," he said
softly.

Clowes advanced into the room and proceeded to pick
up various misplaced articles of furniture in a helpful way.

"I thought so," he said presently, "come and look here."

Tied to a chair, exactly as it had been in the case of
Mill, was a neat white card, and on it were the words,
"With the Compliments of the League".

"What are you going to do about this?" asked Clowes.
"Come into my room and talk it over."

"I'll tidy this place up first," said Trevor. He felt that
the work would be a relief. "I don't want people to see this.
It mustn't get about. I'm not going to have my study
turned into a sort of side-show, like Mill's. You go and
change. I shan't be long."

"I will *never* desert Mr Micawber," said Clowes.
"Friend, my place is by your side. Shut the door and let's
get to work."

Ten minutes later the room had resumed a more or less
—though principally less—normal appearance. The books

and chairs were back in their places. The ink was sopped up. The broken photographs were stacked in a neat pile in one corner, with a rug over them. The mantelpiece was still empty, but, as Clowes pointed out, it now merely looked as if Trevor had been pawning some of his household gods. There was no sign that a devastating secret society had raged through the study.

Then they adjourned to Clowes' study, where Trevor sank into Clowes' second-best chair—Clowes, by an adroit movement, having appropriated the best one—with a sigh of enjoyment. Running and passing, followed by the toil of furniture-shifting, had made him feel quite tired.

"It doesn't look so bad now," he said, thinking of the room they had left. "By the way, what did you do with that card?"

"Here it is. Want it?"

"You can keep it. I don't want it."

"Thanks. If this sort of things goes on, I shall get quite a nice collection of these cards. Start an album some day."

"You know," said Trevor, "this is getting serious."

"It always does get serious when anything bad happens to one's self. It always strikes one as rather funny when things happen to other people. When Mill's study was wrecked, I bet you regarded it as an amusing and original 'turn'. What do you think of the present effort?"

"Who on earth can have done it?"

"The Pres—"

"Oh, dry up. Of course it was. But who the blazes is he?"

"Nay, children, you have me there," quoted Clowes. "I'll tell you one thing, though. You remember what I said about it's probably being Rand-Brown. He can't have done this, that's certain, because he was out in the fields the whole time. Though I don't see who else could have anything to gain by Barry not getting his colours."

"There's no reason to suspect him at all, as far as I can see. I don't know much about him, bar the fact that he can't play footer for nuts, but I've never heard anything against him. Have you?"

"I scarcely know him myself. He isn't liked in Seymour's, I believe."

"Well, anyhow, this can't be his work."

"That's what I said."

"For all we know, the League may have got their knife into Barry for some reason. You said they used to get their knife into fellows in that way. Anyhow, I mean to find out who ragged my room."

"It wouldn't be a bad idea," said Clowes.

O'Hara came round to Donaldson's before morning school next day to tell Trevor that he had not yet succeeded in finding the lost bat. He found Trevor and Clowes in the former's den, trying to put a few finishing touches to the same.

"Hullo, an' what's up with your study?" he inquired. He was quick at noticing things. Trevor looked annoyed. Clowes asked the visitor if he did not think the study presented a neat and gentlemanly appearance.

"Where are all your photographs, Trevor?" persisted the descendant of Irish kings.

"It's no good trying to conceal anything from the bhoy," said Clowes. "Sit down, O'Hara—mind that chair; it's rather wobbly—and I will tell ye the story."

"Can you keep a thing dark?" inquired Trevor.

O'Hara protested that tombs were not in it.

"Well, then, do you remember what happened to Mill's study? That's what's been going on here."

O'Hara nearly fell off his chair with surprise. That some philanthropist should rag Mill's study was only to be expected. Mill was one of the worst. A worm without a saving grace. But Trevor! Captain of football! In the first eleven! The thing was unthinkable.

"But who—?" he began.

"That's just what I want to know," said Trevor, shortly. He did not enjoy discussing the affair.

"How long have you been at Wrykyn, O'Hara?" said Clowes.

O'Hara made a rapid calculation. His fingers twiddled in the air as he worked out the problem.

"Six years," he said at last, leaning back exhausted with brain work.

"Then you must remember the League?"

"Remember the League? Rather."

"Well, it's been revived."

O'Hara whistled.

"This'll liven the old place up," he said. "I've often thought of reviving it meself. An' so has Moriarty. If it's anything like the Old League, there's going to be a sort of Donnybrook before it's done with. I wonder who's running it this time."

"We should like to know that. If you find out, you might tell us."

"I will."

"And don't tell anybody else," said Trevor. "This business has got to be kept quiet. Keep it dark about my study having been ragged."

"I won't tell a soul."

"Not even Moriarty."

"Oh, hang it, man," put in Clowes, "you don't want to kill the poor bhoy, surely? You must let him tell one person."

"All right," said Trevor, "you can tell Moriarty. But nobody else, mind."

O'Hara promised that Moriarty should receive the news exclusively.

"But why did the League go for ye?"

"They happen to be down on me. It doesn't matter why. They are."

"I see," said O'Hara. "Oh," he added, "about that bat.

The search is being 'vigorously prosecuted'—that's a news-paper quotation—"

"*Times?*" inquired Clowes.

"*Wrykyn Patriot,*" said O'Hara, pulling out a bundle of letters. He inspected each envelope in turn, and from the fifth extracted a newspaper cutting.

"Read that," he said.

It was from the local paper, and ran as follows :—

"*Hooligan Outrage*—A painful sensation has been caused in the town by a deplorable ebullition of local Hooliganism, which has resulted in the wanton disfigure-ment of the splendid statue of Sir Eustace Briggs which stands in the New Recreation Grounds. Our readers will recollect that the statue was erected to commemorate the return of Sir Eustace as member for the borough of Wrykyn, by an overwhelming majority, at the last election. Last Tuesday some youths of the town, passing through the Recreation Grounds early in the morning, noticed that the face and body of the statue were completely covered with leaves and some black substance, which on examin-ation proved to be tar. They speedily lodged information at the police station. Everything seems to point to party spite as the motive for the outrage. In view of the forth-coming election, such an act is highly significant, and will serve sufficiently to indicate the tactics employed by our opponents. The search for the perpetrator (or perpetrators) of the dastardly act is being vigorously prosecuted, and we learn with satisfaction that the police have already several clues."

"Clues!" said Clowes, handing back the paper, "that means *the bat.* That gas about 'our opponents' is all a blind to put you off your guard. You wait. There'll be more painful sensations before you've finished with this business."

"They can't have found the bat, or why did they not say so?" observed O'Hara.

"Guile," said Clowes, "pure guile. If I were you, I should escape while I could. Try Callao. There's no extradition there.

> 'On no petition
> Is extradition
> Allowed in Callao.'

Either of you chaps coming over to school?"

VIII

O'HARA ON THE TRACK

Tuesday mornings at Wrykyn were devoted—up to the quarter to eleven interval—to the study of mathematics. That is to say, instead of going to their form-rooms, the various forms visited the out-of-the-way nooks and dens at the top of the buildings where the mathematical masters were wont to lurk, and spent a pleasant two hours there playing round games or reading fiction under the desk. Mathematics being one of the few branches of school learning which are of any use in after life, nobody ever dreamed of doing any work in that direction, least of all O'Hara. It was a theory of O'Hara's that he came to school to enjoy himself. To have done any work during a mathematics lessons would have struck him as a positive waste of time, especially as he was in Mr Banks' class. Mr Banks was a master who simply cried out to be ragged. Everything he did and said seemed to invite the members of his class to amuse themselves, and they amused themselves accordingly. One of the advantages of being under him was that it was possible to predict to a nicety the moment when one would be sent out of the room. This was found very convenient.

O'Hara's ally, Moriarty, was accustomed to take his mathematics with Mr Morgan, whose room was directly opposite Mr Banks'. With Mr Morgan it was not quite so easy to date one's expulsion from the room under ordinary circumstances, and in the normal wear and tear of the morning's work, but there was one particular action which could always be relied upon to produce the desired result.

In one corner of the room stood a gigantic globe. The problem—how did it get into the room?—was one that had exercised the minds of many generations of Wrykinians. It was much too big to have come through the door. Some thought that the block had been built round it, others that it had been placed in the room in infancy, and had since grown. To refer the question to Mr Morgan would, in six cases out of ten, mean instant departure from the room. But to make the event certain, it was necessary to grasp the globe firmly and spin it round on its axis. That always proved successful. Mr Morgan would dash down from his dais, address the offender in spirited terms, and give him his marching orders at once and without further trouble.

Moriarty had arranged with O'Hara to set the globe rolling at ten sharp on this particular morning. O'Hara would then so arrange matters with Mr Banks that they could meet in the passage at that hour, when O'Hara wished to impart to his friend his information concerning the League.

O'Hara promised to be at the trysting-place at the hour mentioned.

He did not think there would be any difficulty about it. The news that the League had been revived meant that there would be trouble in the very near future, and the prospect of trouble was meat and drink to the Irishman in O'Hara. Consequently he felt in particularly good form for mathematics (as he interpreted the word). He thought that he would have no difficulty whatever in keeping Mr Banks bright and amused. The first step had to be to arouse in him an interest in life, to bring him into a frame of mind which would induce him to look severely rather than leniently on the next offender. This was effected as follows : —

It was Mr Banks' practice to set his class sums to work out, and, after some three-quarters of an hour had elapsed, to pass round the form what he called "solutions". These were large sheets of paper, on which he had worked out each sum in his neat handwriting to a happy ending. When the head of the form, to whom they were passed first, had finished with them, he would make a slight tear in one corner, and, having done so, hand them on to his neighbour. The neighbour, before giving them to *his* neighbour, would also tear them slightly. In time they would return to their patentee and proprietor, and it was then that things became exciting.

"Who tore these solutions like this?" asked Mr Banks, in the repressed voice of one who is determined that he *will* be calm.

No answer. The tattered solutions waved in the air.

He turned to Harringay, the head of the form.

"Harringay, did you tear these solutions like this?"

Indignant negative from Harringay. What he had done had been to make the small tear in the top left-hand corner. If Mr Banks had asked, "Did you make this small tear in the top left-hand corner of these solutions?" Harringay would have scorned to deny the impeachment. But to claim the credit for the whole work would, he felt, be an act of flat dishonesty, and an injustice to his gifted *collaborateurs.*

"No, sir," said Harringay.

"Browne!"

"Yes, sir?"

"Did you tear these solutions in this manner?"

"No, sir."

And so on through the form.

Then Harringay rose after the manner of the debater who is conscious that he is going to say the popular thing.

"Sir—" he began.

"Sit down, Harringay."

Harringay gracefully waved aside the absurd command.

"Sir," he said, "I think I am expressing the general consensus of opinion among my—ahem—fellow-students, when I say that this class sincerely regrets the unfortunate state the solutions have managed to get themselves into."

"Hear, hear!" from a back bench.

"It is with—"

"Sit *down*, Harringay."

"It is with heartfelt—"

"Harringay, if you do not sit down—"

"As your ludship pleases." This *sotto voce*.

And Harringay resumed his seat amidst applause. O'Hara got up.

"As me frind who has just sat down was about to observe—"

"Sit *down*, O'Hara. The whole form will remain after the class."

"—the unfortunate state the solutions have managed to get thimsilves into is sincerely regretted by this class. Sir, I think I am ixprissing the general consensus of opinion among my fellow-students whin I say that it is with heartfelt sorrow—"

"O'Hara!"

"Yes, sir?"

"Leave the room instantly."

"Yes, sir."

From the tower across the gravel came the melodious sound of chimes. The college clock was beginning to strike ten. He had scarcely got into the passage, and closed the door after him, when a roar as of a bereaved spirit rang through the room opposite, followed by a string of words, the only intelligible one being the noun-substantive "globe", and the next moment the door opened and Moriarty came out. The last stroke of ten was just booming from the clock.

There was a large cupboard in the passage, the top of which made a very comfortable seat. They climbed on to this, and began to talk business.

"An' what was it ye wanted to tell me?" inquired Moriarty.

O'Hara related what he had learned from Trevor that morning.

"An' do ye know," said Moriarty, when he had finished, "I half suspected, when I heard that Mill's study had been ragged, that it might be the League that had done it. If ye remember, it was what they enjoyed doing, breaking up a man's happy home. They did it frequently."

"But I can't understand them doing it to Trevor at all."

"They'll do it to anybody they choose till they're caught at it."

"If they are caught, there'll be a row."

"We must catch 'em," said Moriarty. Like O'Hara, he revelled in the prospect of a disturbance. O'Hara and he were going up to Aldershot at the end of the term, to try and bring back the light and middle-weight medals respectively. Moriarty had won the light-weight in the previous year, but, by reason of putting on a stone since the competition, was now no longer eligible for that class. O'Hara had not been up before, but the Wrykyn instructor, a good judge of pugilistic form, was of opinion that he ought to stand an excellent chance. As the prize-fighter in *Rodney Stone* says, "When you get a good Irishman, you can't better 'em, but they're dreadful 'asty." O'Hara was attending the gymnasium every night, in order to learn to curb his "dreadful 'astiness", and acquire skill in its place.

"I wonder if Trevor would be any good in a row," said Moriarty.

"He can't box," said O'Hara, "but he'd go on till he was killed entirely. I say, I'm getting rather tired of sitting here, aren't you? Let's go to the other end of the passage and have some cricket."

So, having unearthed a piece of wood from the débris at the top of the cupboard, and rolled a handkerchief into a ball, they adjourned.

Recalling the stirring events of six years back, when the League had first been started, O'Hara remembered that the members of that enterprising society had been wont to hold meetings in a secluded spot, where it was unlikely that they would be disturbed. It seemed to him that the first thing he ought to do, if he wanted to make their nearer acquaintance now, was to find their present rendezvous. They must have one. They would never run the risk involved in holding mass-meetings in one another's studies. On the last occasion, it had been an old quarry away out on the downs. This had been proved by the not-to-be-shaken testimony of three school-house fags, who had wandered out one half-holiday with the unconcealed intention of finding the League's place of meeting. Unfortunately for them, they *had* found it. They were going down the path that led to the quarry before-mentioned, when they were unexpectedly seized, blindfolded, and carried off. An impromptu court-martial was held—in whispers—and the three explorers forthwith received the most spirited "touching-up" they had ever experienced. Afterwards they were released, and returned to their house with their zeal for detection quite quenched. The episode had created a good deal of excitement in the school at the time.

On three successive afternoons, O'Hara and Moriarty scoured the downs, and on each occasion they drew blank. On the fourth day, just before lock-up, O'Hara, who had been to tea with Gregson, of Day's, was going over to the gymnasium to keep a pugilistic appointment with Moriarty, when somebody ran swiftly past him in the direction of the boarding-houses. It was almost dark, for the days were still short, and he did not recognise the runner. But it puzzled him a little to think where he had sprung from. O'Hara was walking quite close to the wall of the College buildings, and the runner had passed between it and him. And he had not heard his footsteps. Then he understood, and his pulse quickened as he felt that he was on the track. Beneath the block was a large sort of cellar-basement. It was used as a store-room for chairs, and was never opened except when prize-day or some similar event occurred, when the chairs were needed. It was supposed to be locked at other times, but never was. The door was just by the spot where he was standing. As he stood there, half-a-dozen other vague forms dashed past him in a knot. One of them almost brushed against him. For a moment he thought of stopping him, but decided not to. He could wait.

On the following afternoon he slipped down into the basement soon after school. It was as black as pitch in the cellar. He took up a position near the door.

It seemed hours before anything happened. He was, indeed, almost giving up the thing as a bad job, when a ray of light cut through the blackness in front of him, and somebody slipped through the door. The next moment, a second form appeared dimly, and then the light was shut off again.

O'Hara could hear them groping their way past him. He waited no longer. It is difficult to tell where sound comes from in the dark. He plunged forward at a venture. His hand, swinging round in a semicircle, met something which felt like a shoulder. He slipped his grasp down to the arm, and clutched it with all the force at his disposal.

MAINLY ABOUT FERRETS

"Ow!" exclaimed the captive, with no uncertain voice. "Let go, you ass, you're hurting."

The voice was a treble voice. This surprised O'Hara. It looked very much as if he had put up the wrong bird. From the dimensions of the arm which he was holding, his prisoner seemed to be of tender years.

"Let go, Harvey, you idiot. I shall kick."

Before the threat could be put into execution, O'Hara, who had been fumbling all this while in his pocket for a match, found one loose, and struck a light. The features of the owner of the arm—he was still holding it—were lit up for a moment.

"Why, it's young Renford!" he exclaimed. "What are you doing down here?"

Renford, however, continued to pursue the topic of his arm, and the effect that the vice-like grip of the Irishman had had upon it.

"You've nearly broken it," he said, complainingly.

"I'm sorry. I mistook you for somebody else. Who's that with you?"

"It's me," said an ungrammatical voice.

"Who's me?"

"Harvey."

At this point a soft yellow light lit up the more immediate neighbourhood. Harvey had brought a bicycle lamp into action.

"That's more like it," said Renford. "Look here, O'Hara, you won't split, will you?"

"I'm not an informer by profession, thanks," said O'Hara.

"Oh, I know it's all right, really, but you can't be too careful, because one isn't allowed down here, and there'd be a beastly row if it got out about our being down here."

"And *they* would be cobbed," put in Harvey.

"Who are they?" asked O'Hara.

"Ferrets. Like to have a look at them?"

"*Ferrets!*"

"Yes. Harvey brought back a couple at the beginning of term. Ripping little beasts. We couldn't keep them in the house, as they'd have got dropped on in a second, so we had to think of somewhere else, and thought why not keep them down here?"

"Why, indeed?" said O'Hara. "Do ye find they like it?"

"Oh, *they* don't mind," said Harvey. "We feed 'em twice a day. Once before breakfast—we take it in turns to get up early—and once directly after school. And on half-holidays and Sundays we take them out on to the downs."

"What for?"

"Why, rabbits, of course. Renford brought back a saloon-pistol with him. We keep it locked up in a box—don't tell any one."

"And what do ye do with the rabbits?"

"We pot at them as they come out of the holes."

"Yes, but when ye hit 'em?"

"Oh," said Renford, with some reluctance, "we haven't exactly hit any yet."

"We've got jolly near, though, lots of times," said Harvey. "Last Saturday I swear I wasn't more than a quarter of an inch off one of them. If it had been a decent-sized rabbit, I should have plugged it middle stump; only it was a small one, so I missed. But come and see them. We keep 'em right at the other end of the place, in case anybody comes in."

"Have you ever seen anybody down here?" asked O'Hara.

"Once," said Renford. "Half-a-dozen chaps came down here once while we were feeding the ferrets. We waited till they'd got well in, then we nipped out quietly. They didn't see us."

"Did you see who they were?"

"No. It was too dark. Here they are. Rummy old crib this, isn't it? Look out for your shins on the chairs. Switch on the light, Harvey. There, aren't they rippers? Quite tame, too. They know us quite well. They know they're going to be fed, too. Hullo, Sir Nigel! This is Sir Nigel. Out of the 'White Company', you know. Don't let him nip your fingers. This other one's Sherlock Holmes."

"Cats-s-s--s!!" said O'Hara. He had a sort of idea that that was the right thing to say to any animal that could chase and bite.

Renford was delighted to be able to show his ferrets off to so distinguished a visitor.

"What were you down here about?" inquired Harvey, when the little animals had had their meal, and had retired once more into private life.

O'Hara had expected this question, but he did not quite know what answer to give. Perhaps, on the whole, he thought, it would be best to tell them the real reason. If he refused to explain, their curiosity would be roused, which would be fatal. And to give any reason except the true one called for a display of impromptu invention of which he was not capable. Besides, they would not be likely to give away his secret while he held this one of theirs connected with the ferrets. He explained the situation briefly, and swore them to silence on the subject.

Renford's comment was brief.

"By Jove!" he observed.

Harvey went more deeply into the question.

"What makes you think they meet down here?" he asked.

"I saw some fellows cutting out of here last night. And you say ye've seen them here, too. I don't see what object they could have down here if they weren't the League holding a meeting. I don't see what else a chap would be after."

"He might be keeping ferrets," hazarded Renford.

"The whole school doesn't keep ferrets," said O'Hara. "You're unique in that way. No, it must be the League, an' I mean to wait here till they come."

"Not all night?" asked Harvey. He had a great respect for O'Hara, whose reputation in the school for out-of-the-way doings was considerable. In the bright lexicon of O'Hara he believed there to be no such word as "impossible."

"No," said O'Hara, "but till lock-up. You two had better cut now."

"Yes, I think we'd better," said Harvey.

"And don't ye breathe a word about this to a soul"—a warning which extracted fervent promises of silence from both youths.

"This," said Harvey, as they emerged on to the gravel, "is something like. I'm jolly glad we're in it."

"Rather. Do you think O'Hara will catch them?"

"He must if he waits down there long enough. They're certain to come again. Don't you wish you'd been here when the League was on before?"

"I should think I did. Race you over to the shop. I want to get something before it shuts."

"Right ho!" And they disappeared.

O'Hara waited where he was till six struck from the clock-tower, followed by the sound of the bell as it rang for lock-up. Then he picked his way carefully through the groves of chairs, barking his shins now and then on their out-turned legs, and, pushing open the door, went out into the open air. It felt very fresh and pleasant after the brand of atmosphere supplied in the vault. He then ran over to the gymnasium to meet Moriarty, feeling a little disgusted at the lack of success that had attended his detective efforts up to the present. So far he had nothing to show for his trouble except a good deal of dust on his clothes, and a dirty collar, but he was full of determination. He could play a waiting game.

It was a pity, as it happened, that O'Hara left the vault when he did. Five minutes after he had gone, six shadowy forms made their way silently and in single file through the doorway of the vault, which they closed carefully behind them. The fact that it was after lock-up was of small consequence. A good deal of latitude in that way was allowed at Wrykyn. It was the custom to go out, after the bell had sounded, to visit the gymnasium. In the winter and Easter terms, the gymnasium became a sort of social club. People went there with a very small intention of doing gymnastics. They went to lounge about, talking to cronies, in front of the two huge stoves which warmed the place. Occasionally, as a concession to the look of the thing, they would do an easy exercise or two on the horse or parallels, but, for the most part, they preferred the *rôle* of spectator. There was plenty to see. In one corner O'Hara and Moriarty would be sparring their nightly six rounds (in two batches of three rounds each). In another, Drummond, who was going up to Aldershot as a feather-weight, would be putting in a little practice with the instructor. On the apparatus, the members of the gymnastic six, including the two experts who were to carry the school colours to Aldershot in the spring, would be performing their usual marvels. It was worth dropping into the gymnasium of an evening. In no other place in the school were so many sights to be seen.

When you were surfeited with sightseeing, you went off to your house. And this was where the peculiar beauty of the gymnasium system came in. You went up to any master who happened to be there—there was always one at least—and observed in suave accents, "Please, sir, can I have a paper?" Whereupon, he, taking a scrap of paper, would write upon it, "J. O. Jones (or A. B. Smith or C. D. Robinson) left gymnasium at such-and-such a time". And, by presenting this to the menial who opened the door to you at your house, you went in rejoicing, and all was peace.

Now, there was no mention on the paper of the hour at which you *came* to the gymnasium—only of the hour at which you left. Consequently, certain lawless spirits would range the neighbourhood after lock-up, and, by putting in a quarter of an hour at the gymnasium before returning to their houses, escape comment. To this class belonged the shadowy forms previously mentioned.

O'Hara had forgotten this custom, with the result that he was not at the vault when they arrived. Moriarty, to whom he confided between the rounds the substance of his evening's discoveries, reminded him of it.

"It's no good watching before lock-up," he said. "After six is the time they'll come, if they come at all."

"Bedad, ye're right," said O'Hara. "One of these nights we'll take a night off from boxing, and go and watch."

"Right," said Moriarty. "Are ye ready to go on?"

"Yes. I'm going to practise that left swing at the body this round. The one Fitzsimmons does." And they "put 'em up" once more.

X

On the evening following O'Hara's adventure in the vaults,
Barry and M'Todd were in their study, getting out the
tea-things. Most Wrykinians brewed in the winter and
Easter terms, when the days were short and lock-up early.
In the summer term there were other things to do—nets,
which lasted till a quarter to seven (when lock-up was),
and the baths—and brewing practically ceased. But just
now it was at its height, and every evening, at a quarter
past five, there might be heard in the houses the sizzling
of the succulent sausage and other rare delicacies. As a
rule, one or two studies would club together to brew,
instead of preparing solitary banquets. This was found both
more convivial and more economical. At Seymour's, studies
numbers five, six, and seven had always combined from
time immemorial, and Barry, on obtaining study six, had
carried on the tradition. In study five were Drummond and
his friend De Bertini. In study seven, which was a smaller
room and only capable of holding one person with any
comfort, one James Rupert Leather-Twigg (that was his
singular name, as Mr Gilbert has it) had taken up his
abode. The name of Leather-Twigg having proved, at an
early date in his career, too great a mouthful for Wrykyn,
he was known to his friends and acquaintances by the
euphonious title of Shoeblossom. The charm about the
genial Shoeblossom was that you could never tell what he
was going to do next. All that you could rely on with any
certainty was that it would be something which would have
been better left undone.

It was just five o'clock when Barry and M'Todd started to get things ready. They were not high enough up in the school to have fags, so that they had to do this for themselves.

Barry was still in football clothes. He had been out running and passing with the first fifteen. M'Todd, whose idea of exercise was winding up a watch, had been spending his time since school ceased in the study with a book. He was in his ordinary clothes. It was therefore fortunate that, when he upset the kettle (he nearly always did at some period of the evening's business), the contents spread themselves over Barry, and not over himself. Football clothes will stand any amount of water, whereas M'Todd's "Youth's winter suiting at forty-two shillings and sixpence" might have been injured. Barry, however, did not look upon the episode in this philosophical light. He spoke to him eloquently for a while, and then sent him downstairs to fetch more water. While he was away, Drummond and De Bertini came in.

"Hullo," said Drummond, "tea ready?"

"Not much," replied Barry, bitterly, "not likely to be, either, at this rate. We'd just got the kettle going when that ass M'Todd plunged against the table and upset the lot over my bags. Lucky the beastly stuff wasn't boiling. I'm soaked."

"While we wait—the sausages—Yes?—a good idea— M'Todd, he is downstairs—but to wait? No, no. Let us. Shall we? Is it not so? Yes?" observed Bertie, lucidly.

"Now construe," said Barry, looking at the linguist with a bewildered expression. It was a source of no little inconvenience to his friends that De Bertini was so very fixed in his determination to speak English. He was a trier all the way, was De Bertini. You rarely caught him helping out his remarks with the language of his native land. It was English or nothing with him. To most of his circle it might as well have been Zulu.

Drummond, either through natural genius or because he spent more time with him, was generally able to act as interpreter. Occasionally there would come a linguistic effort by which even he freely confessed himself baffled, and then they would pass on unsatisfied. But, as a rule, he was equal to the emergency. He was so now.

"What Bertie means," he explained, "is that it's no good us waiting for M'Todd to come back. He never could fill a kettle in less than ten minutes, and even then he's certain to spill it coming upstairs and have to go back again. Let's get on with the sausages."

The pan had just been placed on the fire when M'Todd returned with the water. He tripped over the mat as he entered, and spilt about half a pint into one of his football boots, which stood inside the door, but the accident was comparatively trivial, and excited no remark.

"I wonder where that slacker Shoeblossom has got to," said Barry. "He never turns up in time to do any work. He seems to regard himself as a beastly guest. I wish we could finish the sausages before he comes. It would be a sell for him."

"Not much chance of that," said Drummond, who was kneeling before the fire and keeping an excited eye on the spluttering pan, "*you* see. He'll come just as we've finished cooking them. I believe the man waits outside with his ear to the keyhole. Hullo! Stand by with the plate. They'll be done in half a jiffy."

Just as the last sausage was deposited in safety on the plate, the door opened, and Shoeblossom, looking as if he had not brushed his hair since early childhood, sidled in with an attempt at an easy nonchalance which was rendered quite impossible by the hopeless state of his conscience.

"Ah," he said, "brewing, I see. Can I be of any use?"

"We've finished years ago," said Barry.

"Ages ago," said M'Todd.

A look of intense alarm appeared on Shoeblossom's classical features.

"You've not finished, really?"

"We've finished cooking everything," said Drummond. "We haven't begun tea yet. Now, are you happy?"

Shoeblossom was. So happy that he felt he must do something to celebrate the occasion. He felt like a successful general. There must be *something* he could do to show that he regarded the situation with approval. He looked round the study. Ha! Happy thought—the frying-pan. That useful culinary instrument was lying in the fender, still bearing its cargo of fat, and beside it—a sight to stir the blood and make the heart beat faster—were the sausages, piled up on their plate.

Shoeblossom stooped. He seized the frying-pan. He gave it one twirl in the air. Then, before any one could stop him, he had turned it upside down over the fire. As has been already remarked, you could never predict exactly what James Rupert Leather-Twigg would be up to next.

When anything goes out of the frying-pan into the fire, it is usually productive of interesting by-products. The maxim applies to fat. The fat was in the fire with a vengeance. A great sheet of flame rushed out and up. Shoeblossom leaped back with a readiness highly creditable in one who was not a professional acrobat. The covering of the mantelpiece caught fire. The flames went roaring up the chimney.

Drummond, cool while everything else was so hot, without a word moved to the mantelpiece to beat out the fire with a football shirt. Bertie was talking rapidly to himself in French. Nobody could understand what he was saying, which was possibly fortunate.

By the time Drummond had extinguished the mantelpiece, Barry had also done good work by knocking the fire into the grate with the poker. M'Todd, who had been standing up till now in the far corner of the room, gaping vaguely at things in general, now came into action. Probably it was force of habit that suggested to him that the time had come to upset the kettle. At any rate, upset it he did—most of it over the glowing, blazing mass in the grate, the rest over Barry. One of the largest and most detestable smells the study had ever had to endure instantly assailed their nostrils. The fire in the study was out now, but in the chimney it still blazed merrily.

"Go up on to the roof and heave water down," said Drummond, the strategist. "You can get out from Milton's dormitory window. And take care not to chuck it down the wrong chimney."

Barry was starting for the door to carry out these excellent instructions, when it flew open.

"Pah! *What* have you boys been doing? What an abominable smell. Pah!" said a muffled voice. It was Mr Seymour. Most of his face was concealed in a large handkerchief, but by the look of his eyes, which appeared above, he did not seem pleased. He took in the situation at a glance. Fires in the house were not rarities. One facetious sportsman had once made a rule of setting the senior day-room chimney on fire every term. He had since left (by request), but fires still occurred.

"Is the chimney on fire?"

"Yes, sir," said Drummond.

"Go and find Herbert, and tell him to take some water on to the roof and throw it down." Herbert was the boot and knife cleaner at Seymour's.

Barry went. Soon afterwards a splash of water in the grate announced that the intrepid Herbert was hard at it. Another followed, and another. Then there was a pause. Mr Seymour thought he would look up to see if the fire was out. He stooped and peered into the darkness, and, even as he gazed, splash came the contents of the fourth pail, together with some soot with which they had formed a travelling acquaintance on the way down. Mr Seymour staggered back, grimy and dripping. There was dead silence in the study. Shoeblossom's face might have been seen working convulsively.

The silence was broken by a hollow, sepulchral voice with a strong Cockney accent.

"Did yer see any water come down then, sir?" said the voice.

Shoeblossom collapsed into a chair, and began to sob feebly.

"—disgraceful . . . scandalous . . . get *up*, Leather-Twigg . . . not to be trusted . . . *babies* . . . three hundred lines, Leather-Twigg . . . abominable . . . surprised . . . ought to be ashamed of yourselves . . . *double*, Leather-Twigg . . . not fit to have studies . . . atrocious . . .—"

Such were the main heads of Mr Seymour's speech on the situation as he dabbed desperately at the soot on his face with his handkerchief. Shoeblossom stood and gurgled throughout. Not even the thought of six hundred lines could quench that dauntless spirit.

"Finally," perorated Mr Seymour, as he was leaving the room, "as you are evidently not to be trusted with rooms of your own, I forbid you to enter them till further notice. It is disgraceful that such a thing should happen. Do you hear, Barry? And you, Drummond? You are not to enter your studies again till I give you leave. Move your books down to the senior day-room tonight."

And Mr Seymour stalked off to clean himself.

"Anyhow," said Shoeblossom, as his footsteps died away, "we saved the sausages."

It is this indomitable gift of looking on the bright side that makes us Englishmen what we are.

XI

The House-Matches

It was something of a consolation to Barry and his friends —at any rate, to Barry and Drummond—that directly after they had been evicted from their study, the house-matches began. Except for the Ripton match, the house-matches were the most important event of the Easter term. Even the sports at the beginning of April were productive of less excitement. There were twelve houses at Wrykyn, and they played on the "knocking-out" system. To be beaten once meant that a house was no longer eligible for the competition. It could play "friendlies" as much as it liked, but, play it never so wisely, it could not lift the cup. Thus it often happened that a weak house, by fluking a victory over a strong rival, found itself, much to its surprise, in the semi-final, or sometimes even in the final. This was rarer at football than at cricket, for at football the better team generally wins.

The favourites this year were Donaldson's, though some fancied Seymour's. Donaldson's had Trevor, whose leadership was worth almost more than his play. In no other house was training so rigid. You could tell a Donaldson's man, if he was in his house-team, at a glance. If you saw a man eating oatmeal biscuits in the shop, and eyeing wistfully the while the stacks of buns and pastry, you could put him down as a Donaldsonite without further evidence. The captains of the other houses used to prescribe a certain amount of self-abnegation in the matter of food, but Trevor left his men barely enough to support life—enough, that is, of the things that are really worth eating. The consequence was that Donaldson's would turn out for an important match all muscle and bone, and on such occasions it was bad for those of their opponents who had been taking life more easily. Besides Trevor they had Clowes, and had had bad luck in not having Paget. Had Paget stopped, no other house could have looked at them. But by his departure, the strength of the team had become more nearly on a level with that of Seymour's.

Some even thought that Seymour's were the stronger. Milton was as good a forward as the school possessed. Besides him there were Barry and Rand-Brown on the wings. Drummond was a useful half, and five of the pack had either first or second fifteen colours. It was a team that would take some beating.

Trevor came to that conclusion early. "If we can beat Seymour's, we'll lift the cup," he said to Clowes.

"We'll have to do all we know," was Clowes' reply.

They were watching Seymour's pile up an immense score against a scratch team got up by one of the masters. The first round of the competition was over. Donaldson's had beaten Templar's, Seymour's the School House. Templar's were rather stronger than the School House, and Donaldson's had beaten them by a rather larger score than that which Seymour's had run up in their match. But neither Trevor nor Clowes was inclined to draw any augury from this. Seymour's had taken things easily after half-time; Donaldson's had kept going hard all through.

"That makes Rand-Brown's fourth try," said Clowes, as the wing three-quarter of the second fifteen raced round and scored in the corner.

"Yes. This is the sort of game he's all right in. The man who's marking him is no good. Barry's scored twice, and both good tries, too."

"Oh, there's no doubt which is the best man," said Clowes. "I only mentioned that it was Rand-Brown's fourth as an item of interest."

The game continued. Barry scored a third try.

"We're drawn against Appleby's next round," said Trevor. "We can manage them all right."

"When is it?"

"Next Thursday. Nomads' match on Saturday. Then Ripton, Saturday week."

"Who've Seymour's drawn?"

"Day's. It'll be a good game, too. Seymour's ought to win, but they'll have to play their best. Day's have got some good men."

"Fine scrum," said Clowes.

"Yes. Quick in the open, too, which is always good business. I wish they'd beat Seymour's."

"Oh, we ought to be all right, whichever wins."

Appleby's did not offer any very serious resistance to the Donaldson attack. They were outplayed at every point of the game, and, before half-time, Donaldson's had scored their thirty points. It was a rule in all in-school matches— and a good rule, too—that, when one side led by thirty points, the match stopped. This prevented those massacres which do so much towards crushing all the football out of the members of the beaten team; and it kept the winning team from getting slack, by urging them on to score their thirty points before half-time. There were some houses— notoriously slack—which would go for a couple of seasons without ever playing the second half of a match.

Having polished off the men of Appleby, the Donaldson team trooped off to the other game to see how Seymour's were getting on with Day's. It was evidently an exciting match. The first half had been played to the accompaniment of much shouting from the ropes. Though coming so early in the competition, it was really the semi-final, for whichever team won would be almost certain to get into the final. The school had turned up in large numbers to watch.

"Seymour's looking tired of life," said Clowes. "That would seem as if his fellows weren't doing well."

"What's been happening here?" asked Trevor of an enthusiast in a Seymour's house cap whose face was crimson with yelling.

"One goal all," replied the enthusiast huskily. "Did you beat Appleby's?"

"Yes. Thirty points before half-time. Who's been doing the scoring here?"

"Milton got in for us. He barged through out of touch. We've been pressing the whole time. Barry got over once, but he was held up. Hullo, they're beginning again. Buck up, Sey-*mour's*."

His voice cracking on the high note, he took an immense slab of vanilla chocolate as a remedy for hoarseness.

"Who scored for Day's?" asked Clowes.

"Strachan. Rand-Brown let him through from their twenty-five. You never saw anything so rotten as Rand-Brown. He doesn't take his passes, and Strachan gets past him every time."

"Is Strachan playing on the wing?"

Strachan was the first fifteen full-back.

"Yes. They've put young Bassett back instead of him. Sey-*mour's*. Buck up, Seymour's. We-ell played! There, did you ever see anything like it?" he broke off disgustedly.

The Seymourite playing centre next to Rand-Brown had run through to the back and passed out to his wing, as a good centre should. It was a perfect pass, except that it came at his head instead of his chest. Nobody with any pretensions to decent play should have missed it. Rand-Brown, however, achieved that feat. The ball struck his hands and bounded forward. The referee blew his whistle for a scrum, and a certain try was lost.

From the scrum the Seymour's forwards broke away to the goal-line, where they were pulled up by Bassett. The next minute the defence had been pierced, and Drummond was lying on the ball a yard across the line. The enthusiast standing by Clowes expended the last relics of his voice in commemorating the fact that his side had the lead.

"Drummond'll be good next year," said Trevor. And he made a mental note to tell Allardyce, who would succeed him in the command of the school football, to keep an eye on the player in question.

The triumph of the Seymourites was not long lived. Milton failed to convert Drummond's try. From the drop-out from the twenty-five line Barry got the ball, and punted into touch. The throw-out was not straight, and a scrum was formed. The ball came out to the Day's halves, and went across to Strachan. Rand-Brown hesitated, and then made a futile spring at the first fifteen man's neck. Strachan handed him off easily, and ran. The Seymour's full-back, who was a poor player, failed to get across in time. Strachan ran round behind the posts, the kick succeeded, and Day's now led by two points.

After this the game continued in Day's half. Five minutes before time was up, Drummond got the ball from a scrum nearly on the line, passed it to Barry on the wing instead of opening up the game by passing to his centres, and Barry slipped through in the corner. This put Seymour's just one point ahead, and there they stayed till the whistle blew for no-side.

Milton walked over to the boarding-houses with Clowes and Trevor. He was full of the match, particularly of the iniquity of Rand-Brown.

"I slanged him on the field," he said. "It's a thing I don't often do, but what else *can* you do when a man plays like that? He lost us three certain tries."

"When did you administer your rebuke?" inquired Clowes.

"When he had let Strachan through that second time, in the second half. I asked him why on earth he tried to play footer at all. I told him a good kiss-in-the-ring club

was about his form. It was rather cheap, but I felt so
frightfully sick about it. It's sickening to be let down like
that when you've been pressing the whole time, and ought
to be scoring every other minute."

"What had he to say on the subject?" asked Clowes.

"Oh, he gassed a bit until I told him I'd kick him if he
said another word. That shut him up."

"You ought to have kicked him. You want all the kicking
practice you can get. I never saw anything feebler than that
shot of yours after Drummond's try."

"I'd like to see *you* take a kick like that. It was nearly
on the touch-line. Still, when we play you, we shan't need
to convert any of our tries. We'll get our thirty points
without that. Perhaps you'd like to scratch?"

"As a matter of fact," said Clowes confidentially, "I am
going to score seven tries against you off my own bat.
You'll be sorry you ever turned out when we've finished
with you."

XII

News of the Gold Bat

Shoeblossom sat disconsolately on the table in the senior day-room. He was not happy in exile. Brewing in the senior day-room was a mere vulgar brawl, lacking all the refining influences of the study. You had to fight for a place at the fire, and when you had got it 'twas not always easy to keep it, and there was no privacy, and the fellows were always bear-fighting, so that it was impossible to read a book quietly for ten consecutive minutes without some ass heaving a cushion at you or turning out the gas. Altogether Shoeblossom yearned for the peace of his study, and wished earnestly that Mr Seymour would withdraw the order of banishment. It was the not being able to read that he objected to chiefly. In place of brewing, the ex-proprietors of studies five, six, and seven now made a practice of going to the school shop. It was more expensive and not nearly so comfortable—there is a romance about a study brew which you can never get anywhere else—but it served, and it was not on this score that he grumbled most. What he hated was having to live in a bear-garden. For Shoeblossom was a man of moods. Give him two or three congenial spirits to back him up, and he would lead the revels with the *abandon* of a Mr Bultitude (after his return to his original form). But he liked to choose his accomplices, and the gay sparks of the senior day-room did not appeal to him. They were not intellectual enough. In his lucid intervals, he was accustomed to be almost abnormally solemn and respectable. When not promoting some unholy rag, Shoeblossom resembled an elderly gentleman of studious habits. He liked to sit in a comfortable chair and read a book. It was the impossibility of doing this in the senior day-room that led him to try and think of some other haven where he might rest. Had it been summer, he would have taken some literature out on to the cricket-field or the downs, and put in a little steady reading there, with the aid of a bag of cherries. But with the thermometer low, that was impossible.

He felt very lonely and dismal. He was not a man with many friends. In fact, Barry and the other three were almost the only members of the house with whom he was on speaking-terms. And of these four he saw very little. Drummond and Barry were always out of doors or over at the gymnasium, and as for M'Todd and De Bertini, it was not worth while talking to the one, and impossible to talk to the other. No wonder Shoeblossom felt dull. Once Barry and Drummond had taken him over to the gymnasium with them, but this had bored him worse than ever. They had been hard at it all the time—for, unlike a good many of the school, they went to the gymnasium for business, not to lounge—and he had had to sit about watching them. And watching gymnastics was one of the things he most loathed. Since then he had refused to go.

That night matters came to a head. Just as he had settled down to read, somebody, in flinging a cushion across the room, brought down the gas apparatus with a run, and before light was once more restored it was tea-time. After that there was preparation, which lasted for two hours, and by the time he had to go to bed he had not been able to read a single page of the enthralling work with which he was at present occupied.

He had just got into bed when he was struck with a brilliant idea. Why waste the precious hours in sleep? What was that saying of somebody's, "Five hours for a wise man, six for somebody else—he forgot whom—eight for a fool, nine for an idiot," or words to that effect? Five hours sleep would mean that he need not go to bed till half-past two. In the meanwhile he could be finding out exactly what the hero *did* do when he found out (to his horror) that it was his cousin Jasper who had really killed the old gentleman in the wood. The only question was—how was he to do his reading? Prefects were allowed to work on after lights out in their dormitories by the aid of a candle, but to the ordinary mortal this was forbidden.

Then he was struck with another brilliant idea. It is a curious thing about ideas. You do not get one for over a month, and then there comes a rush of them, all brilliant. Why, he thought, should he not go and read in his study with a dark lantern? He had a dark lantern. It was one of the things he had found lying about at home on the last day of the holidays, and had brought with him to school. It was his custom to go about the house just before the holidays ended, snapping up unconsidered trifles, which might or might not come in useful. This term he had brought back a curious metal vase (which looked Indian, but which had probably been made in Birmingham the year before last), two old coins (of no mortal use to anybody in the world, including himself), and the dark lantern. It was reposing now in the cupboard in his study nearest the window.

He had brought his book up with him on coming to bed, on the chance that he might have time to read a page or two if he woke up early. (He had always been doubtful about that man Jasper. For one thing, he had been seen pawning the old gentleman's watch on the afternoon of the murder, which was a suspicious circumstance, and then he was not a nice character at all, and just the sort of man who would be likely to murder old gentlemen in woods.) He waited till Mr Seymour had paid his nightly visit—he went the round of the dormitories at about eleven—and then he chuckled gently. If Mill, the dormitory prefect, was awake, the chuckle would make him speak, for Mill was of a suspicious nature, and believed that it was only his unintermitted vigilance which prevented the dormitory ragging all night.

Mill *was* awake.

"Be quiet, there," he growled. "Shut up that noise."

Shoeblossom felt that the time was not yet ripe for his departure. Half an hour later he tried again. There was no rebuke. To make certain he emitted a second chuckle, replete with sinister meaning. A slight snore came from the direction of Mill's bed. Shoeblossom crept out of the room, and hurried to his study. The door was not locked, for Mr Seymour had relied on his commands being sufficient to keep the owner out of it. He slipped in, found and lit the dark lantern, and settled down to read. He read with feverish excitement. The thing was, you see, that though Claud Trevelyan (that was the hero) knew jolly well that it was Jasper who had done the murder, the police didn't, and, as he (Claud) was too noble to tell them, he had himself been arrested on suspicion. Shoeblossom was skimming through the pages with starting eyes, when suddenly his attention was taken from his book by a sound. It was a footstep. Somebody was coming down the passage, and under the door filtered a thin stream of light. To snap the dark slide over the lantern and dart to the door, so that if it opened he would be behind it, was with him, as Mr Claud Trevelyan might have remarked, the work of a moment. He heard the door of study number five flung open, and then the footsteps passed on, and stopped opposite his own den. The handle turned, and the light of a candle flashed into the room, to be extinguished instantly as the draught of the moving door caught it.

Shoeblossom heard his visitor utter an exclamation of annoyance, and fumble in his pocket for matches. He recognised the voice. It was Mr Seymour's. The fact was that Mr Seymour had had the same experience as General Stanley in *The Pirates of Penzance*:

The man who finds his conscience ache,
No peace at all enjoys;
And, as I lay in bed awake,
I thought I heard a noise.

Whether Mr Seymour's conscience ached or not, cannot, of course, be discovered. But he had certainly thought he heard a noise, and he had come to investigate.

The search for matches had so far proved fruitless. Shoeblossom stood and quaked behind the door. The reek of hot tin from the dark lantern grew worse momentarily. Mr Seymour sniffed several times, until Shoeblossom thought that he must be discovered. Then, to his immense relief, the master walked away. Shoeblossom's chance had come. Mr Seymour had probably gone to get some matches to relight his candle. It was far from likely that the episode was closed. He would be back again presently. If Shoeblossom was going to escape, he must do it now, so he waited till the footsteps had passed away, and then darted out in the direction of his dormitory.

As he was passing Milton's study, a white figure glided out of it. All that he had ever read or heard of spectres rushed into Shoeblossom's petrified brain. He wished he was safely in bed. He wished he had never come out of it. He wished he had led a better and nobler life. He wished he had never been born.

The figure passed quite close to him as he stood glued against the wall, and he saw it disappear into the dormitory opposite his own, of which Rigby was prefect. He blushed hotly at the thought of the fright he had been in. It was only somebody playing the same game as himself.

He jumped into bed and lay down, having first plunged the lantern bodily into his jug to extinguish it. Its indignant hiss had scarcely died away when Mr Seymour appeared at the door. It had occurred to Mr Seymour that he had smelt something very much out of the ordinary in Shoeblossom's study, a smell uncommonly like that of hot tin. And a suspicion dawned on him that Shoeblossom had been in there with a dark lantern. He had come to the dormitory to confirm his suspicions. But a glance showed him how unjust they had been. There was Shoeblossom fast asleep. Mr Seymour therefore followed the excellent example of my Lord Tomnoddy on a celebrated occasion, and went off to bed.

It was the custom for the captain of football at Wrykyn to select and publish the team for the Ripton match a week before the day on which it was to be played. On the evening after the Nomads' match, Trevor was sitting in his study writing out the names, when there came a knock at the door, and his fag entered with a letter.

"This has just come, Trevor," he said.

"All right. Put it down."

The fag left the room. Trevor picked up the letter. The handwriting was strange to him. The words had been printed. Then it flashed upon him that he had received a letter once before addressed in the same way—the letter from the League about Barry. Was this, too, from that address? He opened it.

It was.

He read it, and gasped. The worst had happened. The gold bat was in the hands of the enemy.

XIII

Victim Number Three

"With reference to our last communication," ran the letter
—the writer evidently believed in the commercial style—
"it may interest you to know that the bat you lost by the
statue on the night of the 26th of January has come into
our possession. *We observe that Barry is still playing for the
first fifteen.*"

"And will jolly well continue to," muttered Trevor,
crumpling the paper viciously into a ball.

He went on writing the names for the Ripton match.
The last name on the list was Barry's.

Then he sat back in his chair, and began to wrestle with
this new development. Barry must play. That was certain.
All the bluff in the world was not going to keep him from
playing the best man at his disposal in the Ripton match.
He himself did not count. It was the school he had to think
of. This being so, what was likely to happen? Though nothing was said on the point, he felt certain that if he persisted in ignoring the League, that bat would find its way
somehow—by devious routes, possibly—to the headmaster
or some one else in authority. And then there would be
questions—awkward questions—and things would begin
to come out. Then a fresh point struck him, which was,
that whatever might happen would affect, not himself, but
O'Hara. This made it rather more of a problem how to
act. Personally, he was one of those dogged characters who
can put up with almost anything themselves. If this had
been his affair, he would have gone on his way without hesi-
tating. Evidently the writer of the letter was under the

impression that he had been the hero (or villain) of the statue escapade.

If everything came out it did not require any great effort of prophecy to predict what the result would be. O'Hara would go. Promptly. He would receive his marching orders within ten minutes of the discovery of what he had done. He would be expelled twice over, so to speak, once for breaking out at night—one of the most heinous offences in the school code—and once for tarring the statue. Anything that gave the school a bad name in the town was a crime in the eyes of the powers, and this was such a particularly flagrant case. Yes, there was no doubt of that. O'Hara would take the first train home without waiting to pack up. Trevor knew his people well, and he could imagine their feelings when the prodigal strolled into their midst— an old Wrykinian *malgré lui.* As the philosopher said of falling off a ladder, it is not the falling that matters : it is the sudden stopping at the other end. It is not the being expelled that is so peculiarly objectionable : it is the sudden homecoming. With this gloomy vision before him, Trevor almost wavered. But the thought that the selection of the team had nothing whatever to do with his personal feelings strengthened him. He was simply a machine, devised to select the fifteen best men in the school to meet Ripton. In his official capacity of football captain he was not supposed to have any feelings. However, he yielded in so far that he went to Clowes to ask his opinion.

Clowes, having heard everything and seen the letter, un-hesitatingly voted for the right course. If fifty mad Irish-men were to be expelled, Barry must play against Ripton. He was the best man, and in he must go.

"That's what I thought," said Trevor. "It's bad for O'Hara, though."

Clowes remarked somewhat tritely that business was business.

"Besides," he went on, "you're assuming that the thing

this letter hints at will really come off. I don't think it will. A man would have to be such an awful blackguard to go as low as that. The least grain of decency in him would stop him. I can imagine a man threatening to do it as a piece of bluff—by the way, the letter doesn't actually say anything of the sort, though I suppose it hints at it—but I can't imagine anybody out of a melodrama doing it."

"You can never tell," said Trevor. He felt that this was but an outside chance. The forbearance of one's antagonist is but a poor thing to trust to at the best of times.

"Are you going to tell O'Hara?" asked Clowes.

"I don't see the good. Would you?"

"No. He can't do anything, and it would only give him a bad time. There are pleasanter things, I should think, than going on from day to day not knowing whether you're going to be sacked or not within the next twelve hours. Don't tell him."

"I won't. And Barry plays against Ripton."

"Certainly. He's the best man."

"I'm going over to Seymour's now," said Trevor, after a pause, "to see Milton. We've drawn Seymour's in the next round of the house-matches. I suppose you knew. I want to get it over before the Ripton match, for several reasons. About half the fifteen are playing on one side or the other, and it'll give them a good chance of getting fit. Running and passing is all right, but a good, hard game's the thing for putting you into form. And then I was thinking that, as the side that loses, whichever it is—"

"Seymour's, of course."

"Hope so. Well, they're bound to be a bit sick at losing, so they'll play up all the harder on Saturday to console themselves for losing the cup."

"My word, what strategy!" said Clowes. "You think of everything. When do you think of playing it, then?"

"Wednesday struck me as a good day. Don't you think so?"

"It would do splendidly. It'll be a good match. For all practical purposes, of course, it's the final. If we beat Seymour's, I don't think the others will trouble us much."

There was just time to see Milton before lock-up. Trevor ran across to Seymour's, and went up to his study.

"Come in," said Milton, in answer to his knock.

Trevor went in, and stood surprised at the difference in the look of the place since the last time he had visited it. The walls, once covered with photographs, were bare. Milton, seated before the fire, was ruefully contemplating what looked like a heap of waste cardboard.

Trevor recognised the symptoms. He had had experience.

"You don't mean to say they've been at you, too!" he cried.

Milton's normally cheerful face was thunderous and gloomy.

"Yes. I was thinking what I'd like to do to the man who ragged it."

"It's the League again, I suppose?"

Milton looked surprised.

"*Again?*" he said, "where did *you* hear of the League? This is the first time I've heard of its existence, whatever it is. What *is* the confounded thing, and why on earth have they played the fool here? What's the meaning of this bally rot?"

He exhibited one of the variety of cards of which Trevor had already seen two specimens. Trevor explained briefly the style and nature of the League, and mentioned that his study also had been wrecked.

"Your study? Why, what have they got against you?"

"I don't know," said Trevor. Nothing was to be gained by speaking of the letters he had received.

"Did they cut up your photographs?"

"Every one."

"I tell you what it is, Trevor, old chap," said Milton, with great solemnity, "there's a lunatic in the school. That's what I make of it. A lunatic whose form of madness is wrecking studies."

"But the same chap couldn't have done yours and mine. It must have been a Donaldson's fellow who did mine, and one of your chaps who did yours and Mill's."

"Mill's? By Jove, of course. I never thought of that. That was the League, too, I suppose?"

"Yes. One of those cards was tied to a chair, but Clowes took it away before anybody saw it."

Milton returned to the details of the disaster.

"Was there any ink spilt in your room?"

"Pints," said Trevor, shortly. The subject was painful.

"So there was here," said Milton, mournfully. "Gallons."

There was silence for a while, each pondering over his wrongs.

"Gallons," said Milton again. "I was ass enough to keep a large pot full of it here, and they used it all, every drop. You never saw such a sight."

Trevor said he had seen one similar spectacle.

"And my photographs! You remember those photographs I showed you? All ruined. Slit across with a knife. Some torn in half. I wish I knew who did that."

Trevor said he wished so, too.

"There was one of Mrs Patrick Campbell," Milton continued in heartrending tones, "which was torn into sixteen pieces. I counted them. There they are on the mantelpiece. And there was one of Little Tich" (here he almost broke down), "which was so covered with ink that for half an hour I couldn't recognise it. Fact."

Trevor nodded sympathetically.

"Yes," said Milton. "Soaked."

There was another silence. Trevor felt it would be almost an outrage to discuss so prosaic a topic as the date of a house-match with one so broken up. Yet time was flying, and lock-up was drawing near.

"Are you willing to play—" he began.

"I feel as if I could never play again," interrupted Milton. "You'd hardly believe the amount of blotting-paper I've used today. It must have been a lunatic, Dick, old man."

When Milton called Trevor "Dick", it was a sign that he was moved. When he called him "Dick, old man", it gave evidence of an internal upheaval without parallel.

"Why, who else but a lunatic would get up in the night to wreck another chap's study? All this was done between eleven last night and seven this morning. I turned in at eleven, and when I came down here again at seven the place was a wreck. It must have been a lunatic."

"How do you account for the printed card from the League?"

Milton murmured something about madmen's cunning and diverting suspicion, and relapsed into silence. Trevor seized the opportunity to make the proposal he had come to make, that Donaldson's *v.* Seymour's should be played on the following Wednesday.

Milton agreed listlessly.

"Just where you're standing," he said, "I found a photograph of Sir Henry Irving so slashed about that I thought at first it was Huntley Wright in *San Toy*."

"Start at two-thirty sharp," said Trevor.

"I had seventeen of Edna May," continued the stricken Seymourite, monotonously. "In various attitudes. All destroyed."

"On the first fifteen ground, of course," said Trevor. "I'll get Aldridge to referee. That'll suit you, I suppose?"

"All right. Anything you like. Just by the fireplace I found the remains of Arthur Roberts in *H.M.S. Irresponsible*. And part of Seymour Hicks. Under the table—"

Trevor departed.

XIV

The White Figure

"Suppose," said Shoeblossom to Barry, as they were walking over to school on the morning following the day on which Milton's study had passed through the hands of the League, "suppose you thought somebody had done something, but you weren't quite certain who, but you knew it was some one, what would you do?"

"What on *earth* do you mean?" inquired Barry.

"I was trying to make an A.B. case of it," explained Shoeblossom.

"What's an A.B. case?"

"I don't know," admitted Shoeblossom, frankly. "But it comes in a book of Stevenson's. I think it must mean a sort of case where you call everyone A. and B. and don't tell their names."

"Well, go ahead."

"It's about Milton's study."

"What! what about it?"

"Well, you see, the night it was ragged I was sitting in my study with a dark lantern——"

"What!"

Shoeblossom proceeded to relate the moving narrative of his night-walking adventure. He dwelt movingly on his state of mind when standing behind the door, waiting for Mr Seymour to come in and find him. He related with appropriate force the hair-raising episode of the weird white figure. And then he came to the conclusions he had since drawn (in calmer moments) from that apparition's movements.

"You see," he said, "I saw it coming out of Milton's study, and that must have been about the time the study was ragged. And it went into Rigby's dorm. So it must have been a chap in that dorm. who did it."

Shoeblossom was quite clever at rare intervals. Even Barry, whose belief in his sanity was of the smallest, was compelled to admit that here, at any rate, he was talking sense.

"What would you do?" asked Shoeblossom.

"Tell Milton, of course," said Barry.

"But he'd give me beans for being out of the dorm. after lights-out."

This was a distinct point to be considered. The attitude of Barry towards Milton was different from that of Shoe-blossom. Barry regarded him—through having played with him in important matches—as a good sort of fellow who had always behaved decently to him. Leather-Twigg, on the other hand, looked on him with undisguised apprehension, as one in authority who would give him lines the first time he came into contact with him, and cane him if he ever did it again. He had a decided disinclination to see Milton on any pretext whatever.

"Suppose I tell him?" suggested Barry.

"You'll keep my name dark?" said Shoeblossom, alarmed.

Barry said he would make an A.B. case of it.

After school he went to Milton's study, and found him still brooding over its departed glories.

"I say, Milton, can I speak to you for a second?"

"Hullo, Barry. Come in."

Barry came in.

"I had forty-three photographs," began Milton, without preamble. "All destroyed. And I've no money to buy any more. I had seventeen of Edna May."

Barry, feeling that he was expected to say something, said, "By Jove! Really?"

"In various positions," continued Milton. "All ruined."

"Not really?" said Barry.

"There was one of Little Tich—"

But Barry felt unequal to playing the part of chorus any longer. It was all very thrilling, but, if Milton was going to run through the entire list of his destroyed photographs, life would be too short for conversation on any other topic.

"I say, Milton," he said, "it was about that that I came. I'm sorry—"

Milton sat up.

"It wasn't you who did this, was it?"

"No, no," said Barry, hastily.

"Oh, I thought from your saying you were sorry—"

"I was going to say I thought I could put you on the track of the chap who did do it—"

For the second time since the interview began Milton sat up.

"Go on," he said.

"—But I'm sorry I can't give you the name of the fellow who told me about it."

"That doesn't matter," said Milton. "Tell me the name of the fellow who did it. That'll satisfy me."

"I'm afraid I can't do that, either."

"Have you any idea what you *can* do?" asked Milton, satirically.

"I can tell you something which may put you on the right track."

"That'll do for a start. Well?"

"Well, the chap who told me—I'll call him A.; I'm going to make an A.B. case of it—was coming out of his study at about one o'clock in the morning—"

"What the deuce was he doing that for?"

"Because he wanted to go back to bed," said Barry.

"About time, too. Well?"

"As he was going past your study, a white figure emerged—"

"I should strongly advise you, young Barry," said Milton, gravely, "not to try and rot me in any way. You're a jolly good wing three-quarters, but you shouldn't presume on it. I'd slay the Old Man himself if he rotted me about this business."

Barry was quite pained at this sceptical attitude in one whom he was going out of his way to assist.

"I'm not rotting," he protested. "This is all quite true."

"Well, go on. You were saying something about white figures emerging."

"Not white figures. A white figure," corrected Barry. "It came out of your study—"

"—And vanished through the wall?"

"It went into Rigby's dorm.," said Barry, sulkily. It was maddening to have an exclusive bit of news treated in this way.

"Did it, by Jove!" said Milton, interested at last. "Are you sure the chap who told you wasn't pulling your leg? Who was it told you?"

"I promised him not to say."

"Out with it, young Barry."

"I won't," said Barry.

"You aren't going to tell me?"

"No."

Milton gave up the point with much cheerfulness. He liked Barry, and he realised that he had no right to try and make him break his promise.

"That's all right," he said. "Thanks very much, Barry. This may be useful."

"I'd tell you his name if I hadn't promised, you know, Milton."

"It doesn't matter," said Milton. "It's not important."

"Oh, there was one thing I forgot. It was a biggish chap the fellow saw."

"How big! My size?"

"Not quite so tall, I should think. He said he was about Seymour's size."

"Thanks. That's worth knowing. Thanks very much, Barry."

When his visitor had gone, Milton proceeded to unearth one of the printed lists of the house which were used for purposes of roll-call. He meant to find out who were in Rigby's dormitory. He put a tick against the names. There were eighteen of them. The next thing was to find out which of them was about the same height as Mr Seymour. It was a somewhat vague description, for the house-master stood about five feet nine or eight, and a good many of the dormitory were that height, or near it. At last, after much brain-work, he reduced the number of "possibles" to seven. These seven were Rigby himself, Linton, Rand-Brown, Griffith, Hunt, Kershaw, and Chapple. Rigby might be scratched off the list at once. He was one of Milton's greatest friends. Exeunt also Griffith, Hunt, and Kershaw. They were mild youths, quite incapable of any deed of devilry. There remained, therefore, Chapple, Linton, and Rand-Brown. Chapple was a boy who was invariably late for breakfast. The inference was that he was not likely to forego his sleep for the purpose of wrecking studies. Chapple might disappear from the list. Now there were only Linton and Rand-Brown to be considered. His suspicions fell on Rand-Brown. Linton was the last person, he thought, to do such a low thing. He was a cheerful, rollicking individual, who was popular with everyone and seemed to like everyone. He was not an orderly member of the house, certainly, and on several occasions Milton had found it necessary to drop on him heavily for creating disturbances. But he was not the sort that bears malice. He took it all in the way of business, and came up smiling after it was over. No, everything pointed to Rand-Brown. He and Milton had never got on well together, and quite recently they had quarrelled openly over the former's play in the Day's match.

Rand-Brown must be the man. But Milton was sensible enough to feel that so far he had no real evidence whatever. He must wait.

On the following afternoon Seymour's turned out to play Donaldson's.

The game, like most house-matches, was played with the utmost keenness. Both teams had good three-quarters, and they attacked in turn. Seymour's had the best of it forward, where Milton was playing a great game, but Trevor in the centre was the best outside on the field, and pulled up rush after rush. By half-time neither side had scored.

After half-time Seymour's, playing downhill, came away with a rush to the Donaldsonites' half, and Rand-Brown, with one of the few decent runs he had made in good class football that term, ran in on the left. Milton took the kick, but failed, and Seymour's led by three points. For the next twenty minutes nothing more was scored. Then, when five minutes more of play remained, Trevor gave Clowes an easy opening, and Clowes sprinted between the posts. The kick was an easy one, and what sporting reporters term "the major points" were easily added.

When there are five more minutes to play in an important house-match, and one side has scored a goal and the other a try, play is apt to become spirited. Both teams were doing all they knew. The ball came out to Barry on the right. Barry's abilities as a three-quarter rested chiefly on the fact that he could dodge well. This eel-like attribute compensated for a certain lack of pace. He was past the Donaldson's three-quarters in an instant, and running for the line, with only the back to pass, and with Clowes in hot pursuit. Another wriggle took him past the back, but it also gave Clowes time to catch him up. Clowes was a far faster runner, and he got to him just as he reached the twenty-five line. They came down together with a crash, Clowes on top, and as they fell the whistle blew.

"No-side," said Mr. Aldridge, the master who was refereeing.

Clowes got up.

"All over," he said. "Jolly good game. Hullo, what's up?"

For Barry seemed to be in trouble.

"You might give us a hand up," said the latter. "I believe I've twisted my beastly ankle or something."

XV

A Sprain and a Vacant Place

"I say," said Clowes, helping him up, "I'm awfully sorry. Did I do it? How did it happen?"

Barry was engaged in making various attempts at standing on the injured leg. The process seemed to be painful.

"Shall I get a stretcher or anything? Can you walk?"

"If you'd help me over to the house, I could manage all right. What a beastly nuisance! It wasn't your fault a bit. Only you tackled me when I was just trying to swerve, and my ankle was all twisted."

Drummond came up, carrying Barry's blazer and sweater.

"Hullo, Barry," he said, "what's up? You aren't crocked?"

"Something gone wrong with my ankle. That my blazer? Thanks. Coming over to the house? Clowes was just going to help me over."

Clowes asked a Donaldson's junior, who was lurking near at hand, to fetch his blazer and carry it over to the house, and then made his way with Drummond and the disabled Barry to Seymour's. Having arrived at the senior day-room, they deposited the injured three-quarter in a chair, and sent M'Todd, who came in at the moment, to fetch the doctor.

Dr Oakes was a big man with a breezy manner, the sort of doctor who hits you with the force of a sledge-hammer in the small ribs, and asks you if you felt anything *then*. It was on this principle that he acted with regard to Barry's ankle. He seized it in both hands and gave it a wrench.

"Did that hurt?" he inquired anxiously.

Barry turned white, and replied that it did.

Dr Oakes nodded wisely.

"Ah! H'm! Just so. 'Myes. Ah."

"Is it bad?" asked Drummond, awed by these mystic utterances.

"My dear boy," replied the doctor, breezily, "it is always bad when one twists one's ankle."

"How long will it do me out of footer?" asked Barry.

"How long? How long? How long? Why, fortnight. Fortnight," said the doctor.

"Then I shan't be able to play next Saturday?"

"Next Saturday? Next Saturday? My dear boy, if you can put your foot to the ground by next Saturday, you may take it as evidence that the age of miracles is not past. Next Saturday, indeed! Ha, ha."

It was not altogether his fault that he treated the matter with such brutal levity. It was a long time since he had been at school, and he could not quite realise what it meant to Barry not to be able to play against Ripton. As for Barry, he felt that he had never loathed and detested any one so thoroughly as he loathed and detested Dr Oakes at that moment.

"I don't see where the joke comes in," said Clowes, when he had gone. "I bar that man."

"He's a beast," said Drummond. "I can't understand why they let a tout like that be the school doctor."

Barry said nothing. He was too sore for words.

What Dr Oakes said to his wife that evening was: "Over at the school, my dear, this afternoon. This afternoon. Boy with a twisted ankle. Nice young fellow. Very much put out when I told him he could not play football for a fortnight. But I chaffed him, and cheered him up in no time. I cheered him up in no time, my dear."

"I'm sure you did, dear," said Mrs Oakes. Which shows how differently the same thing may strike different people.

Barry certainly did not look as if he had been cheered up when Clowes left the study and went over to tell Trevor that he would have to find a substitute for his right wing three-quarter against Ripton.

Trevor had left the field without noticing Barry's accident, and he was tremendously pleased at the result of the game.

"Good man," he said, when Clowes came in, "you saved the match."

"And lost the Ripton match probably," said Clowes, gloomily.

"What do you mean?"

"That last time I brought down Barry I crocked him. He's in his study now with a sprained ankle. I've just come from there. Oakes has seen him, and says he mustn't play for a fortnight."

"Great Scott!" said Trevor, blankly. "What on earth shall we do?"

"Why not move Strachan up to the wing, and put somebody else back instead of him? Strachan is a good wing."

Trevor shook his head.

"No. There's nobody good enough to play back for the first. We mustn't risk it."

"Then I suppose it must be Rand-Brown?"

"I suppose so."

"He may do better than we think. He played quite a decent game today. That try he got wasn't half a bad one."

"He'd be all right if he didn't funk. But perhaps he wouldn't funk against Ripton. In a match like that anybody would play up. I'll ask Milton and Allardyce about it."

"I shouldn't go to Milton today," said Clowes. "I fancy he'll want a night's rest before he's fit to talk to. He must be a bit sick about this match. I know he expected Seymour's to win."

He went out, but came back almost immediately.

"I say," he said, "there's one thing that's just occurred to me. This'll please the League. I mean, this ankle business of Barry's."

The same idea had struck Trevor. It was certainly a respite. But he regretted it for all that. What he wanted was to beat Ripton, and Barry's absence would weaken the team. However, it was good in its way, and cleared the atmosphere for the time. The League would hardly do anything with regard to the carrying out of their threat while Barry was on the sick-list.

Next day, having given him time to get over the bitterness of defeat in accordance with Clowes' thoughtful suggestion, Trevor called on Milton, and asked him what his opinion was on the subject of the inclusion of Rand-Brown in the first fifteen in place of Barry.

"He's the next best man," he added, in defence of the proposal.

"I suppose so," said Milton. "He'd better play, I suppose. There's no one else."

"Clowes thought it wouldn't be a bad idea to shove Strachan on the wing, and put somebody else back."

"Who is there to put?"

"Jervis?"

"Not good enough. No, it's better to be weakish on the wing than at back. Besides, Rand-Brown may do all right. He played well against you."

"Yes," said Trevor. "Study looks a bit better now," he added, as he was going, having looked round the room. "Still a bit bare, though."

Milton sighed. "It will never be what it was."

"Forty-three theatrical photographs want some replacing, of course," said Trevor. "But it isn't bad, considering."

"How's yours?"

"Oh, mine's all right, except for the absence of photographs."

"I say, Trevor."

"Yes?" said Trevor, stopping at the door. Milton's voice had taken on the tone of one who is about to disclose dreadful secrets.

"Would you like to know what I think?"

"What?"

"Why, I'm pretty nearly sure who it was that ragged my study?"

"By Jove! What have you done to him?"

"Nothing as yet. I'm not quite sure of my man."

"Who is the man?"

"Rand-Brown."

"By Jove! Clowes once said he thought Rand-Brown must be the President of the League. But then, I don't see how you can account for *my* study being wrecked. He was out on the field when it was done."

"Why, the League, of course. You don't suppose he's the only man in it? There must be a lot of them."

"But what makes you think it was Rand-Brown?"

Milton told him the story of Shoeblossom, as Barry had told it to him. The only difference was that Trevor listened without any of the scepticism which Milton had displayed on hearing it. He was getting excited. It all fitted in so neatly. If ever there was circumstantial evidence against a man, here it was against Rand-Brown. Take the two cases. Milton had quarrelled with him. Milton's study was wrecked "with the compliments of the League". Trevor had turned him out of the first fifteen. Trevor's study was wrecked "with the compliments of the League". As Clowes had pointed out, the man with the most obvious motive for not wishing Barry to play for the school was Rand-Brown. It seemed a true bill.

"I shouldn't wonder if you're right," he said, "but of course one can't do anything yet. You want a lot more evidence. Anyhow, we must play him against Ripton, I suppose. Which is his study? I'll go and tell him now."

"Ten."

Trevor knocked at the door of study Ten. Rand-Brown was sitting over the fire, reading. He jumped up when he saw that it was Trevor who had come in, and to his visitor it seemed that his face wore a guilty look.

"What do you want?" said Rand-Brown.

It was not the politest way of welcoming a visitor. It increased Trevor's suspicions. The man was afraid. A great idea darted into his mind. Why not go straight to the point and have it out with him here and now? He had the League's letter about the bat in his pocket. He would confront him with it and insist on searching the study there and then. If Rand-Brown were really, as he suspected, the writer of the letter, the bat must be in this room somewhere. Search it now, and he would have no time to hide it. He pulled out the letter.

"I believe you wrote that," he said.

Trevor was always direct.

Rand-Brown seemed to turn a little pale, but his voice when he replied was quite steady.

"That's a lie," he said.

"Then, perhaps," said Trevor, "you wouldn't object to proving it."

"How?"

"By letting me search your study?"

"You don't believe my word?"

"Why should I? You don't believe mine."

Rand-Brown made no comment on this remark.

"Was that what you came here for?" he asked.

"No," said Trevor; "as a matter of fact, I came to tell you to turn out for running and passing with the first tomorrow afternoon. You're playing against Ripton on Saturday."

Rand-Brown's attitude underwent a complete transformation at the news. He became friendliness itself.

"All right," he said. "I say, I'm sorry I said what I did

about lying. I was rather sick that you should think I wrote
that rot you showed me. I hope you don't mind."

"Not a bit. Do you mind my searching your study?"

For a moment Rand-Brown looked vicious. Then he sat
down with a laugh.

"Go on," he said; "I see you don't believe me. Here are
the keys if you want them."

Trevor thanked him, and took the keys. He opened every
drawer and examined the writing-desk. The bat was in
none of these places. He looked in the cupboards. No bat
there.

"Like to take up the carpet?" inquired Rand-Brown.

"No, thanks."

"Search me if you like. Shall I turn out my pockets?"

"Yes, please," said Trevor, to his surprise. He had not
expected to be taken literally.

Rand-Brown emptied them, but the bat was not there.
Trevor turned to go.

"You've not looked inside the legs of the chairs yet," said
Rand-Brown. "They may be hollow. There's no knowing."

"It doesn't matter, thanks," said Trevor. "Sorry for
troubling you. Don't forget tomorrow afternoon."

And he went, with the very unpleasant feeling that he
had been badly scored off.

XVI

THE RIPTON MATCH

It was a curious thing in connection with the matches between Ripton and Wrykyn, that Ripton always seemed to be the bigger team. They always had a gigantic pack of forwards, who looked capable of shoving a hole through one of the pyramids. Possibly they looked bigger to the Wrykinians than they really were. Strangers always look big on the football field. When you have grown accustomed to a person's appearance, he does not look nearly so large. Milton, for instance, never struck anybody at Wrykyn as being particularly big for a school forward, and yet today he was the heaviest man on the field by a quarter of a stone. But, taken in the mass, the Ripton pack were far heavier than their rivals. There was a legend current among the lower forms at Wrykyn that fellows were allowed to stop on at Ripton till they were twenty-five, simply to play football. This is scarcely likely to have been based on fact. Few lower form legends are.

Jevons, the Ripton captain, through having played opposite Trevor for three seasons—he was the Ripton left centre-three-quarter—had come to be quite an intimate of his. Trevor had gone down with Milton and Allardyce to meet the team at the station, and conduct them up to the school.

"How have you been getting on since Christmas?" asked Jevons.

"Pretty well. We've lost Paget, I suppose you know?"

"That was the fast man on the wing, wasn't it?"

"Yes."

"Well, we've lost a man, too."

"Oh, yes, that red-haired forward. I remember him."

"It ought to make us pretty even. What's the ground like?"

"Bit greasy, I should think. We had some rain late last night."

The ground *was* a bit greasy. So was the ball. When Milton kicked off up the hill with what wind there was in his favour, the outsides of both teams found it difficult to hold the ball. Jevons caught it on his twenty-five line, and promptly handed it forward. The first scrum was formed in the heart of the enemy's country.

A deep, swelling roar from either touch-line greeted the school's advantage. A feature of a big match was always the shouting. It rarely ceased throughout the whole course of the game, the monotonous but impressive sound of five hundred voices all shouting the same word. It was worth hearing. Sometimes the evenness of the noise would change to an excited *crescendo* as a school three-quarter got off, or the school back pulled up the attack with a fine piece of defence. Sometimes the shouting would give place to clapping when the school was being pressed and somebody had found touch with a long kick. But mostly the man on the ropes roared steadily and without cessation, and with the full force of his lungs, the word *"Wrykyn!"*

The scrum was a long one. For two minutes the forwards heaved and strained, now one side, now the other, gaining a few inches. The Wrykyn pack were doing all they knew to heel, but their opponents' superior weight was telling. Ripton had got the ball, and were keeping it. Their game was to break through with it and rush. Then suddenly one of their forwards kicked it on, and just at that moment the opposition of the Wrykyn pack gave way, and the scrum broke up. The ball came out on the Wrykyn side, and Allardyce whipped it out to Deacon, who was playing half with him.

"Ball's out," cried the Ripton half who was taking the scrum. "Break up. It's out."

And his colleague on the left darted across to stop Trevor, who had taken Deacon's pass, and was running through on the right.

Trevor ran splendidly. He was a three-quarter who took a lot of stopping when he once got away. Jevons and the Ripton half met him almost simultaneously, and each slackened his pace for the fraction of a second, to allow the other to tackle. As they hesitated, Trevor passed them. He had long ago learned that to go hard when you have once started is the thing that pays.

He could see that Rand-Brown was racing up for the pass, and, as he reached the back, he sent the ball to him, waist-high. Then the back got to him, and he came down with a thud, with a vision, seen from the corner of his eye, of the ball bounding forward out of the wing three-quarter's hands into touch. Rand-Brown had bungled the pass in the old familiar way, and lost a certain try.

The touch-judge ran up with his flag waving in the air, but the referee had other views.

"Knocked on inside," he said; "scrum here."

"Here" was, Trevor saw with unspeakable disgust, some three yards from the goal-line. Rand-Brown had only had to take the pass, and he must have scored.

The Ripton forwards were beginning to find their feet better now, and they carried the scrum. A truculent-looking warrior in one of those ear-guards which are tied on by strings underneath the chin, and which add fifty per cent to the ferocity of a forward's appearance, broke away with the ball at his feet, and swept down the field with the rest of the pack at his heels. Trevor arrived too late to pull up the rush, which had gone straight down the right touch-line, and it was not till Strachan fell on the ball on the Wrykyn twenty-five line that the danger ceased to threaten.

Even now the school were in a bad way. The enemy

were pressing keenly, and a real piece of combination among their three-quarters would only too probably end in a try. Fortunately for them, Allardyce and Deacon were a better pair of halves than the couple they were marking. Also, the Ripton forwards heeled slowly, and Allardyce had generally got his man safely buried in the mud before he could pass.

He was just getting round for the tenth time to bottle his opponent as before, when he slipped. When the ball came out he was on all fours, and the Ripton exponent, finding to his great satisfaction that he had not been tackled, whipped the ball out on the left, where a wing three-quarter hovered.

This was the man Rand-Brown was supposed to be marking, and once again did Barry's substitute prove of what stuff his tackling powers were made. After his customary moment of hesitation, he had at the Riptonian's neck. The Riptonian handed him off in a manner that recalled the palmy days of the old Prize Ring—handing off was always slightly vigorous in the Ripton *v.* Wrykyn match—and dashed over the line in the extreme corner.

There was anguish on the two touch-lines. Trevor looked savage, but made no comment. The team lined up in silence.

It takes a very good kick to convert a try from the touch-line. Jevons' kick was a long one, but it fell short. Ripton led by a try to nothing.

A few more scrums near the halfway line, and a fine attempt at a dropped goal by the Ripton back, and it was half-time, with the score unaltered.

During the interval there were lemons. An excellent thing is your lemon at half-time. It cools the mouth, quenches the thirst, stimulates the desire to be at them again, and improves the play.

Possibly the Wrykyn team had been happier in their choice of lemons on this occasion, for no sooner had the game been restarted than Clowes ran the whole length of the field, dodged through the three-quarters, punted over the back's head, and scored a really brilliant try, of the sort that Paget had been fond of scoring in the previous term. The man on the touch-line brightened up wonderfully, and began to try and calculate the probable score by the end of the game, on the assumption that, as a try had been scored in the first two minutes, ten would be scored in the first twenty, and so on.

But the calculations were based on false premises. After Strachan had failed to convert, and the game had been resumed with the score at one try all, play settled down in the centre, and neither side could pierce the other's defence. Once Jevons got off for Ripton, but Trevor brought him down safely, and once Rand-Brown let his man through, as before, but Strachan was there to meet him, and the effort came to nothing. For Wrykyn, no one did much except tackle. The forwards were beaten by the heavier pack, and seldom let the ball out. Allardyce intercepted a pass when about ten minutes of play remained, and ran through to the back. But the back, who was a capable man and in his third season in the team, laid him low scientifically before he could reach the line.

Altogether it looked as if the match were going to end in a draw. The Wrykyn defence, with the exception of Rand-Brown, was too good to be penetrated, while the Ripton forwards, by always getting the ball in the scrums, kept them from attacking. It was about five minutes from the end of the game when the Ripton right centre-three-quarter, in trying to punt across to the wing, miskicked and sent the ball straight into the hands of Trevor's colleague in the centre. Before his man could get round to him he had slipped through, with Trevor backing him up. The back, as a good back should, seeing two men coming at him, went for the man with the ball. But by the time he had brought him down, the ball was no longer where it had originally been. Trevor had got it, and was running in between the posts.

This time Strachan put on the extra two points without difficulty.

Ripton played their hardest for the remaining minutes, but without result. The game ended with Wrykyn a goal ahead—a goal and a try to a try. For the second time in one season the Ripton match had ended in a victory—a thing it was very rarely in the habit of doing.

The senior day-room at Seymour's rejoiced considerably that night. The air was dark with flying cushions, and darker still, occasionally, when the usual humorist turned the gas out. Milton was out, for he had gone to the dinner which followed the Ripton match, and the man in command of the house in his absence was Mill. And the senior day-room had no respect whatever for Mill.

Barry joined in the revels as well as his ankle would let him, but he was not feeling happy. The disappointment of being out of the first still weighed on him.

At about eight, when things were beginning to grow really lively, and the noise seemed likely to crack the window at any moment, the door was flung open and Milton stalked in.

"What's all this row?" he inquired. "Stop it at once."

As a matter of fact, the row *had* stopped—directly he came in.

"Is Barry here?" he asked.

"Yes," said that youth.

"Congratulate you on your first, Barry. We've just had a meeting and given you your colours. Trevor told me to tell you."

XVII

The Watchers in the Vault

For the next three seconds you could have heard a cannon-ball drop. And that was equivalent, in the senior day-room at Seymour's, to a dead silence. Barry stood in the middle of the room leaning on the stick on which he supported life, now that his ankle had been injured, and turned red and white in regular rotation, as the magnificence of the news came home to him.

Then the small voice of Linton was heard.

"That'll be six d. I'll trouble you for, young Sammy," said Linton. For he had betted an even sixpence with Master Samuel Menzies that Barry would get his first fifteen cap this term, and Barry had got it.

A great shout went up from every corner of the room. Barry was one of the most popular members of the house, and every one had been sorry for him when his sprained ankle had apparently put him out of the running for the last cap.

"Good old Barry," said Drummond, delightedly. Barry thanked him in a dazed way.

Every one crowded in to shake his hand. Barry thanked them all in a dazed way.

And then the senior day-room, in spite of the fact that Milton had returned, gave itself up to celebrating the occasion with one of the most deafening uproars that had ever been heard even in that factory of noise. A babel of voices discussed the match of the afternoon, each trying to outshout the other. In one corner Linton was beating wildly on a biscuit-tin with part of a broken chair. Shoeblossom was busy in the opposite corner executing an intricate step-dance on somebody else's box. M'Todd had got hold of the red-hot poker, and was burning his initials in huge letters on the seat of a chair. Every one, in short, was enjoying himself, and it was not until an advanced hour that comparative quiet was restored. It was a great evening for Barry, the best he had ever experienced.

Clowes did not learn the news till he saw it on the notice-board, on the following Monday. When he saw it he whistled softly.

"I see you've given Barry his first," he said to Trevor, when they met. "Rather sensational."

"Milton and Allardyce both thought he deserved it. If he'd been playing instead of Rand-Brown, they wouldn't have scored at all probably, and we should have got one more try."

"That's all right," said Clowes. "He deserves it right enough, and I'm jolly glad you've given it him. But things will begin to move now, don't you think? The League ought to have a word to say about the business. It'll be a facer for them."

"Do you remember," asked Trevor, "saying that you thought it must be Rand-Brown who wrote those letters?"

"Yes. Well?"

"Well, Milton had an idea that it was Rand-Brown who ragged his study."

"What made him think that?"

Trevor related the Shoeblossom incident.

Clowes became quite excited.

"Then Rand-Brown must be the man," he said. "Why don't you go and tackle him? Probably he's got the bat in his study."

"It's not in his study," said Trevor, "because I looked everywhere for it, and got him to turn out his pockets, too. And yet I'll swear he knows something about it. One thing struck me as a bit suspicious. I went straight into his study and showed him that last letter—about the bat, you know, and accused him of writing it. Now, if he hadn't been in the business somehow, he wouldn't have understood what was meant by their saying 'the bat you lost'. It might have been an ordinary cricket-bat for all he knew. But he offered to let me search the study. It didn't strike me as rum till afterwards. Then it seemed fishy. What do you think?"

Clowes thought so too, but admitted that he did not see of what use the suspicion was going to be. Whether Rand-Brown knew anything about the affair or not, it was quite certain that the bat was not with him.

O'Hara, meanwhile, had decided that the time had come for him to resume his detective duties. Moriarty agreed with him, and they resolved that that night they would patronise the vault instead of the gymnasium, and take a holiday as far as their boxing was concerned. There was plenty of time before the Aldershot competition.

Lock-up was still at six, so at a quarter to that hour they slipped down into the vault, and took up their position.

A quarter of an hour passed. The lock-up bell sounded faintly. Moriarty began to grow tired.

"Is it worth it?" he said, "an' wouldn't they have come before, if they meant to come?"

"We'll give them another quarter of an hour," said O'Hara. "After that—"

"Sh!" whispered Moriarty.

The door had opened. They could see a figure dimly outlined in the semi-darkness. Footsteps passed down into the vault, and there came a sound as if the unknown had cannoned into a chair, followed by a sharp intake of breath, expressive of pain. A scraping sound, and a flash of light, and part of the vault was lit by a candle. O'Hara caught a glimpse of the unknown's face as he rose from lighting the candle, but it was not enough to enable him to recognise him. The candle was standing on a chair, and the light it gave was too feeble to reach the face of any one not on a level with it.

The unknown began to drag chairs out into the neighbourhood of the light. O'Hara counted six.

The sixth chair had scarcely been placed in position when the door opened again. Six other figures appeared in the opening one after the other, and bolted into the vault like rabbits into a burrow. The last of them closed the door after them.

O'Hara nudged Moriarty, and Moriarty nudged O'Hara; but neither made a sound. They were not likely to be seen—the blackness of the vault was too Egyptian for that—but they were so near to the chairs that the least whisper must have been heard. Not a word had proceeded from the occupants of the chairs so far. If O'Hara's suspicion was correct, and this was really the League holding a meeting, their methods were more secret than those of any other secret society in existence. Even the Nihilists probably exchanged a few remarks from time to time, when they met together to plot. But these men of mystery never opened their lips. It puzzled O'Hara.

The light of the candle was obscured for a moment, and a sound of puffing came from the darkness.

O'Hara nudged Moriarty again.

"Smoking!" said the nudge.

Moriarty nudged O'Hara.

"Smoking it is!" was the meaning of the movement.

A strong smell of tobacco showed that the diagnosis had been a true one. Each of the figures in turn lit his pipe at the candle, and sat back, still in silence. It could not have been very pleasant, smoking in almost pitch darkness, but it was breaking rules, which was probably the main consideration that swayed the smokers. They puffed away steadily, till the two Irishmen were wrapped about in invisible clouds.

Then a strange thing happened. I know that I am

infringing copyright in making that statement, but it so exactly suits the occurrence, that perhaps Mr Rider Haggard will not object. It *was* a strange thing that happened.

A rasping voice shattered the silence.

"You boys down there," said the voice, "come here immediately. Come here, I say."

It was the well-known voice of Mr Robert Dexter, O'Hara and Moriarty's beloved house-master.

The two Irishmen simultaneously clutched one another, each afraid that the other would think—from force of long habit—that the house-master was speaking to him. Both stood where they were. It was the men of mystery and tobacco that Dexter was after, they thought.

But they were wrong. What had brought Dexter to the vault was the fact that he had seen two boys, who looked uncommonly like O'Hara and Moriarty, go down the steps of the vault at a quarter to six. He had been doing his usual after-lock-up prowl on the junior gravel, to intercept stragglers, and he had been a witness—from a distance of fifty yards, in a very bad light—of the descent into the vault. He had remained on the gravel ever since, in the hope of catching them as they came up; but as they had not come up, he had determined to make the first move himself. He had not seen the six unknowns go down, for, the evening being chilly, he had paced up and down, and they had by a lucky accident chosen a moment when his back was turned.

"Come up immediately," he repeated.

Here a blast of tobacco-smoke rushed at him from the darkness. The candle had been extinguished at the first alarm, and he had not realised—though he had suspected it—that smoking had been going on.

A hurried whispering was in progress among the unknowns. Apparently they saw that the game was up, for they picked their way towards the door.

As each came up the steps and passed him, Mr Dexter observed "Ha!" and appeared to make a note of his name. The last of the six was just leaving him after this process had been completed, when Mr Dexter called him back.

"That is not all," he said, suspiciously.

"Yes, sir," said the last of the unknowns.

Neither of the Irishmen recognised the voice. Its owner was a stranger to them.

"I tell you it is not," snapped Mr Dexter. "You are concealing the truth from me. O'Hara and Moriarty are down there—two boys in my own house. I saw them go down there."

"They had nothing to do with us, sir. We saw nothing of them."

"I have no doubt," said the house-master, "that you imagine that you are doing a very chivalrous thing by trying to hide them, but you will gain nothing by it. You may go."

He came to the top of the steps, and it seemed as if he intended to plunge into the darkness in search of the suspects. But, probably realising the futility of such a course, he changed his mind, and delivered an ultimatum from the top step.

"O'Hara and Moriarty."

No reply.

"O'Hara and Moriarty, I know perfectly well that you are down there. Come up immediately."

Dignified silence from the vault.

"Well, I shall wait here till you do choose to come up. You would be well advised to do so immediately. I warn you you will not tire me out."

He turned, and the door slammed behind him.

"What'll we do?" whispered Moriarty. It was at last safe to whisper.

"Wait," said O'Hara, "I'm thinking."

O'Hara thought. For many minutes he thought in vain.

At last there came flooding back into his mind a memory of the days of his faghood. It was after that that he had been groping all the time. He remembered now. Once in those days there had been an unexpected function in the middle of term. There were needed for that function certain chairs. He could recall even now his furious disgust when he and a select body of fellow fags had been pounced upon by their form-master, and coerced into forming a line from the junior block to the cloisters, for the purpose of handing chairs. True, his form-master had stood ginger-beer after the event, with princely liberality, but the labour was of the sort that gallons of ginger-beer will not make pleasant. But he ceased to regret the episode now. He had been at the extreme end of the chair-handling chain. He had stood in a passage in the junior block, just by the door that led to the masters' garden, and which—he remembered—was never locked till late at night. And while he stood there, a pair of hands—apparently without a body—had heaved up chair after chair through a black opening in the floor. In other words, a trap-door connected with the vault in which he now was.

He imparted these reminiscences of childhood to Moriarty. They set off to search for the missing door, and, after wanderings and barkings of shins too painful to relate, they found it. Moriarty lit a match. The light fell on the trap-door, and their last doubts were at an end. The thing opened inwards. The bolt was on their side, not in the passage above them. To shoot the bolt took them one second, to climb into the passage one minute. They stood at the side of the opening, and dusted their clothes.

"Bedad!" said Moriarty, suddenly.

"What?"

"Why, how are we to shut it?"

This was a problem that wanted some solving. Eventually they managed it, O'Hara leaning over and fishing for it, while Moriarty held his legs.

As luck would have it—and luck had stood by them well all through—there was a bolt on top of the trap-door, as well as beneath it.

"Supposing that had been shot!" said O'Hara, as they fastened the door in its place.

Moriarty did not care to suppose anything so unpleasant.

Mr Dexter was still prowling about on the junior gravel, when the two Irishmen ran round and across the senior gravel to the gymnasium. Here they put in a few minutes' gentle sparring, and then marched boldly up to Mr Day (who happened to have looked in five minutes after their arrival) and got their paper.

"What time did O'Hara and Moriarty arrive at the gymnasium?" asked Mr Dexter of Mr Day next morning.

"O'Hara and Moriarty? Really, I can't remember. I know they *left* at about a quarter to seven."

That profound thinker, Mr Tony Weller, was never so correct as in his views respecting the value of an *alibi*. There are few better things in an emergency.

XVIII

O'Hara Excels Himself

It was Renford's turn next morning to get up and feed the ferrets. Harvey had done it the day before.

Renford was not a youth who enjoyed early rising, but in the cause of the ferrets he would have endured anything, so at six punctually he slid out of bed, dressed quietly, so as not to disturb the rest of the dormitory, and ran over to the vault. To his utter amazement he found it locked. Such a thing had never been done before in the whole course of his experience. He tugged at the handle, but not an inch or a fraction of an inch would the door yield. The policy of the Open Door had ceased to find favour in the eyes of the authorities.

A feeling of blank despair seized upon him. He thought of the dismay of the ferrets when they woke up and realised that there was no chance of breakfast for them. And then they would gradually waste away, and some day somebody would go down to the vault to fetch chairs, and would come upon two mouldering skeletons, and wonder what they had once been. He almost wept at the vision so conjured up.

There was nobody about. Perhaps he might break in somehow. But then there was nothing to get to work with. He could not kick the door down. No, he must give it up, and the ferrets' breakfast-hour must be postponed. Possibly Harvey might be able to think of something.

"Fed 'em?" inquired Harvey, when they met at breakfast.

"No, I couldn't."

"Why on earth not? You didn't oversleep yourself?"

Renford poured his tale into his friend's shocked ears.

"My hat!" said Harvey, when he had finished, "what on earth are we to do? They'll starve."

Renford nodded mournfully.

"Whatever made them go and lock the door?" he said.

He seemed to think the authorities should have given him due notice of such an action.

"You're sure they have locked it? It isn't only stuck or something?"

"I lugged at the handle for hours. But you can go and see for yourself if you like."

Harvey went, and, waiting till the coast was clear, attached himself to the handle with a prehensile grasp, and put his back into one strenuous tug. It was even as Renford had said. The door was locked beyond possibility of doubt.

Renford and he went over to school that morning with long faces and a general air of acute depression. It was perhaps fortunate for their purpose that they did, for had their appearance been normal it might not have attracted O'Hara's attention. As it was, the Irishman, meeting them on the junior gravel, stopped and asked them what was wrong. Since the adventure in the vault, he had felt an interest in Renford and Harvey.

The two told their story in alternate sentences like the Strophe and Antistrophe of a Greek chorus. ("Steichomuthics," your Greek scholar calls it, I fancy. Ha, yes! Just so.)

"So ye can't get in because they've locked the door, an' ye don't know what to do about it?" said O'Hara, at the conclusion of the narrative.

Renford and Harvey informed him in chorus that that *was* the state of the game up to present date.

"An' ye want me to get them out for you?"

Neither had dared to hope that he would go so far as this. What they had looked for had been at the most a few thoughtful words of advice. That such a master-strategist as O'Hara should take up their cause was an unexampled piece of good luck.

"If you only would," said Harvey.

"We should be most awfully obliged," said Renford.

"Very well," said O'Hara.

They thanked him profusely.

O'Hara replied that it would be a privilege.

He should be sorry, he said, to have anything happen to the ferrets.

Renford and Harvey went on into school feeling more cheerful. If the ferrets could be extracted from their present tight corner, O'Hara was the man to do it.

O'Hara had not made his offer of assistance in any spirit of doubt. He was certain that he could do what he had promised. For it had not escaped his memory that this was a Tuesday—in other words, a mathematics morning up to the quarter to eleven interval. That meant, as has been explained previously, that, while the rest of the school were in the form-rooms, he would be out in the passage, if he cared to be. There would be no witnesses to what he was going to do.

But, by that curious perversity of fate which is so often noticeable, Mr Banks was in a peculiarly lamb-like and long-suffering mood this morning. Actions for which O'Hara would on other days have been expelled from the room without hope of return, today were greeted with a mild "Don't do that, please, O'Hara," or even the ridiculously inadequate "O'Hara!" It was perfectly disheartening. O'Hara began to ask himself bitterly what was the use of ragging at all if this was how it was received. And the moments were flying, and his promise to Renford and Harvey still remained unfulfilled.

He prepared for fresh efforts.

So desperate was he, that he even resorted to crude methods like the throwing of paper balls and the dropping of books. And when your really scientific ragger sinks to this, he is nearing the end of his tether. O'Hara hated to be rude, but there seemed no help for it.

The striking of a quarter past ten improved his chances. It had been privily agreed upon beforehand amongst the members of the class that at a quarter past ten every one was to sneeze simultaneously. The noise startled Mr Banks considerably. The angelic mood began to wear off. A man may be long-suffering, but he likes to draw the line somewhere.

"Another exhibition like that," he said, sharply, "and the class stays in after school, O'Hara!"

"Sir?"

"Silence."

"I said nothing, sir, really."

"Boy, you made a cat-like noise with your mouth."

"What *sort* of noise, sir?"

The form waited breathlessly. This peculiarly insidious question had been invented for mathematical use by one Sandys, who had left at the end of the previous summer. It was but rarely that the master increased the gaiety of nations by answering the question in the manner desired.

Mr Banks, off his guard, fell into the trap.

"A noise like this," he said curtly, and to the delighted audience came the melodious sound of a "Mi-aou", which put O'Hara's effort completely in the shade, and would have challenged comparison with the war-cry of the stoutest mouser that ever trod a tile.

A storm of imitations arose from all parts of the room. Mr Banks turned pink, and, going straight to the root of the disturbance, forthwith evicted O'Hara.

O'Hara left with the satisfying feeling that his duty had been done.

Mr Banks' room was at the top of the middle block. He ran softly down the stairs at his best pace. It was not likely that the master would come out into the passage to see if he was still there, but it might happen, and it would be best to run as few risks as possible.

He sprinted over to the junior block, raised the trap-door, and jumped down. He knew where the ferrets had been placed, and had no difficulty in finding them. In another minute he was in the passage again, with the trap-door bolted behind him.

He now asked himself—what should he do with them? He must find a safe place, or his labours would have been in vain.

Behind the fives-court, he thought, would be the spot. Nobody ever went there. It meant a run of three hundred yards there and the same distance back, and there was more than a chance that he might be seen by one of the Powers. In which case he might find it rather hard to explain what he was doing in the middle of the grounds with a couple of ferrets in his possession when the hands of the clock pointed to twenty minutes to eleven.

But the odds were against his being seen. He risked it.

When the bell rang for the quarter to eleven interval the ferrets were in their new home, happily discussing a piece of meat—Renford's contribution, held over from the morning's meal,—and O'Hara, looking as if he had never left the passage for an instant, was making his way through the departing mathematical class to apologise handsomely to Mr Banks—as was his invariable custom—for his disgraceful behaviour during the morning's lesson.

XIX

The Mayor's Visit

School prefects at Wrykyn did weekly essays for the head-master. Those who had got their scholarships at the 'Varsity, or who were going up in the following year, used to take their essays to him after school and read them to him—an unpopular and nerve-destroying practice, akin to suicide. Trevor had got his scholarship in the previous November. He was due at the headmaster's private house at six o'clock on the present Tuesday. He was looking forward to the ordeal not without apprehension. The essay subject this week had been "One man's meat is another man's poison", and Clowes, whose idea of English Essay was that it should be a medium for intempestive frivolity, had insisted on his beginning with, "While I cannot conscientiously go so far as to say that one man's meat is another man's poison, yet I am certainly of opinion that what is highly beneficial to one man may, on the other hand, to another man, differently constituted, be extremely deleterious, and, indeed, absolutely fatal."

Trevor was not at all sure how the headmaster would take it. But Clowes had seemed so cut up at his suggestion that it had better be omitted, that he had allowed it to stand.

He was putting the final polish on this gem of English literature at half-past five, when Milton came in.

"Busy?" said Milton.

Trevor said he would be through in a minute.

Milton took a chair, and waited.

Trevor scratched out two words and substituted two

others, made a couple of picturesque blots, and, laying down his pen, announced that he had finished.

"What's up?" he said.

"It's about the League," said Milton.

"Found out anything?"

"Not anything much. But I've been making inquiries. You remember I asked you to let me look at those letters of yours?"

Trevor nodded. This had happened on the Sunday of that week.

"Well, I wanted to look at the post-marks."

"By Jove, I never thought of that."

Milton continued with the business-like air of the detective who explains in the last chapter of the book how he did it.

"I found, as I thought, that both letters came from the same place."

Trevor pulled out the letters in question.

"So they do," he said, "Chesterton."

"Do you know Chesterton?" asked Milton.

"Only by name."

"It's a small hamlet about two miles from here across the downs. There's only one shop in the place, which acts as post-office and tobacconist and everything else. I thought that if I went there and asked about those letters, they might remember who it was that sent them, if I showed them a photograph."

"By Jove," said Trevor, "of course! Did you? What happened?"

"I went there yesterday afternoon. I took about half-a-dozen photographs of various chaps, including Rand-Brown."

"But wait a bit. If Chesterton's two miles off, Rand-Brown couldn't have sent the letters. He wouldn't have the time after school. He was on the grounds both the afternoons before I got the letters."

"I know," said Milton; "I didn't think of that at the time."

"Well?"

"One of the points about the Chesterton post-office is that there's no letter-box outside. You have to go into the shop and hand anything you want to post across the counter. I thought this was a tremendous score for me. I thought they would be bound to remember who handed in the letters. There can't be many at a place like that."

"Did they remember?"

"They remembered the letters being given in distinctly, but as for knowing anything beyond that, they were simply futile. There was an old woman in the shop, aged about three hundred and ten, I should think. I shouldn't say she had ever been very intelligent, but now she simply gibbered. I started off by laying out a shilling on some poisonous-looking sweets. I gave the lot to a village kid when I got out. I hope they didn't kill him. Then, having scattered ground-bait in that way, I lugged out the photographs, mentioned the letters and the date they had been sent, and asked her to weigh in and identify the sender."

"Did she?"

"My dear chap, she identified them all, one after the other. The first was one of Clowes. She was prepared to swear on oath that that was the chap who had sent the letters. Then I shot a photograph of you across the counter, and doubts began to creep in. She said she was certain it was one of those two 'la-ads', but couldn't quite say which. To keep her amused I fired in photograph number three—Allardyce's. She identified that, too. At the end of ten minutes she was pretty sure that it was one of the six—the other three were Paget, Clephane, and Rand-Brown—but she was not going to bind herself down to any particular one. As I had come to the end of my stock of photographs, and was getting a bit sick of the game, I got up to go, when in came another ornament of Chesterton from a room at the back of the shop. He was quite a kid, not more than a hundred and fifty at the outside, so, as a last chance, I tackled him on the subject. He looked at the photographs for about half an hour, mumbling something about it not being 'thiccy 'un' or 'that 'un', or 'that 'ere tother 'un', until I began to feel I'd had enough of it. Then it came out that the real chap who had sent the letters was a 'la-ad' with light hair, not so big as me—"

"That doesn't help us much," said Trevor.

"—And a 'prarper little gennlemun'. So all we've got to do is to look for some young duke of polished manners and exterior, with a thatch of light hair."

"There are three hundred and sixty-seven fellows with light hair in the school," said Trevor, calmly.

"Thought it was three hundred and sixty-eight myself," said Milton, "but I may be wrong. Anyhow, there you have the results of my investigations. If you can make anything out of them, you're welcome to it. Good-bye."

"Half a second," said Trevor, as he got up; "had the fellow a cap of any sort?"

"No. Bareheaded. You wouldn't expect him to give himself away by wearing a house-cap?"

Trevor went over to the headmaster's revolving this discovery in his mind. It was not much of a clue, but the smallest clue is better than nothing. To find out that the sender of the League letters had fair hair narrowed the search down a little. It cleared the more raven-locked members of the school, at any rate. Besides, by combining his information with Milton's, the search might be still further narrowed down. He knew that the polite letter-writer must be either in Seymour's or in Donaldson's. The number of fair-haired youths in the two houses was not excessive. Indeed, at the moment he could not recall any; which rather complicated matters.

He arrived at the headmaster's door, and knocked. He was shown into a room at the side of the hall, near the

door. The butler informed him that the headmaster was
engaged at present. Trevor, who knew the butler slightly
through having constantly been to see the headmaster on
business *via* the front door, asked who was there.

"Sir Eustace Briggs," said the butler, and disappeared in
the direction of his lair beyond the green baize partition at
the end of the hall.

Trevor went into the room, which was a sort of spare
study, and sat down, wondering what had brought the
mayor of Wrykyn to see the headmaster at this advanced
hour.

A quarter of an hour later the sound of voices broke in
upon his peace. The headmaster was coming down the
hall with the intention of showing his visitor out. The door
of Trevor's room was ajar, and he could hear distinctly
what was being said. He had no particular desire to play
the eavesdropper, but the part was forced upon him.

Sir Eustace seemed excited.

"It is far from being my habit," he was saying, "to make
unnecessary complaints respecting the conduct of the lads
under your care." (Sir Eustace Briggs had a distaste for the
shorter and more colloquial forms of speech. He would
have perished sooner than have substituted "complain of
your boys" for the majestic formula he had used. He spoke
as if he enjoyed choosing his words. He seemed to pause
and think before each word. Unkind people—who were
jealous of his distinguished career—used to say that he did
this because he was afraid of dropping an aitch if he relaxed
his vigilance.)

"But," continued he, "I am reluctantly forced to the
unpleasant conclusion that the dastardly outrage to which
both I and the Press of the town have called your attention
is to be attributed to one of the lads to whom I 'ave—*have*
(this with a jerk) referred."

"I will make a thorough inquiry, Sir Eustace," said the
bass voice of the headmaster.

"I thank you," said the mayor. "It would, under the circumstances, be nothing more, I think, than what is distinctly advisable. The man Samuel Wapshott, of whose narrative I have recently afforded you a brief synopsis, stated in no uncertain terms that he found at the foot of the statue on which the dastardly outrage was perpetrated a diminutive ornament, in shape like the bats that are used in the game of cricket. This ornament, he avers (with what truth I know not), was handed by him to a youth of an age coeval with that of the lads in the upper division of this school. The youth claimed it as his property, I was given to understand."

"A thorough inquiry shall be made, Sir Eustace."

"I thank you."

And then the door shut, and the conversation ceased.

XX

The Finding of the Bat

Trevor waited till the headmaster had gone back to his library, gave him five minutes to settle down, and then went in.

The headmaster looked up inquiringly.

"My essay, sir," said Trevor.

"Ah, yes. I had forgotten."

Trevor opened the notebook and began to read what he had written. He finished the paragraph which owed its insertion to Clowes, and raced hurriedly on to the next. To his surprise the flippancy passed unnoticed, at any rate, verbally. As a rule the headmaster preferred that quotations form back numbers of *Punch* should be kept out of the prefects' English Essays. And he generally said as much. But today he seemed strangely preoccupied. A split infinitive in paragraph five, which at other times would have made him sit up in his chair stiff with horror, elicited no remark. The same immunity was accorded to the insertion (inspired by Clowes, as usual) of a popular catch phrase in the last few lines. Trevor finished with the feeling that luck had favoured him nobly.

"Yes," said the headmaster, seemingly roused by the silence following on the conclusion of the essay. "Yes." Then, after a long pause, "Yes," again.

Trevor said nothing, but waited for further comment.

"Yes," said the headmaster once more, "I think that is a very fair essay. Very fair. It wants a little more—er—not quite so much—um—yes."

Trevor made a note in his mind to effect these improvements in future essays, and was getting up, when the headmaster stopped him.

"Don't go, Trevor. I wish to speak to you."

Trevor's first thought was, perhaps naturally, that the bat was going to be brought into discussion. He was wondering helplessly how he was going to keep O'Hara and his midnight exploit out of the conversation, when the headmaster resumed. "An unpleasant thing has happened, Trevor—"

"Now we're coming to it," thought Trevor.

"It appears, Trevor, that a considerable amount of smoking has been going on in the school."

Trevor breathed freely once more. It was only going to be a mere conventional smoking row after all. He listened with more enjoyment as the headmaster, having stopped to turn down the wick of the reading-lamp which stood on the table at his side, and which had begun, appropriately enough, to smoke, resumed his discourse.

"Mr Dexter—"

Of course, thought Trevor. If there ever was a row in the school, Dexter was bound to be at the bottom of it.

"Mr Dexter has just been in to see me. He reported six boys. He discovered them in the vault beneath the junior block. Two of them were boys in your house."

Trevor murmured something wordless, to show that the story interested him.

"You knew nothing of this, of course—"

"No, sir."

"No. Of course not. It is difficult for the head of a house to know all that goes on in that house."

Was this his beastly sarcasm? Trevor asked himself. But he came to the conclusion that it was not. After all, the head of a house is only human. He cannot be expected to keep an eye on the private life of every member of his house.

"This must be stopped, Trevor. There is no saying how widespread the practice has become or may become. What I want you to do is to go straight back to your house and begin a complete search of the studies."

"Tonight, sir?" It seemed too late for such amusement.

"Tonight. But before you go to your house, call at Mr Seymour's, and tell Milton I should like to see him. And, Trevor."

"Yes, sir?"

"You will understand that I am leaving this matter to you to be dealt with by you. I shall not require you to make any report to me. But if you should find tobacco in any boy's room, you must punish him well, Trevor. Punish him well."

This meant that the culprit must be "touched up" before the house assembled in the dining-room. Such an event did not often occur. The last occasion had been in Paget's first term as head of Donaldson's, when two of the senior day-room had been discovered attempting to revive the ancient and dishonourable custom of bullying. This time, Trevor foresaw, would set up a record in all probability. There might be any number of devotees of the weed, and he meant to carry out his instructions to the full, and make the criminals more unhappy than they had been since the day of their first cigar. Trevor hated the habit of smoking at school. He was so intensely keen on the success of the house and the school at games, that anything which tended to damage the wind and eye filled him with loathing. That anybody should dare to smoke in a house which was going to play in the final for the House Football Cup made him rage internally, and he proposed to make things bad and unrestful for such.

To smoke at school is to insult the divine weed. When you are obliged to smoke in odd corners, fearing every moment that you will be discovered, the whole meaning, poetry, romance of a pipe vanishes, and you become like those lost beings who smoke when they are running to catch trains. The boy who smokes at school is bound to come to a bad end. He will degenerate gradually into a person that plays dominoes in the smoking-rooms of A.B.C. shops with friends who wear bowler hats and frock coats.

Much of this philosophy Trevor expounded to Clowes in energetic language when he returned to Donaldson's after calling at Seymour's to deliver the message for Milton.

Clowes became quite animated at the prospect of a real row.

"We shall be able to see the skeletons in their cupboards," he observed. "Every man has a skeleton in his cupboard, which follows him about wherever he goes. Which study shall we go to first?"

"We?" said Trevor.

"We," repeated Clowes firmly. "I am not going to be left out of this jaunt. I need bracing up—I'm not strong, you know—and this is just the thing to do it. Besides, you'll want a bodyguard of some sort, in case the infuriated occupant turns and rends you."

"I don't see what there is to enjoy in the business," said Trevor, gloomily. "Personally, I bar this kind of thing. By the time we've finished, there won't be a chap in the house I'm on speaking terms with."

"Except me, dearest," said Clowes. "I will never desert you. It's of no use asking me, for I will never do it. Mr Micawber has his faults, but I will *never* desert Mr Micawber."

"You can come if you like," said Trevor; "we'll take the studies in order. I suppose we needn't look up the prefects?"

"A prefect is above suspicion. Scratch the prefects."

"That brings us to Dixon."

Dixon was a stout youth with spectacles, who was popularly supposed to do twenty-two hours' work a day. It was believed that he put in two hours sleep from eleven to one, and then got up and worked in his study till breakfast.

He was working when Clowes and Trevor came in. He dived head foremost into a huge Liddell and Scott as the door opened. On hearing Trevor's voice he slowly emerged, and a pair of round and spectacled eyes gazed blankly at the visitors. Trevor briefly explained his errand, but the interview lost in solemnity owing to the fact that the bare notion of Dixon storing tobacco in his room made Clowes roar with laughter. Also, Dixon stolidly refused to understand what Trevor was talking about, and at the end of ten minutes, finding it hopeless to try and explain, the two went. Dixon, with a hazy impression that he had been asked to join in some sort of round game, and had refused the offer, returned again to his Liddell and Scott, and continued to wrestle with the somewhat obscure utterances of the chorus in Æschylus' *Agamemnon*. The results of this fiasco on Trevor and Clowes were widely different. Trevor it depressed horribly. It made him feel savage. Clowes, on the other hand, regarded the whole affair in a spirit of rollicking farce, and refused to see that this was a serious matter, in which the honour of the house was involved.

The next study was Ruthven's. This fact somewhat toned down the exuberances of Clowes's demeanour. When one particularly dislikes a person, one has a curious objection to seeming in good spirits in his presence. One feels that he may take it as a sort of compliment to himself, or, at any rate, contribute grins of his own, which would be hateful. Clowes was as grave as Trevor when they entered the study.

Ruthven's study was like himself, overdressed and rather futile. It ran to little china ornaments in a good deal of profusion. It was more like a drawing-room than a school study.

"Sorry to disturb you, Ruthven," said Trevor.

"Oh, come in," said Ruthven, in a tired voice. "Please

shut the door; there is a draught. Do you want anything?"

"We've got to have a look round," said Clowes.

"Can't you see everything there is?"

Ruthven hated Clowes as much as Clowes hated him.

Trevor cut into the conversation again.

"It's like this, Ruthven," he said. "I'm awfully sorry, but the Old Man's just told me to search the studies in case any of the fellows have got baccy."

Ruthven jumped up, pale with consternation.

"You can't. I won't have you disturbing my study."

"This is rot," said Trevor, shortly, "I've got to. It's no good making it more unpleasant for me than it is."

"But I've no tobacco. I swear I haven't."

"Then why mind us searching?" said Clowes affably.

"Come on, Ruthven," said Trevor, "chuck us over the keys. You might as well."

"I won't."

"Don't be an ass, man."

"We have here," observed Clowes, in his sad, solemn way, "a stout and serviceable poker." He stooped, as he spoke, to pick it up.

"Leave that poker alone," cried Ruthven.

Clowes straightened himself.

"I'll swop it for your keys," he said.

"Don't be a fool."

"Very well, then. We will now crack our first crib."

Ruthven sprang forward, but Clowes, handing him off in football fashion with his left hand, with his right dashed the poker against the lock of the drawer of the table by which he stood.

The lock broke with a sharp crack. It was not built with an eye to such onslaught.

"Neat for a first shot," said Clowes, complacently. "Now for the Umustaphas and shag."

But as he looked into the drawer he uttered a sudden

cry of excitement. He drew something out, and tossed it over to Trevor.

"Catch, Trevor," he said quietly. "Something that'll interest you."

Trevor caught it neatly in one hand, and stood staring at it as if he had never seen anything like it before. And yet he had—often. For what he had caught was a little golden bat, about an inch long by an eighth of an inch wide.

XXI

The League Revealed

"What do you think of that?" said Clowes.

Trevor said nothing. He could not quite grasp the situation. It was not only that he had got the idea so firmly into his head that it was Rand-Brown who had sent the letters and appropriated the bat. Even supposing he had not suspected Rand-Brown, he would never have dreamed of suspecting Ruthven. They had been friends. Not very close friends—Trevor's keenness for games and Ruthven's dislike of them prevented that—but a good deal more than acquaintances. He was so constituted that he could not grasp the frame of mind required for such an action as Ruthven's. It was something absolutely abnormal.

Clowes was equally surprised, but for a different reason. It was not so much the enormity of Ruthven's proceedings that took him aback. He believed him, with that cheerful intolerance which a certain type of mind affects, capable of anything. What surprised him was the fact that Ruthven had had the ingenuity and even the daring to conduct a campaign of this description. Cribbing in examinations he would have thought the limit of his crimes. Something backboneless and underhand of that kind would not have surprised him in the least. He would have said that it was just about what he had expected all along. But that Ruthven should blossom out suddenly as quite an ingenious and capable criminal in this way, was a complete surprise.

"Well, perhaps *you*'ll make a remark?" he said, turning to Ruthven.

Ruthven, looking very much like a passenger on a

Channel steamer who has just discovered that the motion of the vessel is affecting him unpleasantly, had fallen into a chair when Clowes handed him off. He sat there with a look on his pasty face which was not good to see, as silent as Trevor. It seemed that whatever conversation there was going to be would have to take the form of a soliloquy from Clowes.

Clowes took a seat on the corner of the table.

"It seems to me, Ruthven," he said, "that you'd better say *something*. At present there's a lot that wants explaining. As this bat has been found lying in your drawer, I suppose we may take it that you're the impolite letter-writer?"

Ruthven found his voice at last.

"I'm not," he cried; "I never wrote a line."

"Now we're getting at it," said Clowes. "I thought you couldn't have had it in you to carry this business through on your own. Apparently you've only been the sleeping partner in this show, though I suppose it was you who ragged Trevor's study? Not much sleeping about that. You took over the acting branch of the concern for that day only, I expect. Was it you who ragged the study?"

Ruthven stared into the fire, but said nothing.

"Must be polite, you know, Ruthven, and answer when you're spoken to. Was it you who ragged Trevor's study?"

"Yes," said Ruthven.

"Thought so."

"Why, of course, I met you just outside," said Trevor, speaking for the first time. "You were the chap who told me what had happened."

Ruthven said nothing.

"The ragging of the study seems to have been all the active work he did," remarked Clowes.

"No," said Trevor, "he posted the letters, whether he wrote them or not. Milton was telling me—you remember?

I told you. No, I didn't. Milton found out that the letters were posted by a small, light-haired fellow."

"That's him," said Clowes, as regardless of grammar as the monks of Rheims, pointing with the poker at Ruthven's immaculate locks. "Well, you ragged the study and posted the letters. That was all your share. Am I right in thinking Rand-Brown was the other partner?"

Silence from Ruthven.

"Am I?" persisted Clowes.

"You may think what you like. I don't care."

"Now we're getting rude again," complained Clowes. "*Was* Rand-Brown in this?"

"Yes," said Ruthven.

"Thought so. And who else?"

"No one."

"Try again."

"I tell you there was no one else. Can't you believe a word a chap says?"

"A word here and there, perhaps," said Clowes, as one making a concession, "but not many, and this isn't one of them. Have another shot."

Ruthven relapsed into silence.

"All right, then," said Clowes, "we'll accept that statement. There's just a chance that it may be true. And that's about all, I think. This isn't my affair at all, really. It's yours, Trevor. I'm only a spectator and camp-follower. It's your business. You'll find me in my study." And putting the poker carefully in its place, Clowes left the room. He went into his study, and tried to begin some work. But the beauties of the second book of Thucydides failed to appeal to him. His mind was elsewhere. He felt too excited with what had just happened to translate Greek. He pulled up a chair in front of the fire, and gave himself up to speculating how Trevor was getting on in the neighbouring study. He was glad he had left him to finish the business. If he had been in Trevor's place, there was nothing he would so greatly have disliked as to have some one—however familiar a friend—interfering in his wars and settling them for him. Left to himself, Clowes would probably have ended the interview by kicking Ruthven into the nearest approach to pulp compatible with the laws relating to manslaughter. He had an uneasy suspicion that Trevor would let him down far too easily.

The handle turned. Trevor came in, and pulled up another chair in silence. His face wore a look of disgust. But there were no signs of combat upon him. The toe of his boot was not worn and battered, as Clowes would have liked to have seen it. Evidently he had not chosen to adopt active and physical measures for the improvement of Ruthven's moral well-being.

"Well?" said Clowes.

"My word, what a hound!" breathed Trevor, half to himself.

"My sentiments to a hair," said Clowes, approvingly. "But what have you done?"

"I didn't do anything."

"I was afraid you wouldn't. Did he give any explanation? What made him go in for the thing at all? What earthly motive could he have for not wanting Barry to get his colours, bar the fact that Rand-Brown didn't want him to? And why should he do what Rand-Brown told him? I never even knew they were pals, before today."

"He told me a good deal," said Trevor. "It's one of the beastliest things I ever heard. They neither of them come particularly well out of the business, but Rand-Brown comes worse out of it even than Ruthven. My word, that man wants killing."

"That'll keep," said Clowes, nodding. "What's the yarn?"

"Do you remember about a year ago a chap named Patterson getting sacked?"

Clowes nodded again. He remembered the case well.

Patterson had had gambling transactions with a Wrykyn tradesman, had been found out, and had gone.

"You remember what a surprise it was to everybody. It wasn't one of those cases where half the school suspects what's going on. Those cases always come out sooner or later. But Patterson nobody knew about."

"Yes. Well?"

"Nobody," said Trevor, "except Ruthven, that is. Ruthven got to know somehow. I believe he was a bit of a pal of Patterson's at the time. Anyhow,—they had a row, and Ruthven went to Dexter—Patterson was in Dexter's— and sneaked. Dexter promised to keep his name out of the business, and went straight to the Old Man, and Patterson got turfed out on the spot. Then somehow or other Rand-Brown got to know about it—I believe Ruthven must have told him by accident some time or other. After that he simply had to do everything Rand-Brown wanted him to. Otherwise he said that he would tell the chaps about the Patterson affair. That put Ruthven in a dead funk."

"Of course," said Clowes; "I should imagine friend Ruthven would have got rather a bad time of it. But what made them think of starting the League? It was a jolly smart idea. Rand-Brown's, of course?"

"Yes. I suppose he'd heard about it, and thought something might be made out of it if it were revived."

"And were Ruthven and he the only two in it?"

"Ruthven swears they were, and I shouldn't wonder if he wasn't telling the truth, for once in his life. You see, everything the League's done so far could have been done by him and Rand-Brown, without anybody else's help. The only other studies that were ragged were Mill's and Milton's—both in Seymour's."

"Yes," said Clowes.

There was a pause. Clowes put another shovelful of coal on the fire.

"What are you going to do to Ruthven?"

"Nothing."

"Nothing? Hang it, he doesn't deserve to get off like that. He isn't as bad as Rand-Brown—quite—but he's pretty nearly as finished a little beast as you could find."

"Finished is just the word," said Trevor. "He's going at the end of the week."

"Going? What! sacked?"

"Yes. The Old Man's been finding out things about him, apparently, and this smoking row has just added the finishing-touch to his discoveries. He's particularly keen against smoking just now for some reason."

"But was Ruthven in it?"

"Yes. Didn't I tell you? He was one of the fellows Dexter caught in the vault. There were two in this house, you remember?"

"Who was the other?"

"That man Dashwood. Has the study next to Paget's old one. He's going, too."

"Scarcely knew him. What sort of a chap was he?"

"Outsider. No good to the house in any way. He won't be missed."

"And what are you going to do about Rand-Brown?"

"Fight him, of course. What else could I do?"

"But you're no match for him."

"We'll see."

"But you *aren't*," persisted Clowes. "He can give you a stone easily, and he's not a bad boxer either. Moriarty didn't beat him so very cheaply in the middle-weight this year. You wouldn't have a chance."

Trevor flared up.

"Heavens, man," he cried, "do you think I don't know all that myself? But what on earth would you have me do? Besides, he may be a good boxer, but he's got no pluck at all. I might outstay him."

"Hope so," said Clowes.

But his tone was not hopeful.

XXII

A Dress Rehearsal

Some people in Trevor's place might have taken the earliest opportunity of confronting Rand-Brown, so as to settle the matter in hand without delay. Trevor thought of doing this, but finally decided to let the matter rest for a day, until he should have found out with some accuracy what chance he stood.

After four o'clock, therefore, on the next day, having had tea in his study, he went across to the baths, in search of O'Hara. He intended that before the evening was over the Irishman should have imparted to him some of his skill with the hands. He did not know that for a man absolutely unscientific with his fists there is nothing so fatal as to take a boxing lesson on the eve of battle. A little knowledge is a dangerous thing. He is apt to lose his recklessness—which might have stood by him well—in exchange for a little quite useless science. He is neither one thing nor the other, neither a natural fighter nor a skilful boxer.

This point O'Hara endeavoured to press upon him as soon as he had explained why it was that he wanted coaching on this particular afternoon.

The Irishman was in the gymnasium, punching the ball, when Trevor found him. He generally put in a quarter of an hour with the punching-ball every evening, before Moriarty turned up for the customary six rounds.

"Want me to teach ye a few tricks?" he said. "What's that for?"

"I've got a mill coming on soon," explained Trevor, trying to make the statement as if it were the most ordinary thing in the world for a school prefect, who was also captain of football, head of a house, and in the cricket eleven, to be engaged for a fight in the near future.

"Mill!" exclaimed O'Hara. "You! An' why?"

"Never mind why," said Trevor. "I'll tell you afterwards, perhaps. Shall I put on the gloves now?"

"Wait," said O'Hara, "I must do my quarter of an hour with the ball before I begin teaching other people how to box. Have ye a watch?"

"Yes."

"Then time me. I'll do four rounds of three minutes each, with a minute's rest in between. That's more than I'll do at Aldershot, but it'll get me fit. Ready?"

"Time," said Trevor.

He watched O'Hara assailing the swinging ball with considerable envy. Why, he wondered, had he not gone in for boxing? Everybody ought to learn to box. It was bound to come in useful some time or other. Take his own case. He was very much afraid—no, afraid was not the right word, for he was not that. He was very much of opinion that Rand-Brown was going to have a most enjoyable time when they met. And the final house-match was to be played next Monday. If events turned out as he could not help feeling they were likely to turn out, he would be too battered to play in that match. Donaldson's would probably win whether he played or not, but it would be bitter to be laid up on such an occasion. On the other hand, he must go through with it. He did not believe in letting other people take a hand in settling his private quarrels.

But he wished he had learned to box. If only he could hit that dancing, jumping ball with a fifth of the skill that O'Hara was displaying, his wiriness and pluck might see him through. O'Hara finished his fourth round with his leathern opponent, and sat down, panting.

"Pretty useful, that," commented Trevor, admiringly.

"Ye should see Moriarty," gasped O'Hara.

"Now, will ye tell me why it is you're going to fight, and with whom you're going to fight?"

"Very well. It's with Rand-Brown."

"Rand-Brown!" exclaimed O'Hara. "But, me dearr man, he'll ate you."

Trevor gave a rather annoyed laugh. "I must say I've got a nice, cheery, comforting lot of friends," he said. "That's just what Clowes has been trying to explain to me."

"Clowes is quite right," said O'Hara, seriously. "Has the thing gone too far for ye to back out? Without climbing down, of course," he added.

"Yes," said Trevor, "there's no question of my getting out of it. I daresay I could. In fact, I know I could. But I'm not going to."

"But, me dearr man, ye haven't an earthly chance. I assure ye ye haven't. I've seen Rand-Brown with the gloves on. That was last term. He's not put them on since Moriarty bate him in the middles, so he may be out of practice. But even then he'd be a bad man to tackle. He's big an' he's strong, an' if he'd only had the heart in him he'd have been going up to Aldershot instead of Moriarty. That's what he'd be doing. An' you can't box at all. Never even had the gloves on."

"Never. I used to scrap when I was a kid, though."

"That's no use," said O'Hara, decidedly. "But you haven't said what it is that ye've got against Rand-Brown. What is it?"

"I don't see why I shouldn't tell you. You're in it as well. In fact, if it hadn't been for the bat turning up, you'd have been considerably more in it than I am."

"What!" cried O'Hara. "Where did you find it? Was it in the grounds? When was it you found it?"

Whereupon Trevor gave him a very full and exact account of what had happened. He showed him the two letters from the League, touched on Milton's connection with the affair, traced the gradual development of his suspicions, and described with some approach to excitement the scene in Ruthven's study, and the explanations that had followed it.

"Now do you wonder," he concluded, "that I feel as if a few rounds with Rand-Brown would do me good."

O'Hara breathed hard.

"My word!" he said, "I'd like to see ye kill him."

"But," said Trevor, "as you and Clowes have been pointing out to me, if there's going to be a corpse, it'll be me. However, I mean to try. Now perhaps you wouldn't mind showing me a few tricks."

"Take my advice," said O'Hara, "and don't try any of that foolery."

"Why, I thought you were such a believer in science," said Trevor in surprise.

"So I am, if you've enough of it. But it's the worst thing ye can do to learn a trick or two just before a fight, if you don't know anything about the game already. A tough, rushing fighter is ten times as good as a man who's just begun to learn what he oughtn't to do."

"Well, what do you advise me to do, then?" asked Trevor, impressed by the unwonted earnestness with which the Irishman delivered this pugilistic homily, which was a paraphrase of the views dinned into the ears of every novice by the school instructor. "I must do something."

"The best thing ye can do," said O'Hara, thinking for a moment, "is to put on the gloves and have a round or two with me. Here's Moriarty at last. We'll get him to time us."

As much explanation as was thought good for him having been given to the newcomer, to account for Trevor's newly-acquired taste for things pugilistic, Moriarty took the watch, with instructions to give them two minutes for the first round.

"Go as hard as you can," said O'Hara to Trevor, as they

faced one another, "and hit as hard as you like. It won't
be any practice if you don't. I sha'n't mind being hit. It'll
do me good for Aldershot. See?"

Trevor said he saw.

"Time," said Moriarty.

Trevor went in with a will. He was a little shy at first
of putting all his weight into his blows. It was hard to
forget that he felt friendly towards O'Hara. But he speedily
awoke to the fact that the Irishman took his boxing very
seriously, and was quite a different person when he had
the gloves on. When he was so equipped, the man opposite him ceased to be either friend or foe in a private way.
He was simply an opponent, and every time he hit him
was one point. And, when he entered the ring, his only
object in life for the next three minutes was to score points.
Consequently Trevor, sparring lightly and in rather a futile
manner at first, was woken up by a stinging flush hit between the eyes. After that he, too, forgot that he liked the
man before him, and rushed him in all directions. There
was no doubt as to who would have won if it had been a
competition. Trevor's guard was of the most rudimentary
order, and O'Hara got through when and how he liked.
But though he took a good deal, he also gave a good deal,
and O'Hara confessed himself not altogether sorry when
Moriarty called "Time".

"Man," he said regretfully, "why ever did ye not take
up boxing before? Ye'd have made a splendid middle-
weight."

"Well, have I a chance, do you think?" inquired Trevor.

"Ye might do it with luck," said O'Hara, very doubt-
fully. "But," he added, "I'm afraid ye've not much
chance."

And with this poor encouragement from his trainer and
sparring-partner, Trevor was forced to be content.

XXIII

What Renford Saw

The health of Master Harvey of Seymour's was so delicately constituted that it was an absolute necessity that he should consume one or more hot buns during the quarter of an hour's interval which split up morning school. He was tearing across the junior gravel towards the shop on the morning following Trevor's sparring practice with O'Hara, when a melodious treble voice called his name. It was Renford. He stopped, to allow his friend to come up with him, and then made as if to resume his way to the shop. But Renford proposed an amendment. "Don't go to the shop," he said, "I want to talk."

"Well, can't you talk in the shop?"

"Not what I want to tell you. It's private. Come for a stroll."

Harvey hesitated. There were few things he enjoyed so much as exclusive items of school gossip (scandal preferably), but hot new buns were among those few things. However, he decided on this occasion to feed the mind at the expense of the body. He accepted Renford's invitation.

"What is it?" he asked, as they made for the football field. "What's been happening?"

"It's frightfully exciting," said Renford.

"What's up?"

"You mustn't tell any one."

"All right. Of course not."

"Well, then, there's been a big fight, and I'm one of the only chaps who know about it so far."

"A fight?" Harvey became excited. "Who between?"

Renford paused before delivering his news, to emphasise the importance of it.

"It was between O'Hara and Rand-Brown," he said at length.

"*By Jove!*" said Harvey. Then a suspicion crept into his mind.

"Look here, Renford," he said, "if you're trying to green me—"

"I'm not, you ass," replied Renford indignantly. "It's perfectly true. I saw it myself."

"By Jove, did you really? Where was it? When did it come off? Was it a good one? Who won?"

"It was the best one I've ever seen."

"Did O'Hara beat him? I hope he did. O'Hara's a jolly good sort."

"Yes. They had six rounds. Rand-Brown got knocked out in the middle of the sixth."

"What, do you mean really knocked out, or did he just chuck it?"

"No. He was really knocked out. He was on the floor for quite a time. By Jove, you should have seen it. O'Hara was ripping in the sixth round. He was all over him."

"Tell us about it," said Harvey, and Renford told.

"I'd got up early," he said, "to feed the ferrets, and I was just cutting over to the fives-courts with their grub, when, just as I got across the senior gravel, I saw O'Hara and Moriarty standing waiting near the second court. O'Hara knows all about the ferrets, so I didn't try and cut or anything. I went up and began talking to him. I noticed he didn't look particularly keen on seeing me at first. I asked him if he was going to play fives. Then he said no, and told me what he'd really come for. He said he and Rand-Brown had had a row, and they'd agreed to have it out that morning in one of the fives-courts. Of course, when I heard that, I was all on to see it, so I said I'd wait, if he didn't mind. He said he didn't care, so long as I didn't tell everybody, so I said I wouldn't tell anybody except you, so he said all right, then, I could stop if I wanted to. So that was how I saw it. Well, after we'd been waiting a few minutes, Rand-Brown came in sight, with that beast Merrett in our house, who'd come to second him. It was just like one of those duels you read about, you know. Then O'Hara said that as I was the only one there with a watch —he and Rand-Brown were in footer clothes, and Merrett and Moriarty hadn't got their tickers on them—I'd better act as timekeeper. So I said all right, I would, and we went to the second fives-court. It's the biggest of them, you know. I stood outside on the bench, looking through the wire netting over the door, so as not to be in the way when they started scrapping. O'Hara and Rand-Brown took off their blazers and sweaters, and chucked them to Moriarty and Merrett, and then Moriarty and Merrett went and stood in two corners, and O'Hara and Rand-Brown walked into the middle and stood up to one another. Rand-Brown was miles the heaviest—by a stone, I should think—and he was taller and had a longer reach. But O'Hara looked much fitter. Rand-Brown looked rather flabby.

"I sang out 'Time' through the wire netting, and they started off at once. O'Hara offered to shake hands, but Rand-Brown wouldn't. So they began without it.

"The first round was awfully fast. They kept having long rallies all over the place. O'Hara was a jolly sight quicker, and Rand-Brown didn't seem able to guard his hits at all. But he hit frightfully hard himself, great, heavy slogs, and O'Hara kept getting them in the face. At last he got one bang in the mouth which knocked him down flat. He was up again in a second, and was starting to rush, when I looked at the watch, and found that I'd given them nearly half a minute too much already. So I shouted 'Time', and made up my mind I'd keep more of an eye on the watch next round. I'd got so jolly excited, watching them, that I'd forgot I was supposed to be keeping time for them.

They had only asked for a minute between the rounds, but as I'd given them half a minute too long in the first round, I chucked in a bit extra in the rest, so that they were both pretty fit by the time I started them again.

"The second round was just like the first, and so was the third. O'Hara kept getting the worst of it. He was knocked down three or four times more, and once, when he'd rushed Rand-Brown against one of the walls, he hit out and missed, and barked his knuckles jolly badly against the wall. That was in the middle of the third round, and Rand-Brown had it all his own way for the rest of the round—for about two minutes, that is to say. He hit O'Hara about all over the shop. I was so jolly keen on O'Hara's winning, that I had half a mind to call time early, so as to give him time to recover. But I thought it would be a low thing to do, so I gave them their full three minutes.

"Directly they began the fourth round, I noticed that things were going to change a bit. O'Hara had given up his rushing game, and was waiting for his man, and when he came at him he'd put in a hot counter, nearly always at the body. After a bit Rand-Brown began to get cautious, and wouldn't rush, so the fourth round was the quietest there had been. In the last minute they didn't hit each other at all. They simply sparred for openings. It was in the fifth round that O'Hara began to forge ahead. About half way through he got in a ripper, right in the wind, which almost doubled Rand-Brown up, and then he started rushing again. Rand-Brown looked awfully bad at the end of the round. Round six was ripping. I never saw two chaps go for each other so. It was one long rally. Then—how it happened I couldn't see, they were so quick—just as they had been at it a minute and a half, there was a crack, and the next thing I saw was Rand-Brown on the ground, looking beastly. He went down absolutely flat; his heels and head touched the ground at the same time.

"I counted ten out loud in the professional way like they do at the National Sporting Club, you know, and then said 'O'Hara wins'. I felt an awful swell. After about another half-minute, Rand-Brown was all right again, and he got up and went back to the house with Merrett, and O'Hara and Moriarty went off to Dexter's, and I gave the ferrets their grub, and cut back to breakfast."

"Rand-Brown wasn't at breakfast," said Harvey.

"No. He went to bed. I wonder what'll happen. Think there'll be a row about it?"

"Shouldn't think so," said Harvey. "They never do make rows about fights, and neither of them is a prefect, so I don't see what it matters if they *do* fight. But, I say—"

"What's up?"

"I wish," said Harvey, his voice full of acute regret, "that it had been my turn to feed those ferrets."

"I don't," said Renford cheerfully. "I wouldn't have missed that mill for something. Hullo, there's the bell. We'd better run."

When Trevor called at Seymour's that afternoon to see Rand-Brown, with a view to challenging him to deadly combat, and found that O'Hara had been before him, he ought to have felt relieved. His actual feeling was one of acute annoyance. It seemed to him that O'Hara had exceeded the limits of friendship. It was all very well for him to take over the Rand-Brown contract, and settle it himself, in order to save Trevor from a very bad quarter of an hour, but Trevor was one of those people who object strongly to the interference of other people in their private business. He sought out O'Hara and complained. Within two minutes O'Hara's golden eloquence had soothed him and made him view the matter in quite a different light. What O'Hara pointed out was that it was not Trevor's affair at all, but his own. Who, he asked, had been likely to be damaged most by Rand-Brown's manoeuvres in connection with the lost bat? Trevor was bound to admit that O'Hara was that person. Very well, then, said O'Hara, then who had a better right to fight Rand-Brown? And Trevor confessed that no one else had a better.

"Then I suppose," he said, "that I shall have to do nothing about it?"

"That's it," said O'Hara.

"It'll be rather beastly meeting the man after this," said Trevor, presently. "Do you think he might possibly leave at the end of term?"

"He's leaving at the end of the week," said O'Hara. "He was one of the fellows Dexter caught in the vault that evening. You won't see much more of Rand-Brown."

"I'll try and put up with that," said Trevor.

"And so will I," replied O'Hara. "And I shouldn't think Milton would be so very grieved."

"No," said Trevor. "I tell you what will make him sick, though, and that is your having milled with Rand-Brown. It's a job he'd have liked to have taken on himself."

XXIV

CONCLUSION

Into the story at this point comes the narrative of Charles Mereweather Cook, aged fourteen, a day-boy.

Cook arrived at the school on the tenth of March, at precisely nine o'clock, in a state of excitement.

He said there was a row on in the town.

Cross-examined, he said there was no end of a row on in the town.

During morning school he explained further, whispering his tale into the attentive ear of Knight of the School House, who sat next to him.

What sort of a row, Knight wanted to know.

Cook deposed that he had been riding on his bicycle past the entrance to the Recreation Grounds on his way to school, when his eye was attracted by the movements of a mass of men just inside the gate. They appeared to be fighting. Witness did not stop to watch, much as he would have liked to do so. Why not? Why, because he was late already, and would have had to scorch anyhow, in order to get to school in time. And he had been late the day before, and was afraid that old Appleby (the master of the form) would give him beans if he were late again. Wherefore he had no notion of what the men were fighting about, but he betted that more would be heard about it. Why? Because, from what he saw of it, it seemed a jolly big thing. There must have been quite three hundred men fighting. (Knight, satirically, "*Pile* it on!") Well, quite a hundred, anyhow. Fifty a side. And fighting like anything. He betted there would be something about it in the *Wrykyn*

Patriot tomorrow. He shouldn't wonder if somebody had
been killed. What were they scrapping about? How should
he know!

Here Mr Appleby, who had been trying for the last five
minutes to find out where the whispering noise came from,
at length traced it to its source, and forthwith requested
Messrs Cook and Knight to do him two hundred lines,
adding that, if he heard them talking again, he would put
them into the extra lesson. Silence reigned from that
moment.

Next day, while the form was wrestling with the moderately exciting account of Caesar's doings in Gaul, Master
Cook produced from his pocket a newspaper cutting. This,
having previously planted a forcible blow in his friend's
ribs with an elbow to attract the latter's attention, he
handed to Knight, and in dumb show requested him to
peruse the same. Which Knight, feeling no interest whatever in Caesar's doings in Gaul, and having, in consequence, a good deal of time on his hands, proceeded to
do. The cutting was headed "Disgraceful Fracas", and
was written in the elegant style that was always so marked
a feature of the *Wrykyn Patriot*.

"We are sorry to have to report," it ran, "another of
those deplorable ebullitions of local Hooliganism, to which
it has before now been our painful duty to refer. Yesterday
the Recreation Grounds were made the scene of as brutal
an exhibition of savagery as has ever marred the fair fame
of this town. Our readers will remember how on a previous
occasion, when the fine statue of Sir Eustace Briggs was
found covered with tar, we attributed the act to the
malevolence of the Radical section of the community.
Events have proved that we were right. Yesterday a body
of youths, belonging to the rival party, was discovered in
the very act of repeating the offence. A thick coating of
tar had already been administered, when several members of the rival faction appeared. A free fight of a pecu-

liarly violent nature immediately ensued, with the result that, before the police could interfere, several of the combatants had received severe bruises. Fortunately the police then arrived on the scene, and with great difficulty succeeded in putting a stop to the *fracas*. Several arrests were made.

"We have no desire to discourage legitimate party rivalry, but we feel justified in strongly protesting against such dastardly tricks as those to which we have referred. We can assure our opponents that they can gain nothing by such conduct."

There was a good deal more to the effect that now was the time for all good men to come to the aid of the party, and that the constituents of Sir Eustace Briggs must look to it that they failed not in the hour of need, and so on. That was what the *Wrykyn Patriot* had to say on the subject.

O'Hara managed to get hold of a copy of the paper, and showed it to Clowes and Trevor.

"So now," he said, "it's all right, ye see. They'll never suspect it wasn't the same people that tarred the statue both times. An' ye've got the bat back, so it's all right, ye see."

"The only thing that'll trouble you now," said Clowes, "will be your conscience."

O'Hara intimated that he would try and put up with that.

"But isn't it a stroke of luck," he said, "that they should have gone and tarred Sir Eustace again so soon after Moriarty and I did it?"

Clowes said gravely that it only showed the force of good example.

"Yes. They wouldn't have thought of it, if it hadn't been for us," chortled O'Hara. "I wonder, now, if there's anything else we could do to that statue!" he added, meditatively.

"My good lunatic," said Clowes, "don't you think you've done almost enough for one term?"

"Well, 'myes," replied O'Hara thoughtfully, "perhaps we have, I suppose."

The term wore on. Donaldson's won the final house-match by a matter of twenty-six points. It was, as they had expected, one of the easiest games they had had to play in the competition. Bryant's, who were their opponents, were not strong, and had only managed to get into the final owing to their luck in drawing weak opponents for the trial heats. The real final, that had decided the ownership of the cup, had been Donaldson's *v.* Seymour's.

Aldershot arrived, and the sports. Drummond and O'Hara covered themselves with glory, and brought home silver medals. But Moriarty, to the disappointment of the school, which had counted on his pulling off the middles, met a strenuous gentleman from St Paul's in the final, and was prematurely outed in the first minute of the third round. To him, therefore, there fell but a medal of bronze.

It was on the Sunday after the sports that Trevor's connection with the bat ceased—as far, that is to say, as concerned its unpleasant character (as a piece of evidence that might be used to his disadvantage). He had gone to supper with the headmaster, accompanied by Clowes and Milton. The headmaster nearly always invited a few of the house prefects to Sunday supper during the term. Sir Eustace Briggs happened to be there. He had withdrawn his insinuations concerning the part supposedly played by a member of the school in the matter of the tarred statue, and the headmaster had sealed the *entente cordiale* by asking him to supper.

An ordinary man might have considered it best to keep off the delicate subject. Not so Sir Eustace Briggs. He was on to it like glue. He talked of little else throughout the whole course of the meal.

"My suspicions," he boomed, towards the conclusion of the feast, "which have, I am rejoiced to say, proved so entirely void of foundation and significance, were aroused in the first instance, as I mentioned before, by the narrative of the man Samuel Wapshott."

Nobody present showed the slightest desire to learn what the man Samuel Wapshott had had to say for himself, but Sir Eustace, undismayed, continued as if the whole table were hanging on his words.

"The man Samuel Wapshott," he said, "distinctly asserted that a small gold ornament, shaped like a bat, was handed by him to a lad of age coeval with these lads here."

The headmaster interposed. He had evidently heard more than enough of the man Samual Wapshott.

"He must have been mistaken," he said briefly. "The bat which Trevor is wearing on his watch-chain at this moment is the only one of its kind that I know of. You have never lost it, Trevor?"

Trevor thought for a moment. *He* had never lost it. He replied diplomatically, "It has been in a drawer nearly all the term, sir," he said.

"A drawer, hey?" remarked Sir Eustace Briggs. "Ah! A very sensible place to keep it in, my boy. You could have no better place, in my opinion."

And Trevor agreed with him, with the mental reservation that it rather depended on whom the drawer belonged to.

THE HEAD OF KAY'S

CONTENTS

I

Mainly about Fenn

"When we get licked tomorrow by half-a-dozen wickets," said Jimmy Silver, tilting his chair until the back touched the wall, "don't say I didn't warn you. If you fellows take down what I say from time to time in note-books, as you ought to do, you'll remember that I offered to give anyone odds that Kay's would out us in the final. I always said that a really hot man like Fenn was more good to a side than half-a-dozen ordinary men. He can do all the bowling and all the batting. All the fielding, too, in the slips."

Tea was just over at Blackburn's, and the bulk of the house had gone across to preparation in the school buildings. The prefects, as was their custom, lingered on to finish the meal at their leisure. These after-tea conversations were quite an institution at Blackburn's. The labours of the day were over, and the time for preparation for the morrow had not yet come. It would be time to be thinking of that in another hour. Meanwhile, a little relaxation might be enjoyed. Especially so as this was the last day but two of the summer term, and all necessity for working after tea had ceased with the arrival of the last lap of the examinations.

Silver was head of the house, and captain of its cricket team, which was nearing the end of its last match, the final for the inter-house cup, and—on paper—getting decidedly the worst of it. After riding in triumph over the School House, Bedell's, and Mulholland's, Blackburn's had met its next door neighbour, Kay's, in the final, and, to the surprise of the great majority of the school, was showing up badly. The match was affording one more example of how a team of average merit all through may sometimes fall before a one-man side. Blackburn's had the three last men on the list of the first eleven, Silver, Kennedy, and Challis, and at least nine of its representatives had the reputation of being able to knock up a useful twenty or thirty at any time. Kay's, on the other hand, had one man, Fenn. After him the tail started. But Fenn was such an exceptional all-round man that, as Silver had said, he was as good as half-a-dozen of the Blackburn's team, equally formidable whether batting or bowling—he headed the school averages at both. He was one of those batsmen who seem to know exactly what sort of ball you are going to bowl before it leaves your hand, and he could hit like another Jessop. As for his bowling, he bowled left hand— always a puzzling eccentricity to an undeveloped batsman —and could send them down very fast or very slow, as he thought best, and it was hard to see which particular brand he was going to serve up before it was actually in mid-air.

But it is not necessary to enlarge on his abilities. The figures against his name in *Wisden* prove a good deal. The fact that he had steered Kay's through into the last round of the house-matches proves still more. It was perfectly obvious to everyone that, if only you could get Fenn out for under ten, Kay's total for that innings would be nearer twenty than forty. They were an appalling side. But then no house bowler had as yet succeeded in getting Fenn out for under ten. In the six innings he had played in the competition up to date, he had made four centuries, an eighty, and a seventy.

Kennedy, the second prefect at Blackburn's, paused in the act of grappling with the remnant of a pot of jam belonging to some person unknown, to reply to Silver's remarks.

"We aren't beaten yet," he said, in his solid way. Kennedy's chief characteristics were solidity, and an infinite capacity for taking pains. Nothing seemed to tire or discourage him. He kept pegging away till he arrived. The ordinary person, for instance, would have considered the jam-pot, on which he was then engaged, an empty jam-pot. Kennedy saw that there was still a strawberry (or it may have been a section of a strawberry) at the extreme end, and he meant to have that coy vegetable if he had to squeeze the pot to get at it. To take another instance, all the afternoon of the previous day he had bowled patiently at Fenn while the latter lifted every other ball into space. He had been taken off three times, and at every fresh attack he had plodded on doggedly, until at last, as he had expected, the batsman had misjudged a straight one, and he had bowled him all over his wicket. Kennedy generally managed to get there sooner or later.

"It's no good chucking the game up simply because we're in a tight place," he said, bringing the spoon to the surface at last with the section of strawberry adhering to the end of it. "That sort of thing's awfully feeble."

"He calls me feeble!" shouted Jimmy Silver. "By James, I've put a man to sleep for less."

It was one of his amusements to express himself from time to time in a melodramatic fashion, sometimes accompanying his words with suitable gestures. It was on one of these occasions—when he had assumed at a moment's notice the *rôle* of the "Baffled Despot", in an argument with Kennedy in his study on the subject of the house football team—that he broke what Mr Blackburn considered a valuable door with a poker. Since then he had moderated his transports.

"They've got to make seventy-nine," said Kennedy.

Challis, the other first eleven man, was reading a green scoring-book.

"I don't think Kay's ought to have the face to stick the cup up in their dining-room," he said, "considering the little

they've done to win it. If they *do* win it, that is. Still, as
they made two hundred first innings, they ought to be able
to knock off seventy-nine. But I was saying that the pot
ought to go to Fenn. Lot the rest of the team had to do
with it. Blackburn's, first innings, hundred and fifty-one;
Fenn, eight for forty-nine. Kay's, two hundred and one;
Fenn, a hundred and sixty-four not out. Second innings,
Blackburn's hundred and twenty-eight; Fenn ten for eighty.
Bit thick, isn't it? I suppose that's what you'd call a one-
man team."

Williams, one of the other prefects, who had just sat
down at the piano for the purpose of playing his one tune
—a cake-walk, of which, through constant practice, he had
mastered the rudiments—spoke over his shoulder to Silver.

"I tell you what, Jimmy," he said, "you've probably lost
us the pot by getting your people to send brother Billy to
Kay's. If he hadn't kept up his wicket yesterday, Fenn
wouldn't have made half as many."

When his young brother had been sent to Eckleton two
terms before, Jimmy Silver had strongly urged upon his
father the necessity of placing him in some house other
than Blackburn's. He felt that a head of a house, even of
so orderly and perfect a house as Blackburn's, has enough
worries without being saddled with a small brother. And
on the previous afternoon young Billy Silver, going in
eighth wicket for Kay's, had put a solid bat in front of
everything for the space of one hour, in the course of which
he made ten runs and Fenn sixty. By scoring odd numbers
off the last ball of each over, Fenn had managed to secure
the majority of the bowling in the most masterly way.

"These things will happen," said Silver, resignedly. "We
Silvers, you know, can't help making runs. Come on,
Williams, let's have that tune, and get it over."

Williams obliged. It was a classic piece called "The
Coon Band Contest", remarkable partly for a taking

melody, partly for the vast possibilities of noise which it afforded. Williams made up for his failure to do justice to the former by a keen appreciation of the latter. He played the piece through again, in order to correct the mistakes he had made at his first rendering of it. Then he played it for the third time to correct a new batch of errors.

"I should like to hear Fenn play that," said Challis. "You're awfully good, you know, Williams, but he might do it better still."

"Get him to play it as an encore at the concert," said Williams, starting for the fourth time.

The talented Fenn was also a musician,—not a genius at the piano, as he was at cricket, but a sufficiently sound performer for his age, considering that he had not made a special study of it. He was to play at the school concert on the following day.

"I believe Fenn has an awful time at Kay's," said Jimmy Silver. "It must be a fair sort of hole, judging from the specimens you see crawling about in Kay caps. I wish I'd known my people were sending young Billy there. I'd have warned them. I only told them not to sling him in here. I had no idea they'd have picked Kay's."

"Fenn was telling me the other day," said Kennedy, "that being in Kay's had spoiled his whole time at the school. He always wanted to come to Blackburn's, only there wasn't room that particular term. Bad luck, wasn't it? I don't think he found it so bad before he became head of the house. He didn't come into contact with Kay so much. But now he finds that he can't do a thing without Kay buzzing round and interfering."

"I wonder," said Jimmy Silver, thoughtfully, "if that's why he bowls so fast. To work it off, you know."

In the course of a beautiful innings of fifty-three that afternoon, the captain of Blackburn's had received two of Fenn's speediest on the same spot just above the pad in rapid succession, and he now hobbled painfully when he moved about.

The conversation that evening had dealt so largely with Fenn—the whole school, indeed, was talking of nothing but his great attempt to win the cricket cup single-handed—that Kennedy, going out into the road for a breather before the rest of the boarders returned from preparation, made his way to Kay's to see if Fenn was imitating his example, and taking the air too.

He found him at Kay's gate, and they strolled towards the school buildings together. Fenn was unusually silent.

"Well?" said Kennedy, after a minute had passed without a remark.

"Well, what?"

"What's up?"

Fenn laughed what novelists are fond of calling a mirthless laugh.

"Oh, I don't know," he said; "I'm sick of this place."

Kennedy inspected his friend's face anxiously by the light of the lamp over the school gate. There was no mistake about it. Fenn certainly did look bad. His face always looked lean and craggy, but tonight there was a difference. He looked used up.

"Fagged?" asked Kennedy.

"No. Sick."

"What about?"

"Everything. I wish you could come into Kay's for a bit just to see what it's like. Then you'd understand. At present I don't suppose you've an idea of it. I'd like to write a book on 'Kay Day by Day'. I'd have plenty to put in it."

"What's he been doing?"

"Oh, nothing out of the ordinary run. It's the fact that he's always at it that does me. You get a houseful of—well, you know the sort of chap the average Kayite is. They'd keep me busy even if I were allowed a free hand. But I'm not. Whenever I try and keep order and stop things a bit, out springs the man Kay from nowhere, and takes the job out of my hands, makes a ghastly mess of everything, and retires purring. Once in every three times, or thereabouts, he slangs me in front of the kids for not keeping order. I'm glad this is the end of the term. I couldn't stand it much longer. Hullo, here come the chaps from prep. We'd better be getting back."

II

An Evening at Kay's

They turned, and began to walk towards the houses. Kennedy felt miserable. He never allowed himself to be put out, to any great extent, by his own worries, which, indeed, had not been very numerous up to the present, but the misfortunes of his friends always troubled him exceedingly. When anything happened to him personally, he found the discomfort of being in a tight place largely counterbalanced by the excitement of trying to find a way out. But the impossibility of helping Fenn in any way depressed him.

"It must be awful," he said, breaking the silence.

"It is," said Fenn, briefly.

"But haven't the house-matches made any difference? Blackburn's always frightfully bucked when the house does anything. You can do anything you like with him if you lift a cup. I should have thought Kay would have been all right when he saw you knocking up centuries, and getting into the final, and all that sort of thing."

Fenn laughed.

"Kay!" he said. "My dear man, he doesn't *know*. I don't suppose he's got the remotest idea that we are in the final at all, or, if he has, he doesn't understand what being in the final means."

"But surely he'll be glad if you lick us tomorrow?" asked Kennedy. Such indifference on the part of a house-master respecting the fortunes of his house seemed to him, having before him the bright example of Mr Blackburn almost incredible.

"I don't suppose so," said Fenn. "Or, if he is, I'll bet he

doesn't show it. He's not like Blackburn. I wish he was. Here he comes, so perhaps we'd better talk about something else."

The vanguard of the boys returning from preparation had passed them, and they were now standing at the gate of the house. As Fenn spoke, a little, restless-looking man in cap and gown came up. His clean-shaven face wore an expression of extreme alertness—the sort of look a ferret wears as he slips in at the mouth of a rabbit-hole. A doctor, called upon to sum up Mr Kay at a glance, would probably have said that he suffered from nerves, which would have been a perfectly correct diagnosis, though none of the members of his house put his manners and customs down to that cause. They considered that the methods he pursued in the management of the house were the outcome of a naturally malignant disposition. This was, however, not the case. There is no reason to suppose that Mr Kay did not mean well. But there is no doubt that he was extremely fussy. And fussiness—with the possible exceptions of homicidal mania and a taste for arson—is quite the worst characteristic it is possible for a house-master to possess.

He caught sight of Fenn and Kennedy at the gate, and stopped in his stride.

"What are you doing here, Fenn?" he asked, with an abruptness which brought a flush to the latter's face. "Why are you outside the house?"

Kennedy began to understand why it was that his friend felt so strongly on the subject of his house-master. If this was the sort of thing that happened every day, no wonder that there was dissension in the house of Kay. He tried to imagine Blackburn speaking in that way to Jimmy Silver or himself, but his imagination was unequal to the task. Between Mr Blackburn and his prefects there existed a perfect understanding. He relied on them to see that order was kept, and they acted accordingly. Fenn, by the exercise of considerable self-control, had always been scrupulously polite to Mr Kay.

"I came out to get some fresh air before lock-up, sir," he replied.

"Well, go in. Go in at once. I cannot allow you to be outside the house at this hour. Go indoors directly."

Kennedy expected a scene, but Fenn took it quite quietly.

"Good night, Kennedy," he said.

"So long," said Kennedy.

Fenn caught his eye, and smiled painfully. Then he turned and went into the house.

Mr Kay's zeal for reform was apparently still unsatisfied. He directed his batteries towards Kennedy.

"Go to your house at once, Kennedy. You have no business out here at this time."

This, thought Kennedy, was getting a bit too warm. Mr Kay might do as he pleased with his own house, but he was hanged if he was going to trample on *him*.

"Mr Blackburn is my house-master, sir," he said with great respect.

Mr Kay stared.

"My house-master," continued Kennedy with gusto, slightly emphasising the first word, "knows that I always go out just before lock-up, and he has no objection."

And, to emphasise this point, he walked towards the school buildings again. For a moment it seemed as if Mr Kay intended to call him back, but he thought better of it. Mr Blackburn, in normal circumstances a pacific man, had one touchy point—his house. He resented any interference with its management, and was in the habit of saying so. Mr Kay remembered one painful scene in the Masters' Common Room, when he had ventured to let fall a few well-meant hints as to how a house should be ruled. Really, he had thought Blackburn would have choked. Better, perhaps, to leave him to look after his own affairs.

So Mr Kay followed Fenn indoors, and Kennedy, having watched him vanish, made his way to Blackburn's.

Quietly as Fenn had taken the incident at the gate, it nevertheless rankled. He read prayers that night in a distinctly unprayerful mood. It seemed to him that it would be lucky if he could get through to the end of the term before Mr Kay applied that last straw which does not break the backs of camels only. Eight weeks' holiday, with plenty of cricket, would brace him up for another term. And he had been invited to play for the county against Middlesex four days after the holidays began. That should have been a soothing thought. But it really seemed to make matters worse. It was hard that a man who on Monday would be bowling against Warner and Beldam, or standing up to Trott and Hearne, should on the preceding Tuesday be sent indoors like a naughty child by a man who stood five-feet-one in his boots, and was devoid of any sort of merit whatever.

It seemed to him that it would help him to sleep peacefully that night if he worked off a little of his just indignation upon somebody. There was a noise going on in the fags' room. There always was at Kay's. It was not a particularly noisy noise—considering; but it had better be stopped. Badly as Kay had treated him, he remembered that he was head of the house, and as such it behoved him to keep order in the house.

He went downstairs, and, on arriving on the scene of action, found that the fags were engaged upon spirited festivities, partly in honour of the near approach of the summer holidays, partly because—miracles barred—the house was going on the morrow to lift the cricket-cup. There were a good many books flying about, and not a few slippers. There was a confused mass rolling in combat on the floor, and the table was occupied by a scarlet-faced individual, who passed the time by kicking violently at certain hands, which were endeavouring to drag him from his post, and shrieking frenzied abuse at the owners of the said hands. It was an animated scene, and to a deaf man might have been most enjoyable.

Fenn's appearance was the signal for a temporary suspension of hostilities.

"What the dickens is all this row about?" he inquired.

No one seemed ready at the moment with a concise explanation. There was an awkward silence. One or two of the weaker spirits even went so far as to sit down and begin to read. All would have been well but for a bright idea which struck some undiscovered youth at the back of the room.

"Three cheers for Fenn!" observed this genial spirit, in no uncertain voice.

The idea caught on. It was just what was wanted to give a finish to the evening's festivities. Fenn had done well by the house. He had scored four centuries and an eighty, and was going to knock off the runs against Blackburn's tomorrow off his own bat. Also, he had taken eighteen wickets in the final house-match. Obviously Fenn was a person deserving of all encouragement. It would be a pity to let him think that his effort had passed unnoticed by the fags' room. Happy thought! Three cheers and one more, and then "He's a jolly good fellow", to wind up with.

It was while those familiar words, "It's a way we have in the public scho-o-o-o-l-s", were echoing through the room in various keys, that a small and energetic form brushed past Fenn as he stood in the doorway, vainly trying to stop the fags' choral efforts.

It was Mr Kay.

The singing ceased gradually, very gradually. It was some time before Mr Kay could make himself heard. But after a couple of minutes there was a lull, and the house-master's address began to be audible.

". . . unendurable noise. What is the meaning of it? I will not have it. Do you hear? It is disgraceful. Every boy in this room will write me two hundred lines by tomorrow evening. It is abominable, Fenn." He wheeled round towards the head of the house. "Fenn, I am surprised at you standing here and allowing such a disgraceful disturbance to go on. Really, if you cannot keep order better— It is disgraceful, disgraceful."

Mr Kay shot out of the room. Fenn followed in his wake, and the procession made its way to the house-masters' study. It had been a near thing, but the last straw had arrived before the holidays.

Mr Kay wheeled round as he reached his study door.

"Well, Fenn?"

Fenn said nothing.

"Have you anything you wish to say, Fenn?"

"I thought you might have something to say to me, sir."

"I do not understand you, Fenn."

"I thought you might wish to apologise for slanging me in front of the fags."

It is wonderful what a difference the last straw will make in one's demeanour to a person.

"Apologise! I think you forget whom it is you are speaking to."

When a master makes this well-worn remark, the wise youth realises that the time has come to close the conversation. All Fenn's prudence, however, had gone to the four winds.

"If you wanted to tell me I was not fit to be head of the house, you needn't have done it before a roomful of fags. How do you think I can keep order in the house if you do that sort of thing?"

Mr Kay overcame his impulse to end the interview abruptly in order to put in a thrust.

"You do not keep order in the house, Fenn," he said, acidly.

"I do when I am not interfered with."

"You will be good enough to say 'sir' when you speak

to me, Fenn," said Mr Kay, thereby scoring another point. In the stress of the moment, Fenn had not noticed the omission.

He was silenced. And before he could recover himself, Mr Kay was in his study, and there was a closed, forbidding door between them.

And as he stared at it, it began slowly to dawn upon Fenn that he had not shown up to advantage in the recent interview. In a word, he had made a fool of himself.

III

THE FINAL HOUSE-MATCH

Blackburn's took the field at three punctually on the following afternoon, to play out the last act of the final house-match. They were not without some small hope of victory, for curious things happen at cricket, especially in the fourth innings of a match. And runs are admitted to be easier saved than made. Yet seventy-nine seemed an absurdly small score to try and dismiss a team for, and in view of the fact that that team contained a batsman like Fenn, it seemed smaller still. But Jimmy Silver, resolutely as he had declared victory impossible to his intimate friends, was not the man to depress his team by letting it become generally known that he considered Blackburn's chances small.

"You must work like niggers in the field," he said; "don't give away a run. Seventy-nine isn't much to make, but if we get Fenn out for a few, they won't come near it."

He did not add that in his opinion Fenn would take very good care that he did not get out for a few. It was far more likely that he would make that seventy-nine off his own bat in a dozen overs.

"You'd better begin, Kennedy," he continued, "from the top end. Place your men where you want 'em. I should have an extra man in the deep, if I were you. That's where Fenn kept putting them last innings. And you'll want a short leg, only for goodness sake keep them off the leg-side if you can. It's a safe four to Fenn every time if you don't. Look out, you chaps. Man in."

Kay's first pair were coming down the pavilion steps.

Challis, going to his place at short slip, called Silver's attention to a remarkable fact.

"Hullo," he said, "why isn't Fenn coming in first?"

"What! By Jove, nor he is. That's queer. All the better for us. You might get a bit finer, Challis, in case they snick 'em."

Wayburn, who had accompanied Fenn to the wicket at the beginning of Kay's first innings, had now for his partner one Walton, a large, unpleasant-looking youth, said to be a bit of a bruiser, and known to be a black sheep. He was one of those who made life at Kay's so close an imitation of an Inferno. His cricket was of a rustic order. He hit hard and high. When allowed to do so, he hit often. But, as a rule, he left early, a prey to the slips or deep fields. Today was no exception to that rule.

Kennedy's first ball was straight and medium-paced. It was a little too short, however, and Walton, letting go at it with a semi-circular sweep like the drive of a golfer, sent it soaring over mid-on's head and over the boundary. Cheers from the pavilion.

Kennedy bowled his second ball with the same purposeful air, and Walton swept at it as before. There was a click, and Jimmy Silver, who was keeping wicket, took the ball comfortably on a level with his chin.

"How's that?"

The umpire's hand went up, and Walton went out—reluctantly, murmuring legends of how he had not gone within a yard of the thing.

It was only when the next batsman who emerged from the pavilion turned out to be his young brother and not Fenn, that Silver began to see that something was wrong. It was conceivable that Fenn might have chosen to go in first wicket down instead of opening the batting, but not that he should go in second wicket. If Kay's were to win it was essential that he should begin to bat as soon as possible.

Otherwise there might be no time for him to knock off the runs. However good a batsman is, he can do little if no one can stay with him.

There was no time to question the newcomer. He must control his curiosity until the fall of the next wicket.

"Man in," he said.

Billy Silver was in many ways a miniature edition of his brother, and he carried the resemblance into his batting. The head of Blackburn's was stylish, and took no risks. His brother had not yet developed a style, but he was very settled in his mind on the subject of risks. There was no tempting him with half-volleys and long-hops. His motto was defence, not defiance. He placed a straight bat in the path of every ball, and seemed to consider his duty done if he stopped it.

The remainder of the over was, therefore, quiet. Billy played Kennedy's fastest like a book, and left the more tempting ones alone.

Challis's first over realised a single, Wayburn snicking him to leg. The first ball of Kennedy's second over saw him caught at the wicket, as Walton had been.

"Every *time* a coconut," said Jimmy Silver complacently, as he walked to the other end. "We're a powerful combination, Kennedy. Where's Fenn? Does anybody know? Why doesn't he come in?"

Billy Silver, seated on the grass by the side of the crease, fastening the top strap of one of his pads, gave tongue with the eagerness of the well-informed man.

"What, don't you know?" he said. "Why, there's been an awful row. Fenn won't be able to play till four o'clock. I believe he and Kay had a row last night, and he cheeked Kay, and the old man's given him a sort of extra. I saw him going over to the School House, and I heard him tell Wayburn that he wouldn't be able to play till four."

The effect produced by this communication would be

most fittingly expressed by the word "sensation" in brackets.
It came as a complete surprise to everyone. It seemed to
knock the bottom out of the whole match. Without Fenn
the thing would be a farce. Kay's would have no chance.

"What a worm that man is," said Kennedy. "Do you
know, I had a sort of idea Fenn wouldn't last out much
longer. Kay's been ragging him all the term. I went round
to see him last night, and Kay behaved like a bounder
then. I expect Fenn had it out with him when they got
indoors. What a beastly shame, though."

"Beastly," agreed Jimmy Silver. "Still, it can't be helped.
The sins of the house-master are visited on the house. I'm
afraid it will be our painful duty to wipe the floor with
Kay's this day. Speaking at a venture, I should say that we
have got them where the hair's short. Yea. Even on toast,
if I may be allowed to use the expression. Who is this
coming forth now? Curtis, or me old eyes deceive me. And
is not Curtis's record score three, marred by ten chances?
Indeed yes. A fastish yorker should settle Curtis's young
hash. Try one."

Kennedy followed the recipe. A ball later the middle
and leg stumps were lying in picturesque attitudes some
yards behind the crease, and Curtis was beginning that
"sad, unending walk to the pavilion", thinking, with the
poet,

"Thou wast not made to play, infernal ball!"

Blackburn's non-combatants, dotted round the boundary,
shrieked their applause. Three wickets had fallen for five
runs, and life was worth living. Kay's were silent and
gloomy.

Billy Silver continued to occupy one end in an immov-
able manner, but at the other there was no monotony. Man
after man came in, padded and gloved, and looking capable
of mighty things. They took guard, patted the ground

lustily, as if to make it plain that they were going to stand no nonsense, settled their caps over their eyes, and prepared to receive the ball. When it came it usually took a stump or two with it before it stopped. It was a procession such as the school grounds had not often seen. As the tenth man walked from the pavilion, four sounded from the clock over the Great Hall, and five minutes later the weary eyes of the supporters of Kay's were refreshed by the sight of Fenn making his way to the arena from the direction of the School House.

Just as he arrived on the scene, Billy Silver's defence broke down. One of Challis's slows, which he had left alone with the idea that it was going to break away to the off, came in quickly instead, and removed a bail. Billy Silver had only made eight; but, as the full score, including one bye, was only eighteen, this was above the average, and deserved the applause it received.

Fenn came in in the unusual position of eleventh man, with an expression on his face that seemed to suggest that he meant business. He was curiously garbed. Owing to the shortness of the interval allowed him for changing, he had only managed to extend his cricket costume as far as white buckskin boots. He wore no pads or gloves. But even in the face of these sartorial deficiencies, he looked like a cricketer. The field spread out respectfully, and Jimmy Silver moved a man from the slips into the country.

There were three more balls of Challis's over, for Billy Silver's collapse had occurred at the third delivery. Fenn mistimed the first. Two hours' writing indoors does not improve the eye. The ball missed the leg stump by an inch.

About the fifth ball he made no mistake. He got the full face of the bat to it, and it hummed past coverpoint to the boundary. The last of the over he put to leg for three.

A remarkable last-wicket partnership now took place, remarkable not so much for tall scoring as for the fact that one of the partners did not receive a single ball from beginning to end of it, with the exception of the one that bowled him. Fenn seemed to be able to do what he pleased with the bowling. Kennedy he played with a shade more respect than the others, but he never failed to score a three or a single off the last ball of each of his overs. The figures on the telegraph-board rose from twenty to thirty, from thirty to forty, from forty to fifty. Williams went on at the lower end instead of Challis, and Fenn made twelve off his first over. The pavilion was filled with howling enthusiasts, who cheered every hit in a frenzy.

Jimmy Silver began to look worried. He held a hasty consultation with Kennedy. The telegraph-board now showed the figures 60—9—8.

"This won't do," said Silver. "It would be too foul to get licked after having nine of them out for eighteen. Can't you manage to keep Fenn from scoring odd figures off the last ball of your over? If only that kid at the other end would get some of the bowling, we should do it."

"I'll try," said Kennedy, and walked back to begin his over.

Fenn reached his fifty off the third ball. Seventy went up on the board. Ten more and Kay's would have the cup. The fourth ball was too good to hit. Fenn let it pass. The fifth he drove to the on. It was a big hit, but there was a fieldsman in the neighbourhood. Still, it was an easy two. But to Kennedy's surprise Fenn sent his partner back after they had run a single. Even the umpire was surprised. Fenn's policy was so obvious that it was strange to see him thus deliberately allow his partner to take a ball.

"That's not over, you know, Fenn," said the umpire—Lang, of the School House, a member of the first eleven.

Fenn looked annoyed. He had miscounted the balls, and now his partner, who had no pretensions to be considered a bat, would have to face Kennedy.

That mistake lost Kay's the match.

Impossible as he had found it to defeat Fenn, Kennedy

had never lost his head or his length. He was bowling fully as well as he had done at the beginning of the innings.

The last ball of the over beat the batsman all the way. He scooped blindly forward, missed it by a foot, and the next moment the off stump lay flat. Blackburn's had won by seven runs.

IV

Harmony and Discord

What might be described as a mixed reception awaited the
players as they left the field. The pavilion and the parts
about the pavilion rails were always packed on the last day
of a final house-match, and even in normal circumstances
there was apt to be a little sparring between the juniors of
the two houses which had been playing for the cup. In the
present case, therefore, it was not surprising that Kay's
fags took the defeat badly. The thought that Fenn's presence at the beginning of the innings, instead of at the end,
would have made all the difference between a loss and a
victory, maddened them. The crowd that seethed in front
of the pavilion was a turbulent one.

For a time the operation of chairing Fenn up the steps
occupied the active minds of the Kayites. When he had
disappeared into the first eleven room, they turned their
attention in other directions. Caustic and uncomplimentary
remarks began to fly to and fro between the representatives
of Kay's and Blackburn's. It is not known who actually
administered the first blow. But, when Fenn came out of
the pavilion with Kennedy and Silver, he found a stirring
battle in progress. The members of the other houses who
had come to look on at the match stood in knots, and gazed
with approval at the efforts of Kay's and Blackburn's
juniors to wipe each other off the face of the earth. The
air was full of shrill battle-cries, varied now and then by a
smack or a thud, as some young but strenuous fist found a
billet. The fortune of war seemed to be distributed equally

so far, and the combatants were just warming to their work.

"Look here," said Kennedy, "we ought to stop this."

"What's the good," said Fenn, without interest. "It pleases them, and doesn't hurt anybody else."

"All the same," observed Jimmy Silver, moving towards the nearest group of combatants, "free fights aren't quite the thing, somehow. For, children, you should never let your angry passions rise; your little hands were never made to tear each other's eyes. Dr Watts' *Advice to Young Pugilists*. Drop it, you little beasts."

He separated two heated youths who were just beginning a fourth round. The rest of the warriors, seeing Silver and the others, called a truce, and Silver, having read a sort of Riot Act, moved on. The juniors of the beaten house, deciding that it would be better not to resume hostilities, consoled themselves by giving three groans for Mr Kay.

"What happened after I left you last night, Fenn?" asked Kennedy.

"Oh, I had one of my usual rows with Kay, only rather worse than usual. I said one or two things he didn't like, and today the old man sent for me and told me to come to his room from two till four. Kay had run me in for being 'grossly rude'. Listen to those kids. What a row they're making!"

"It's a beastly shame," said Kennedy despondently.

At the school shop Morrell, of Mulholland's, met them. He had been spending the afternoon with a rug and a novel on the hills at the back of the school, and he wanted to know how the final house-match had gone. Blackburn's had beaten Mulholland's in one of the early rounds. Kennedy explained what had happened.

"We should have lost if Fenn had turned up earlier," he said. "He had a row with Kay, and Kay gave him a sort of extra between two and four."

Fenn, busily occupied with an ice, added no comment of his own to this plain tale.

"Rough luck," said Morrell. "What's all that row out in the field?"

"That's Kay's kids giving three groans for Kay," explained Silver. "At least, they started with the idea of giving three groans. They've got up to about three hundred by this time. It seems to have fascinated them. They won't leave off. There's no school rule against groaning in the grounds, and they mean to groan till the end of the term. Personally, I like the sound. But then, I'm fond of music."

Morrell's face beamed with sudden pleasure. "I knew there was something I wanted to tell you," he said, "only I couldn't remember what. Your saying you're fond of music reminds me. Mulholland's crocked himself, and won't be able to turn out for the concert."

"What!" cried Kennedy. "How did it happen? What's he done?"

Mr Mulholland was the master who looked after the music of the school, a fine cricketer and keen sportsman. Had nothing gone wrong, he would have conducted at the concert that night.

"I heard it from the matron at our place," said Morrell. "She's full of it. Mulholland was batting at the middle net, and somebody else—I forget who—was at the one next to it on the right. The bowler sent down a long-hop to leg, and this Johnny had a smack at it, and sent it slap through the net, and it got Mulholland on the side of the head. He was stunned for a bit, but he's getting all right again now. But he won't be able to conduct tonight. Rather bad luck on the man, especially as he's so keen on the concert."

"Who's going to sub for him?" asked Silver. "Perhaps they'll scratch the show," suggested Kennedy.

"Oh, no," said Morrell, "it's all right. Kay is going to conduct. He's often done it at choir practices when Mulholland couldn't turn up."

Fenn put down his empty saucer with an emphatic crack on the counter.

"If Kay's going to run the show, I'm hanged if I turn up," he said.

"My dear chap, you can't get out of it now," said Kennedy anxiously. He did not want to see Fenn plunging into any more strife with the authorities this term.

"Think of the crowned heads who are coming to hear you," pleaded Jimmy Silver. "Think of the nobility and gentry. Think of me. You must play."

"Ah, there you are, Fenn."

Mr Kay had bustled in in his energetic way.

Fenn said nothing. He *was* there. It was idle to deny it.

"I thought I should find you here. Yes, I wanted to see you about the concert tonight. Mr Mulholland has met with an unfortunate accident, and I am looking after the entertainment in his place. Come with me and play over your piece. I should like to see that you are perfect in it. Dear me, dear me, what a noise those boys are making. Why *are* they behaving in that extraordinary way, I wonder!"

Kay's juniors had left the pavilion, and were trooping back to their house. At the present moment they were passing the school shop, and their tuneful voices floated in through the open window.

"This is very unusual. Why, they seem to be boys in my house. They are groaning."

"I think they are a little upset at the result of the match, sir," said Jimmy Silver suavely. "Fenn did not arrive, for some reason, till the end of the innings, so Mr Blackburn's won. The wicket was good, but a little fiery."

"Thank you, Silver," replied Mr Kay with asperity. "When I require explanations I will ask for them."

He darted out of the shop, and a moment later they heard him pouring out a flood of recriminations on the groaning fags.

"There was *once* a man who snubbed me," said Jimmy Silver. "They buried him at Brookwood. Well, what are you going to do, Fenn? Going to play tonight? Harkee, boy. Say but the word, and I will beard this tyrant to his face."

Fenn rose.

"Yes," he said briefly, "I shall play. You'd better turn up. I think you'll enjoy it."

Silver said that no human power should keep him away.

The School concert was always one of the events of the summer term. There was a concert at the end of the winter term, too, but it was not so important. To a great many of those present the summer concert marked, as it were, the last flutter of their school life. On the morrow they would be Old Boys, and it behoved them to extract as much enjoyment from the function as they could. Under Mr Mullholland's rule the concert had become a very flourishing institution. He aimed at a high standard, and reached it. There was more than a touch of the austere about the music. A glance at the programme was enough to show the lover of airs of the trashy, clashy order that this was no place for him. Most of the items were serious. When it was thought necessary to introduce a lighter touch, some staidly rollicking number was inserted, some song that was saved —in spite of a catchy tune—by a halo of antiquity. Anything modern was taboo, unless it were the work of Gotsuchakoff, Thingummyowsky, or some other eminent foreigner. Foreign origin made it just possible.

The school prefects lurked during the performance at the doors and at the foot of the broad stone steps that led to the Great Hall. It was their duty to supply visitors with programmes.

Jimmy Silver had foregathered with Kennedy, Challis, and Williams at the junior door. The hall was full now, and their labours consequently at an end.

"Pretty good 'gate'," said Silver, looking in through the open door. "It must be warm up in the gallery."

Across the further end of the hall a dais had been erected. On this the bulk of the school sat, leaving the body of the hall to the crowned heads, nobility, and gentry to whom Silver had referred in his conversation with Fenn.

"It always is warm in the gallery," said Challis. "I lost about two stone there every concert when I was a kid. We simply used to sit and melt."

"And I tell you what," broke in Silver, "it's going to get warmer before the end of the show. Do you notice that all Kay's house are sitting in a lump at the back. I bet they're simply spoiling for a row. Especially now Kay's running the concert. There's going to be a hot time in the old town tonight—you see if there isn't. Hark at 'em."

The choir had just come to the end of a little thing of Handel's. There was no reason to suppose that the gallery appreciated Handel. Nevertheless, they were making a deafening noise. Clouds of dust rose from the rhythmical stamping of many feet. The noise was loudest and the dust thickest by the big window, beneath which sat the men from Kay's. Things were warming up.

The gallery, with one last stamp which nearly caused the dais to collapse, quieted down. The masters in the audience looked serious. One or two of the visitors glanced over their shoulders with a smile. How excited the dear boys were at the prospect of holidays! Young blood! Young blood! Boys *would* be boys.

The concert continued. Half-way through the programme there was a ten minutes' interval. Fenn's pianoforte solo was the second item of the second half.

He mounted the platform amidst howls of delight from the gallery. Applause at the Eckleton concerts was granted more for services in the playing-fields than merit as a musician. Kubelik or Paderewski would have been welcomed with a few polite handclaps. A man in the eleven or fifteen was certain of two minutes' unceasing cheers.

"Evidently one of their heroes, my dear," said Paterfamilias to Materfamilias. "I suppose he has won a scholarship at the University."

Paterfamilias' mind was accustomed to run somewhat upon scholarships at the University. What the school wanted was a batting average of forty odd or a bowling analysis in single figures.

Fenn played the "Moonlight Sonata". A trained musical critic would probably have found much to cavil at in his rendering of the piece, but it was undoubtedly good for a public school player. Of course he was encored. The gallery would have encored him if he had played with one finger, three mistakes to every bar.

"I told Fenn," said Jimmy Silver, "if he got an encore, that he ought to play the— My aunt! *He is!*"

Three runs and half-a-dozen crashes, and there was no further room for doubt. Fenn was playing the "Coon Band Contest".

"He's gone mad," gasped Kennedy.

Whether he had or not, it is certain that the gallery had. All the evening they had been stewing in an atmosphere like that of the inner room of a Turkish bath, and they were ready for anything. It needed but a trifle to set them off. The lilt of that unspeakable Yankee melody supplied that trifle. Kay's malcontents, huddled in their seats by the window, were the first to break out. Feet began to stamp in time to the music—softly at first, then more loudly. The wooden dais gave out the sound like a drum.

Other rioters joined in from the right. The noise spread through the gallery as a fire spreads through gorse. Soon three hundred pairs of well-shod feet were rising and falling. Somebody began to whistle. Everybody whistled. Mr Kay was on his feet, gesticulating wildly. His words were lost in the uproar.

For five minutes the din prevailed. Then, with a final crash, Fenn finished. He got up from the music-stool, bowed, and walked back to his place by the senior door. The musical efforts of the gallery changed to a storm of cheering and clapping.

The choir rose to begin the next piece.

Still the noise continued.

People began to leave the Hall—in ones and twos first, then in a steady stream which blocked the doorways. It was plain to the dullest intelligence that if there was going to be any more concert, it would have to be performed in dumb show. Mr Kay flung down his bâton.

The visitors had left by now, and the gallery was beginning to follow their example, howling as it went.

"Well," said Jimmy Silver cheerfully, as he went with Kennedy down the steps, "I *think* we may call that a record. By my halidom, there'll be a row about this later on."

V

Camp

With the best intentions in the world, however, a head-master cannot make a row about a thing unless he is given a reasonable amount of time to make it in. The concert being on the last evening of term, there was only a single morning before the summer holidays, and that morning was occupied with the prize-giving. The school assembled at ten o'clock with a shadowy hope that this prize-day would be more exciting than the general run of prize-days, but they were disappointed. The function passed off without sensation. The headmaster did not denounce the school in an impassioned speech from the dais. He did not refer to the events of the previous evening. At the same time, his demeanour was far from jovial. It lacked that rollicking bonhomie which we like to see in headmasters on prize-day. It was evident to the most casual observer that the affair was not closed. The school would have to pay the bill sooner or later. But eight weeks would elapse before the day of reckoning, which was a comforting thought.

The last prize was handed over to its rightful owner. The last and dullest vote of thanks had been proposed by the last and dullest member of the board of governors. The Bishop of Rumtifoo (who had been selected this year to distribute the prizes) had worked off his seventy minutes' speech (inaudible, of course, as usual), and was feeling much easier. The term had been formally declared at an end, and those members of the school corps who were going to camp were beginning to assemble in front of the buildings.

"I wonder why it always takes about three hours to get us off to the station," said Jimmy Silver. "I've been to camp two years now, and there's always been this rotting about in the grounds before we start. Nobody's likely to turn up to inspect us for the next hour or so. If any gent cares to put in a modest ginger-beer at the shop, I'm with him."

"I don't see why we shouldn't," said Kennedy. He had seen Fenn go into the shop, and wished to talk to him. He had not seen him after the concert, and he thought it would be interesting to know how Kay had taken it, and what his comments had been on meeting Fenn in the house that night.

Fenn had not much to say.

"He was rather worried," he said, grinning as if the recollection of the interview amused him. "But he couldn't do anything. Of course, there'll be a row next term, but it can't be helped."

"If I were you," said Silver, "I should point out to them that you'd a perfect right to play what you liked for an encore. How were you to know the gallery would go off like that? You aren't responsible for them. Hullo, there's that bugle. Things seem to be on the move. We must go."

"So long," said Fenn.

"Goodbye. Mind you come off against Middlesex."

Kennedy stayed for a moment.

"Has the Old Man said anything to you yet?" he asked.

"Not yet. He'll do that next term. It'll be something to look forward to."

Kennedy hurried off to take his place in the ranks.

Getting to camp at the end of the summer term is always a nuisance. Aldershot seems a long way from everywhere, and the trains take their time over the journey. Then, again, the heat always happens to be particularly oppressive on that day. Snow may have fallen on the day before, but directly one sets out for camp, the thermometer goes up into three figures. The Eckleton contingent marched into the lines damp and very thirsty.

Most of the other schools were already on the spot, and looked as if they had been spending the last few years there. There was nothing particular going on when the Eckleton warriors arrived, and everybody was lounging about in khaki and shirt-sleeves, looking exasperatingly cool. The only consolation which buoyed up the spirits of Eckleton was the reflection that in a short space of time, when the important-looking gentleman in uniform who had come to meet them had said all he wanted to say on the subject of rules and regulations, they would be like that too. Happy thought! If the man bucked up and cut short the peroration, there would be time for a bathe in Cove Reservoir. Those of the corps who had been to camp in previous years felt quite limp with the joy of the thought. Why couldn't he get through with it, and give a fellow a chance of getting cool again?

The gist of the oration was apparently that the Eckleton cadets were to consider themselves not only as soldiers—and as such subject to military discipline, and the rules for the conduct of troops quartered in the Aldershot district—but also as members of a public school. In short, that if they misbehaved themselves they would get cells, and a hundred lines in the same breath, as it were.

The corps knew all this ages ago. The man seemed to think he was telling them something fresh. They began positively to dislike him after a while.

He finished at last. Eckleton marched off wearily, but in style, to its lines.

"Dis-miss!"

They did.

"And about time, too," said Jimmy Silver. "I wish they would tie that man up, or something. He's one of the worst bores I know. He may be full of bright conversation in private life, but in public he will talk about his beastly military regulations. You can't stop him. It's a perfect mania with him. Now, I believe—that's to say, I have a sort of dim idea—that there's a place round about here called a canteen. I seem to remember such a thing vaguely. We might go and look for it."

Kennedy made no objection.

This was his first appearance at camp. Jimmy Silver, on the other hand, was a veteran. He had been there twice before, and meant to go again. He had a peculiar and extensive knowledge of the ins and outs of the place. Kennedy was quite willing to take him as his guide. He was full of information. Kennedy was surprised to see what a number of men from the other schools he seemed to know. In the canteen there were, amongst others, a Carthusian, two Tonbridge men, and a Haileyburian. They all greeted Silver with the warmth of old friends.

"You get to know a lot of fellows in camp," explained Jimmy, as they strolled back to the Eckleton lines. "That's the best of the place. Camp's the best place on earth, if only you have decent weather. See that chap over there? He came here last year. He'd never been before, and one of the things he didn't know was that Cove Reservoir's only about three feet deep round the sides. He took a running dive, and almost buried himself in the mud. It's about two feet deep. He told me afterwards he swallowed pounds of it. Rather bad luck. Somebody ought to have told him. You can't do much diving here."

"Glad you mentioned it," said Kennedy. "I should have dived myself if you hadn't."

Many other curious and diverting facts did the expert drag from the bonded warehouse of his knowledge. Nothing changes at camp. Once get to know the ropes, and you know them for all time.

"The one thing I bar," he said, "is having to get up at half-past five. And one day in the week, when there's a divisional field-day, it's half-past four. It's hardly worth while going to sleep at all. Still, it isn't so bad as it used to be. The first year I came to camp we used to have to do a three hours' field-day before brekker. We used to have coffee before it, and nothing else till it was over. By Jove, you felt you'd had enough of it before you got back. This is Laffan's Plain. The worst of Laffan's Plain is that you get to know it too well. You get jolly sick of always starting on field-days from the same place, and marching across the same bit of ground. Still, I suppose they can't alter the scenery for our benefit. See that man there? He won the sabres at Aldershot last year. That chap with him is in the Clifton footer team."

When a school corps goes to camp, it lives in a number of tents, and, as a rule, each house collects in a tent of its own. Blackburn's had a tent, and further down the line Kay's had assembled. The Kay contingent were under Wayburn, a good sort, as far as he himself was concerned, but too weak to handle a mob like Kay's. Wayburn was not coming back after the holidays, a fact which perhaps still further weakened his hold on the Kayites. They had nothing to fear from him next term.

Kay's was represented at camp by a dozen or so of its members, of whom young Billy Silver alone had any pretensions to the esteem of his fellow man. Kay's was the rowdiest house in the school, and the cream of its rowdy members had come to camp. There was Walton, for one, a perfect specimen of the public school man at his worst. There was Mortimer, another of Kay's gems. Perry, again, and Callingham, and the rest. A pleasant gang, fit for anything, if it could be done in safety.

Kennedy observed them, and—the spectacle starting a train of thought—asked Jimmy Silver, as they went into their tent just before lights-out, if there was much ragging in camp.

"Not very much," said the expert. "Chaps are generally too done up at the end of the day to want to do anything

except sleep. Still, I've known cases. You sometimes get one
tent mobbing another. They loose the ropes, you know.
Low trick, I think. It isn't often done, and it gets dropped
on like bricks when it's found out. But why? Do you feel
as if you wanted to do it?"

"It only occurred to me that we've got a lively gang from
Kay's here. I was wondering if they'd get any chances of
ragging, or if they'd have to lie low."

"I'd forgotten Kay's for the moment. Now you mention
it, they are rather a crew. But I shouldn't think they'd find
it worth while to rot about here. It isn't as if they were
on their native heath. People have a prejudice against
having their tent-ropes loosed, and they'd get beans if they
did anything in that line. I remember once there was a
tent which made itself objectionable, and it got raided in
the night by a sort of vigilance committee from the other
schools, and the chaps in it got the dickens of a time. None
of them ever came to camp again. I hope Kay's 'll try and
behave decently. It'll be an effort for them; but I hope
they'll make it. It would be an awful nuisance if young
Billy made an ass of himself in any way. He loves making
an ass of himself. It's a sort of hobby of his."

As if to support the statement, a sudden volley of subdued shouts came from the other end of the Eckleton lines.

"Go it, Wren!"

"Stick to it, Silver!"

"Wren!"

"Silver!"

"S-s-h!"

Silence, followed almost immediately by a gruff voice
inquiring with simple directness what the dickens all this
noise was about.

"Hullo!" said Kennedy. "Did you hear that? I wonder
what's been up? Your brother was in it, whatever it was."

"Of course," said Jimmy Silver, "he would be. We can't

find out about it now, though. I'll ask him tomorrow, if I remember. I shan't remember, of course. Good night."

"Good night."

Half an hour later, Kennedy, who had been ruminating over the incident in his usual painstaking way, reopened the debate.

"Who's Wren?" he asked.

"Wha'?" murmured Silver, sleepily.

"Who's Wren?" repeated Kennedy.

"I d'know.... Oh.... Li'l' beast.... Kay's.... Red hair.... G'-ni'."

And sleep reigned in Blackburn's tent.

VI

The Raid on the Guard-Tent

Wren and Billy Silver had fallen out over a question of
space. It was Silver's opinion that Wren's nest ought to
have been built a foot or two further to the left. He stated
baldly that he had not room to breathe, and requested the
red-headed one to ease off a point or so in the direction of
his next-door neighbour. Wren had refused, and, after a
few moments' chatty conversation, smote William earnestly
in the wind. Trouble had begun upon the instant. It had
ceased almost as rapidly owing to interruptions from without, but the truce had been merely temporary. They
continued the argument outside the tent at five-thirty the
next morning, after the *réveille* had sounded, amidst shouts
of approval from various shivering mortals who were
tubbing preparatory to embarking on the labours of the
day.

A brisk first round had just come to a conclusion when
Walton lounged out of the tent, yawning.

Walton proceeded to separate the combatants. After
which he rebuked Billy Silver with a swagger-stick. Wren's
share in the business he overlooked. He was by way of being
a patron of Wren's, and he disliked Billy Silver, partly for
his own sake and partly because he hated his brother, with
whom he had come into contact once or twice during his
career at Eckleton, always with unsatisfactory results.

So Walton dropped on to Billy Silver, and Wren continued his toilet rejoicing.

Camp was beginning the strenuous life now. Tent after
tent emptied itself of its occupants, who stretched themselves

vigorously, and proceeded towards the tubbing-ground, where there were tin baths for those who cared to wait until the same were vacant, and a good, honest pump for those who did not. Then there was that unpopular job, the piling of one's bedding outside the tent, and the rolling up of the tent curtains. But these unpleasant duties came to an end at last, and signs of breakfast began to appear.

Breakfast gave Kennedy his first insight into life in camp. He happened to be tent-orderly that day, and it therefore fell to his lot to join the orderlies from the other tents in their search for the Eckleton rations. He returned with a cargo of bread (obtained from the quartermaster), and, later, with a great tin of meat, which the cook-house had supplied, and felt that this was life. Hitherto breakfast had been to him a thing of white cloths, tables, and food that appeared from nowhere. This was the first time he had ever tracked his food to its source, so to speak, and brought it back with him. After breakfast, when he was informed that, as tent-orderly for the day, it was his business to wash up, he began to feel as if he were on a desert island. He had never quite realised before what washing-up implied, and he was conscious of a feeling of respect for the servants at Blackburn's, who did it every day as a matter of course, without complaint. He had had no idea before this of the intense stickiness of a jammy plate.

One day at camp is much like another. The schools opened the day with parade drill at about eight o'clock, and, after an instruction series of "changing direction half-left in column of double companies", and other pleasant movements of a similar nature, adjourned for lunch. Lunch was much like breakfast, except that the supply of jam was cut off. The people who arrange these things—probably the War Office, or Mr Brodrick, or someone—have come to the conclusion that two pots of jam per tent are sufficient for breakfast and lunch. The unwary devour theirs recklessly at the earlier meal, and have to go jamless until tea at six o'clock, when another pot is served out.

The afternoon at camp is perfect or otherwise, according to whether there is a four o'clock field-day or not. If there is, there are more manoeuvrings until tea-time, and the time is spent profitably, but not so pleasantly as it might be. If there is no field-day, you can take your time about your bathe in Cove Reservoir. And a really satisfactory bathe on a hot day should last at least three hours. Kennedy and Jimmy Silver strolled off in the direction of the Reservoir as soon as they felt that they had got over the effects of the beef, potatoes, and ginger-beer which a generous commissariat had doled out to them for lunch. It was a glorious day, and bathing was the only thing to do for the next hour or so. Stump-cricket, that fascinating sport much indulged in in camp, would not be at its best until the sun had cooled off a little.

After a pleasant half hour in the mud and water of the Reservoir, they lay on the bank and watched the rest of the schools take their afternoon dip. Kennedy had laid in a supply of provisions from the stall which stood at the camp end of the water. Neither of them felt inclined to move.

"This *is* decent," said Kennedy, wriggling into a more comfortable position in the long grass. "Hullo!"

"What's up?" inquired Jimmy Silver, lazily.

He was almost asleep.

"Look at those idiots. They're certain to get spotted."

Jimmy Silver tilted his hat off his face, and sat up.

"What's the matter? Which idiot?"

Kennedy pointed to a bush on their right. Walton and Perry were seated beside it. Both were smoking.

"Oh, that's all right," said Silver. "Masters never come to Cove Reservoir. It's a sort of unwritten law. They're rotters to smoke, all the same. Certain to get spotted some day.... Not worth it.... Spoils lungs.... Beastly bad ... training."

He dozed off. The sun was warm, and the grass very soft and comfortable. Kennedy turned his gaze to the Reservoir again. It was no business of his what Walton and Perry did.

Walton and Perry were discussing ways and means. The conversation changed as they saw Kennedy glance at them. They were the sort of persons who feel a vague sense of injury when anybody looks at them, perhaps because they feel that those whose attention is attracted to them must say something to their discredit when they begin to talk about them.

"There's that beast Kennedy," said Walton. "I can't stick that man. He's always hanging round the house. What he comes for, I can't make out."

"Pal of Fenn's," suggested Perry.

"He hangs on to Fenn. I bet Fenn bars him really."

Perry doubted this in his innermost thoughts, but it was not worth while to say so.

"Those Blackburn chaps," continued Walton, reverting to another grievance, "will stick on no end of side next term about that cup. They wouldn't have had a look in if Kay hadn't given Fenn that extra. Kay ought to be kicked. I'm hanged if I'm going to care what I do next term. Somebody ought to do something to take it out of Kay for getting his own house licked like that."

Walton spoke as if the line of conduct he had mapped out for himself would be a complete reversal of his customary mode of life. As a matter of fact, he had never been in the habit of caring very much what he did.

Walton's last remarks brought the conversation back to where it had been before the mention of Kennedy switched it off on to new lines. Perry had been complaining that he thought camp a fraud, that it was all drilling and getting up at unearthly hours. He reminded Walton that he had only come on the strength of the latter's statement that it would

be a rag. Where did the rag come in? That was what Perry
wanted to know.

"When it's not a ghastly sweat," he concluded, "it's
slow. Like it is now. Can't we do something for a change?"

"As a matter of fact," said Walton, "nearly all the best
rags are played out. A chap at a crammer's told me last
holidays that when he was at camp he and some other
fellows loosed the ropes of the guard-tent. He said it was
grand sport."

Perry sat up.

"That's the thing," he said, excitedly. "Let's do that.
Why not?"

"It's beastly risky," objected Walton.

"What's that matter? They can't do anything, even if
they spot us."

"That's all you know. We should get beans."

"Still, it's worth risking. It would be the biggest rag
going. Did the chap tell you how they did it?"

"Yes," said Walton, becoming animated as he recalled
the stirring tale, "they bagged the sentry. Chucked a cloth
or something over his head, you know. Then they shoved
him into the ditch, and one of them sat on him while the
others loosed the ropes. It took the chaps inside no end of a
time getting out."

"That's the thing. We'll do it. We only need one other
chap. Leveson would come if we asked him. Let's get back
to the lines. It's almost tea-time. Tell him after tea."

Leveson proved agreeable. Indeed, he jumped at it. His
life, his attitude suggested, had been a hollow mockery until
he heard the plan, but now he could begin to enjoy himself
once more.

The lights-out bugle sounded at ten o'clock; the last post
at ten-thirty. At a quarter to twelve the three adventurers,
who had been keeping themselves awake by the exercise of
great pains, satisfied themselves that the other occupants of
the tent were asleep, and stole out.

It was an excellent night for their purpose. There was no moon, and the stars were hidden by clouds.

They crept silently towards the guard-tent. A dim figure loomed out of the blackness. They noted with satisfaction, as it approached, that it was small. Sentries at the public-school camp vary in physique. They felt that it was lucky that the task of sentry-go had not fallen that night to some muscular forward from one of the school fifteens, or worse still, to a boxing expert who had figured in the Aldershot competition at Easter. The present sentry would be an easy victim.

They waited for him to arrive.

A moment later Private Jones, of St Asterisk's—for it was he—turning to resume his beat, found himself tackled from behind. Two moments later he was reclining in the ditch. He would have challenged his adversary, but, unfortunately, that individual happened to be seated on his face.

He struggled, but to no purpose.

He was still struggling when a muffled roar of indignation from the direction of the guard-tent broke the stillness of the summer night. The roar swelled into a crescendo. What seemed like echoes came from other quarters out of the darkness. The camp was waking.

The noise from the guard-tent waxed louder.

The unknown marauder rose from his seat on Private Jones, and vanished.

Private Jones also rose. He climbed out of the ditch, shook himself, looked round for his assailant, and, not finding him, hurried to the guard-tent to see what was happening.

VII

A Clue

The guard-tent had disappeared.

Private Jones' bewildered eye, rolling in a fine frenzy from heaven to earth, and from earth to heaven, in search of the missing edifice, found it at last in a tangled heap upon the ground. It was too dark to see anything distinctly, but he perceived that the canvas was rising and falling spasmodically like a stage sea, and for a similar reason— because there were human beings imprisoned beneath it.

By this time the whole camp was up and doing. Figures in *déshabillé*, dashing the last vestiges of sleep away with their knuckles, trooped on to the scene in twos and threes, full of inquiry and trenchant sarcasm.

"What are you men playing at? What's all the row about? Can't you finish that game of footer some other time, when we aren't trying to get to sleep? What on earth's up?"

Then the voice of one having authority.

"What's the matter? What are you doing?"

It was perfectly obvious what the guard was doing. It was trying to get out from underneath the fallen tent. Private Jones explained this with some warmth.

"Somebody jumped at me and sat on my head in the ditch. I couldn't get up. And then some blackguard cut the ropes of the guard-tent. I couldn't see who it was. He cut off directly the tent went down."

Private Jones further expressed a wish that he could find the chap. When he did, there would, he hinted, be trouble in the old homestead.

The tent was beginning to disgorge its prisoners.

"Guard, turn out!" said a facetious voice from the darkness.

The camp was divided into two schools of thought. Those who were watching the guard struggle out thought the episode funny. The guard did not. It was pathetic to hear them on the subject of their mysterious assailants.

Matters quieted down rapidly after the tent had been set up again. The spectators were driven back to their lines by their officers. The guard turned in again to try and restore their shattered nerves with sleep until their time for sentry-go came round. Private Jones picked up his rifle and resumed his beat. The affair was at an end as far as that night was concerned.

Next morning, as might be expected, nothing else was talked about. Conversation at breakfast was confined to the topic. No halfpenny paper, however many times its circulation might exceed that of any penny morning paper, ever propounded so fascinating and puzzling a breakfast-table problem. It was the utter impossibility of detecting the culprits that appealed to the schools. They had swooped down like hawks out of the night, and disappeared like eels into mud, leaving no traces.

Jimmy Silver, of course, had no doubts.

"It was those Kay's men," he said. "What does it matter about evidence? You've only got to look at 'em. That's all the evidence you want. The only thing that makes it at all puzzling is that they did nothing worse. You'd naturally expect them to slay the sentry, at any rate."

But the rest of the camp, lacking that intimate knowledge of the Kayite which he possessed, did not turn the eye of suspicion towards the Eckleton lines. The affair remained a mystery. Kennedy, who never gave up a problem when everybody else did, continued to revolve the mystery in his mind.

"I shouldn't wonder," he said to Silver, two days later, "if you were right."

Silver, who had not made any remark for the last five minutes, with the exception of abusive comments on the toughness of the meat which he was trying to carve with a blunt knife for the tent, asked for an explanation.

"I mean about that row the other night."

"What row?"

"That guard-tent business."

"Oh, that! I'd forgotten. Why don't you move with the times? You're always thinking of something that's been dead and buried for years."

"You remember you said you thought it was those Kay's chaps who did it. I've been thinking it over, and I believe you're right. You see, it was probably somebody who'd been to camp before, or he wouldn't have known that dodge of loosing the ropes."

"I don't see why. Seems to me it's the sort of idea that might have occurred to anybody. You don't want to study the thing particularly deeply to know that the best way of making a tent collapse is to loose the ropes. Of course it was Kay's lot who did it. But I don't see how you're going to have them simply because one or two of them have been here before."

"No, I suppose not," said Kennedy.

After tea the other occupants of the tent went out of the lines to play stump-cricket. Silver was in the middle of a story in one of the magazines, so did not accompany them. Kennedy cried off on the plea of slackness.

"I say," he said, when they were alone.

"Hullo," said Silver, finishing his story, and putting down the magazine. "What do you say to going after those chaps? I thought that story was going to be a long one that would take half an hour to get through. But it collapsed. Like that guard-tent."

"About that tent business," said Kennedy. "Of course

that was all rot what I was saying just now. I suddenly remembered that I didn't particularly want anybody but you to hear what I was going to say, so I had to invent any rot that I could think of."

"But now," said Jimmy Silver, sinking his voice to a melodramatic whisper, "the villagers have left us to continue their revels on the green, our wicked uncle has gone to London, his sinister retainer, Jasper Murgleshaw, is washing his hands in the scullery sink, and—*we are alone!*"

"Don't be an ass," pleaded Kennedy.

"Tell me your dreadful tale. Conceal nothing. Spare me not. In fact, say on."

"I've had a talk with the chap who was sentry that night," began Kennedy.

"Astounding revelations by our special correspondent," murmured Silver.

"You might listen."

"I *am* listening. Why don't you begin? All this hesitation strikes me as suspicious. Get on with your shady story."

"You remember the sentry was upset—"

"Very upset."

"Somebody collared him from behind, and upset him into the ditch. They went in together, and the other man sat on his head."

"A touching picture. Proceed, friend."

"They rolled about a bit, and this sentry chap swears he scratched the man. It was just after that that the man sat on his head. Jones says he was a big chap, strong and heavy."

"He was in a position to judge, anyhow."

"Of course, he didn't mean to scratch him. He was rather keen on having that understood. But his fingers came up against the fellow's cheek as he was falling. So you see we've only got to look for a man with a scratch on his cheek. It was the right cheek, Jones was almost certain. I don't see what you're laughing at."

"I wish you wouldn't spring these good things of yours on me suddenly," gurgled Jimmy Silver, rolling about the wooden floor of the tent. "You ought to give a chap some warning. Look here," he added, imperatively, "swear you'll take me with you when you go on your tour through camp examining everybody's right cheek to see if it's got a scratch on it."

Kennedy began to feel the glow and pride of the successful sleuth-hound leaking out of him. This aspect of the case had not occurred to him. The fact that the sentry had scratched his assailant's right cheek, added to the other indubitable fact that Walton, of Kay's, was even now walking abroad with a scratch on his right cheek, had seemed to him conclusive. He had forgotten that there might be others. Still, it was worth while just to question him. He questioned him at Cove Reservoir next day.

"Hullo, Walton," he said, with a friendly carelessness which would not have deceived a prattling infant, "nasty scratch you've got on your cheek. How did you get it?"

"Perry did it when we were ragging a few days ago," replied Walton, eyeing him distrustfully.

"Oh," said Kennedy.

"Silly fool," said Walton.

"Talking about me?" inquired Kennedy politely.

"No," replied Walton, with the suavity of a Chesterfield, "Perry."

They parted, Kennedy with the idea that Walton was his man still more deeply rooted, Walton with an uncomfortable feeling that Kennedy knew too much, and that, though he had undoubtedly scored off him for the moment, a time (as Jimmy Silver was fond of observing with a satanic laugh) would come, and then—!

He felt that it behoved him to be wary.

VIII

A Night Adventure—The Dethronement of Fenn

One of the things which make life on this planet more or less agreeable is the speed with which alarums, excursions, excitement, and rows generally, blow over. A nine-days' wonder has to be a big business to last out its full time nowadays. As a rule the third day sees the end of it, and the public rushes whooping after some other hare that has been started for its benefit. The guard-tent row, as far as the bulk of camp was concerned, lasted exactly two days; at the end of which period it was generally agreed that all that could be said on the subject had been said, and that it was now a back number. Nobody, except possibly the authorities, wanted to find out the authors of the raid, and even Private Jones had ceased to talk about it—this owing to the unsympathetic attitude of his tent.

"Jones," the corporal had observed, as the ex-sentry's narrative of his misfortunes reached a finish for the third time since *réveille* that morning, "if you can't manage to switch off that infernal chestnut of yours, I'll make you wash up all day and sit on your head all night."

So Jones had withdrawn his yarn from circulation. Kennedy's interest in detective work waned after his interview with Walton. He was quite sure that Walton had been one of the band, but it was not his business to find out; even had he found out, he would have done nothing. It was more for his own private satisfaction than for the furtherance of justice that he wished to track the offenders down. But he did not look on the affair, as Jimmy Silver did, as rather sporting; he had a tender feeling for the good name of the school, and he felt that it was not likely to make Eckleton popular with the other schools that went to camp if they got the reputation of practical jokers. Practical jokers are seldom popular until they have been dead a hundred years or so.

As for Walton and his colleagues, to complete the list of those who were interested in this matter of the midnight raid, they lay remarkably low after their successful foray. They imagined that Kennedy was spying on their every movement. In which they were quite wrong, for Kennedy was doing nothing of the kind. Camp does not allow a great deal of leisure for the minding of other people's businesses. But this reflection did not occur to Walton, and he regarded Kennedy, whenever chance or his duties brought him into the neighbourhood of that worthy's tent, with a suspicion which increased whenever the latter looked at him.

On the night before camp broke up, a second incident of a sensational kind occurred, which, but for the fact that they never heard of it, would have given the schools a good deal to talk about. It happened that Kennedy was on sentry-go that night. The manner of sentry-go is thus. At seven in the evening the guard falls in, and patrols the fringe of the camp in relays till seven in the morning. A guard consists of a sergeant, a corporal, and ten men. They are on duty for two hours at a time, with intervals of four hours between each spell, in which intervals they sleep the sleep of tired men in the guard-tent, unless, as happened on the occasion previously described, some miscreant takes it upon himself to loose the ropes. The ground to be patrolled by the sentries is divided into three parts, each of which is entrusted to one man.

Kennedy was one of the ten privates, and his first spell of sentry-go began at eleven o'clock.

On this night there was no moon. It was as black as pitch. It is always unpleasant to be on sentry-go on such a night. The mind wanders, in spite of all effort to check it, through a long series of all the ghastly stories one has ever read. There is one in particular of Conan Doyle's about a mummy that came to life and chased people on lonely roads—but enough! However courageous one may be, it is difficult not to speculate on the possible horrors which may spring out on one from the darkness. That feeling that there is somebody—or something—just behind one can only be experienced in all its force by a sentry on an inky night at camp. And the thought that, of all the hundreds there, he and two others are the only ones awake, puts a sort of finishing touch to the unpleasantness of the situation.

Kennedy was not a particularly imaginative youth, but he looked forward with no little eagerness to the time when he should be relieved. It would be a relief in two senses of the word. His beat included that side of the camp which faces the road to Aldershot. Between camp and this road is a ditch and a wood. After he had been on duty for an hour this wood began to suggest a variety of possibilities, all grim. The ditch, too, was not without associations. It was into this that Private Jones had been hurled on a certain memorable occasion. Such a thing was not likely to happen again in the same week, and, even if it did, Kennedy flattered himself that he would have more to say in the matter than Private Jones had had; but nevertheless he kept a careful eye in that direction whenever his beat took him along the ditch.

It was about half-past twelve, and he had entered upon the last section of his two hours, when Kennedy distinctly heard footsteps in the wood. He had heard so many mysterious sounds since his patrol began at eleven o'clock that at first he was inclined to attribute this to imagination. But a crackle of dead branches and the sound of soft breathing convinced him that this was the real thing for once, and that, as a sentry of the Public Schools' Camp on duty, it behoved him to challenge the unknown.

He stopped and waited, peering into the darkness in a futile endeavour to catch a glimpse of his man. But the night was too black for the keenest eye to penetrate it. A slight thud put him on the right track. It showed him two things; first, that the unknown had dropped into the ditch, and, secondly, that he was a camp man returning to his tent after an illegal prowl about the town at lights-out. Nobody save one belonging to the camp would have cause to cross the ditch.

Besides, the man walked warily, as one not ignorant of the danger of sentries. The unknown had crawled out of the ditch now. As luck would have it he had chosen a spot immediately opposite to where Kennedy stood. Now that he was nearer Kennedy could see the vague outline of him.

"Who goes there?" he said.

From an instinctive regard for the other's feelings he did not shout the question in the regulation manner. He knew how he would feel himself if he were out of camp at half-past twelve, and the voice of the sentry were to rip suddenly through the silence *fortissimo*.

As it was, his question was quite loud enough to electrify the person to whom it was addressed. The unknown started so violently that he nearly leapt into the air. Kennedy was barely two yards from him when he spoke.

The next moment this fact was brought home to him in a very practical manner. The unknown, sighting the sentry, perhaps more clearly against the dim whiteness of the tents than Kennedy could sight him against the dark wood, dashed in with a rapidity which showed that he knew something of the art of boxing. Kennedy dropped his rifle and flung up his arm. He was altogether too late. A sudden blaze of light, and he was on the ground, sick and dizzy, a feeling he had often experienced before in a slighter degree, when sparring in the Eckleton gymnasium with the boxing instructor.

The immediate effect of a flush hit in the regions about

the jaw is to make the victim lose for the moment all interest in life. Kennedy lay where he had fallen for nearly half a minute before he fully realised what it was that had happened to him. When he did realise the situation, he leapt to his feet, feeling sick and shaky, and staggered about in all directions in a manner which suggested that he fancied his assailant would be waiting politely until he had recovered. As was only natural, that wily person had vanished, and was by this time doing a quick change into garments of the night. Kennedy had the satisfaction of knowing—for what it was worth—that his adversary was in one of those tents, but to place him with any greater accuracy was impossible.

So he gave up the search, found his rifle, and resumed his patrol. And at one o'clock his successor relieved him.

On the following day camp broke up.

Kennedy always enjoyed going home, but, as he travelled back to Eckleton on the last day of these summer holidays, he could not help feeling that there was a great deal to be said for term. He felt particularly cheerful. He had the carriage to himself, and he had also plenty to read and eat. The train was travelling at forty miles an hour. And there were all the pleasures of a first night after the holidays to look forward to, when you dashed from one friend's study to another's, comparing notes, and explaining—five or six of you at a time—what a good time you had had in the holidays. This was always a pleasant ceremony at Blackburn's, where all the prefects were intimate friends, and all good sorts, without that liberal admixture of weeds, worms, and outsiders which marred the list of prefects in most of the other houses. Such as Kay's! Kennedy could not restrain a momentary gloating as he contrasted the state of affairs in Blackburn's with what existed at Kay's. Then this feeling was merged in one of pity for Fenn's hard case. How he must hate the beginning of term, thought Kennedy.

All the well-known stations were flashing by now. In a few minutes he would be at the junction, and in another half-hour back at Blackburn's. He began to collect his baggage from the rack.

Nobody he knew was at the junction. This was the late train that he had come down by. Most of the school had returned earlier in the afternoon.

He reached Blackburn's at eight o'clock, and went up to his study to unpack. This was always his first act on coming back to school. He liked to start the term with all his books in their shelves, and all his pictures and photographs in their proper places on the first day. Some of the studies looked like lumber-rooms till near the end of the first week.

He had filled the shelves, and was arranging the artistic decorations, when Jimmy Silver came in. Kennedy had been surprised that he had not met him downstairs, but the matron had answered his inquiry with the statement that he was talking to Mr Blackburn in the other part of the house.

"When did you arrive?" asked Silver, after the conclusion of the first outbreak of holiday talk.

"I've only just come."

"Seen Blackburn yet?"

"No. I was thinking of going up after I had got this place done properly."

Jimmy Silver ran his eye over the room.

"I haven't started mine yet," he said. "You're such an energetic man. Now, are all those books in their proper places?"

"Yes," said Kennedy.

"Sure?"

"Yes."

"How about the pictures? Got them up?"

"All but this lot here. Shan't be a second. There you are. How's that for effect?"

"Not bad. Got all your photographs in their places?"

"Yes."

"Then," said Jimmy Silver, calmly, "you'd better start now to pack them all up again. And why, my son? Because you are no longer a Blackburnite. That's what."

Kennedy stared.

"I've just had the whole yarn from Blackburn," continued Jimmy Silver. "Our dear old pal, Mr Kay, wanting somebody in his house capable of keeping order, by way of a change, has gone to the Old Man and borrowed you. So *you're* head of Kay's now. There's an honour for you."

IX

THE SENSATIONS OF AN EXILE

"What" shouted Kennedy.

He sprang to his feet as if he had had an electric shock.

Jimmy Silver, having satisfied his passion for the dramatic by the abruptness with which he had exploded his mine, now felt himself at liberty to be sympathetic.

"It's quite true," he said. "And that's just how I felt when Blackburn told me. Blackburn's as sick as anything. Naturally he doesn't see the point of handing you over to Kay. But the Old Man insisted, so he caved in. He wanted to see you as soon as you arrived. You'd better go now. I'll finish your packing."

This was noble of Jimmy, for of all the duties of life he loathed packing most.

"Thanks awfully," said Kennedy, "but don't you bother. I'll do it when I get back. But what's it all about? What made Kay want a man? Why won't Fenn do? And why me?"

"Well, it's easy to see why they chose you. They reflected that you'd had the advantage of being in Blackburn's with me, and seeing how a house really should be run. Kay wants a head for his house. Off he goes to the Old Man. 'Look here,' he says, 'I want somebody shunted into my happy home, or it'll bust up. And it's no good trying to put me off with an inferior article, because I won't have it. It must be somebody who's been trained from youth up by Silver.' 'Then,' says the Old Man, reflectively, 'you can't do better than take Kennedy. I happen to know that Silver has spent years in showing him the straight and narrow path. You

take Kennedy.' 'All right,' says Kay; 'I always thought
Kennedy a bit of an ass myself, but if he's studied under
Silver he ought to know how to manage a house. I'll take
him. Advise our Mr Blackburn to that effect, and ask him
to deliver the goods at his earliest convenience. Adoo, mess-
mate, adoo!' And there you are—that's how it was."

"But what's wrong with Fenn?"

"My dear chap! Remember last term. Didn't Fenn have
a regular scrap with Kay, and get shoved into extra for it?
And didn't he wreck the concert in the most sportsmanlike
way with that encore of his? Think the Old Man is going
to take that grinning? Not much! Fenn made a ripping
fifty against Kent in the holidays—I saw him do it—but
they don't count that. It's a wonder they didn't ask him to
leave. Of course, I think it's jolly rough on Fenn, but I
don't see that you can blame them. Not the Old Man, at
any rate. He couldn't do anything else. It's all Kay's fault
that all this has happened, of course. I'm awfully sorry for
you having to go into that beastly hole, but from Kay's
point of view it's a jolly sound move. You may reform the
place."

"I doubt it."

"So do I—very much. I didn't say you would—I said
you might. I wonder if Kay means to give you a free hand.
It all depends on that."

"Yes. If he's going to interfere with me as he used to
with Fenn, he'll want to bring in another head to improve
on me."

"Rather a good idea, that," said Jimmy Silver, laughing,
as he always did when any humorous possibilities suggested
themselves to him. "If he brings in somebody to improve
on you, and then somebody else to improve on him, and
then another chap to improve on him, he ought to have a
decent house in half-a-dozen years or so."

"The worst of it is," said Kennedy, "that I've got to go
to Kay's as a sort of rival to Fenn. I shouldn't mind so

much if it wasn't for that. I wonder how he'll take it! Do you think he knows about it yet? He didn't enjoy being head, but that's no reason why he shouldn't cut up rough at being shoved back to second prefect. It's a beastly situation."

"Beastly," agreed Jimmy Silver. "Look here," he added, after a pause, "there's no reason, you know, why this should make any difference. To us, I mean. What I mean to say is, I don't see why we shouldn't see each other just as often, and so on, simply because you are in another house, and all that sort of thing. You know what I mean."

He spoke shamefacedly, as was his habit whenever he was serious. He liked Kennedy better than anyone he knew, and hated to show his feelings. Anything remotely connected with sentiment made him uncomfortable.

"Of course," said Kennedy, awkwardly.

"You'll want a refuge," said Silver, in his normal manner, "now that you're going to see wild life in Kay's. Don't forget that I'm always at home in my study in the afternoons—admission on presentation of a visiting-card."

"All right," said Kennedy, "I'll remember. I suppose I'd better go and see Blackburn now."

Mr Blackburn was in his study. He was obviously disgusted and irritated by what had happened. Loyalty to the headmaster, and an appreciation of his position as a member of the staff led him to try and conceal his feelings as much as possible in his interview with Kennedy, but the latter understood as plainly as if his house-master had burst into a flow of abuse and complaint. There had always been an excellent understanding—indeed, a friendship—between Kennedy and Mr Blackburn, and the master was just as sorry to lose his second prefect as the latter was to go.

"Well, Kennedy," he said, pleasantly. "I hope you had a good time in the holidays. I suppose Silver has told you the melancholy news—that you are to desert us this term? It is a great pity. We shall all be very sorry to lose you. I don't look forward to seeing you bowl us all out in the house-matches next summer," he added, with a smile, "though we shall expect a few full-pitches to leg, for the sake of old times."

He meant well, but the picture he conjured up almost made Kennedy break down. Nothing up to the present had made him realise the completeness of his exile so keenly as this remark of Mr Blackburn's about his bowling against the side for which he had taken so many wickets in the past. It was a painful thought.

"I am afraid you won't have quite such a pleasant time in Mr Kay's as you have had here," resumed the house-master. "Of course, I know that, strictly speaking, I ought not to talk like this about another master's house; but you can scarcely be unaware of the reasons that have led to this change. You must know that you are being sent to pull Mr Kay's house together. This is strictly between ourselves, of course. I think you have a difficult task before you, but I don't fancy that you will find it too much for you. And mind you come here as often as you please. I am sure Silver and the others will be glad to see you. Goodbye, Kennedy. I think you ought to be getting across now to Mr Kay's. I told him that you would be there before half-past nine. Good night."

"Good night, sir," said Kennedy.

He wandered out into the house dining-room. Somehow, though Kay's was only next door, he could not get rid of the feeling that he was about to start on a long journey, and would never see his old house again. And in a sense this was so. He would probably visit Blackburn's tomorrow afternoon, but it would not be the same. Jimmy Silver would greet him like a brother, and he would brew in the same study in which he had always brewed, and sit in the same chair; but it would not be the same. He would be an outsider, a visitor, a stranger within the gates, and—worst of all—a Kayite. Nothing could alter that.

The walls of the dining-room were covered with photographs of the house cricket and football teams for the last fifteen years. Looking at them, he felt more than ever how entirely his school life had been bound up in his house. From his first day at Eckleton he had been taught the simple creed of the Blackburnite, that Eckleton was the finest school in the three kingdoms, and that Blackburn's was the finest house in the finest school.

Under the gas-bracket by the door hung the first photograph in which he appeared, the cricket team of four years ago. He had just got the last place in front of Challis on the strength of a tremendous catch for the house second in a scratch game two days before the house-matches began. It had been a glaring fluke, but it had impressed Denny, the head of the house, who happened to see it, and had won him his place.

He walked round the room, looking at each photograph in turn. It seemed incredible that he had no longer any right to an interest in the success of Blackburn's. He could have endured leaving all this when his time at school was up, for that would have been the natural result of the passing of years. But to be transplanted abruptly and with a wrench from his native soil was too much. He went upstairs to pack, suffering from as severe an attack of the blues as any youth of eighteen had experienced since blues were first invented.

Jimmy Silver hovered round, while he packed, with expressions of sympathy and bitter remarks concerning Mr Kay and his wicked works, and, when the operation was concluded, helped Kennedy carry his box over to his new house with the air of one seeing a friend off to the parts beyond the equator.

It was ten o'clock by the time the front door of Kay's closed upon its new head. Kennedy went to the matron's sanctum to be instructed in the geography of the house. The matron, a severe lady, whose faith in human nature had been terribly shaken by five years of office in Kay's, showed him his dormitory and study with a lack of geniality which added a deeper tinge of azure to Kennedy's blues. "So you've come to live here, have you?" her manner seemed to say; "well, I pity you, that's all. A nice time *you're* going to have."

Kennedy spent the half-hour before going to bed in unpacking his box for the second time, and arranging his books and photographs in the study which had been Wayburn's. He had nothing to find fault with in the study. It was as large as the one he had owned at Blackburn's, and, like it, looked out over the school grounds.

At half-past ten the gas gave a flicker and went out, turned off at the main. Kennedy lit a candle and made his way to his dormitory. There now faced him the more than unpleasant task of introducing himself to its inmates. He knew from experience the disconcerting way in which a dormitory greets an intruder. It was difficult to know how to begin matters. It would take a long time, he thought, to explain his presence to their satisfaction.

Fortunately, however, the dormitory was not unprepared. Things get about very quickly in a house. The matron had told the housemaids; the housemaids had handed it on to their ally, the boot boy; the boot boy had told Wren, whom he happened to meet in the passage, and Wren had told everybody else.

There was an uproar going on when Kennedy opened the door, but it died away as he appeared, and the dormitory gazed at the newcomer in absolute and embarrassing silence. Kennedy had not felt so conscious of the public eye being upon him since he had gone out to bat against the M.C.C., on his first appearance in the ranks of the Eckleton eleven. He went to his bed and began to undress without a word, feeling rather than seeing the eyes that were peering at him. When he had completed the performance of disrobing, he blew out the candle and got into bed. The silence was broken by numerous coughs, of that short, suggestive type with which the public schoolboy loves to embarrass his fellow man. From some unidentified corner of the room came a subdued giggle. Then a whispered, "Shut *up*, you fool!" To which a low voice replied, "All *right*. I'm not doing anything."

More coughs, and another outbreak of giggling from a fresh quarter.

"Good night," said Kennedy, to the room in general.

There was no reply. The giggler appeared to be rapidly approaching hysterics.

"Shut up that row," said Kennedy.

The giggling ceased.

The atmosphere was charged with suspicion. Kennedy fell asleep fearing that he was going to have trouble with his dormitory before many nights had passed.

X

Further Experiences of an Exile

Breakfast on the following morning was a repetition of the dormitory ordeal. Kennedy walked to his place on Mr Kay's right, feeling that everyone was looking at him, as indeed they were. He understood for the first time the meaning of the expression, "the cynosure of all eyes". He was modest by nature, and felt his position a distinct trial.

He did not quite know what to say or do with regard to his new house-master at this their first meeting in the latter's territory. "Come aboard, sir," occurred to him for a moment as a happy phrase, but he discarded it. To make the situation more awkward, Mr Kay did not observe him at first, being occupied in assailing a riotous fag at the other end of the table, that youth having succeeded, by a dexterous drive in the ribs, in making a friend of his spill half a cup of coffee. Kennedy did not know whether to sit down without a word or to remain standing until Mr Kay had time to attend to him. He would have done better to have sat down; Mr Kay's greeting, when it came, was not worth waiting for.

"Sit down, Kennedy," he said, irritably—rebuking people on an empty stomach always ruffled him. "Sit down, sit down."

Kennedy sat down, and began to toy diffidently with a sausage, remembering, as he did so, certain diatribes of Fenn's against the food at Kay's. As he became more intimate with the sausage, he admitted to himself that Fenn had had reason. Mr Kay meanwhile pounded away in moody silence at a plate of kidneys and bacon. It was one of the many grievances which gave the Kayite material for conversation that Mr Kay had not the courage of his opinions in the matter of food. He insisted that he fed his house luxuriously, but he refused to brave the mysteries of its bill of fare himself.

Fenn had not come down when Kennedy went in to breakfast. He arrived some ten minutes later, when Kennedy had vanquished the sausage, and was keeping body and soul together with bread and marmalade.

"I cannot have this, Fenn," snapped Mr Kay; "you must come down in time."

Fenn took the rebuke in silence, cast one glance at the sausage which confronted him, and then pushed it away with such unhesitating rapidity that Mr Kay glared at him as if about to take up the cudgels for the rejected viand. Perhaps he remembered that it scarcely befitted the dignity of a house-master to enter upon a wrangle with a member of his house on the subject of the merits and demerits of sausages, for he refrained, and Fenn was allowed to go on with his meal in peace.

Kennedy's chief anxiety had been with regard to Fenn. True, the latter could hardly blame him for being made head of Kay's, since he had not been consulted in the matter, and, if he had been, would have refused the post with horror; but nevertheless the situation might cause a coolness between them. And if Fenn, the only person in the house with whom he was at all intimate, refused to be on friendly terms, his stay in Kay's would be rendered worse than even he had looked for.

Fenn had not spoken to him at breakfast, but then there was little table talk at Kay's. Perhaps the quality of the food suggested such gloomy reflections that nobody liked to put them into words.

After the meal Fenn ran upstairs to his study. Kennedy followed him, and opened conversation in his direct way with the subject which he had come to discuss.

"I say," he said, "I hope you aren't sick about this. You know I didn't want to bag your place as head of the house."

"My dear chap," said Fenn, "don't apologise. You're welcome to it. Being head of Kay's isn't such a soft job that one is keen on sticking to it."

"All the same—" began Kennedy.

"I knew Kay would get at me somehow, of course. I've been wondering how all the holidays. I didn't think of this. Still, I'm jolly glad it's happened. I now retire into private life, and look on. I've taken years off my life sweating to make this house decent, and now I'm going to take a rest and watch you tearing your hair out over the job. I'm awfully sorry for you. I wish they'd roped in some other victim."

"But you're still a house prefect, I suppose?"

"I believe so. Kay couldn't very well make me a fag again."

"Then you'll help manage things?"

Fenn laughed.

"Will I, by Jove! I'd like to see myself! I don't want to do the heavy martyr business and that sort of thing, but I'm hanged if I'm going to take any more trouble over the house. Haven't you any respect for Mr Kay's feelings? He thinks I can't keep order. Surely you don't want me to go and shatter his pet beliefs? Anyhow, I'm not going to do it. I'm going to play 'villagers and retainers' to your 'hero'. If you do anything wonderful with the house, I shall be standing by ready to cheer. But you don't catch me shoving myself forward. 'Thank 'eaven I knows me place,' as the butler in the play says."

Kennedy kicked moodily at the leg of the chair which he was holding. The feeling that his whole world had fallen about his ears was increasing with every hour he spent in Kay's. Last term he and Fenn had been as close friends as you could wish to see. If he had asked Fenn to help him in a tight place then, he knew he could have relied on him.

Now his chief desire seemed to be to score off the human race in general, his best friend included. It was a depressing beginning.

"Do you know what the sherry said to the man when he was just going to drink it?" inquired Fenn. "It said, '*Nemo me impune lacessit*'. That's how I feel. Kay went out of his way to give me a bad time when I was doing my best to run his house properly, so I don't see that I'm called upon to go out of my way to work for him."

"It's rather rough on me—" Kennedy began. Then a sudden indignation rushed through him. Why should he grovel to Fenn? If Fenn chose to stand out, let him. He was capable of running the house by himself.

"I don't care," he said, savagely. "If you can't see what a cad you're making of yourself, I'm not going to try to show you. You can do what you jolly well please. I'm not dependent on you. I'll make this a decent house off my own bat without your help. If you like looking on, you'd better look on. I'll give you something to look at soon."

He went out, leaving Fenn with mixed feelings. He would have liked to have followed him, taken back what he had said, and formed an offensive alliance against the black sheep of the house—and also, which was just as important, against the slack sheep, who were good for nothing, either at work or play. But his bitterness against the house-master prevented him. He was not going to take his removal from the leadership of Kay's as if nothing had happened.

Meanwhile, in the dayrooms and studies, the house had been holding indignation meetings, and at each it had been unanimously resolved that Kay's had been abominably treated, and that the deposition of Fenn must not be tolerated. Unfortunately, a house cannot do very much when it revolts. It can only show its displeasure in little things, and by an increase of rowdiness. This was the line that Kay's took. Fenn became a popular hero. Fags, until he kicked them for it, showed a tendency to cheer him whenever they saw him. Nothing could paint Mr Kay blacker in the eyes of his house, so that Kennedy came in for all the odium. The same fags who had cheered Fenn hooted him on one occasion as he passed the junior dayroom. Kennedy stopped short, went in, and presented each inmate of the room with six cuts with a swagger-stick. This summary and Captain Kettle-like move had its effect. There was no more hooting. The fags bethought themselves of other ways of showing their disapproval of their new head.

One genius suggested that they might kill two birds with one stone—snub Kennedy and pay a stately compliment to Fenn by applying to the latter for leave to go out of bounds instead of to the former. As the giving of leave "down town" was the prerogative of the head of the house, and of no other, there was a suggestiveness about this mode of procedure which appealed to the junior dayroom.

But the star of the junior dayroom was not in the ascendant. Fenn might have quarrelled with Kennedy, and be extremely indignant at his removal from the headship of the house, but he was not the man to forget to play the game. His policy of non-interference did not include underhand attempts to sap Kennedy's authority. When Gorrick, of the Lower Fourth, the first of the fags to put the ingenious scheme into practice, came to him, still smarting from Kennedy's castigation, Fenn promptly gave him six more cuts, worse than the first, and kicked him out into the passage. Gorrick naturally did not want to spoil a good thing by giving Fenn's game away, so he lay low and said nothing, with the result that Wren and three others met with the same fate, only more so, because Fenn's wrath increased with each visit.

Kennedy, of course, heard nothing of this, or he might perhaps have thought better of Fenn. As for the junior dayroom, it was obliged to work off its emotion by jeering

Jimmy Silver from the safety of the touchline when the head of Blackburn's was refereeing in a match between the juniors of his house and those of Kay's. Blackburn's happened to win by four goals and eight tries, a result which the patriotic Kay fag attributed solely to favouritism on the part of the referee.

"I like the kids in your house," said Jimmy to Kennedy, after the match, when telling the latter of the incident; "there's no false idea of politeness about them. If they don't like your decisions, they say so in a shrill treble."

"Little beasts," said Kennedy. "I wish I knew who they were. It's hopeless to try and spot them, of course."

The Senior Dayroom opens Fire

Curiously enough, it was shortly after this that the junior dayroom ceased almost entirely to trouble the head of the house. Not that they turned over new leaves, and modelled their conduct on that of the hero of the Sunday-school story. They were still disorderly, but in a lesser degree; and ragging became a matter of private enterprise among the fags instead of being, as it had threatened to be, an organised revolt against the new head. When a Kay's fag rioted now, he did so with the air of one endeavouring to amuse himself, not as if he were carrying on a holy war against the oppressor.

Kennedy's difficulties were considerably diminished by this change. A head of a house expects the juniors of his house to rag. It is what they are put into the world to do, and there is no difficulty in keeping the thing within decent limits. A revolution is another case altogether. Kennedy was grateful for the change, for it gave him more time to keep an eye on the other members of the house, but he had no idea what had brought it about. As a matter of fact, he had Billy Silver to thank for it. The chief organiser of the movement against Kennedy in the junior dayroom had been the red-haired Wren, who preached war to his fellow fags, partly because he loved to create a disturbance, and partly because Walton, who hated Kennedy, had told him to. Between Wren and Billy Silver a feud had existed since their first meeting. The unsatisfactory conclusion to their encounter in camp had given another lease of life to the feud, and Billy had come back to Kay's with the fixed intention of smiting his auburn-haired foe hip and thigh at the earliest opportunity. Wren's attitude with respect to Kennedy gave him a decent excuse. He had no particular regard for Kennedy. The fact that he was a friend of his brother's was no recommendation. There existed between the two Silvers that feeling which generally exists between an elder and a much younger brother at the same school. Each thought the other a bit of an idiot, and though equal to tolerating him personally, was hanged if he was going to do the same by his friends. In Billy's circle of acquaintances, Jimmy's friends were looked upon with cold suspicion as officious meddlers who would give them lines if they found them out of bounds. The aristocrats with whom Jimmy foregathered barely recognised the existence of Billy's companions. Kennedy's claim to Billy's good offices rested on the fact that they both objected to Wren.

So that, when Wren lifted up his voice in the junior dayroom, and exhorted the fags to go and make a row in the passage outside Kennedy's study, and—from a safe distance, and having previously ensured a means of rapid escape—to fling boots at his door, Billy damped the popular enthusiasm which had been excited by the proposal by kicking Wren with some violence, and begging him not to be an ass. Whereupon they resumed their battle at the point at which it had been interrupted at camp. And when, some five minutes later, Billy, from his seat on his adversary's chest, offered to go through the same performance with anybody else who wished, the junior dayroom came to the conclusion that his feelings with regard to the new head of the house, however foolish and unpatriotic, had better be respected. And the revolution of the fags had fizzled out from that moment.

In the senior dayroom, however, the flag of battle was still unfurled. It was so obvious that Kennedy had been put into the house as a reformer, and the seniors of Kay's had such an objection to being reformed, that trouble was only to be expected. It was the custom in most houses for the head of the house, by right of that position, to be also captain of football. The senior dayroom was aggrieved at Kennedy's taking this post from Fenn. Fenn was in his second year in the school fifteen, and he was the three-quarter who scored most frequently for Eckleton, whereas Kennedy, though practically a certainty for one of the six vacant places in the school scrum, was at present entitled to wear only a second fifteen cap. The claims of Fenn to be captain of Kay's football were strong. Kennedy had begged him to continue in that position more than once. Fenn's persistent refusal had helped to increase the coolness between them, and it had also made things more difficult for Kennedy in the house.

It was on the Monday of the third week of term that Kennedy, at Jimmy Silver's request, arranged a "friendly" between Kay's and Blackburn's. There could be no doubt as to which was the better team (for Blackburn's had been runners up for the Cup the season before), but the better one's opponents the better the practice. Kennedy wrote out the list and fixed it on the notice board. The match was to be played on the following afternoon.

A football team must generally be made up of the biggest men at the captain's disposal, so it happened that Walton, Perry, Callingham, and the other leaders of dissension in Kay's, all figured on the list. The consequence was that the list came in for a good deal of comment in the senior dayroom. There were games every Saturday and Wednesday, and it annoyed Walton and friends that they should have to turn out on an afternoon that was not a half holiday. It was trouble enough playing football on the days when it was compulsory. As for patriotism, no member of the house even pretended to care whether Kay's put a good team into the field or not. The senior dayroom sat talking over the matter till lights-out. When Kennedy came down next morning, he found his list scribbled over with blue pencil, while across it in bold letters ran the single word,

ROT.

He went to his study, wrote out a fresh copy, and pinned it up in place of the old one. He had been early in coming down that morning, and the majority of the Kayites had not seen the defaced notice. The match was fixed for half-past four. At four a thin rain was falling. The weather had been bad for some days, but on this particular afternoon it reached the limit. In addition to being wet, it was also cold, and Kennedy, as he walked over to the grounds, felt that he would be glad when the game was over. He hoped that Blackburn's would be punctual, and congratulated himself on his foresight in securing Mr Blackburn as referee. Some of the staff, when they consented to hold the whistle in a scratch game, invariably kept the teams waiting on the field for half an hour before turning up. Mr Blackburn, on the other hand, was always punctual. He came out of his house just as Kennedy turned in at the school gates.

"Well, Kennedy," he said from the depths of his ulster, the collar of which he had turned up over his ears with a prudence which Kennedy, having come out with only a blazer on over his football clothes, distinctly envied, "I hope your men are not going to be late. I don't think I ever saw a worse day for football. How long were you thinking of playing? Two twenty-fives would be enough for a day like this, I think."

Kennedy consulted with Jimmy Silver, who came up at this moment, and they agreed without argument that twenty-five minutes each way would be the very thing.

"Where are your men?" asked Jimmy. "I've got all our chaps out here, bar Challis, who'll be out in a few minutes. I left him almost changed."

Challis appeared a little later, and joined the rest of Blackburn's team, who were putting in the time and trying to keep warm by running and passing and dropping desultory goals. But, with the exception of Fenn, who stood brooding by himself in the centre of the field, wrapped to the eyes in a huge overcoat, and two other house prefects of Kay's, who strolled up and down looking as if they wished they were in their studies, there was no sign of the missing team.

"I can't make it out," said Kennedy.

"You're sure you put up the right time?" asked Jimmy Silver.

"Yes, quite."

It certainly could not be said that Kay's had had any room for doubt as to the time of the match, for it had appeared in large figures on both notices.

A quarter to five sounded from the college clock.

"We must begin soon," said Mr Blackburn, "or there will not be light enough even for two twenty-fives."

Kennedy felt wretched. Apart from the fact that he was frozen to an icicle and drenched by the rain, he felt responsible for his team, and he could see that Blackburn's men were growing irritated at the delay, though they did their best to conceal it.

"Can't we lend them some subs?" suggested Challis, hopefully.

"All right—if you can raise eleven subs," said Silver. "They've only got four men on the field at present."

Challis subsided.

"Look here," said Kennedy, "I'm going back to the house to see what's up. I'll be back as soon as I can. They must have mistaken the time or something after all."

He rushed back to the house, and flung open the door of the senior dayroom. It was empty.

Kennedy had expected to find his missing men huddled in a semicircle round the fire, waiting for some one to come and tell them that Blackburn's had taken the field, and that they could come out now without any fear of having to wait in the rain for the match to begin. This, he thought, would have been the unselfish policy of Kay's senior dayroom.

But to find nobody was extraordinary.

The thought occurred to him that the team might be changing in their dormitories. He ran upstairs. But all the dormitories were locked, as he might have known they would have been. Coming downstairs again he met his fag, Spencer.

Spencer replied to his inquiry that he had only just come in. He did not know where the team had got to. No, he had not seen any of them.

"Oh, yes, though," he added, as an afterthought, "I met Walton just now. He looked as if he was going down town."

Walton had once licked Spencer, and that vindictive youth thought that this might be a chance of getting back at him.

"Oh," said Kennedy, quietly, "Walton? Did you? Thanks."

Spencer was disappointed at his lack of excitement. His news did not seem to interest him.

Kennedy went back to the football field to inform Jimmy Silver of the result of his investigations.

XII

KENNEDY INTERVIEWS WALTON

"I'm very sorry," he said, when he rejoined the shivering group, "but I'm afraid we shall have to call this match off. There seems to have been a mistake. None of my team are anywhere about. I'm awfully sorry, sir," he added, to Mr Blackburn, "to have given you all this trouble for nothing."

"Not at all, Kennedy. We must try another day."

Mr Blackburn suspected that something untoward had happened in Kay's to cause this sudden defection of the first fifteen of the house. He knew that Kennedy was having a hard time in his new position, and he did not wish to add to his discomfort by calling for an explanation before an audience. It could not be pleasant for Kennedy to feel that his enemies had scored off him. It was best to preserve a discreet silence with regard to the whole affair, and leave him to settle it for himself.

Jimmy Silver was more curious. He took Kennedy off to tea in his study, sat him down in the best chair in front of the fire, and proceeded to urge him to confess everything.

"Now, then, what's it all about?" he asked, briskly, spearing a muffin on the fork and beginning to toast.

"It's no good asking me," said Kennedy. "I suppose it's a put-up job to make me look a fool. I ought to have known something of this kind would happen when I saw what they did to my first notice."

"What was that?"

Kennedy explained.

"This is getting thrilling," said Jimmy. "Just pass that plate. Thanks. What are you going to do about it?"

"I don't know. What would you do?"

"My dear chap, I'd first find out who was at the bottom of it—there's bound to be one man who started the whole thing—and I'd make it my aim in life to give him the warmest ten minutes he'd ever had."

"That sounds all right. But how would you set about it?"

"Why, touch him up, of course. What else would you do? Before the whole house, too."

"Supposing he wouldn't be touched up?"

"Wouldn't *be!* He'd have to."

"You don't know Kay's, Jimmy. You're thinking what you'd do if this had happened in Blackburn's. The two things aren't the same. Here the man would probably take it like a lamb. The feeling of the house would be against him. He'd find nobody to back him up. That's because Blackburn's is a decent house instead of being a sink like Kay's. If I tried the touching-up before the whole house game with our chaps, the man would probably reply by going for me, assisted by the whole strength of the company."

"Well, dash it all then, all you've got to do is to call a prefects' meeting, and he'll get ten times worse beans from them than he'd have got from you. It's simple."

Kennedy stared into the fire pensively.

"I don't know," he said. "I bar that prefects' meeting business. It always seems rather feeble to me, lugging in a lot of chaps to help settle some one you can't manage yourself. I want to carry this job through on my own."

"Then you'd better scrap with the man."

"I think I will."

Silver stared.

"Don't be an ass," he said. "I was only rotting. You can't go fighting all over the shop as if you were a fag. You'd lose your prefect's cap if it came out."

"I could wear my topper," said Kennedy, with a grin. "You see," he added, "I've not much choice. I must do

something. If I took no notice of this business there'd be
no holding the house. I should be ragged to death. It's no
good talking about it. Personally, I should prefer touching
the chap up to fighting him, and I shall try it on. But he's
not likely to meet me half-way. And if he doesn't there'll
be an interesting turn-up, and you shall hold the watch.
I'll send a kid round to fetch you when things look like
starting. I must go now to interview my missing men. So
long. Mind you slip round directly I send for you."

"Wait a second. Don't be in such a beastly hurry. Who's
the chap you're going to fight?"

"I don't know yet. Walton, I should think. But I don't
know."

"Walton! By Jove, it'll be worth seeing, anyhow, if we
are both sacked for it when the Old Man finds out."

Kennedy returned to his study and changed his football
boots for a pair of gymnasium shoes. For the job he had in
hand it was necessary that he should move quickly, and
football boots are a nuisance on a board floor. When he had
changed, he called Spencer.

"Go down to the senior dayroom," he said, "and tell
MacPherson I want to see him."

MacPherson was a long, weak-looking youth. He had
been put down to play for the house that day, and had not
appeared.

"MacPherson!" said the fag, in a tone of astonishment,
"not Walton?"

He had been looking forward to the meeting between
Kennedy and his ancient foe, and to have a miserable being
like MacPherson offered as a substitute disgusted him.

"If you have no objection," said Kennedy, politely, "I
may want you to fetch Walton later on."

Spencer vanished, hopeful once more.

"Come in, MacPherson," said Kennedy, on the arrival
of the long one; "shut the door."

MacPherson did so, feeling as if he were paying a visit

to the dentist. As long as there had been others with him in this affair he had looked on it as a splendid idea. But to be singled out like this was quite a different thing.

"Now," said Kennedy, "Why weren't you on the field this afternoon?"

"I—er—I was kept in."

"How long?"

"Oh—er—till about five."

"What do you call about five?"

"About twenty-five to," he replied, despondently.

"Now look here," said Kennedy, briskly, "I'm just going to explain to you exactly how I stand in this business, so you'd better attend. I didn't ask to be made head of this sewage depôt. If I could have had any choice, I wouldn't have touched a Kayite with a barge-pole. But since I am head, I'm going to be it, and the sooner you and your senior dayroom crew realise it the better. This sort of thing isn't going on. I want to know now who it was put up this job. You wouldn't have the cheek to start a thing like this yourself. Who was it?"

"Well—er—"

"You'd better say, and be quick, too. I can't wait. Whoever it was, I shan't tell him you told me. And I shan't tell Kay. So now you can go ahead. Who was it?"

"Well—er—Walton."

"I thought so. Now you can get out. If you see Spencer, send him here."

Spencer, curiously enough, was just outside the door. So close to it, indeed, that he almost tumbled in when Mac-Pherson opened it.

"Go and fetch Walton," said Kennedy.

Spencer dashed off delightedly, and in a couple of minutes Walton appeared. He walked in with an air of subdued defiance, and slammed the door.

"Don't bang the door like that," said Kennedy. "Why didn't you turn out today?"

"I was kept in."

"Couldn't you get out in time to play?"

"No."

"When did you get out?"

"Six."

"Not before?"

"I said six."

"Then how did you manage to go down town—without leave, by the way, but that's a detail—at half-past five?"

"All right," said Walton; "better call me a liar."

"Good suggestion," said Kennedy, cheerfully; "I will."

"It's all very well," said Walton. "You know jolly well you can say anything you like. I can't do anything to you. You'd have me up before the prefects."

"Not a bit of it. This is a private affair between ourselves. I'm not going to drag the prefects into it. You seem to want to make this house worse than it is. I want to make it more or less decent. We can't both have what we want."

There was a pause.

"When would it be convenient for you to be touched up before the whole house?" inquired Kennedy, pleasantly.

"What?"

"Well, you see, it seems the only thing. I must take it out of some one for this house-match business, and you started it. Will tonight suit you, after supper?"

"You'll get it hot if you try to touch me."

"We'll see."

"You'd funk taking me on in a scrap," said Walton.

"Would I? As a matter of fact, a scrap would suit me just as well. Better. Are you ready now?"

"Quite, thanks," sneered Walton. "I've knocked you out before, and I'll do it again."

"Oh, then it was you that night at camp? I thought so. I spotted your style. Hitting a chap when he wasn't ready, you know, and so on. Now, if you'll wait a minute, I'll send across to Blackburn's for Silver. I told him I should probably want him as a time-keeper tonight."

"What do you want with Silver. Why won't Perry do?"

"Thanks, I'm afraid Perry's time-keeping wouldn't be impartial enough. Silver, I think, if you don't mind."

Spencer was summoned once more, and despatched to Blackburn's. He returned with Jimmy.

"Come in, Jimmy," said Kennedy. "Run away, Spencer. Walton and I are just going to settle a point of order which has arisen, Jimmy. Will you hold the watch? We ought just to have time before tea."

"Where?" asked Silver.

"My dormitory would be the best place. We can move the beds. I'll go and get the keys."

Kennedy's dormitory was the largest in the house. After the beds had been moved back, there was a space in the middle of fifteen feet one way, and twelve the other—not a large ring, but large enough for two fighters who meant business.

Walton took off his coat, waistcoat, and shirt. Kennedy, who was still in football clothes, removed his blazer.

"Half a second," said Jimmy Silver—"what length rounds?"

"Two minutes?" said Kennedy to Walton.

"All right," growled Walton.

"Two minutes, then, and half a minute in between."

"Are you both ready?" asked Jimmy, from his seat on the chest of drawers.

Kennedy and Walton advanced into the middle of the impromptu ring.

There was dead silence for a moment.

"Time!" said Jimmy Silver.

XIII

THE FIGHT IN THE DORMITORY

Stating it broadly, fighters may be said to be divided into
two classes—those who are content to take two blows if
they can give three in return, and those who prefer to
receive as little punishment as possible, even at the expense
of scoring fewer points themselves. Kennedy's position,
when Jimmy Silver called time, was peculiar. On all the
other occasions on which he had fought—with the gloves
on in the annual competition, and at the assault-at-arms—
he had gone in for the policy of taking all that the other
man liked to give him, and giving rather more in exchange.
Now, however, he was obliged to alter his whole style. For
a variety of reasons it was necessary that he should come
out of this fight with as few marks as possible. To begin
with, he represented, in a sense, the Majesty of the Law.
He was tackling Walton more by way of an object-lesson
to the Kayite mutineers than for his own personal satisfaction. The object-lesson would lose in impressiveness if he
were compelled to go about for a week or so with a pair
of black eyes, or other adornments of a similar kind. Again
—and this was even more important—if he was badly
marked the affair must come to the knowledge of the
headmaster. Being a prefect, and in the sixth form, he came
into contact with the Head every day, and the disclosure
of the fact that he had been engaged in a pitched battle
with a member of his house, who was, in addition to other
disadvantages, very low down in the school, would be likely
to lead to unpleasantness. A school prefect of Eckleton was
supposed to be hedged about with so much dignity that he

could quell turbulent inferiors with a glance. The idea of one of the august body lowering himself to the extent of emphasising his authority with the bare knuckle would scandalise the powers.

So Kennedy, rising at the call of time from the bed on which he sat, came up to the scratch warily.

Walton, on the other hand, having everything to gain and nothing to lose, and happy in the knowledge that no amount of bruises could do him any harm, except physically, came on with the evident intention of making a hurricane fight of it. He had very little science as a boxer. Heavy two-handed slogging was his forte, and, as the majority of his opponents up to the present had not had sufficient skill to discount his strength, he had found this a very successful line of action. Kennedy and he had never had the gloves on together. In the competition of the previous year both had entered in their respective classes, Kennedy as a lightweight, Walton in the middles, and both, after reaching the semi-final, had been defeated by the narrowest of margins by men who had since left the school. That had been in the previous Easter term, and, while Walton had remained much the same as regards weight and strength, Kennedy, owing to a term of hard bowling and a summer holiday spent in the open, had filled out. They were now practically on an equality, as far as weight was concerned. As for condition, that was all in favour of Kennedy. He played football in his spare time. Walton, on the days when football was not compulsory, smoked cigarettes.

Neither of the pair showed any desire to open the fight by shaking hands. This was not a friendly spar. It was business. The first move was made by Walton, who feinted with his right and dashed in to fight at close quarters. It was not a convincing feint. At any rate, it did not deceive Kennedy. He countered with his left, and swung his right at the body with all the force he could put into the hit.

Walton went back a pace, sparred for a moment, then came in again, hitting heavily. Kennedy's counter missed its mark this time. He just stopped a round sweep of Walton's right, ducked to avoid a similar effort of his left, and they came together in a clinch.

In a properly regulated glove-fight, the referee, on observing the principals clinch, says, "Break away there, break away," in a sad, reproachful voice, and the fighters separate without demur, being very much alive to the fact that, as far as that contest is concerned, their destinies are in his hands, and that any bad behaviour in the ring will lose them the victory. But in an impromptu turn-up like this one, the combatants show a tendency to ignore the rules so carefully mapped out by the present Marquess of Queensberry's grandfather, and revert to the conditions of warfare under which Cribb and Spring won their battles. Kennedy and Walton, having clinched, proceeded to wrestle up and down the room, while Jimmy Silver looked on from his eminence in pained surprise at the sight of two men, who knew the rules of the ring, so far forgetting themselves.

To do Kennedy justice, it was not his fault. He was only acting in self-defence. Walton had started the hugging. Also, he had got the under-grip, which, when neither man knows a great deal of the science of wrestling, generally means victory. Kennedy was quite sure that he could not throw his antagonist, but he hung on in the knowledge that the round must be over shortly, when Walton would have to loose him.

"Time," said Jimmy Silver.

Kennedy instantly relaxed his grip, and in that instant Walton swung him off his feet, and they came down together with a crash that shook the room. Kennedy was underneath, and, as he fell, his head came into violent contact with the iron support of a bed.

Jimmy Silver sprang down from his seat.

"What are you playing at, Walton? Didn't you hear me

call time? It was a beastly foul—the worst I ever saw. You ought to be sacked for a thing like that. Look here, Kennedy, you needn't go on. I disqualify Walton for fouling."

The usually genial James stammered with righteous indignation.

Kennedy sat down on a bed, dizzily.

"No," he said; "I'm going on."

"But he fouled you."

"I don't care. I'll look after myself. Is it time yet?"

"Ten seconds more, if you really are going on."

He climbed back on to the chest of drawers.

"Time."

Kennedy came up feeling weak and sick. The force with which he had hit his head on the iron had left him dazed.

Walton rushed in as before. He had no chivalrous desire to spare his man by way of compensation for fouling him. What monopolised his attention was the evident fact that Kennedy was in a bad way, and that a little strenuous infighting might end the affair in the desired manner.

It was at this point that Kennedy had reason to congratulate himself on donning gymnasium shoes. They gave him that extra touch of lightness which enabled him to dodge blows which he was too weak to parry. Everything was vague and unreal to him. He seemed to be looking on at a fight between Walton and some stranger.

Then the effect of his fall began to wear off. He could feel himself growing stronger. Little by little his head cleared, and he began once more to take a personal interest in the battle. It is astonishing what a power a boxer, who has learnt the art carefully, has of automatic fighting. The expert gentleman who fights under the pseudonym of "Kid M'Coy" once informed the present writer that in one of his fights he was knocked down by such a severe hit that he remembered nothing further, and it was only on reading the paper next morning that he found, to his surprise, that he had fought four more rounds after the blow, and won the battle handsomely on points. Much the same thing happened to Kennedy. For the greater part of the second round he fought without knowing it. When Jimmy Silver called time he was in as good case as ever, and the only effects of the blow on his head were a vast lump underneath the hair, and a settled determination to win or perish. In a few minutes the bell would ring for tea, and all his efforts would end in nothing. It was no good fighting a draw with Walton if he meant to impress the house. He knew exactly what Rumour, assisted by Walton, would make of the affair in that case. "Have you heard the latest?" A would ask of B. "Why, Kennedy tried to touch Walton up for not playing footer, and Walton went for him and would have given him frightful beans, only they had to go down to tea." There must be none of that sort of thing.

"Time," said Jimmy Silver, breaking in on his meditations.

It was probably the suddenness and unexpectedness of it that took Walton aback. Up till now his antagonist had been fighting strictly on the defensive, and was obviously desirous of escaping punishment as far as might be possible. And then the fall at the end of round one had shaken him up, so that he could hardly fight at all at their second meeting. Walton naturally expected that it would be left to him to do the leading in round three. Instead of this, however, Kennedy opened the round with such a lightning attack that Walton was all abroad in a moment. In his most scientific mood he had never had the remotest notion of how to guard. He was aggressive and nothing else. Attacked by a quick hitter, he was useless. Three times Kennedy got through his guard with his left. The third hit staggered him. Before he could recover, Kennedy had got his right in, and down went Walton in a heap.

He was up again as soon as he touched the boards, and down again almost as soon as he was up. Kennedy was always a straight hitter, and now a combination of good cause and bad temper—for the thought of the foul in the first round had stirred what was normally a more or less placid nature into extreme viciousness—lent a vigour to his left arm to which he had hitherto been a stranger. He did not use his right again. It was not needed.

Twice more Walton went down. He was still down when Jimmy Silver called time. When the half-minute interval between the rounds was over, he stated that he was not going on.

Kennedy looked across at him as he sat on a bed dabbing tenderly at his face with a handkerchief, and was satisfied with the success of his object-lesson. From his own face the most observant of headmasters could have detected no evidence that he had been engaged in a vulgar fight. Walton, on the other hand, looked as if he had been engaged in several—all violent. Kennedy went off to his study to change, feeling that he had advanced a long step on the thorny path that led to the Perfect House.

XIV

FENN RECEIVES A LETTER

But the step was not such a very long one after all. What it amounted to was simply this, that open rebellion ceased in Kay's. When Kennedy put up the list on the notice-board for the third time, which he did on the morning following his encounter with Walton, and wrote on it that the match with Blackburn's would take place that after-noon, his team turned out like lambs, and were duly defeated by thirty-one points. He had to play a substitute for Walton, who was rather too battered to be of any real use in the scrum; but, with that exception, the team that entered the field was the same that should have entered it the day before.

But his labours in the Augean stables of Kay's were by no means over. Practically they had only begun. The state of the house now was exactly what it had been under Fenn. When Kennedy had taken over the reins, Kay's had become on the instant twice as bad as it had been before. By his summary treatment of the revolution, he had, so to speak, wiped off this deficit. What he had to do now was to begin to improve things. Kay's was now in its normal state—slack, rowdy in an underhand way, and utterly useless to the school. It was "up to" Kennedy, as they say in America, to start in and make something pre-sentable and useful out of these unpromising materials.

What annoyed him more than anything else was the knowledge that if only Fenn chose to do the square thing and help him in his work, the combination would be irresistible. It was impossible to make any leeway to speak of by himself. If Fenn would only forget his grievances and join forces with him, they could electrify the house.

Fenn, however, showed no inclination to do anything of the kind. He and Kennedy never spoke to one another now except when it was absolutely unavoidable, and then they behaved with that painful politeness in which the public schoolman always wraps himself as in a garment when dealing with a friend with whom he has quarrelled.

On the Walton episode Fenn had made no comment, though it is probable that he thought a good deal.

It was while matters were in this strained condition that Fenn received a letter from his elder brother. This brother had been at Eckleton in his time—School House—and had left five years before to go to Cambridge. Cambridge had not taught him a great deal, possibly because he did not meet the well-meant efforts of his tutor half-way. The net result of his three years at King's was—*imprimis*, a cricket blue, including a rather lucky eighty-three at Lord's; secondly, a very poor degree; thirdly and lastly, a taste for literature and the drama—he had been a prominent member of the Footlights Club. When he came down he looked about him for some occupation which should combine in happy proportions a small amount of work and a large amount of salary, and, finding none, drifted into journalism, at which calling he had been doing very fairly ever since.

"Dear Bob," the letter began. Fenn's names were Robert Mowbray, the second of which he had spent much of his time in concealing. "Just a line."

The elder Fenn always began his letters with these words, whether they ran to one sheet or eight. In the present case the screed was not particularly long.

"Do you remember my reading you a bit of an opera I was writing? Well, I finished it, and, after going the round of most of the managers, who chucked it with wonderful unanimity, it found an admirer in Higgs, the man who took the part of the duke in *The Outsider*. Luckily, he happened to be thinking of starting on his own in opera instead of farce, and there's a part in mine which fits him like a glove. So he's going to bring it out at the Imperial in the spring, and by way of testing the piece—trying it on the dog, as it were—he means to tour with it. Now, here's the point of this letter. We start at Eckleton next Wednesday. We shall only be there one night, for we go on to Southampton on Thursday. I suppose you couldn't come and see it? I remember Peter Brown, who got the last place in the team the year I got my cricket colours, cutting out of his house (Kay's, by the way) and going down town to see a piece at the theatre. I'm bound to admit he got sacked for it, but still, it shows that it can be done. All the same, I shouldn't try it on if I were you. You'll be able to read all about the 'striking success' and 'unrestrained enthusiasm' in the *Eckleton Mirror* on Thursday. Mind you buy a copy."

The rest of the letter was on other subjects. It took Fenn less than a minute to decide to patronise that opening performance. He was never in the habit of paying very much attention to risks when he wished to do anything, and now he felt as if he cared even less than usual what might be the outcome of the adventure. Since he had ceased to be on speaking terms with Kennedy, he had found life decidedly dull. Kennedy had been his only intimate friend. He had plenty of acquaintances, as a first eleven and first fifteen man usually has, but none of them were very entertaining. Consequently he welcomed the idea of a break in the monotony of affairs. The only thing that had broken it up to the present had been a burglary at the school house. Some enterprising marauder had broken in a week before and gone off with a few articles of value from the headmaster's drawing-room. But the members of the school house had talked about this episode to such an extent that the rest of the school had dropped

off the subject, exhausted, and declined to discuss it further.
And things had become monotonous once more.

Having decided to go, Fenn began to consider how he
should do it. And here circumstances favoured him. It
happened that on the evening on which his brother's play
was to be produced the headmaster was giving his once-a-
term dinner to the house-prefects. This simplified matters
wonderfully. The only time when his absence from the
house was at all likely to be discovered would be at prayers,
which took place at half-past nine. The prefects' dinner
solved this difficulty for him. Kay would not expect him
to be at prayers, thinking he was over at the Head's, while
the Head, if he noticed his absence at all, would imagine
that he was staying away from the dinner owing to a head-
ache or some other malady. It seemed tempting Providence
not to take advantage of such an excellent piece of
luck. For the rest, detection was practically impossible.
Kennedy's advent to the house had ousted Fenn from the
dormitory in which he had slept hitherto, and, there being
no bed available in any of the other dormitories, he had
been put into the spare room usually reserved for invalids
whose invalidism was not of a sufficiently infectious kind
to demand their removal to the infirmary. As for getting
back into the house, he would leave the window of his
study unfastened. He could easily climb on to the window-
ledge, and so to bed without let or hindrance.

The distance from Kay's to the town was a mile and a
half. If he started at the hour when he should have been
starting for the school house, he would arrive just in time
to see the curtain go up.

Having settled these facts definitely in his mind, he got
his books together and went over to school.

XV

Down Town

Fenn arrived at the theatre a quarter of an hour before
the curtain rose. Going down a gloomy alley of the High
Street, he found himself at the stage door, where he made
inquiries of a depressed-looking man with a bad cold in
the head as to the whereabouts of his brother. It seemed
that he was with Mr Higgs. If he would wait, said the
door-keeper, his name should be sent up. Fenn waited,
while the door-keeper made polite conversation by describ-
ing his symptoms to him in a hoarse growl. Presently the
minion who had been despatched to the upper regions with
Fenn's message returned. Would he go upstairs, third door
on the left. Fenn followed the instructions, and found himself in a small room, a third of which was filled by a huge
iron-bound chest, another third by a very stout man and a
dressing-table, while the rest of the space was comparatively empty, being occupied by a wooden chair with three
legs. On this seat his brother was trying to balance himself,
giving what part of his attention was not required for this
feat to listening to some story the fat man was telling him.
Fenn had heard his deep voice booming as he went up
the passage.

His brother did the honours.

"Glad to see you, glad to see you," said Mr Higgs, for
the fat man was none other than that celebrity. "Take a
seat."

Fenn sat down on the chest and promptly tore his
trousers on a jagged piece of iron.

"These provincial dressing-rooms!" said Mr Higgs, by

way of comment. "No room! Never any room! No chairs! Nothing!"

He spoke in short, quick sentences, and gasped between each. Fenn said it really didn't matter—he was quite comfortable.

"Haven't they done anything about it?" asked Fenn's brother, resuming the conversation which Fenn's entrance had interrupted. "We've been having a burglary here," he explained. "Somebody got into the theatre last night through a window. I don't know what they expected to find."

"Why," said Fenn, "we've had a burglar up our way too. Chap broke into the school house and went through the old man's drawing-room. The school house men have been talking about nothing else ever since. I wonder if it's the same crew."

Mr Higgs turned in his chair, and waved a stick of grease paint impressively to emphasise his point.

"There," he said. "There! What I've been saying all along. No doubt of it. Organised gang. And what are the police doing? Nothing, sir, nothing. Making inquiries. Rot! What's the good of inquiries?"

Fenn's brother suggested mildly that inquiries were a good beginning. You *must* start somewhere. Mr Higgs scouted the idea.

"There ought not to be any doubt, sir. They ought to *know*. To KNOW," he added, with firmness.

At this point there filtered through the closed doors the strains of the opening chorus.

"By Jove, it's begun!" said Fenn's brother. "Come on, Bob."

"Where are we going to?" asked Fenn, as he followed. "The wings?"

But it seemed that the rules of Mr Higgs' company prevented any outsider taking up his position in that desirable quarter. The only place from which it was possible to watch the performance, except by going to the front of the house, was the "flies," situated near the roof of the building.

Fenn found all the pleasures of novelty in watching the players from this lofty position. Judged by the cold light of reason, it was not the best place from which to see a play. It was possible to gain only a very foreshortened view of the actors. But it was a change after sitting "in front".

The piece was progressing merrily. The gifted author, at first silent and pale, began now to show signs of gratification. Now and again he chuckled as some *jeu de mots* hit the mark and drew a quick gust of laughter from the unseen audience. Occasionally he would nudge Fenn to draw his attention to some good bit of dialogue which was approaching. He was obviously enjoying himself.

The advent of Mr Higgs completed his satisfaction, for the audience greeted the comedian with roars of applause. As a rule Eckleton took its drama through the medium of third-rate touring companies, which came down with plays that had not managed to attract London to any great extent, and were trying to make up for failures in the metropolis by long tours in the provinces. It was seldom that an actor of the Higgs type paid the town a visit, and in a play, too, which had positively never appeared before on any stage. Eckleton appreciated the compliment.

"Listen," said Fenn's brother. "Isn't that just the part for him? It's just like he was in the dressing-room, eh? Short sentences and everything. The funny part of it is that I didn't know the man when I wrote the play. It was all luck."

Mr Higgs' performance sealed the success of the piece. The house laughed at everything he said. He sang a song in his gasping way, and they laughed still more. Fenn's brother became incoherent with delight. The verdict of Eckleton was hardly likely to affect London theatre-goers, but it was very pleasant notwithstanding. Like every playwright with his first piece, he had been haunted by the idea that his dialogue "would not act", that, however humorous it might be to a reader, it would fall flat when spoken. There was no doubt now as to whether the lines sounded well.

At the beginning of the second act the great Higgs was not on the stage, Fenn's brother knowing enough of the game not to bring on his big man too soon. He had not to enter for ten minutes or so. The author, who had gone down to see him during the interval, stayed in the dressing-room. Fenn, however, who wanted to see all of the piece that he could, went up to the "flies" again.

It occurred to him when he got there that he would see more if he took the seat which his brother had been occupy-ing. It would give him much the same view of the stage, and a wider view of the audience. He thought it would be amusing to see how the audience looked from the "flies".

Mr W. S. Gilbert once wrote a poem about a certain bishop who, while fond of amusing himself, objected to his clergy doing likewise. And the consequence was that when-ever he did so amuse himself, he was always haunted by a phantom curate, who joined him in his pleasures, much to his dismay. On one occasion he stopped to watch a Punch and Judy show,

> And heard, as Punch was being treated penally,
> That phantom curate laughing all hyænally.

The disgust and panic of this eminent cleric was as nothing compared with that of Fenn, when, shifting to his brother's seat, he got the first clear view he had had of the audience. In a box to the left of the dress-circle sat, "laugh-ing all hyænally", the following distinguished visitors:

Mr Mulholland of No. 7 College Buildings.

Mr Raynes of No. 4 ditto.

and

Mr Kay.

Fenn drew back like a flash, knocking his chair over as he did so.

"Giddy, sir?" said a stage hand, pleasantly. "Bless you, lots of gents is like that when they comes up here. Can't stand the 'eight, they can't. You'll be all right in a jiffy."

"Yes. It—it is rather high, isn't it?" said Fenn. "Awful glare, too."

He picked up his chair and sat down well out of sight of the box. Had they seen him? he wondered. Then common sense returned to him. They could not possibly have seen him. Apart from any other reasons, he had only been in his brother's seat for half-a-dozen seconds. No. He was all right so far. But he would have to get back to the house, and at once. With three of the staff, including his own house-master, ranging the town, things were a trifle too warm for comfort. He wondered it had not occurred to him that, with a big attraction at the theatre, some of the staff might feel an inclination to visit it.

He did not stop to say goodbye to his brother. Descending from his perch, he hurried to the stage door.

"It's in the toobs that I feel it, sir," said the door-keeper, as he let him out, resuming their conversation as if they had only just parted. Fenn hurried off without waiting to hear more.

It was drizzling outside, and there was a fog. Not a "London particular", but quite thick enough to make it difficult to see where one was going. People and vehicles passed him, vague phantoms in the darkness. Occasionally the former collided with him. He began to wish he had not accepted his brother's invitation. The unexpected sight of the three masters had shaken his nerve. Till then only the romantic, adventurous side of the expedition had struck him. Now the risks began to loom larger in his mind. It was all very well, he felt, to think, as he had done, that he would be expelled if found out, but that all the same he would risk it. Detection then had seemed a remote contingency. With three masters in the offing it became at least a possibility. The melancholy case of Peter Brown seemed to him now to have a more personal significance for him.

Wrapped in these reflections, he lost his way.

He did not realise this for some time. It was borne in upon him when the road he was taking suddenly came to an abrupt end in a blank wall. Instead of being, as he had fancied, in the High Street, he must have branched off into some miserable blind alley.

More than ever he wished he had not come. Eckleton was not a town that took up a great deal of room on the map of England, but it made up for small dimensions by the eccentricity with which it had been laid out. On a dark and foggy night, to one who knew little of its geography, it was a perfect maze.

Fenn had wandered some way when the sound of someone whistling a popular music-hall song came to him through the gloom. He had never heard anything more agreeable.

"I say," he shouted at a venture, "can you tell me the way to the High Street?"

The whistler stopped in the middle of a bar, and presently Fenn saw a figure sidling towards him in what struck him as a particularly furtive manner.

"Wot's thet, gav'nor?"

"Can you tell me where the High Street is? I've lost my way."

The vague figure came closer.

" 'Igh Street? Yus; yer go—"

A hand shot out, Fenn felt a sharp wrench in the region of his waistcoat, and a moment later the stranger had vanished into the fog with the prefect's watch and chain.

Fenn forgot his desire to return to the High Street. He forgot everything except that he wished to catch the fugitive, maltreat him, and retrieve his property. He tore in the direction whence came the patter of retreating foot-steps.

There were moments when he thought he had him, when he could hear the sound of his breathing. But the fog was against him. Just as he was almost on his man's heels, the fugitive turned sharply into a street which was moderately well lighted. Fenn turned after him. He had just time to recognise the street as his goal, the High Street, when somebody, walking unexpectedly out of the corner house, stood directly in his path. Fenn could not stop himself. He charged the man squarely, clutched him to save himself, and they fell in a heap on the pavement.

XVI

What Happened to Fenn

Fenn was up first. Many years' experience of being tackled at full speed on the football field had taught him how to fall. The stranger, whose football days, if he had ever had any, were long past, had gone down with a crash, and remained on the pavement, motionless. Fenn was conscious of an ignoble impulse to fly without stopping to chat about the matter. Then he was seized with a gruesome fear that he had injured the man seriously, which vanished when the stranger sat up. His first words were hardly of the sort that one would listen to from choice. His first printable expression, which did not escape him until he had been speaking some time, was in the nature of an official bulletin.

"You've broken my neck," said he.

Fenn renewed his apologies and explanations.

"Your watch!" cried the man in a high, cracked voice. "Don't stand there talking about your watch, but help me up. What do I care about your watch? Why don't you look where you are going to? Now then, now then, don't hoist me as if I were a hod of bricks. That's right. Now help me indoors, and go away."

Fenn supported him while he walked lamely into the house. He was relieved to find that there was nothing more the matter with him than a shaking and a few bruises.

"Door on the left," said the injured one.

Fenn led him down the passage and into a small sitting-room. The gas was lit, and as he turned it up he saw that the stranger was a man well advanced in years. He had grey hair that was almost white. His face was not a pleasant one. It was a mass of lines and wrinkles from which a physiognomist would have deduced uncomplimentary conclusions as to his character. Fenn had little skill in that way, but he felt that for some reason he disliked the man, whose eyes, which were small and extraordinarily bright, gave rather an eerie look to his face.

"Go away, go away," he kept repeating savagely from his post on the shabby sofa on which Fenn had deposited him.

"But are you all right? Can't I get you something?" asked the Eckletonian.

"Go away, go away," repeated the man.

Conversation on these lines could never be really attractive. Fenn turned to go. As he closed the door and began to feel his way along the dark passage, he heard the key turn in the lock behind him. The man could not, he felt, have been very badly hurt if he were able to get across the room so quickly. The thought relieved him somewhat. Nobody likes to have the maiming even of the most complete stranger on his mind. The sensation of relief lasted possibly three seconds. Then it flashed upon him that in the excitement of the late interview he had forgotten his cap. That damaging piece of evidence lay on the table in the sitting-room, and between him and it was a locked door.

He groped his way back, and knocked. No sound came from the room.

"I say," he cried, "you might let me have my cap. I left it on the table."

No reply.

Fenn half thought of making a violent assault on the door. He refrained on reflecting that it would be useless. If he could break it open—which, in all probability, he could not—there would be trouble such as he had never come across in his life. He was not sure it would not be an offence for which he would be rendered liable to fine or imprisonment. At any rate, it would mean the certain detection of his visit to the town. So he gave the thing up, resolving to return on the morrow and reopen negotiations. For the present, what he had to do was to get safely back to his house. He had lost his watch, his cap with his name in it was in the hands of an evil old man who evidently bore him a grudge, and he had to run the gauntlet of three house-masters and get to bed *viâ* a study-window. Few people, even after the dullest of plays, have returned from the theatre so disgusted with everything as did Fenn. Reviewing the situation as he ran with long, easy strides over the road that led to Kay's, he found it devoid of any kind of comfort. Unless his mission in quest of the cap should prove successful, he was in a tight place.

It is just as well that the gift of second sight is accorded to but few. If Fenn could have known at this point that his adventures were only beginning, that what had taken place already was but as the overture to a drama, it is possible that he would have thrown up the sponge for good and all, entered Kay's by way of the front door—after knocking up the entire household—and remarked, in answer to his house-master's excited questions, "Enough! Enough! I am a victim of Fate, a Toad beneath the Harrow. Sack me tomorrow, if you like, but for goodness' sake let me get quietly to bed now."

As it was, not being able to "peep with security into futurity," he imagined that the worst was over.

He began to revise this opinion immediately on turning in at Kay's gate. He had hardly got half-way down the drive when the front door opened and two indistinct figures came down the steps. As they did so his foot slipped off the grass border on which he was running to deaden the noise of his steps, and grated sharply on the gravel.

"What's that?" said a voice. The speaker was Mr Kay.

"What's what?" replied a second voice which he recognised as Mr Mulholland's.

"Didn't you hear a noise?"

" 'I heard the water lapping on the crag,' " replied Mr Mulholland, poetically.

"It was over there," persisted Mr Kay. "I am certain I heard something—positively certain, Mulholland. And after that burglary at the school house—"

He began to move towards the spot where Fenn lay crouching behind a bush. Mr Mulholland followed, mildly amused. They were a dozen yards away when Fenn, debating in his mind whether it would not be better—as it would certainly be more dignified—for him to rise and deliver himself up to justice instead of waiting to be discovered wallowing in the damp grass behind a laurel bush, was aware of something soft and furry pressing against his knuckles. A soft purring sound reached his ears.

He knew at once who it was—Thomas Edward, the matron's cat, ever a staunch friend of his. Many a time had they taken tea together in his study in happier days. The friendly animal had sought him out in his hiding-place, and was evidently trying to intimate that the best thing they could do now would be to make a regular night of it.

Fenn, as I have said, liked and respected Thomas. In ordinary circumstances he would not have spoken an unfriendly word to him. But things were desperate now, and needed remedies to match.

Very softly he passed his hand down the delighted animal's back until he reached his tail. Then, stifling with an effort all the finer feelings which should have made such an act impossible, he administered so vigorous a tweak to that appendage that Thomas, with one frenzied yowl, sprang through the bush past the two masters and vanished at full speed into the opposite hedge.

"My goodness!" said Mr Kay, starting back.

It was a further shock to Fenn to find how close he was to the laurel.

" 'Goodness me,
    Why, what was that?
Silent be,
    It was the cat,' "

chanted Mr Mulholland, who was in poetical vein after the theatre.

"It was a cat!" gasped Mr Kay.

"So I am disposed to imagine. What lungs! We shall be having the R.S.P.C.A. down on us if we aren't careful. They must have heard that noise at the headquarters of the Society, wherever they are. Well, if your zeal for big game hunting is satisfied, and you don't propose to follow the vocalist through that hedge, I think I will be off. Good night. Good piece, wasn't it?"

"Excellent. Good night, Mulholland."

"By the way, I wonder if the man who wrote it is a relation of our Fenn. It may be his brother—I believe he writes. You probably remember him when he was here. He was before my time. Talking of Fenn, how do you find the new arrangement answer? Is Kennedy an improvement?"

"Kennedy," said Mr Kay, "is a well-meaning boy, I think. Quite well-meaning. But he lacks ability, in my opinion. I have had to speak to him on several occasions on account of disturbances amongst the juniors. Once I found two boys actually fighting in the junior dayroom. I was very much annoyed about it."

"And where was Kennedy while this was going on? Was he holding the watch?"

"The watch?" said Mr Kay, in a puzzled tone of voice. "Kennedy was over at the gymnasium when it occurred."

"Then it was hardly his fault that the fight took place."

"My dear Mulholland, if the head of a house is efficient, fights should be impossible. Even when he is not present, his influence, his prestige, so to speak, should be sufficient to restrain the boys under him."

Mr Mulholland whistled softly.

"So that's your idea of what the head of your house should be like, is it? Well, I know of one fellow who would have been just your man. Unfortunately, he is never likely to come to school at Eckleton."

"Indeed?" said Mr Kay, with interest. "Who is that? Where did you meet him? What school is he at?"

"I never said I had met him. I only go by what I have heard of him. And as far as I know, he is not at any school. He was a gentleman of the name of Napoleon Bonaparte. He might just have been equal to the arduous duties which devolve upon the head of your house. Goodnight."

And Fenn heard his footsteps crunch the gravel as he walked away. A minute later the front door shut, and there was a rattle. Mr Kay had put the chain up and retired for the night.

Fenn lay where he was for a short while longer. Then he rose, feeling very stiff and wet, and crept into one of the summer-houses which stood in Mr Kay's garden. Here he sat for an hour and a half, at the end of which time, thinking that Mr Kay must be asleep, he started out to climb into the house.

His study was on the first floor. A high garden-seat stood directly beneath the window and acted as a convenient ladder. It was easy to get from this on to the window-ledge. Once there he could open the window, and the rest would be plain sailing.

Unhappily, there was one flaw in his scheme. He had conceived that scheme in the expectation that the window would be as he had left it.

But it was not.

During his absence somebody had shot the bolt. And, try his hardest, he could not move the sash an inch.

XVII

FENN HUNTS FOR HIMSELF

Nobody knows for certain the feelings of the camel when
his proprietor placed that last straw on his back. The
incident happened so long ago. If it had occurred in
modern times, he would probably have contributed a first-
hand report to the *Daily Mail*. But it is very likely that he
felt on that occasion exactly as Fenn felt when, after a
night of unparalleled misadventure, he found that somebody had cut off his retreat by latching the window. After
a gruelling race Fate had just beaten him on the tape.

There was no doubt about its being latched. The sash
had not merely stuck. He put all he knew into the effort
to raise it, but without a hint of success. After three
attempts he climbed down again and, sitting on the garden-
seat, began to review his position.

If one has an active mind and a fair degree of optimism,
the effect of the "staggerers" administered by Fate passes
off after a while. Fenn had both. The consequence was
that, after ten minutes of grey despair, he was relieved by
a faint hope that there might be some other way into the
house than through his study. Anyhow, it would be worth
while to investigate.

His study was at the side of the house. At the back were
the kitchen, the scullery, and the dining-room, and above
these more studies and a couple of dormitories. As a last
resort he might fling rocks and other solids at the windows
until he woke somebody up. But he did not feel like trying
this plan until every other had failed. He had no desire to
let a garrulous dormitory into the secret of his wanderings.

What he hoped was that he might find one of the lower windows open.

And so he did.

As he turned the corner of the house he saw what he had been looking for. The very first window was wide open. His spirits shot up, and for the first time since he had left the theatre he was conscious of taking a pleasure in his adventurous career. Fate was with him after all. He could not help smiling as he remembered how he had felt during that ten minutes on the garden-seat, when the future seemed blank and devoid of any comfort whatsoever. And all the time he could have got in without an effort, if he had only thought of walking half a dozen yards.

Now that the way was open to him, he wasted no time. He climbed through into the dark room. He was not certain which room it was, in spite of his lengthy residence at Kay's.

He let himself down softly till his foot touched the floor. After a moment's pause he moved forward a step. Then another. At the third step his knee struck the leg of a table. He must be in the dining-room. If so, he was all right. He could find his way up to his room with his eyes shut. It was easy to find out for certain. The walls of the dining-room at Kay's, as in the other houses, were covered with photographs. He walked gingerly in the direction in which he imagined the nearest wall to be, reached it, and passed his hand along it. Yes, there were photographs. Then all he had to do was to find the table again, make his way along it, and when he got to the end the door would be a yard or so to his left. The programme seemed simple and attractive. But it was added to in a manner which he had not foreseen. Feeling his way back to the table, he upset a chair. If he had upset a cart-load of coal on to a sheet of tin it could not, so it seemed to him in the disordered state of his nerves, have made more noise. It went down with an appalling crash, striking the table on its way.

"This," thought Fenn, savagely, as he waited, listening, "is where I get collared. What a fool I am to barge about like this."

He felt that the echoes of that crash must have penetrated to every corner of the house. But no one came. Perhaps, after all, the noise had not been so great. He proceeded on his journey down the table, feeling every inch of the way. The place seemed one bristling mass of chairs. But, by the exercise of consummate caution, he upset no more and won through at last in safety to the door.

It was at this point that the really lively and exciting part of his adventure began. Compared with what was to follow, his evening had been up to the present dull and monotonous.

As he opened the door there was a sudden stir and crash at the other end of the room. Fenn had upset one chair and the noise had nearly deafened him. Now chairs seemed to be falling in dozens. Bang! Bang! Crash!! (two that time). And then somebody shot through the window like a harlequin and dashed away across the lawn. Fenn could hear his footsteps thudding on the soft turf. And at the same moment other footsteps made themselves heard.

Somebody was coming downstairs.

"Who is that? Is anybody there?"

It was Mr Kay's voice, unmistakably nervous. Fenn darted from the door and across the passage. At the other side was a boot-cupboard. It was his only refuge in that direction. What he ought to have done was to leave the dining-room by the opposite door, which led *via* a corridor to the junior dayroom. But he lost his head, and instead of bolting away from the enemy, went towards him.

The stairs down which Mr Kay was approaching were at the end of the passage. To reach the dining-room one turned to the right. Beyond the stairs on the left the passage ended in a wall, so that Mr Kay was bound to take the right direction in the search. Fenn wondered if he had a pistol. Not that he cared very much. If the house-master was going to find him, it would be very little extra discomfort to be shot at. And Mr Kay's talents as a marksman were in all probability limited to picking off sitting haystacks. The important point was that he had a candle. A faint yellow glow preceded him down the stairs. Playing hide-and-seek with him in the dark, Fenn might have slipped past in safety; but the candle made that impossible.

He found the boot-room door and slipped through just as Mr Kay turned the corner. With a thrill of pleasure he found that there was a key inside. He turned it as quietly as he could, but nevertheless it grated. Having done this, and seeing nothing else that he could do except await developments, he sat down on the floor among the boots. It was not a dignified position for a man who had played for his county while still at school, but just then he would not have exchanged it for a throne—if the throne had been placed in the passage or the dining-room.

The only question was—had he been seen or heard? He thought not; but his heart began to beat furiously as the footsteps stopped outside the cupboard door and unseen fingers rattled the handle.

Twice Mr Kay tried the handle, but, finding the cupboard locked, passed on into the dining-room. The light of the candle ceased to shine under the door, and Fenn was once more in inky darkness.

He listened intently. A minute later he had made his second mistake. Instead of waiting, as he should have done, until Mr Kay had retired for good, he unlocked the door directly he had passed, and when a muffled crash told him that the house-master was in the dining-room among the chairs, out he came and fled softly upstairs towards his bedroom. He thought that Mr Kay might possibly take it into his head to go round the dormitories to make certain that all the members of his house were in. In which case all would be discovered.

When he reached his room he began to fling off his clothes with feverish haste. Once in bed all would be well.

He had got out of his boots, his coat, and his waistcoat, and was beginning to feel that electric sensation of triumph which only comes to the man who *just* pulls through, when he heard Mr Kay coming down the corridor towards his room. The burglar-hunter, returning from the dining-room in the full belief that the miscreant had escaped through the open window, had had all his ardour for the chase redoubled by the sight of the cupboard door, which Fenn in his hurry had not remembered to close. Mr Kay had made certain by two separate trials that that door had been locked. And now it was wide open. Ergo, the apostle of the jemmy and the skeleton key must still be in the house. Mr Kay, secure in the recollection that burglars never show fight if they can possibly help it, determined to search the house.

Fenn made up his mind swiftly. There was no time to finish dressing. Mr Kay, peering round, might note the absence of the rest of his clothes from their accustomed pegs if he got into bed as he was. There was only one thing to be done. He threw back the bed-clothes, ruffled the sheets till the bed looked as if it had been slept in, and opened the door just as Mr Kay reached the threshold.

"Anything the matter, sir?" asked Fenn, promptly. "I heard a noise downstairs. Can I help you?"

Mr Kay looked carefully at the ex-head of his house. Fenn was a finely-developed youth. He stood six feet, and all of him that was not bone was muscle. A useful colleague to have by one in a hunt for a possibly ferocious burglar.

So thought Mr Kay.

"So *you* heard the noise?" he said. "Well, perhaps you had better come with me. There is no doubt that a burglar has entered the house tonight, in spite of the fact that I locked all the windows myself. Your study window was unlocked, Fenn. It was extremely careless of you to leave it in such a condition, and I hope you will be more careful in future. Why, somebody might have got in through it."

Fenn thought it was not at all unlikely.

"Come along, then. I am sure the man is still in the house. He was hiding in the cupboard by the dining-room. I know it. I am sure he is still in the house."

But, in spite of the fact that Fenn was equally sure, half an hour's search failed to discover any lurking evil-doer.

"You had better go to bed, Fenn," said Mr Kay, disgustedly, at the end of that period. "He must have got back in some extraordinary manner."

"Yes, sir," agreed Fenn.

He himself had certainly got back in a very extraordinary manner.

However, he *had* got back, which was the main point.

XVIII

A Vain Quest

After all he had gone through that night, it disturbed Fenn very little to find on the following morning that the professional cracksman had gone off with one of the cups in his study. Certainly, it was not as bad as it might have been, for he had only abstracted one out of the half dozen that decorated the room. Fenn was a fine runner, and had won the "sprint" events at the sports for two years now.

The news of the burglary at Kay's soon spread about the school. Mr Kay mentioned it to Mr Mulholland, and Mr Mulholland discussed it at lunch with the prefects of his house. The juniors of Kay's were among the last to hear of it, but when they did, they made the most of it, to the disgust of the School House fags, to whom the episode seemed in the nature of an infringement of copyright. Several spirited by-battles took place that day owing to this, and at the lower end of the table of Kay's dining-room at tea that evening there could be seen many swollen countenances. All, however, wore pleased smiles. They had proved to the School House their right to have a burglary of their own if they liked. It was the first occasion since Kennedy had become head of the house that Kay's had united in a common and patriotic cause.

Directly afternoon school was over that day, Fenn started for the town. The only thing that caused him any anxiety now was the fear lest the cap which he had left in the house in the High Street might rise up as evidence against him later on. Except for that, he was safe. The headmaster had evidently not remembered his absence from the festive board, or he would have spoken to him on the subject before now. If he could but recover the lost cap, all would be right with the world. Give him back that cap, and he would turn over a new leaf with a rapidity and emphasis which would lower the world's record for that performance. He would be a reformed character. He would even go to the extent of calling a truce with Mr Kay, climbing down to Kennedy, and offering him his services in his attempt to lick the house into shape.

As a matter of fact, he had had this idea before. Jimmy Silver, who was in the position—common at school—of being very friendly with two people who were not on speaking terms, had been at him on the topic.

"It's rot," James had said, with perfect truth, "to see two chaps like you making idiots of themselves over a house like Kay's. And it's all your fault, too," he had added frankly. "You know jolly well you aren't playing the game. You ought to be backing Kennedy up all the time. Instead of which, you go about trying to look like a Christian martyr—"

"I don't," said Fenn, indignantly.

"Well, like a stuffed frog, then—it's all the same to me. It's perfect rot. If I'm walking with Kennedy, you stalk past as if we'd both got the plague or something. And if I'm with you, Kennedy suddenly remembers an appointment, and dashes off at a gallop in the opposite direction. If I had to award the bronze medal for drivelling lunacy in this place, you would get it by a narrow margin, and Kennedy would be *proxime*, and honourably mentioned. Silly idiots!"

"Don't stop, Jimmy. Keep it up," said Fenn, settling himself in his chair. The dialogue was taking place in Silver's study.

"My dear chap, you didn't think I'd finished, surely! I was only trying to find some description that would suit you. But it's no good. I can't. Look here, take my advice—

the advice," he added, in the melodramatic voice he was in the habit of using whenever he wished to conceal the fact that he was speaking seriously, "of an old man who wishes ye both well. Go to Kennedy, fling yourself on his chest, and say, 'We have done those things which we ought not to have done—' No. As you were! Compn'y, 'shun! Say 'J. Silver says that I am a rotter. I am a worm. I have made an ass of myself. But I will be good. Shake, pard!' That's what you've got to do. Come in."

And in had come Kennedy. The attractions of Kay's were small, and he usually looked in on Jimmy Silver in the afternoons.

"Oh, sorry," he said, as he saw Fenn. "I thought you were alone, Jimmy."

"I was just going," said Fenn, politely.

"Oh, don't let me disturb you," protested Kennedy, with winning courtesy.

"Not at all," said Fenn.

"Oh, if you really were—"

"Oh, yes, really."

"Get out, then," growled Jimmy, who had been listening in speechless disgust to the beautifully polite conversation just recorded. "I'll forward that bronze medal to you, Fenn."

And as the door closed he had turned to rend Kennedy as he had rent Fenn; while Fenn walked back to Kay's feeling that there was a good deal in what Jimmy had said.

So that when he went down town that afternoon in search of his cap, he pondered as he walked over the advisability of making a fresh start. It would not be a bad idea. But first he must concentrate his energies on recovering what he had lost.

He found the house in the High Street without a great deal of difficulty, for he had marked the spot carefully as far as that had been possible in the fog.

The door was opened to him, not by the old man with

whom he had exchanged amenities on the previous night, but by a short, thick fellow, who looked exactly like a picture of a loafer from the pages of a comic journal. He eyed Fenn with what might have been meant for an inquiring look. To Fenn it seemed merely menacing.

"Wodyer want?" he asked, abruptly.

Eckleton was not a great distance from London, and, as a consequence, many of London's choicest blackguards migrated there from time to time. During the hopping season, and while the local races were on, one might meet with two Cockney twangs for every country accent.

"I want to see the old gentleman who lives here," said Fenn.

"Wot old gentleman?"

"I'm afraid I don't know his name. Is this a home for old gentlemen? If you'll bring out all you've got, I'll find my one."

"Wodyer want see the old gentleman for?"

"To ask for my cap. I left it here last night."

"Oh, yer left it 'ere last night! Well, yer cawn't see 'im."

"Not from here, no," agreed Fenn. "Being only eyes, you see," he quoted happily, "my wision's limited. But if you wouldn't mind moving out of the way—"

"Yer cawn't see 'im. Blimey, 'ow much more of it, I should like to know. Gerroutovit, cawn't yer! You and yer caps."

And he added a searching expletive by way of concluding the sentence fittingly. After which he slipped back and slammed the door, leaving Fenn waiting outside like the Peri at the gate of Paradise.

His resemblance to the Peri ceased after the first quarter of a minute. That lady, we read, took her expulsion lying down. Fenn was more vigorous. He seized the knocker, and banged lustily on the door. He had given up all hope of getting back the cap. All he wanted was to get the door-keeper out into the open again, when he would proceed to show him, to the best of his ability, what was what. It would not be the first time he had taken on a gentleman of the same class and a similar type of conversation.

But the man refused to be drawn. For all the reply Fenn's knocking produced, the house might have been empty. At last, having tired his wrist and collected a small crowd of Young Eckleton, who looked as if they expected him to proceed to further efforts for their amusement, he gave it up, and retired down the High Street with what dignity he could command—which, as he was followed for the first fifty yards by the silent but obviously expectant youths, was not a great deal.

They left him, disappointed, near the Town Hall, and Fenn continued on his way alone. The window of the grocer's shop, with its tins of preserved apricots and pots of jam, recalled to his mind what he had forgotten, that the food at Kay's, though it might be wholesome (which he doubted), was undeniably plain, and, secondly, that he had run out of jam. Now that he was here he might as well supply that deficiency.

Now it chanced that Master Wren, of Kay's, was down town—without leave, as was his habit—on an errand of a very similar nature. Walton had found that he, like Fenn, lacked those luxuries of life which are so much more necessary than necessities, and, being unable to go himself, owing to the unfortunate accident of being kept in by his form-master, had asked Wren to go for him. Wren's visit to the grocer's was just ending when Fenn's began.

They met in the doorway.

Wren looked embarrassed, and nearly dropped a pot of honey, which he secured low down after the manner of a catch in the slips. Fenn, on the other hand, took no notice of his fellow-Kayite, but walked on into the shop and began to inspect the tins of biscuits which were stacked on the floor by the counter.

XIX

The Guile of Wren

Wren did not quite know what to make of this. Why had not Fenn said a word to him? There were one or two prefects in the school whom he might have met even at such close quarters and yet have cherished a hope that they had not seen him. Once he had run right into Drew, of the School House, and escaped unrecognised. But with Fenn it was different. Compared to Fenn, lynxes were astigmatic. He must have spotted him.

There was a vein of philosophy in Wren's composition. He felt that he might just as well be hanged for a sheep as a lamb. In other words, having been caught down town without leave, he might as well stay there and enjoy himself a little while longer before going back to be executed. So he strolled off down the High Street, bought a few things at a stationer's, and wound up with an excellent tea at the confectioner's by the post-office.

It was as he was going to this meal that Kennedy caught sight of him. Kennedy had come down town to visit the local photographer, to whom he had entrusted a fortnight before the pleasant task of taking his photograph. As he had heard nothing from him since, he was now coming to investigate. He entered the High Street as Wren was turning into the confectioner's, saw him, and made a note of it for future reference.

When Wren returned to the house just before lock-up, he sought counsel of Walton.

"I say," he said, as he handed over the honey he had saved so neatly from destruction, "what would you do?

Just as I was coming out of the shop, I barged into Fenn. He must have twigged me."

"Didn't he say anything?"

"Not a word. I couldn't make it out, because he must have seen me. We weren't a yard away from one another."

"It's dark in the shop," suggested Walton.

"Not at the door; which is where we met."

Before Walton could find anything to say in reply to this, their conversation was interrupted by Spencer.

"Kennedy wants you, Wren," said Spencer. "You'd better buck up; he's in an awful wax."

Next to Walton, the vindictive Spencer objected most to Wren, and he did not attempt to conceal the pleasure he felt in being the bearer of this ominous summons.

The group broke up. Wren went disconsolately upstairs to Kennedy's study; Walton smacked Spencer's head— more as a matter of form than because he had done anything special to annoy him—and retired to the senior day-room; while Spencer, muttering darkly to himself, avoided a second smack and took cover in the junior room, where he consoled himself by toasting a piece of india-rubber in the gas till it made the atmosphere painful to breathe in, and recalling with pleasure the condition Walton's face had been in for the day or two following his encounter with Kennedy in the dormitory.

Kennedy was working when Wren knocked at his door. He had not much time to spare on a bounds-breaking fag; and his manner was curt.

"I saw you going into Rose's, in the High Street, this afternoon, Wren," he said, looking up from his Greek prose. "I didn't give you leave. Come up here after prayers tonight. Shut the door."

Wren went down to consult Walton again. His attitude with regard to a licking from the head of the house was much like that of the other fags. Custom had, to a certain extent, inured him to these painful interviews, but still, if it was possible, he preferred to keep out of them. Under Fenn's rule he had often found a tolerably thin excuse serve his need. Fenn had so many other things to do that he was not unwilling to forego an occasional licking, if the excuse was good enough. And he never took the trouble to find out whether the ingenious stories Wren was wont to serve up to him were true or not. Kennedy, Wren reflected uncomfortably, had given signs that this easy-going method would not do for him. Still, it might be possible to hunt up some story that would meet the case. Walton had a gift in that direction.

"He says I'm to go to his study after prayers," reported Wren. "Can't you think of any excuse that would do?"

"Can't understand Fenn running you in," said Walton. "I thought he never spoke to Kennedy."

Wren explained.

"It wasn't Fenn who ran me in. Kennedy was down town, too, and twigged me going into Rose's. I went there and had tea after I got your things at the grocer's."

"Oh, he spotted you himself, did he?" said Walton. "And he doesn't know Fenn saw you?"

"I don't think so."

"Then I've got a ripping idea. When he has you up tonight, swear that you got leave from Fenn to go down town."

"But he'll ask him."

"The odds are that he won't. He and Fenn had a row at the beginning of term, and never speak to one another if they can help it. It's ten to one that he will prefer taking your yarn to going and asking Fenn if it's true or not. Then he's bound to let you off."

Wren admitted that the scheme was sound.

At the conclusion of prayers, therefore, he went up again to Kennedy's study, with a more hopeful air than he had worn on his previous visit.

"Come in," said Kennedy, reaching for the swagger-stick which he was accustomed to use at these ceremonies.

"Please, Kennedy," said Wren, glibly. "I did get leave to go down town this afternoon."

"What!"

Wren repeated the assertion.

"Who gave you leave?"

"Fenn."

The thing did not seem to be working properly. When he said the word "Fenn", Wren expected to see Kennedy retire baffled, conscious that there was nothing more to be said or done. Instead of this, the remark appeared to infuriate him.

"It's just like your beastly cheek," he said, glaring at the red-headed delinquent, "to ask Fenn for leave instead of me. You know perfectly well that only the head of the house can give leave to go down town. I don't know how often you and the rest of the junior dayroom have played this game, but it's going to stop now. You'd better remember another time when you want to go to Rose's that I've got to be consulted first."

With which he proceeded to ensure to the best of his ability that the memory of Master Wren should not again prove treacherous in this respect.

"How did it work?" asked Walton, when Wren returned.

"It didn't," said Wren, briefly.

Walton expressed an opinion that Kennedy was a cad; which, however sound in itself, did little to improve the condition of Wren.

Having disposed of Wren, Kennedy sat down seriously to consider this new development of a difficult situation. Hitherto he had imagined Fenn to be merely a sort of passive resister who confined himself to the Achilles-in-his-tent business, and was only a nuisance because he refused to back him up. To find him actually aiding and abetting the house in its opposition to its head was something of a shock. And yet, if he had given Wren leave to go down town, he had probably done the same kind office by others. It irritated Kennedy more than the most overt act of enmity would have done. It was not good form. It was hitting below the belt. There was, of course, the chance that Wren's story had not been true. But he did not build much on that. He did not yet know his Wren well, and believed that such an audacious lie would be beyond the daring of a fag. But it would be worth while to make inquiries. He went down the passage to Fenn's study. Fenn, however, had gone to bed, so he resolved to approach him on the subject next day. There was no hurry.

He went to his dormitory, feeling very bitter towards Fenn, and rehearsing home truths with which to confound him on the morrow.

XX

JIMMY THE PEACEMAKER

In these hustling times it is not always easy to get ten minutes' conversation with an acquaintance in private. There was drill in the dinner hour next day for the corps, to which Kennedy had to go directly after lunch. It did not end till afternoon school began. When afternoon school was over, he had to turn out and practise scrummaging with the first fifteen, in view of an important school match which was coming off on the following Saturday. Kennedy had not yet received his cap, but he was playing regularly for the first fifteen, and was generally looked upon as a certainty for one of the last places in the team. Fenn, being a three-quarter, had not to participate in this practice. While the forwards were scrummaging on the second fifteen ground, the outsides ran and passed on the first fifteen ground over at the other end of the field. Fenn's training for the day finished earlier than Kennedy's, the captain of the Eckleton fifteen, who led the scrum, not being satisfied with the way in which the forwards wheeled. He kept them for a quarter of an hour after the outsides had done their day's work, and when Kennedy got back to the house and went to Fenn's study, the latter was not there. He had evidently changed and gone out again, for his football clothes were lying in a heap in a corner of the room. Going back to his own study, he met Spencer.

"Have you seen Fenn?" he asked.

"No," said the fag. "He hasn't come in."

"He's come in all right, but he's gone out again. Go and ask Taylor if he knows where he is."

Taylor was Fenn's fag.

Spencer went to the junior dayroom, and returned with the information that Taylor did not know.

"Oh, all right, then—it doesn't matter," said Kennedy, and went into his study to change.

He had completed this operation, and was thinking of putting his kettle on for tea, when there was a knock at the door.

It was Baker, Jimmy Silver's fag.

"Oh, Kennedy," he said, "Silver says, if you aren't doing anything special, will you go over to his study to tea?"

"Why, is there anything on?"

It struck him as curious that Jimmy should take the trouble to send his fag over to Kay's with a formal invitation. As a rule the head of Blackburn's kept open house. His friends were given to understand that they could drop in whenever they liked. Kennedy looked in for tea three times a week on an average.

"I don't think so," said Baker.

"Who else is going to be there?"

Jimmy Silver sometimes took it into his head to entertain weird beings from other houses whose brothers or cousins he had met in the holidays. On such occasions he liked to have some trusty friend by him to help the conversation along. It struck Kennedy that this might be one of those occasions. If so, he would send back a polite but firm refusal of the invitation. Last time he had gone to help Jimmy entertain a guest of this kind, conversation had come to a dead standstill a quarter of an hour after his arrival, the guest refusing to do anything except eat prodigiously, and reply "Yes" or "No", as the question might demand, when spoken to. Also he had declined to stir from his seat till a quarter to seven. Kennedy was not going to be let in for another orgy of that nature if he knew it.

"Who's with Silver?" he asked.

"Only Fenn," said Baker.

Kennedy pondered for a moment.

"All right," he said, at last, "tell him I'll be round in a few minutes."

He sat thinking the thing over after Baker had gone back to Blackburn's with the message. He saw Silver's game, of course. Jimmy had made no secret for some time of his disgust at the coolness between Kennedy and Fenn. Not knowing all the circumstances, he considered it absolute folly. If only he could get the two together over a quiet pot of tea, he imagined that it would not be a difficult task to act effectively as a peacemaker.

Kennedy was sorry for Jimmy. He appreciated his feelings in the matter. He would not have liked it himself if his two best friends had been at daggers drawn. Still, he could not bring himself to treat Fenn as if nothing had happened, simply to oblige Silver. There had been a time when he might have done it, but now that Fenn had started a deliberate campaign against him by giving Wren—and probably, thought Kennedy, half the other fags in the house—leave down town when he ought to have sent them on to him, things had gone too far. However, he could do no harm by going over to Jimmy's to tea, even if Fenn was there. He had not looked to interview Fenn before an audience, but if that audience consisted only of Jimmy, it would not matter so much.

His advent surprised Fenn. The astute James, fancying that if he mentioned that he was expecting Kennedy to tea, Fenn would make a bolt for it, had said nothing about it.

When Kennedy arrived there was one of those awkward pauses which are so difficult to fill up in a satisfactory manner.

"Now you're up, Fenn," said Jimmy, as the latter rose, evidently with the intention of leaving the study, "you might as well reach down that toasting-fork and make some toast."

"I'm afraid I must be off now, Jimmy," said Fenn.

"No you aren't," said Silver. "You bustle about and make yourself useful, and don't talk rot. You'll find your cup on that shelf over there, Kennedy. It'll want a wipe round. Better use the table-cloth."

There was silence in the study until tea was ready. Then Jimmy Silver spoke.

"Long time since we three had tea together," he said, addressing the remark to the teapot.

"Kennedy's a busy man," said Fenn, suavely. "He's got a house to look after."

"And I'm going to look after it," said Kennedy, "as you'll find."

Jimmy Silver put in a plaintive protest.

"I wish you two men wouldn't talk shop," he said. "It's bad enough having Kay's next door to one, without your dragging it into the conversation. How were the forwards this evening, Kennedy?"

"Not bad," said Kennedy, shortly.

"I wonder if we shall lick Tuppenham on Saturday?"

"I don't know," said Kennedy; and there was silence again.

"Look here, Jimmy," said Kennedy, after a long pause, during which the head of Blackburn's tried to fill up the blank in the conversation by toasting a piece of bread in a way which was intended to suggest that if he were not so busy, the talk would be unchecked and animated, "it's no good. We must have it out some time, so it may as well be here as anywhere else. I've been looking for Fenn all day."

"Sorry to give you all that trouble," said Fenn, with a sneer. "Got something important to say?"

"Yes."

"Go ahead, then."

Jimmy Silver stood between them with the toasting-fork in his hand, as if he meant to plunge it into the one who first showed symptoms of flying at the other's throat. He was unhappy. His peace-making tea-party was not proving a success.

"I wanted to ask you," said Kennedy, quietly, "what you meant by giving the fags leave down town when you knew that they ought to come to me?"

The gentle and intelligent reader will remember (though that miserable worm, the vapid and irreflective reader, will have forgotten) that at the beginning of the term the fags of Kay's had endeavoured to show their approval of Fenn and their disapproval of Kennedy by applying to the former for leave when they wished to go to the town; and that Fenn had received them in the most ungrateful manner with blows instead of exeats. Strong in this recollection, he was not disturbed by Kennedy's question. Indeed, it gave him a comfortable feeling of rectitude. There is nothing more pleasant than to be accused to your face of something which you can deny on the spot with an easy conscience. It is like getting a very loose ball at cricket. Fenn felt almost friendly towards Kennedy.

"I meant nothing," he replied, "for the simple reason that I didn't do it."

"I caught Wren down town yesterday, and he said you had given him leave."

"Then he lied, and I hope you licked him."

"There you are, you see," broke in Jimmy Silver triumphantly, "it's all a misunderstanding. You two have got no right to be cutting one another. Why on earth can't you stop all this rot, and behave like decent members of society again?"

"As a matter of fact," said Fenn, "they did try it on earlier in the term. I wasted a lot of valuable time pointing out to them with a swagger-stick—that I was the wrong person to come to. I'm sorry you should have thought I could play it as low down as that."

Kennedy hesitated. It is not very pleasant to have to

climb down after starting a conversation in a stormy and wrathful vein. But it had to be done.

"I'm sorry, Fenn," he said; "I was an idiot."

Jimmy Silver cut in again.

"You were," he said, with enthusiasm. "You both were. I used to think Fenn was a bigger idiot than you, but now I'm inclined to call it a dead heat. What's the good of going on trying to see which of you can make the bigger fool of himself? You've both lowered all previous records."

"I suppose we have," said Fenn. "At least, I have."

"No, I have," said Kennedy.

"You both have," said Jimmy Silver. "Another cup of tea, anybody? Say when."

Fenn and Kennedy walked back to Kay's together, and tea-d together in Fenn's study on the following afternoon, to the amazement—and even scandal—of Master Spencer, who discovered them at it. Spencer liked excitement; and with the two leaders of the house at logger-heads, things could never be really dull. If, as appearances seemed to suggest, they had agreed to settle their differences, life would become monotonous again—possibly even unpleasant.

This thought flashed through Spencer's brain (as he called it) when he opened Fenn's door and found him helping Kennedy to tea.

"Oh, the headmaster wants to see you, please, Fenn," said Spencer, recovering from his amazement, "and told me to give you this."

"This" was a prefect's cap. Fenn recognised it without difficulty. It was the cap he had left in the sitting-room of the house in the High Street.

XXI

In Which an Episode is Closed

"Thanks," said Fenn.

He stood twirling the cap round in his hand as Spencer closed the door. Then he threw it on to the table. He did not feel particularly disturbed at the thought of the interview that was to come. He had been expecting the cap to turn up, like the corpse of Eugene Aram's victim, at some inconvenient moment. It was a pity that it had come just as things looked as if they might be made more or less tolerable in Kay's. He had been looking forward with a grim pleasure to the sensation that would be caused in the house when it became known that he and Kennedy had formed a combine for its moral and physical benefit. But that was all over. He would be sacked, beyond a doubt. In the history of Eckleton, as far as he knew it, there had never been a case of a fellow breaking out at night and not being expelled when he was caught. It was one of the cardinal sins in the school code. There had been the case of Peter Brown, which his brother had mentioned in his letter. And in his own time he had seen three men vanish from Eckleton for the same offence. He did not flatter himself that his record at the school was so good as to make it likely that the authorities would stretch a point in his favour.

"So long, Kennedy," he said. "You'll be here when I get back, I suppose?"

"What does he want you for, do you think?" asked Kennedy, stretching himself, with a yawn. It never struck him that Fenn could be in any serious trouble. Fenn was a prefect; and when the headmaster sent for a prefect, it was generally to tell him that he had got a split infinitive in his English Essay that week.

"Glad I'm not you," he added, as a gust of wind rattled the sash, and the rain dashed against the pane. "Beastly evening to have to go out."

"It isn't the rain I mind," said Fenn; "it's what's going to happen when I get indoors again," and refused to explain further. There would be plenty of time to tell Kennedy the whole story when he returned. It was better not to keep the headmaster waiting.

The first thing he noticed on reaching the School House was the strange demeanour of the butler. Whenever Fenn had had occasion to call on the headmaster hitherto, Watson had admitted him with the air of a high priest leading a devotee to a shrine of which he was the sole managing director. This evening he seemed restless, excited.

"Good evening, Mr Fenn," he said. "This way, sir."

Those were his actual words. Fenn had not known for certain until now that he *could* talk. On previous occasions their conversations had been limited to an "Is the head-master in?" from Fenn, and a stately inclination of the head from Watson. The man was getting a positive babbler.

With an eager, springy step, distantly reminiscent of a shopwalker heading a procession of customers, with a touch of the style of the winner in a walking-race to Brighton, the once slow-moving butler led the way to the headmaster's study.

For the first time since he started out, Fenn was conscious of a tremor. There is something about a closed door, behind which somebody is waiting to receive one, which appeals to the imagination, especially if the ensuing meet-ing is likely to be an unpleasant one.

"Ah, Fenn," said the headmaster. "Come in."

Fenn wondered. It was not in this tone of voice that the Head was wont to begin a conversation which was going to prove painful.

"You've got your cap, Fenn? I gave it to a small boy in your house to take to you."

"Yes, sir."

He had given up all hope of understanding the Head's line of action. Unless he was playing a deep game, and intended to flash out suddenly with a keen question which it would be impossible to parry, there seemed nothing to account for the strange absence of anything unusual in his manner. He referred to the cap as if he had borrowed it from Fenn, and had returned it by bearer, hoping that its loss had not inconvenienced him at all.

"I daresay," continued the Head, "that you are wondering how it came into my possession. You missed it, of course?"

"Very much, sir," said Fenn, with perfect truth.

"It has just been brought to my house, together with a great many other things, more valuable, perhaps,"—here he smiled a head-magisterial smile—"by a policeman from Eckleton."

Fenn was still unequal to the intellectual pressure of the conversation. He could understand, in a vague way, that for some unexplained reason things were going well for him, but beyond that his mind was in a whirl.

"You will remember the unfortunate burglary of Mr Kay's house and mine. Your cap was returned with the rest of the stolen property."

"Just so," thought Fenn. "The rest of the stolen property? Exactly. *Go* on. Don't mind me. I shall begin to understand soon, I suppose."

He condensed these thoughts into the verbal reply, "Yes, sir."

"I sent for you to identify your own property. I see there is a silver cup belonging to you. Perhaps there are also other articles. Go and see. You will find them on that table. They are in a hopeless state of confusion, having been conveyed here in a sack. Fortunately, nothing is broken."

He was thinking of certain valuables belonging to himself which had been abstracted from his drawing-room on the occasion of the burglar's visit to the School House.

Fenn crossed the room, and began to inspect the table indicated. On it was as mixed a collection of valuable and useless articles as one could wish to see. He saw his cup at once, and attached himself to it. But of all the other exhibits in this private collection, he could recognise nothing else as his property.

"There is nothing of mine here except the cup, sir," he said.

"Ah. Then that is all, I think. You are going back to Mr Kay's. Then please send Kennedy to me. Good night, Fenn."

"Good night, sir."

Even now Fenn could not understand it. The more he thought it over, the more his brain reeled. He could grasp the fact that his cap and his cup were safe again, and that there was evidently going to be no sacking for the moment. But how it had all happened, and how the police had got hold of his cap, and why they had returned it with the loot gathered in by the burglar who had visited Kay's and the School House, were problems which, he had to confess, were beyond him.

He walked to Kay's through the rain with the cup under his mackintosh, and freely admitted to himself that there were things in heaven and earth—and particularly earth—which no fellow could understand.

"I don't know," he said, when Kennedy pressed for an explanation of the reappearance of the cup. "It's no good asking me. I'm going now to borrow the matron's smelling-salts : I feel faint. After that I shall wrap a wet towel round my head, and begin to think it out. Meanwhile, you're to go over to the Head. He's had enough of me, and he wants to have a look at you."

"Me?" said Kennedy. "Why?"

"Now, is it any good asking *me*?" said Fenn. "If you can find out what it's all about, I'll thank you if you'll come and tell me."

Ten minutes later Kennedy returned. He carried a watch and chain.

"I couldn't think what had happened to my watch," he said. "I missed it on the day after that burglary here, but I never thought of thinking it had been collared by a professional. I thought I must have lost it somewhere."

"Well, have you grasped what's been happening?"

"I've grasped my ticker, which is good enough for me. Half a second. The old man wants to see the rest of the prefects. He's going to work through the house in batches, instead of man by man. I'll just go round the studies and rout them out, and then I'll come back and explain. It's perfectly simple."

"Glad you think so," said Fenn.

Kennedy went and returned.

"Now," he said, subsiding into a deck-chair, "what is it you don't understand?"

"I don't understand anything. Begin at the beginning."

"I got the yarn from the butler—what's his name?"

"Those who know him well enough to venture to give him a name—I've never dared to myself—call him Watson," said Fenn.

"I got the yarn from Watson. He was as excited as anything about it. I never saw him like that before."

"I noticed something queer about him."

"He's awfully bucked, and is doing the Ancient Mariner business all over the place. Wants to tell the story to everyone he sees."

"Well, suppose you follow his example. I want to hear about it."

"Well, it seems that the police have been watching a house at the corner of the High Street for some time— what's up?"

"Nothing. Go on."

"But you said, 'By Jove!'"

"Well, why shouldn't I say 'By Jove'? When you are telling sensational yarns, it's my duty to say something of the sort. Buck along."

"It's a house not far from the Town Hall, at the corner of Pegwell Street—you've probably been there scores of times."

"Once or twice, perhaps," said Fenn. "Well?"

"About a month ago two suspicious-looking bounders went to live there. Watson says their faces were enough to hang them. Anyhow, they must have been pretty bad, for they made even the Eckleton police, who are pretty average-sized rotters, suspicious, and they kept an eye on them. Well, after a bit there began to be a regular epidemic of burglary round about here. Watson says half the houses round were broken into. The police thought it was getting a bit too thick, but they didn't like to raid the house without some jolly good evidence that these two men were the burglars, so they lay low and waited till they should give them a decent excuse for jumping on them. They had had a detective chap down from London, by the way, to see if he couldn't do something about the burglaries, and he kept his eye on them, too."

"They had quite a gallery. Didn't they notice any of the eyes?"

"No. Then after a bit one of them nipped off to London with a big bag. The detective chap was after him like a shot. He followed him from the station, saw him get into a cab, got into another himself, and stuck to him hard. The front cab stopped at about a dozen pawnbrokers' shops. The detective Johnny took the names and addresses, and hung on to the burglar man all day, and finally saw him return to the station, where he caught a train back to Eckleton. Directly he had seen him off, the detective got into a cab, called on the dozen pawnbrokers, showed his card, with 'Scotland Yard' on it, I suppose, and asked to see what the other chap had pawned. He identified every single thing as something that had been collared from one of the houses round Eckleton way. So he came back here, told the police, and they raided the house, and there they found stacks of loot of all descriptions."

"Including my cap," said Fenn, thoughtfully. "I see now."

"Rummy the man thinking it worth his while to take an old cap," said Kennedy.

"Very," said Fenn. "But it's been a rum business all along."

XXII

KAY'S CHANGES ITS NAME

For the remaining weeks of the winter term, things went
as smoothly in Kay's as Kay would let them. That restless
gentleman still continued to burst in on Kennedy from time
to time with some sensational story of how he had found
a fag doing what he ought not to have done. But there
was a world of difference between the effect these visits
had now and that which they had had when Kennedy had
stood alone in the house, his hand against all men. Now
that he could work off the effects of such encounters by
going straight to Fenn's study and picking the house-master
to pieces, the latter's peculiar methods ceased to be irritat-
ing, and became funny. Mr Kay was always ferreting out
the weirdest misdoings on the part of the members of his
house, and rushing to Kennedy's study to tell him about
them at full length, like a rather indignant dog bringing a
rat he has hunted down into a drawing-room, to display it
to the company. On one occasion, when Fenn and Jimmy
Silver were in Kennedy's study, Mr Kay dashed in to
complain bitterly that he had discovered that the junior
dayroom kept mice in their lockers. Apparently this fact
seemed to him enough to cause an epidemic of typhoid
fever in the place, and he hauled Kennedy over the coals,
in a speech that lasted five minutes, for not having detected
this plague-spot in the house.

"So that's the celebrity at home, is it?" said Jimmy
Silver, when he had gone. "I now begin to understand
more or less why this house wants a new Head every two
terms. Is he often taken like that?"

"He's never anything else," said Kennedy. "Fenn keeps a list of the things he rags me about, and we have an even shilling on, each week, that he will beat the record of the previous week. At first I used to get the shilling if he lowered the record; but after a bit it struck us that it wasn't fair, so now we take it on alternate weeks. This is my week, by the way. I think I can trouble you for that bob, Fenn?"

"I wish I could make it more," said Fenn, handing over the shilling.

"What sort of things does he rag you about generally?" inquired Silver.

Fenn produced a slip of paper.

"Here are a few," he said, "for this month. He came in on the 10th because he found two kids fighting. Kennedy was down town when it happened, but that made no difference. Then he caught the senior dayroom making a row of some sort. He said it was perfectly deafening; but we couldn't hear it in our studies. I believe he goes round the house, listening at keyholes. That was on the 16th. On the 22nd he found a chap in Kennedy's dormitory wandering about the house at one in the morning. He seemed to think that Kennedy ought to have sat up all night on the chance of somebody cutting out of the dormitory. At any rate, he ragged him. I won the weekly shilling on that; and deserved it, too."

Fenn had to go over to the gymnasium shortly after this. Jimmy Silver stayed on, talking to Kennedy.

"And bar Kay," said Jimmy, "how do you find the house doing? Any better?"

"Better! It's getting a sort of model establishment. I believe, if we keep pegging away at them, we may win some sort of a cup sooner or later."

"Well, Kay's very nearly won the cricket cup last year. You ought to get it next season, now that you and Fenn are both in the team."

"Oh, I don't know. It'll be a fluke if we do. Still, we're

hoping. It isn't every house that's got a county man in it. But we're breaking out in another place. Don't let it get about, for goodness' sake, but we're going for the sports' cup."

"Hope you'll get it. Blackburn's won't have a chance, anyhow, and I should like to see somebody get it away from the School House. They've had it much too long. They're beginning to look on it as their right. But who are your men?"

"Well, Fenn ought to be a cert for the hundred and the quarter, to start with."

"But the School House must get the long run, and the mile, and the half, too, probably."

"Yes. We haven't anyone to beat Milligan, certainly. But there are the second and third places. Don't forget those. That's where we're going to have a look in. There's all sorts of unsuspected talent in Kay's. To look at Peel, for instance, you wouldn't think he could do the hundred in eleven, would you? Well, he can, only he's been too slack to go in for the race at the sports, because it meant training. I had him up here and reasoned with him, and he's promised to do his best. Eleven is good enough for second place in the hundred, don't you think? There are lots of others in the house who can do quite decently on the track, if they try. I've been making strict inquiries. Kay's are hot stuff, Jimmy. Heap big medicine. That's what they are."

"You're a wonderful man, Kennedy," said Jimmy Silver. And he meant it. Kennedy's uphill fight at Kay's had appealed to him strongly. He himself had never known what it meant to have to manage a hostile house. He had stepped into his predecessor's shoes at Blackburn's much as the heir to a throne becomes king. Nobody had thought of disputing his right to the place. He was next man in; so, directly the departure of the previous head of Blackburn's left a vacancy, he stepped into it, and the machinery of

the house had gone on as smoothly as if there had been
no change at all. But Kennedy had gone in against a slack
and antagonistic house, with weak prefects to help him,
and a fussy house-master; and he had fought them all for
a term, and looked like winning. Jimmy admired his friend
with a fervour which nothing on earth would have
tempted him to reveal. Like most people with a sense of
humour, he had a fear of appearing ridiculous, and he hid
his real feelings as completely as he was able.

"How is the footer getting on?" inquired Jimmy, remembering the difficulties Kennedy had encountered earlier
in the term in connection with his house team.

"It's better," said Kennedy. "Keener, at any rate. We
shall do our best in the house-matches. But we aren't a
good team."

"Any more trouble about your being captain instead of
Fenn?"

"No. We both sign the lists now. Fenn didn't want to,
but I thought it would be a good idea, so we tried it. It
seems to have worked all right."

"Of course, your getting your first has probably made
a difference."

"A bit, perhaps."

"Well, I hope you won't get the footer cup, because I
want it for Blackburn's. Or the cricket cup. I want that,
too. But you can have the sports' cup with my blessing."

"Thanks," said Kennedy. "It's very generous of you."

"Don't mention it," said Jimmy.

From which conversation it will be seen that Kay's was
gradually pulling itself together. It had been asleep for
years. It was now waking up.

When the winter term ended, there were distinct symptoms of an outbreak of public spirit in the house.

The Easter term opened auspiciously in one way.
Neither Walton nor Perry returned. The former had been
snapped up in the middle of the holidays—to his enormous

disgust—by a bank, which wanted his services so much that it was prepared to pay him £40 a year simply to enter the addresses of its outgoing letters in a book, and post them when he had completed this ceremony. After a spell of this he might hope to be transferred to another sphere of bank life and thought, and at the end of his first year he might even hope for a rise in his salary of ten pounds, if his conduct was good, and he had not been late on more than twenty mornings in the year. I am aware that in a properly-regulated story of school-life Walton would have gone to the Eckleton races, returned in a state of speechless intoxication, and been summarily expelled; but facts are facts, and must not be tampered with. The ingenious but not industrious Perry had been super-annuated. For three years he had been in the Lower Fourth. Probably the master of that form went to the Head, and said that his constitution would not stand another year of him, and that either he or Perry must go. So Perry had departed. Like a poor play, he had "failed to attract," and was withdrawn. There was also another departure of an even more momentous nature.

Mr Kay had left Eckleton.

Kennedy was no longer head of Kay's. He was now head of Dencroft's.

Mr Dencroft was one of the most popular masters in the school. He was a keen athlete and a tactful master. Fenn and Kennedy knew him well, through having played at the nets and in scratch games with him. They both liked him. If Kennedy had had to select a house-master, he would have chosen Mr Blackburn first. But Mr Dencroft would have been easily second.

Fenn learned the facts from the matron, and detailed them to Kennedy.

"Kay got the offer of a headmastership at a small school in the north, and jumped at it. I pity the fellows there. They are going to have a lively time."

"I'm jolly glad Dencroft has got the house," said Kennedy. "We might have had some awful rotter put in. Dencroft will help us buck up the house games."

The new house-master sent for Kennedy on the first evening of term. He wished to find out how the Head of the house and the ex-Head stood with regard to one another. He knew the circumstances, and comprehended vaguely that there had been trouble.

"I hope we shall have a good term," he said.

"I hope so, sir," said Kennedy.

"You—er—you think the house is keener, Kennedy, than when you first came in?"

"Yes, sir. They are getting quite keen now. We might win the sports."

"I hope we shall. I wish we could win the football cup, too, but I am afraid Mr Blackburn's are very heavy metal."

"It's hardly likely we shall have very much chance with them; but we might get into the final!"

"It would be an excellent thing for the house if we could. I hope Fenn is helping you get the team into shape?" he added.

"Oh, yes, sir," said Kennedy. "We share the captaincy. We both sign the lists."

"A very good idea," said Mr Dencroft, relieved. "Good night, Kennedy."

"Good night, sir," said Kennedy.

XXIII

The House-Matches

The chances of Kay's in the inter-house Football Competition were not thought very much of by their rivals. Of late years each of the other houses had prayed to draw Kay's for the first round, it being a certainty that this would mean that they got at least into the second round, and so a step nearer the cup. Nobody, however weak compared to Blackburn's, which was at the moment the crack football house, ever doubted the result of a match with Kay's. It was looked on as a sort of gentle trial trip.

But the efforts of the two captains during the last weeks of the winter term had put a different complexion on matters. Football is not like cricket. It is a game at which anybody of average size and a certain amount of pluck can make himself at least moderately proficient. Kennedy, after consultations with Fenn, had picked out what he considered the best fifteen, and the two set themselves to knock it into shape. In weight there was not much to grumble at. There were several heavy men in the scrum. If only these could be brought to use their weight to the last ounce when shoving, all would be well as far as the forwards were concerned. The outsides were not so satisfactory. With the exception, of course, of Fenn, they lacked speed. They were well-meaning, but they could not run any faster by virtue of that. Kay's would have to trust to its scrum to pull it through. Peel, the sprinter whom Kennedy had discovered in his search for athletes, had to be put in the pack on account of his weight, which deprived the three-quarter line of what would have been a good man in that position. It was a drawback, too, that Fenn was accustomed to play on the wing. To be of real service, a wing three-quarter must be fed by his centres, and, unfortunately, there was no centre in Kay's—or Dencroft's, as it should now be called—who was capable of making openings enough to give Fenn a chance. So he had to play in the centre, where he did not know the game so well.

Kennedy realised at an early date that the one chance of the house was to get together before the house-matches and play as a coherent team, not as a collection of units. Combination will often make up for lack of speed in a three-quarter line. So twice a week Dencroft's turned out against scratch teams of varying strength.

It delighted Kennedy to watch their improvement. The first side they played ran through them to the tune of three goals and four tries to a try, and it took all the efforts of the Head of the house to keep a spirit of pessimism from spreading in the ranks. Another frost of this sort, and the sprouting keenness of the house would be nipped in the bud. He conducted himself with much tact. Another captain might have made the fatal error of trying to stir his team up with pungent abuse. He realised what a mistake this would be. It did not need a great deal of discouragement to send the house back to its old slack ways. Another such defeat, following immediately in the footsteps of the first, and they would begin to ask themselves what was the good of mortifying the flesh simply to get a licking from a scratch team by twenty-four points. Kay's, they would feel, always had got beaten, and they always would, to the end of time. A house that has once got thoroughly slack does not change its views of life in a moment.

Kennedy acted craftily.

"You played jolly well," he told his despondent team, as they trooped off the field. "We haven't got together yet,

that's all. And it was a hot side we were playing today.
They would have licked Blackburn's."

A good deal more in the same strain gave the house
team the comfortable feeling that they had done uncommonly well to get beaten by only twenty-four points.
Kennedy fostered the delusion, and in the meantime
arranged with Mr Dencroft to collect fifteen innocents and
lead them forth to be slaughtered by the house on the
following Friday. Mr Dencroft entered into the thing with
a relish. When he showed Kennedy the list of his team on
the Friday morning, that diplomatist chuckled. He foresaw
a good time in the near future. "You must play up like
the dickens," he told the house during the dinner-hour.
"Dencroft is bringing a hot lot this afternoon. But I think
we shall lick them."

They did. When the whistle blew for No-side, the house
had just finished scoring its fourteenth try. Six goals and
eight tries to nil was the exact total. Dencroft's returned to
headquarters, asking itself in a dazed way if these things
could be. They saw that cup on their mantelpiece already.
Keenness redoubled. Football became the fashion in
Dencroft's. The play of the team improved weekly. And
its spirit improved too. The next scratch team they played
beat them by a goal and a try to a goal. Dencroft's was
not depressed. It put the result down to a fluke. Then they
beat another side by a try to nothing; and by that time
they had got going as an organised team, and their heart
was in the thing.

They had improved out of all knowledge when the
house-matches began. Blair's was the lucky house that drew
against them in the first round.

"Good business," said the men of Blair. "Wonder who
we'll play in the second round."

They left the field marvelling. For some unaccountable
reason, Dencroft's had flatly refused to act in the good old
way as a doormat for their opponents. Instead, they had

played with a dash and knowledge of the game which for the first quarter of an hour quite unnerved Blair's. In that quarter of an hour they scored three times, and finished the game with two goals and three tries to their name.

The School looked on it as a huge joke. "Heard the latest?" friends would say on meeting one another the day after the game. "Kay's—I mean Dencroft's—have won a match. They simply sat on Blair's. First time they've ever won a house-match, I should think. Blair's are awfully sick. We shall have to be looking out."

Whereat the friend would grin broadly. The idea of Dencroft's making a game of it with his house tickled him.

When Dencroft's took fifteen points off Mulholland's, the joke began to lose its humour.

"Why, they must be some good," said the public, startled at the novelty of the idea. "If they win another match, they'll be in the final!"

Kay's in the final! Cricket? Oh, yes, they had got into the final at cricket, of course. But that wasn't the house. It was Fenn. Footer was different. One man couldn't do everything there. The only possible explanation was that they had improved to an enormous extent.

Then people began to remember that they had played in scratch games against the house. There seemed to be a tremendous number of fellows who had done this. At one time or another, it seemed, half the School had opposed Dencroft's in the ranks of a scratch side. It began to dawn on Eckleton that in an unostentatious way Dencroft's had been putting in about seven times as much practice as any other three houses rolled together. No wonder they combined so well.

When the School House, with three first fifteen men in its team, fell before them, the reputation of Dencroft's was established. It had reached the final, and only Blackburn's stood now between it and the cup.

All this while Blackburn's had been doing what was

expected of them by beating each of their opponents with great ease. There was nothing sensational about this as there was in the case of Dencroft's. The latter were, therefore, favourites when the two teams lined up against one another in the final. The School felt that a house that had had such a meteoric flight as Dencroft's must—by all that was dramatic—carry the thing through to its obvious conclusion, and pull off the final.

But Fenn and Kennedy were not so hopeful. A certain amount of science, a great deal of keeness, and excellent condition, had carried them through the other rounds in rare style, but, though they would probably give a good account of themselves, nobody who considered the two teams impartially could help seeing that Dencroft's was a weaker side than Blackburn's. Nothing but great good luck could bring them out victorious today.

And so it proved. Dencroft's played up for all they were worth from the kick-off to the final solo on the whistle, but they were over-matched. Blackburn's scrum was too heavy for them, with its three first fifteen men and two seconds. Dencroft's pack were shoved off the ball time after time, and it was only keen tackling that kept the score down. By half-time Blackburn's were a couple of tries ahead. Fenn scored soon after the interval with a great run from his own twenty-five, and for a quarter of an hour it looked as if it might be anybody's game. Kennedy converted the try, so that Blackburn's only led by a single point. A fluky kick or a mistake on the part of a Blackburnite outside might give Dencroft's the cup.

But the Blackburn outsides did not make mistakes. They played a strong, sure game, and the forwards fed them well. Ten minutes before No-side, Jimmy Silver ran in, increasing the lead to six points. And though Dencroft's never went to pieces, and continued to show fight to the very end, Blackburn's were not to be denied, and Challis scored a final try in the corner. Blackburn's won the cup by the comfortable, but not excessive, margin of a goal and three tries to a goal.

Dencroft's had lost the cup; but they had lost it well. Their credit had increased in spite of the defeat.

"I thought we shouldn't be able to manage Blackburn's," said Kennedy, "What we must do now is win that sports' cup."

XXIV

THE SPORTS

There were certain houses at Eckleton which had, as it were, specialised in certain competitions. Thus, Gay's, who never by any chance survived the first two rounds of the cricket and football housers, invariably won the shooting shield. All the other houses sent their brace of men to the range to see what they could do, but every year it was the same. A pair of weedy obscurities from Gay's would take the shield by a comfortable margin. In the same way Mulholland's had only won the cricket cup once since they had become a house, but they had carried off the swimming cup three years in succession, and six years in all out of the last eight. The sports had always been looked on as the perquisite of the School House; and this year, with Milligan to win the long distances, and Maybury the high jump and the weight, there did not seem much doubt at their success. These two alone would pile up fifteen points. Three points were given for a win, two for second place, and one for third. It was this that encouraged Kennedy in the hope that Dencroft's might have a chance. Nobody in the house could beat Milligan or Maybury, but the School House second and third strings were not so invincible. If Dencroft's, by means of second and third places in the long races and the other events which were certainties for their opponents, could hold the School House, Fenn's sprinting might just give them the cup. In the meantime they trained hard, but in an unobtrusive fashion which aroused no fear in School House circles.

The sports were fixed for the last Saturday of term, but

not all the races were run on that day. The half-mile came
off on the previous Thursday, and the long steeplechase on
the Monday after.

The School House won the half-mile, as they were
expected to do. Milligan led from the start, increased his
lead at the end of the first lap, doubled it half-way through
the second, and finally, with a dazzling sprint in the last
seventy yards, lowered the Eckleton record by a second and
three-fifths, and gave his house three points. Kennedy, who
stuck gamely to his man for half the first lap, was beaten
on the tape by Crake, of Mulholland's. When sports' day
came, therefore, the score was School House three points,
Mulholland's two, Dencroft's one. The success of Mulholland's in the half was to the advantage of Dencroft's.
Mulholland's was not likely to score many more points, and
a place to them meant one or two points less to the School
House.

The sports opened all in favour of Dencroft's, but those
who knew drew no great consolation from this. School
sports always begin with the sprints, and these were
Dencroft's certainties. Fenn won the hundred yards as
easily as Milligan had won the half. Peel was second, and
a Beddell's man got third place. So that Dencroft's had
now six points to their rival's three. Ten minutes later they
had increased their lead by winning the first two places at
throwing the cricket ball, Fenn's throw beating Kennedy's
by ten yards, and Kennedy's being a few feet in front of
Jimmy Silver's, which, by gaining third place, represented
the only point Blackburn's managed to amass during the
afternoon.

It now began to dawn upon the School House that their
supremacy was seriously threatened. Dencroft's, by its
success in the football competition, had to a great extent
lived down the reputation the house had acquired when it
had been Kay's, but even now the notion of its winning a
cup seemed somehow vaguely improper. But the fact had

to be faced that it now led by eleven points to the School House's three.

"It's all right," said the School House, "our spot events haven't come off yet. Dencroft's can't get much more now."

And, to prove that they were right, the gap between the two scores began gradually to be filled up. Dencroft's struggled hard, but the School House total crept up and up. Maybury brought it to six by winning the high jump. This was only what had been expected of him. The discomforting part of the business was that the other two places were filled by Morrell, of Mulholland's, and Smith, of Daly's. And when, immediately afterwards, Maybury won the weight, with another School House man second, leaving Dencroft's with third place only, things began to look black for the latter. They were now only one point ahead, and there was the mile to come : and Milligan could give any Dencroftian a hundred yards at that distance.

But to balance the mile there was the quarter, and in the mile Kennedy contrived to beat Crake by much the same number of feet as Crake had beaten him by in the half. The scores of the two houses were now level, and a goodly number of the School House certainties were past.

Dencroft's forged ahead again by virtue of the quarter-mile. Fenn won it; Peel was second; and a dark horse from Denny's got in third. With the greater part of the sports over, and a lead of five points to their name, Dencroft's could feel more comfortable. The hurdle-race was productive of some discomfort. Fenn should have won it, as being blessed with twice the pace of any of his opponents. But Maybury, the jumper, made up for lack of pace by the scientific way in which he took his hurdles, and won off him by a couple of feet. Smith, Dencroft's second string, finished third, thus leaving the totals unaltered by the race.

By this time the public had become alive to the fact that

Dencroft's were making a great fight for the cup. They had noticed that Dencroft's colours always seemed to be coming in near the head of the procession, but the School House had made the cup so much their own, that it took some time for the school to realise that another house—especially the late Kay's—was running them hard for first place. Then, just before the hurdle-race, fellows with "correct cards" hastily totted up the points each house had won up-to-date. To the general amazement it was found that, while the School House had fourteen, Dencroft's had reached nineteen, and, barring the long run to be decided on the Monday, there was nothing now that the School House must win without dispute.

A house that will persist in winning a cup year after year has to pay for it when challenged by a rival. Dencroft's instantly became warm favourites. Whenever Dencroft's brown and gold appeared at the scratch, the school shouted for it wildly till the event was over. By the end of the day the totals were more nearly even, but Dencroft's were still ahead. They had lost on the long jump, but not unexpectedly. The totals at the finish were, School House twenty-three, Dencroft's twenty-five. Everything now depended on the long run.

"We might do it," said Kennedy to Fenn, as they changed. "Milligan's a cert for three points, of course, but if we can only get two we win the cup."

"There's one thing about the long run," said Fenn; "you never quite know what's going to happen. Milligan might break down over one of the hedges or the brook. There's no telling."

Kennedy felt that such a remote possibility was something of a broken reed to lean on. He had no expectation of beating the School House long distance runner, but he hoped for second place; and second place would mean the cup, for there was nobody to beat either himself or Crake.

The distance of the long run was as nearly as possible

five miles. The course was across country to the village of Ledby in a sort of semicircle of three and a half miles, and then back to the school gates by road. Every Eckletonian who ran at all knew the route by heart. It was the recognised training run if you wanted to train particularly hard. If you did not, you took a shorter spin. At the milestone nearest the school—it was about half a mile from the gates —a good number of fellows used to wait to see the first of the runners and pace their men home. But, as a rule, there were few really hot finishes in the long run. The man who got to Ledby first generally kept the advantage, and came in a long way ahead of the field.

On this occasion the close fight Kennedy and Crake had had in the mile and the half, added to the fact that Kennedy had only to get second place to give Dencroft's the cup, lent a greater interest to the race than usual. The crowd at the milestone was double the size of the one in the previous year, when Milligan had won for the first time. And when, amidst howls of delight from the School House, the same runner ran past the stone with his long, effortless stride, before any of the others were in sight, the crowd settled down breathlessly to watch for the second man.

Then a yell, to which the other had been nothing, burst from the School House as a white figure turned the corner. It was Crake. Waddling rather than running, and breathing in gasps; but still Crake. He toiled past the crowd at the milestone.

"By Jove, he looks bad," said someone.

And, indeed, he looked very bad. But he was ahead of Kennedy. That was the great thing.

He had passed the stone by thirty yards, when the cheering broke out again. Kennedy this time, in great straits, but in better shape than Crake. Dencroft's in a body trotted along at the side of the road, shouting as they went. Crake, hearing the shouts, looked round, almost fell, and then pulled himself together and staggered on again.

There were only a hundred yards to go now, and the school gates were in sight at the end of a long lane of spectators. They looked to Kennedy like two thick, black hedges. He could not sprint, though a hundred voices were shouting to him to do so. It was as much as he could do to keep moving. Only his will enabled him to run now. He meant to get to the gates, if he had to crawl.

The hundred yards dwindled to fifty, and he had diminished Crake's lead by a third. Twenty yards from the gates, and he was only half-a-dozen yards behind.

Crake looked round again, and this time did what he had nearly done before. His legs gave way; he rolled over; and there he remained, with the School House watching him in silent dismay, while Kennedy went on and pitched in a heap on the other side of the gates.

"Feeling bad?" said Jimmy Silver, looking in that evening to make inquiries.

"I'm feeling good," said Kennedy.

"That the cup?" asked Jimmy.

Kennedy took the huge cup from the table.

"That's it. Milligan has just brought it round. Well, they can't say they haven't had their fair share of it. Look here. School House. School House. School House. School House. Daly's. School House. Denny's. School House. School House. *Ad infinitum.*"

They regarded the trophy in silence.

"First pot the house has won," said Kennedy at length. "The very first."

"It won't be the last," returned Jimmy Silver, with decision.

THE WHITE FEATHER

To
MY BROTHER
DICK

The time of this story is a year and a term later than that of *The Gold Bat*. The history of Wrykyn in between these two books is dealt with in a number of short stories, some of them brainy in the extreme, which have appeared in various magazines. I wanted Messrs Black to publish these, but they were light on their feet and kept away—a painful exhibition of the White Feather.

P. G. WODEHOUSE

CONTENTS

I

"With apologies to gent opposite," said Clowes, "I must say I don't think much of the team."

"Don't apologise to *me*," said Allardyce disgustedly, as he filled the teapot, "I think they're rotten."

"They ought to have got into form by now, too," said Trevor. "It's not as if this was the first game of the term."

"First game!" Allardyce laughed shortly. "Why, we've only got a couple of club matches and the return match with Ripton to end the season. It is about time they got into form, as you say."

Clowes stared pensively into the fire.

"They struck me," he said, "as the sort of team who'd get into form somewhere in the middle of the cricket season."

"That's about it," said Allardyce. "Try those biscuits, Trevor. They're about the only good thing left in the place."

"School isn't what it was?" inquired Trevor, plunging a hand into the tin that stood on the floor beside him.

"No," said Allardyce, "not only in footer but in everything. The place seems absolutely rotten. It's bad enough losing all our matches, or nearly all. Did you hear that Ripton took thirty-seven points off us last term? And we only just managed to beat Greenburgh by a try to nil."

"We got thirty points last year," he went on. "Thirty-three, and forty-two the year before. Why, we've always simply walked them. It's an understood thing that we smash them. And this year they held us all the time, and it was only a fluke that we scored at all. Their back mis-kicked, and let Barry in."

"Barry struck me as the best of the outsides today," said Clowes. "He's heavier than he was, and faster."

"He's all right," agreed Allardyce. "If only the centres would feed him, we might do something occasionally. But did you ever see such a pair of rotters?"

"The man who was marking me certainly didn't seem particularly brilliant. I don't even know his name. He didn't do anything at footer in my time," said Trevor.

"He's a chap called Attell. He wasn't here with you. He came after the summer holidays. I believe he was sacked from somewhere. He's no good, but there's nobody else. Colours have been simply a gift this year to anyone who can do a thing. Only Barry and myself left from last year's team. I never saw such a clearance as there was after the summer term."

"Where are the boys of the Old Brigade?" sighed Clowes.

"I don't know. I wish they were here," said Allardyce.

Trevor and Clowes had come down, after the Easter term had been in progress for a fortnight, to play for an Oxford A team against the school. The match had resulted in an absurdly easy victory for the visitors by over forty points. Clowes had scored five tries off his own bat, and Trevor, if he had not fed his wing so conscientiously, would probably have scored an equal number. As it was, he had got through twice, and also dropped a goal. The two were now having a late tea with Allardyce in his study. Allardyce had succeeded Trevor as Captain of Football at Wrykyn, and had found the post anything but a sinecure.

For Wrykyn had fallen for the time being on evil days. It was experiencing the reaction which so often takes place in a school in the year following a season of exceptional athletic prosperity. With Trevor as captain of football, both the Ripton matches had been won, and also three out of the four other school matches. In cricket the eleven had had an even finer record, winning all their school matches, and likewise beating the M.C.C. and Old Wrykinians. It was too early to prophesy concerning the fortunes of next term's cricket team, but, if they were going to resemble the fifteen, Wrykyn was doomed to the worst athletic year it had experienced for a decade.

"It's a bit of a come-down after last season, isn't it?" resumed Allardyce, returning to his sorrows. It was a relief to him to discuss his painful case without restraint.

"We were a fine team last year," agreed Clowes, "and especially strong on the left wing. By the way, I see you've moved Barry across."

"Yes. Attell can't pass much, but he passes better from right to left than from left to right; so, Barry being our scoring man, I shifted him across. The chap on the other wing, Stanning, isn't bad at times. Do you remember him? He's in Appleby's. Then Drummond's useful at half."

"Jolly useful," said Trevor. "I thought he would be. I recommended you last year to keep your eye on him."

"Decent chap, Drummond," said Clowes.

"About the only one there is left in the place," observed Allardyce gloomily.

"Our genial host," said Clowes, sawing at the cake, "appears to have that tired feeling. He seems to have lost that *joie de vivre* of his, what?"

"It must be pretty sickening," said Trevor sympathetically. "I'm glad I wasn't captain in a bad year."

"The rummy thing is that the worse they are, the more side they stick on. You see chaps who wouldn't have been in the third in a good year walking about in first fifteen blazers, and first fifteen scarves, and first fifteen stockings, and sweaters with first fifteen colours round the edges. I wonder they don't tattoo their faces with first fifteen colours."

"It would improve some of them," said Clowes.

Allardyce resumed his melancholy remarks. "But, as I was saying, it's not only that the footer's rotten. That you can't help, I suppose. It's the general beastliness of things that I bar. Rows with the town, for instance. We've been having them on and off ever since you left. And it'll be worse now, because there's an election coming off soon. Are you fellows stopping for the night in the town? If so, I should advise you to look out for yourselves."

"Thanks," said Clowes. "I shouldn't like to see Trevor sand-bagged. Nor indeed, should I—for choice—care to be sand-bagged myself. But, as it happens, the good Donaldson is putting us up, so we escape the perils of the town."

"Everybody seems so beastly slack now," continued Allardyce. "It's considered the thing. You're looked on as an awful blood if you say you haven't done a stroke of work for a week. I shouldn't mind that so much if they were some good at anything. But they can't do a thing. The footer's rotten, the gymnasium six is made up of kids an inch high—we shall probably be about ninetieth at the Public Schools' Competition—and there isn't any one who can play racquets for nuts. The only thing that Wrykyn'll do this year is to get the Light-Weights at Aldershot. Drummond ought to manage that. He won the Feathers last time. He's nearly a stone heavier now, and awfully good. But he's the only man we shall send up, I expect. Now that O'Hara and Moriarty are both gone, he's the only chap we have who's up to Aldershot form. And nobody else'll take the trouble to practice. They're all too slack."

"In fact," said Clowes, getting up, "as was only to be expected, the school started going to the dogs directly I left. We shall have to be pushing on now, Allardyce. We promised to look in on Seymour before we went to bed. Friend let us away."

"Good night," said Allardyce.

"What you want," said Clowes solemnly, "is a liver pill. You are looking on life too gloomily. Take a pill. Let there be no stint. Take two. Then we shall hear your merry laugh ringing through the old cloisters once more. Buck up and be a bright and happy lad, Allardyce."

"Take more than a pill to make me that," growled that soured footballer.

Mr Seymour's views on the school resembled those of Allardyce. Wrykyn, in his opinion, was suffering from a reaction.

"It's always the same," he said, "after a very good year. Boys leave, and it's hard to fill their places. I must say I did not expect quite such a clearing out after the summer. We have had bad luck in that way. Maurice, for instance, and Robinson both ought to have had another year at school. It was quite unexpected, their leaving. They would have made all the difference to the forwards. You must have somebody to lead the pack who has had a little experience of first fifteen matches."

"But even then" said Clowes, "they oughtn't to be so rank as they were this afternoon. They seemed such slackers."

"I'm afraid that's the failing of the school just now," agreed Mr Seymour. "They don't play themselves out. They don't put just that last ounce into their work which makes all the difference."

Clowes thought of saying that, to judge by appearances, they did not put in even the first ounce; but refrained. However low an opinion a games' master may have—and even express—of his team, he does not like people to agree too cordially with his criticisms.

"Allardyce seems rather sick about it," said Trevor.

"I am sorry for Allardyce. It is always unpleasant to be the only survivor of an exceptionally good team. He can't forget last year's matches, and suffers continual disappointments because the present team does not play up to the same form."

"He was saying something about rows with the town," said Trevor, after a pause.

"Yes, there has certainly been some unpleasantness lately. It is the penalty we pay for being on the outskirts of a town. Four years out of five nothing happens. But in the fifth, when the school has got a little out of hand—"

"Oh, then it really *has* got out of hand?" asked Clowes.

"Between ourselves, yes," admitted Mr Seymour.

"What sort of rows?" asked Trevor.

Mr Seymour couldn't explain exactly. Nothing, as it were, definite—as yet. No actual complaints so far. But still—well, trouble—yes, trouble.

"For instance," he said, "a boy in my house, Linton—you remember him?—is moving in society at this moment with a swollen lip and minus a front tooth. Of course, I know nothing about it, but I fancy he got into trouble in the town. That is merely a straw which shows how the wind is blowing, but if you lived on the spot you would see more what I mean. There is trouble in the air. And now that this election is coming on, I should not wonder if things came to a head. I can't remember a single election in Wrykyn when there was not disorder in the town. And if the school is going to join in, as it probably will, I shall not be sorry when the holidays come. I know the headmaster is only waiting for an excuse to put the town out of bounds.'

"But the kids have always had a few rows on with that school in the High Street—what's it's name—St Something?" said Clowes.

"Jude's," supplied Trevor.

"St Jude's!" said Mr Seymour. "Have they? I didn't know that."

"Oh yes. I don't know how it started, but it's been going on for two or three years now. It's a School House feud really, but Dexter's are mixed up in it somehow. If a School House fag goes down town he runs like an antelope along the High Street, unless he's got one or two friends with him. I saved dozens of kids from destruction when I was at school. The St Jude's fellows lie in wait, and dash out on them. I used to find School House fags fighting for their lives in back alleys. The enemy fled on my approach. My air of majesty overawed them."

"But a junior school feud matters very little," said Mr Seymour. "You say it has been going on for three years; and I have never heard of it till now. It is when the bigger fellows get mixed up with the town that we have to interfere. I wish the headmaster would put the place out of bounds entirely until the election is over. Except at election time, the town seems to go to sleep."

"That's what we ought to be doing," said Clowes to Trevor. "I think we had better be off now, sir. We promised Mr Donaldson to be in some time tonight."

"It's later than I thought," said Mr Seymour. "Good night, Clowes. How many tries was it that you scored this afternoon? Five? I wish you were still here, to score them for instead of against us. Good night, Trevor. I was glad to see they tried you for Oxford, though you didn't get your blue. You'll be in next year all right. Good night."

The two Old Wrykinians walked along the road towards Donaldson's. It was a fine night, but misty.

"Jove, I'm quite tired," said Clowes. "Hullo!"

"What's up?"

They were opposite Appleby's at the moment. Clowes drew him into the shadow of the fence.

"There's a chap breaking out. I saw him shinning down a rope. Let's wait, and see who it is."

A moment later somebody ran softly through the gateway and disappeared down the road that led to the town.

"Who was it? said Trevor. "I couldn't see."

"I spotted him all right. It was that chap who was marking me today, Stanning. Wonder what he's after. Perhaps he's gone to tar the statue, like O'Hara. Rather a sportsman."

"Rather a silly idiot," said Trevor. "I hope he gets caught."

"You always were one of those kind sympathetic chaps," said Clowes. "Come on, or Donaldson'll be locking us out."

II

SHEEN AT HOME

On the afternoon following the Oxford A match, Sheen, of
Seymour's, was sitting over the gas-stove in his study with
a Thucydides. He had been staying in that day with a cold.
He was always staying in. Everyone has his hobby. That
was Sheen's.

Nobody at Wrykyn, even at Seymour's, seemed to know
Sheen very well, with the exception of Drummond; and
those who troubled to think about the matter at all rather
wondered what Drummond saw in him. To the superficial
observer the two had nothing in common. Drummond was
good at games—he was in the first fifteen and the second
eleven, and had won the Feather Weights at Aldershot—
and seemed to have no interests outside them. Sheen, on
the other hand, played fives for the house, and that was all.
He was bad at cricket, and had given up football by special
arrangement with Allardyce, on the plea that he wanted all
his time for work. He was in for an in-school scholarship,
the Gotford. Allardyce, though professing small sympathy
with such a degraded ambition, had given him a special
dispensation, and since then Sheen had retired from public
life even more than he had done hitherto. The examination
for the Gotford was to come off towards the end of the
term.

The only other Wrykinians with whom Sheen was known
to be friendly were Stanning and Attell, of Appleby's. And
here those who troubled to think about it wondered still
more, for Sheen, whatever his other demerits, was not of the
type of Stanning and Attell. There are certain members of
every public school, just as there are certain members of
every college at the universities, who are "marked men".
They have never been detected in any glaring breach of the

rules, and their manner towards the powers that be is, as a rule, suave, even deferential. Yet it is one of the things which everybody knows, that they are in the black books of the authorities, and that sooner or later, in the picturesque phrase of the New Yorker, they will "get it in the neck". To this class Stanning and Attell belonged. It was plain to all that the former was the leading member of the firm. A glance at the latter was enough to show that, whatever ambitions he may have had in the direction of villainy, he had not the brains necessary for really satisfactory evil-doing, As for Stanning, he pursued an even course of life, always rigidly obeying the eleventh commandment, "thou shalt not be found out". This kept him from collisions with the authorities; while a ready tongue and an excellent knowledge of the art of boxing—he was, after Drummond, the best Light-Weight in the place—secured him at least tolerance at the hand of the school : and, as a matter of fact, though most of those who knew him disliked him, and particularly those who, like Drummond, were what Clowes had called the Old Brigade, he had, nevertheless, a tolerably large following. A first fifteen man, even in a bad year, can generally find boys anxious to be seen about with him.

That Sheen should have been amongst these surprised one or two people, notably Mr Seymour, who, being games' master had come a good deal into contact with Stanning, and had not been favourably impressed. The fact was that the keynote of Sheen's character was a fear of giving offence. Within limits this is not a reprehensible trait in a person's character, but Sheen overdid it, and it frequently complicated his affairs. There come times when one has to choose which of two people one shall offend. By acting in one way, we offend A. By acting in the opposite way, we annoy B. Sheen had found himself faced by this problem when he began to be friendly with Drummond. Their acquaintance, begun over a game of fives, had progressed. Sheen admired Drummond, as the type of what he would have liked to have been, if he could have managed it. And Drummond felt interested in Sheen because nobody knew much about him. He was, in a way, mysterious. Also, he played the piano really well; and Drummond at that time would have courted anybody who could play for his benefit "Mumblin' Mose", and didn't mind obliging with unlimited encores.

So the two struck up an alliance, and as Drummond hated Stanning only a shade less than Stanning hated him, Sheen was under the painful necessity of choosing between them. He chose Drummond. Whereby he undoubtedly did wisely.

Sheen sat with his Thucydides over the gas-stove, and tried to interest himself in the doings of the Athenian expedition at Syracuse. His brain felt heavy and flabby. He realised dimly that this was because he took too little exercise, and he made a resolution to diminish his hours of work per diem by one, and to devote that one to fives. He would mention it to Drummond when he came in. He would probably come in to tea. The board was spread in anticipation of a visit from him. Herbert, the boot-boy, had been despatched to the town earlier in the afternoon, and had returned with certain food-stuffs which were now stacked in an appetising heap on the table.

Sheen was just making something more or less like sense out of an involved passage of Nikias' speech, in which that eminent general himself seemed to have only a hazy idea of what he was talking about, when the door opened.

He looked up, expecting to see Drummond, but it was Stanning. He felt instantly that "warm shooting" sensation from which David Copperfield suffered in moments of embarrassment. Since the advent of Drummond he had avoided Stanning, and he could not see him without feeling uncomfortable. As they were both in the sixth form, and sat within a couple of yards of one another every day, it will be realised that he was frequently uncomfortable.

"Great Scott!" said Stanning, "swotting?"

Sheen glanced almost guiltily at his Thucydides. Still, it was something of a relief that the other had not opened the conversation with an indictment of Drummond.

"You see," he said apologetically, "I'm in for the Gotford."

"So am I. What's the good of swotting, though? I'm not going to do a stroke."

As Stanning was the only one of his rivals of whom he had any real fear, Sheen might have replied with justice that, if that was the case, the more he swotted the better. But he said nothing. He looked at the stove, and dog's-eared the Thucydides.

"What a worm you are, always staying in!" said Stanning.

"I caught a cold watching the match yesterday."

"You're as flabby as—" Stanning looked round for a simile, "as a dough-nut. Why don't you take some exercise?"

"I'm going to play fives, I think. I do need some exercise."

"Fives? Why don't you play footer?"

"I haven't time. I want to work."

"What rot. I'm not doing a stroke."

Stanning seemed to derive a spiritual pride from this admission.

"Tell you what, then," said Stanning, "I'll play you tomorrow after school.

Sheen looked a shade more uncomfortable, but he made an effort, and declined the invitation.

"I shall probably be playing Drummond," he said.

"Oh, all right," said Stanning. "*I* don't care. Play whom you like."

There was a pause.

"As a matter of fact," resumed Stanning, "what I came here for was to tell you about last night. I got out, and went to Mitchell's. Why didn't you come? Didn't you get my note? I sent a kid with it."

Mitchell was a young gentleman of rich but honest parents, who had left the school at Christmas. He was in his father's office, and lived in his father's house on the outskirts of the town. From time to time his father went up to London on matters connected with business, leaving him alone in the house. On these occasions Mitchell the younger would write to Stanning, with whom when at school he had been on friendly terms; and Stanning, breaking out of his house after everybody had gone to bed, would make his way to the Mitchell residence, and spend a pleasant hour or so there. Mitchell senior owned Turkish cigarettes and a billiard table. Stanning appreciated both. There was also a piano, and Stanning had brought Sheen with him one night to play it. The getting-out and the subsequent getting-in had nearly whitened Sheen's hair, and it was only by a series of miracles that he had escaped detection. Once, he felt, was more than enough; and when a fag from Appleby's had brought him Stanning's note, containing an invitation to a second jaunt of the kind, he had refused to be lured into the business again.

"Yes, I got the note," he said.

"Then why didn't you come? Mitchell was asking where you were."

"It's so beastly risky."

"Risky! Rot."

"We should get sacked if we were caught."

"Well, don't get caught, then."

Sheen registered an internal vow that he would not.

"He wanted us to go again on Monday. Will you come?"

"I—don't think I will, Stanning," said Sheen. "It isn't worth it."

"You mean you funk it. That's what's the matter with you."

"Yes, I do," admitted Sheen.

As a rule—in stories—the person who owns that he is afraid gets unlimited applause and adulation, and feels a glow of conscious merit. But with Sheen it was otherwise. The admission made him if possible, more uncomfortable than he had been before.

"Mitchell will be sick," said Stanning.

Sheen said nothing.

Stanning changed the subject.

"Well, at anyrate," he said, "give us some tea. You seem to have been victualling for a siege."

"I'm awfully sorry," said Sheen, turning a deeper shade

of red and experiencing a redoubled attack of the warm shooting, "but the fact is, I'm waiting for Drummond."

Stanning got up, and expressed his candid opinion of Drummond in a few words.

He said more. He described Sheen, too in unflattering terms.

"Look here," he said, "you may think it jolly fine to drop me just because you've got to know Drummond a bit, but you'll be sick enough that you've done it before you've finished."

"It isn't that—" began Sheen.

"I don't care what it is. You slink about trying to avoid me all day, and you won't do a thing I ask you to do."

"But you see—"

"Oh, shut up," said Stanning.

III

While Sheen had been interviewing Stanning, in study twelve, farther down the passage, Linton and his friend Dunstable, who was in Day's house, were discussing ways and means. Like Stanning, Dunstable had demanded tea, and had been informed that there was none for him.

"Well, you are a bright specimen, aren't you?" said Dunstable, seating himself on the table which should have been groaning under the weight of cake and biscuits. "I should like to know where you expect to go to. You lure me in here, and then have the cheek to tell me you haven't got anything to eat. What have you done with it all?"

"There was half a cake——"

"Bring it on."

"Young Menzies bagged it after the match yesterday. His brother came down with the Oxford A team, and he had to give him tea in his study. Then there were some biscuits——"

"What's the matter with biscuits? *They're* all right. Bring them on. Biscuits forward. Show biscuits."

"Menzies took them as well."

Dunstable eyed him sorrowfully.

You always were a bit of a maniac," he said, "but I never thought you were quite such a complete gibberer as to let Menzies get away with all your grub. Well, the only thing to do is to touch him for tea. He owes us one. Come on."

They proceeded down the passage and stopped at the door of study three.

"Hullo!" said Menzies, as they entered.

"We've come to tea," said Dunstable. "Cut the satisfying sandwich. Let's see a little more of that hissing urn of yours, Menzies. Bustle about, and be the dashing host."

"I wasn't expecting you."

"I can't help your troubles," said Dunstable.

"I've not got anything. I was thinking of coming to you, Linton."

"Where's that cake?"

"Finished. My brother simply walked into it."

"Greed," said Dunstable unkindly, "seems to be the besetting sin of the Menzies'. Well, what are you going to do about it? I don't wish to threaten, but I'm a demon when I'm roused. Being done out of my tea is sure to rouse me. And owing to unfortunate accident of being stonily broken, I can't go to the shop. You're responsible for the slump in provisions, Menzies, and you must see us through this. What are you going to do about it?"

"Do either of you chaps know Sheen at all?"

"I don't," said Linton. "Not to speak to."

"You can't expect us to know all your shady friends," said Dunstable. "Why?"

"He's got a tea on this evening. If you knew him well enough, you might borrow something from him. I met Herbert in the dinner-hour carrying in all sorts of things to his study. Still, if you don't know him——"

"Don't let a trifle of that sort stand in the way," said Dunstable. "Which is his study?"

"Come on, Linton," said Dunstable. "Be a man, and lead the way. Go in as if he'd invited us. Ten to one he'll think he did, if you don't spoil the thing by laughing."

"What, invite ourselves to tea?" asked Linton, beginning to grasp the idea.

"That's it. Sheen's the sort of ass who won't do a thing. Anyhow, its worth trying. Smith in our house got a tea out of him that way last term. Coming, Menzies?"

"Not much. I hope he kicks you out."

"Come on, then, Linton. If Menzies cares to chuck away a square meal, let him."

Thus, no sooner had the door of Sheen's study closed upon Stanning than it was opened again to admit Linton and Dunstable.

"Well," said Linton, affably, "here we are."

"Hope we're not late," said Dunstable. "You said some-where about five. It's just struck. Shall we start?"

He stooped, and took the kettle from the stove.

"Don't you bother," he said to Sheen, who had watched this manoeuvre with an air of amazement, "I'll do all the dirty work."

"But—" began Sheen.

"That's all right," said Dunstable soothingly. "I like it."

The intellectual pressure of the affair was too much for Sheen. He could not recollect having invited Linton, with whom he had exchanged only about a dozen words that term, much less Dunstable, whom he merely knew by sight. Yet here they were, behaving like honoured guests. It was plain that there was a misunderstanding somewhere, but he shrank from grappling with it. He did not want to hurt their feelings. It would be awkward enough if they dis-covered their mistake for themselves.

So he exerted himself nervously to play the host, and the first twinge of remorse which Linton felt came when Sheen pressed upon him a bag of biscuits which, he knew, could not have cost less than one and sixpence a pound. His heart warmed to one who could do the thing in such style.

Dunstable, apparently, was worried by no scruples. He leaned back easily in his chair, and kept up a bright flow of conversation.

"You're not looking well, Sheen," he said. "You ought to take more exercise. Why don't you come down town with us one of these days and do a bit of canvassing? It's a rag. Linton lost a tooth at it the other day. We're going down on Saturday to do a bit more."

"Oh!" said Sheen, politely.

"We shall get one or two more chaps to help next time. It isn't good enough, only us two. We had four great beefy hooligans on to us when Linton got his tooth knocked out. We had to run. There's a regular gang of them going about the town, now that the election's on. A red-headed fellow, who looks like a butcher, seems to boss the show. They call him Albert. He'll have to be slain one of these days, for the credit of the school. I should like to get Drummond on to him."

"I was expecting Drummond to tea," said Sheen.

"He's running and passing with the fifteen," said Linton. "He ought to be in soon. Why, here he is. Hullo, Drummond!"

"Hullo!" said the newcomer, looking at his two fellow-visitors as if he were surprised to see them there.

"How were the First?" asked Dunstable.

"Oh, rotten. Any tea left?"

Conversation flagged from this point, and shortly afterwards Dunstable and Linton went.

"Come and tea with me some time," said Linton.

"Oh, thanks," said Sheen. "Thanks awfully."

"It was rather a shame," said Linton to Dunstable, as they went back to their study, "rushing him like that. I shouldn't wonder if he's quite a good sort, when one gets to know him."

"He must be a rotter to let himself be rushed. By Jove, I should like to see someone try that game on with me."

In the study they had left, Drummond was engaged in pointing this out to Sheen.

"The First are rank bad," he said. "The outsides were passing rottenly today. We shall have another forty points taken off us when we play Ripton. By the way, I didn't know you were a pal of Linton's."

"I'm not," said Sheen.

"Well, he seemed pretty much at home just now."

"I can't understand it. I'm certain I never asked him to tea. Or Dunstable either. Yet they came in as if I had. I didn't like to hurt their feelings by telling them."

Drummond stared.

"What, they came without being asked! Heavens! man, you must buck up a bit and keep awake, or you'll have an awful time. Of course those two chaps were simply trying it on. I had an idea it might be that when I came in. Why did you let them? Why didn't you scrag them?"

"Oh, I don't know," said Sheen uncomfortably.

"But, look here, it's rot. You *must* keep your end up in a place like this, or everybody in the house'll be ragging you.

Chaps will, naturally, play the goat if you let them. Has this ever happened before?"

Sheen admitted reluctantly that it had. He was beginning to see things. It is never pleasant to feel one has been bluffed.

"Once last term," he said, "Smith, a chap in Day's, came to tea like that. I couldn't very well do anything."

"And Dunstable is in Day's. They compared notes. I wonder you haven't had the whole school dropping in on you, lining up in long queues down the passage. Look here, Sheen, you really must pull yourself together. I'm not ragging. You'll have a beastly time if you're so feeble. I hope you won't be sick with me for saying it, but I can't help that. It's all for your own good. And it's really pure slackness that's the cause of it all."

"I hate hurting people's feelings," said Sheen.

"Oh, rot. As if anybody here had any feelings. Besides, it doesn't hurt a chap's feelings being told to get out, when he knows he's no business in a place."

"Oh, all right," said Sheen shortly.

"Glad you see it," said Drummond. "Well, I'm off. Wonder if there's anybody in that bath.

He reappeared a few moments later. During his absence Sheen overheard certain shrill protestations which were apparently being uttered in the neighbourhood of the bath-room door.

"There was," he said, putting his head into the study and grinning cheerfully at Sheen. "There was young Renford, who had no earthly business to be there. I've just looked in to point the moral. Suppose you'd have let him bag all the hot water, which ought to have come to his elders and betters, for fear of hurting his feelings; and gone without your bath. I went on my theory that nobody at Wrykyn, least of all a fag, has any feelings. I turfed him out without a touch of remorse. You get much the best results my way. So long."

And the head disappeared; and shortly afterwards there came from across the passage muffled but cheerful sounds of splashing.

IV

The Better Part of Valour

The borough of Wrykyn had been a little unfortunate—or fortunate, according to the point of view—in the matter of elections. The latter point of view was that of the younger and more irresponsible section of the community, which liked elections because they were exciting. The former was that of the tradespeople, who disliked them because they got their windows broken.

Wrykyn had passed through an election and its attendant festivities in the previous year, when Sir Eustace Briggs, the mayor of the town, had been returned by a comfortable majority. Since then ill-health had caused that gentleman to resign his seat, and the place was once more in a state of unrest. This time the school was deeply interested in the matter. The previous election had not stirred them. They did not care whether Sir Eustace Briggs defeated Mr Saul Pedder, or whether Mr Saul Pedder wiped the political floor with Sir Eustace Briggs. Mr Pedder was an energetic Radical; but owing to the fact that Wrykyn had always returned a Conservative member, and did not see its way to a change as yet, his energy had done him very little good. The school had looked on him as a sportsman, and read his speeches in the local paper with amusement; but they were not interested. Now, however, things were changed. The Conservative candidate, Sir William Bruce, was one of themselves—an Old Wrykinian, a governor of the school, a man who always watched school-matches, and the donor of the Bruce Challenge Cup for the school mile. In fine, one of the best. He was also the father of Jack Bruce, a day-boy on the engineering side. The school would have liked to have made a popular hero of Jack Bruce. If he had liked, he could have gone about with quite a suite of retainers. But he was a quiet, self-sufficing youth, and was rarely to be seen in public. The engineering side of a public school has workshops and other weirdnesses which keep it occupied after the ordinary school hours. It was generally understood that Bruce was a good sort of chap if you knew him, but you had got to know him first; brilliant at his work, and devoted to it; a useful slow bowler; known to be able to drive and repair the family motor-car; one who seldom spoke unless spoken to, but who, when he did speak, generally had something sensible to say. Beyond that, report said little.

As he refused to allow the school to work off its enthusiasm on him, they were obliged to work it off elsewhere. Hence the disturbances which had become frequent between school and town. The inflammatory speeches of Mr Saul Pedder had caused a swashbuckling spirit to spread among the rowdy element of the town. Gangs of youths, to adopt the police-court term, had developed a habit of parading the streets arm-in-arm, shouting "Good old Pedder!" When these met some person or persons who did not consider Mr Pedder good and old, there was generally what the local police-force described as a "frakkus".

It was in one of these frakkuses that Linton had lost a valuable tooth.

Two days had elapsed since Dunstable and Linton had looked in on Sheen for tea. It was a Saturday afternoon, and roll-call was just over. There was no first fifteen match, only a rather uninteresting house-match, Templar's *versus* Donaldson's, and existence in the school grounds showed signs of becoming tame.

"What a beastly term the Easter term is," said Linton, yawning. "There won't be a thing to do till the house-matches begin properly."

Seymour's had won their first match, as had Day's. They would not be called upon to perform for another week or more.

"Let's get a boat out," suggested Dunstable.

"Such a beastly day."

"Let's have tea at the shop."

"Rather slow. How about going to Cook's?"

"All right. Toss you who pays."

Cook's was a shop in the town to which the school most resorted when in need of refreshment.

"Wonder if we shall meet Albert."

Linton licked the place where his tooth should have been, and said he hoped so.

Sergeant Cook, the six-foot proprietor of the shop, was examining a broken window when they arrived, and muttering to himself.,

"Hullo!" said Dunstable, "what's this? New idea for ventilation? Golly, massa, who frew dat brick?"

"Done it at ar-parse six last night, he did," said Sergeant Cook, "the red-'eaded young scallywag. Ketch 'im—I'll give 'im—"

"Sounds like dear old Albert," said Linton. "Who did it, sergeant?"

"Red-headed young mongrel. 'Good old Pedder,' he says. 'I'll give you Pedder,' I says. Then bang it comes right on top of the muffins, and when I doubled out after 'im 'e'd gone."

Mrs Cook appeared and corroborated witness's evidence. Dunstable ordered tea.

"We may meet him on our way home," said Linton. "If we do, I'll give him something from you with your love. I owe him a lot for myself."

Mrs Cook clicked her tongue compassionately at the sight of the obvious void in the speaker's mouth.

"You'll 'ave to 'ave a forlse one, Mr Linton," said Sergeant Cook with gloomy relish.

The back shop was empty. Dunstable and Linton sat down and began tea. Sergeant Cook came to the door from time to time and dilated further on his grievances.

"Gentlemen from the school they come in 'ere and says ain't it all a joke and exciting and what not. But I says to them, you 'aven't got to live in it, I says. That's what it is. You 'aven't got to live in it, I says. Glad when it's all over, that's what I'll be."

" 'Nother jug of hot water, please," said Linton.

The Sergeant shouted the order over his shoulder, as if he were addressing a half-company on parade, and returned to his woes.

"You 'aven't got to live in it, I says. That's what it is. It's this everlasting worry and flurry day in and day out, and not knowing what's going to 'appen next, and one man coming in and saying 'Vote for Bruce', and another 'Vote for Pedder', and another saying how it's the poor man's loaf he's fighting for—if he'd only *buy* a loaf, now—'ullo, 'ullo, wot's this?"

There was a "confused noise without", as Shakespeare would put it, and into the shop came clattering Barry and McTodd, of Seymour's, closely followed by Stanning and Attell.

"This is getting a bit too thick," said Barry, collapsing into a chair.

From the outer shop came the voice of Sergeant Cook.

"Let me jest come to you, you red-'eaded—"

Roars of derision from the road.

"That's Albert," said Linton, jumping up.

"Yes, I heard them call him that," said Barry. "McTodd and I were coming down here to tea, when they started going for us, so we nipped in here, hoping to find reinforcements."

"We were just behind you," said Stanning. "I got one of them a beauty. He went down like a shot."

"Albert?" inquired Linton.

"No. A little chap."

"Let's go out, and smash them up," suggested Linton excitedly.

Dunstable treated the situation more coolly.

"Wait a bit," he said. "No hurry. Let's finish tea at any rate. You'd better eat as much as you can now Linton. You may have no teeth left to do it with afterwards," he added cheerfully.

"Let's chuck things at them," said McTodd.

"Don't be an ass," said Barry. "What on earth's the good of that?"

"Well, it would be something," said McTodd vaguely.

"Hit 'em with a muffin," suggested Stanning. "Dash, I barked my knuckles on that man. But I bet he felt it."

"Look here, I'm going out," said Linton. "Come on, Dunstable."

Dunstable continued his meal without hurry.

"What's the excitement?" he said. "There's plenty of time. Dear old Albert's not the sort of chap to go away when he's got us cornered here. The first principle of warfare is to get a good feed before you start."

"And anyhow," said Barry, "I came here for tea, and I'm going to have it."

Sergeant Cook was recalled from the door, and received the orders.

"They've just gone round the corner," he said, "and that red-'eaded one 'e says he's goin' to wait if he 'as to wait all night."

"Quite right," said Dunstable, approvingly. "Sensible chap, Albert. If you see him, you might tell him we shan't be long, will you?"

A quarter of an hour passed.

"Kerm out," shouted a voice from the street.

Dunstable looked at the others.

"Perhaps we might be moving now," he said, getting up "Ready?"

"We must keep together," said Barry.

"You goin' out, Mr Dunstable?" inquired Sergeant Cook.

"Yes. Good bye. You'll see that we're decently buried won't you?"

The garrison made its sortie.

It happened that Drummond and Sheen were also among those whom it had struck that afternoon that tea at Cook's would be pleasant; and they came upon the combatants some five minutes after battle had been joined. The town contingent were filling the air with strange cries, Albert's voice being easily heard above the din, while the Wrykinians, as public-school men should, were fighting quietly and without unseemly tumult.

"By Jove," said Drummond, "here's a row on."

Sheen stopped dead, with a queer, sinking feeling within him. He gulped. Drummond did not notice these portents. He was observing the battle.

Suddenly he uttered an exclamation.

"Why, it's some of our chaps! There's a Seymour's cap. Isn't that McTodd? And, great Scott! there's Barry. Come on, man!"

Sheen did not move.

"Ought we . . . to get . . . mixed up . . . ?" he began.

Drummond looked at him with open eyes. Sheen babbled on.

"The old man might not like—sixth form, you see—oughtn't we to—?"

There was a yell of triumph from the town army as the red-haired Albert, plunging through the fray, sent Barry staggering against the wall. Sheen caught a glimpse of Albert's grinning face as he turned. He had a cut over one eye. It bled.

"Come on," said Drummond, beginning to run to the scene of action.

Sheen paused for a moment irresolutely. Then he walked rapidly in the opposite direction.

V

THE WHITE FEATHER

It was not until he had reached his study that Sheen
thoroughly realised what he had done. All the way home
he had been defending himself eloquently against an
imaginary accuser; and he had built up a very sound,
thoughtful, and logical series of arguments to show that he
was not only not to blame for what he had done, but had
acted in highly statesmanlike and praiseworthy manner.
After all, he was in the sixth. Not a prefect, it was true,
but, still, practically a prefect. The headmaster disliked
unpleasantness between school and town, much more so
between the sixth form of the school and the town. Therefore, he had done his duty in refusing to be drawn into a
fight with Albert and friends. Besides, why should he be
expected to join in whenever he saw a couple of fellows
fighting? It wasn't reasonable. It was no business of his.
Why, it was absurd. He had no quarrel with those fellows.
It wasn't cowardice. It was simply that he had kept his
head better than Drummond, and seen further into the
matter. Besides . . .

But when he sat down in his chair, this mood changed.
There is a vast difference between the view one takes of
things when one is walking briskly, and that which comes
when one thinks the thing over coldly. As he sat there, the
wall of defence which he had built up slipped away brick
by brick, and there was the fact staring at him, without
covering or disguise.

It was no good arguing against himself. No amount of
argument could wipe away the truth. He had been afraid,
and had shown it. And he had shown it when, in a sense,
he was representing the school, when Wrykyn looked to
him to help it keep its end up against the town.

The more he reflected, the more he saw how far-reaching were the consequences of that failure in the hour of need. He had disgraced himself. He had disgraced Seymour's. He had disgraced the school. He was an outcast.

This mood, the natural reaction from his first glow of almost jaunty self-righteousness, lasted till the lock-up bell rang, when it was succeeded by another. This time he took a more reasonable view of the affair. It occurred to him that there was a chance that his defection had passed unnoticed. Nothing could make his case seem better in his own eyes, but it might be that the thing would end there. The house might not have lost credit.

An overwhelming curiosity seized him to find out how it had all ended. The ten minutes of grace which followed the ringing of the lock-up bell had passed. Drummond and the rest must be back by now.

He went down the passage to Drummond's study. Somebody was inside. He could hear him.

He knocked at the door.

Drummond was sitting at the table reading. He looked up, and there was a silence. Sheen's mouth felt dry. He could not think how to begin. He noticed that Drummond's face was unmarked. Looking down, he saw that one of the knuckles of the hand that held the book was swollen and cut.

"Drummond, I—"

Drummond lowered the book.

"Get out," he said. He spoke without heat, calmly, as if he were making some conventional remark by way of starting a conversation.

"I only came to ask—"

"Get out," said Drummond again.

There was another pause. Drummond raised his book and went on reading.

Sheen left the room.

Outside he ran into Linton. Unlike Drummond, Linton bore marks of the encounter. As in the case of the hero of Calverley's poem, one of his speaking eyes was sable. The swelling of his lip was increased. There was a deep red bruise on his forehead. In spite of these injuries, however, he was cheerful. He was whistling when Sheen collided with him.

"Sorry," said Linton, and went on into the study.

"Well," he said, "how are you feeling, Drummond? Lucky beggar, you haven't got a mark. I wish I could duck like you. Well, we have fought the good fight. Exit Albert —sweep him up. You gave him enough to last him for the rest of the term. I couldn't tackle the brute. He's as strong as a horse. My word, it was lucky you happened to come up. Albert was making hay of us. Still, all's well that ends well. We have smitten the Philistines this day. By the way—"

"What's up now?"

"Who was that chap with you when you came up?"

"Which chap?"

"I thought I saw some one."

"You shouldn't eat so much tea. You saw double."

"There wasn't anybody?"

"No," said Drummond.

"Not Sheen?"

"No," said Drummond, irritably. "How many more times do you want me to say it?"

"All right," said Linton, "I only asked I met him outside."

"Who?"

"Sheen."

"Oh!"

"You might be sociable."

"I know I might. But I want to read."

"Lucky man. Wish I could. I can hardly see. Well, good bye, then. I'm off."

"Good," grunted Drummond. "You know your way out, don't you?"

Linton went back to his own study.

"It's all very well," he said to himself, "for Drummond to deny it, but I'll swear I saw Sheen with him. So did Dunstable. I'll cut out and ask him about it after prep. If he really was there, and cut off, something ought to be done about it. The chap ought to be kicked. He's a disgrace to the house."

Dunstable, questioned after preparation, refused to commit himself.

"I thought I saw somebody with Drummond," he said, "and I had a sort of idea it was Sheen. Still, I was pretty busy at the time, and wasn't paying much attention to anything, except that long, thin bargee with the bowler. I wish those men would hit straight. It's beastly difficult to guard a round-arm swing. My right ear feels like a cauliflower. Does it look rum?"

"Beastly. But what about this? You can't swear to Sheen then?"

"No. Better give him the benefit of the doubt. What does Drummond say? You ought to ask him."

"I have. He says he was alone."

"Well, that settles it. What an ass you are. If Drummond doesn't know, who does?"

"I believe he's simply hushing it up."

"Well, let us hush it up, too. It's no good bothering about it. We licked them all right."

"But it's such a beastly thing for the house."

"Then why the dickens do you want it to get about? Surely the best thing you can do is to dry up and say nothing about it."

"But something ought to be done."

"What's the good of troubling about a man like Sheen? He never was any good, and this doesn't make him very much worse. Besides, he'll probably be sick enough on his own account. I know I should, if I'd done it. And, anyway, we don't know that he did do it."

"I'm certain he did. I could swear it was him."

"Anyhow, for goodness' sake let the thing drop."

"All right. But I shall cut him."

"Well, that would be punishment enough for anybody, whatever he'd done. Fancy existence without your bright conversation. It doesn't bear thinking of. You do look a freak with that eye and that lump on your forehead. You ought to wear a mask."

"That ear of yours," said Linton with satisfaction, "will be about three times its ordinary size tomorrow. And it always was too large. Good night."

On his way back to Seymour's Mason of Appleby's, who was standing at his house gate imbibing fresh air, preparatory to going to bed, accosted him.

"I say, Linton," he said, "—hullo, you look a wreck, don't you! — I say, what's all this about your house?"

"What about my house?"

"Funking, and all that. Sheen, you know. Stanning has just been telling me."

"Then he saw him, too!" exclaimed Linton, involuntarily.

"Oh, it's true, then? Did he really cut off like that? Stanning said he did, but I wouldn't believe him at first. You aren't going? Good night."

So the thing was out. Linton had not counted on Stanning having seen what he and Dunstable had seen. It was impossible to hush it up now. The scutcheon of Seymour's was definitely blotted. The name of the house was being held up to scorn in Appleby's probably everywhere else as well. It was a nuisance, thought Linton, but it could not be helped. After all, it was a judgment on the house for harbouring such a specimen as Sheen.

In Seymour's there was tumult and an impromptu indignation meeting. Stanning had gone to work scientifically. From the moment that, ducking under the guard of a sturdy town youth, he had caught sight of Sheen retreating from the fray, he had grasped the fact that here, readymade, was his chance of working off his grudge against him. All he had to do was to spread the news abroad, and the school would do the rest. On his return from the town he had mentioned the facts of the case to one or two of the more garrulous members of his house, and they had passed it on to everybody they met during the interval in the middle of preparation. By the end of preparation half the school knew what had happened.

Seymour's was furious. The senior day-room to a man condemned Sheen. The junior day-room was crimson in the face and incoherent. The demeanour of a junior in moments of excitement generally lacks that repose which marks the philosopher.

"He ought to be kicked," shrilled Renford.

"We shall get rotted by those kids in Dexter's," moaned Harvey.

"Disgracing the house!" thundered Watson.

"Let's go and chuck things at his door," suggested Renford.

A move was made to the passage in which Sheen's study was situated, and, with divers groans and howls, the junior day-room hove football boots and cricket stumps at the door.

The success of the meeting, however, was entirely neutralised by the fact that in the same passage stood the study of Rigby, the head of the house. Also Rigby was trying at the moment to turn into idiomatic Greek verse the words : "The Days of Peace and Slumberous calm have fled", and this corroboration of the statement annoyed him to the extent of causing him to dash out and sow lines among the revellers like some monarch scattering largesse. The junior day-room retired to its lair to inveigh against the brutal ways of those in authority, and begin working off the commission it had received.

The howls in the passage were the first official intimation Sheen had received that his shortcomings were public property. The word "Funk!" shouted through his keyhole, had not unnaturally given him an inkling as to the state of affairs.

So Drummond had given him away, he thought. Probably he had told Linton the whole story the moment after he, Sheen, had met the latter at the door of the study. And perhaps he was now telling it to the rest of the house. Of all the mixed sensations from which he suffered as he went to his dormitory that night, one of resentment against Drummond was the keenest.

Sheen was in the fourth dormitory, where the majority of the day-room slept. He was in the position of a sort of extra house prefect, as far as the dormitory was concerned. It was a large dormitory, and Mr Seymour had fancied that it might, perhaps, be something of a handful for a single prefect. As a matter of fact, however, Drummond, who was in charge, had shown early in the term that he was more than capable of managing the place single handed. He was popular and determined. The dormitory was orderly, partly because it liked him, principally because it had to be.

He had an opportunity of exhibiting his powers of control that night. When Sheen came in, the room was full. Drummond was in bed, reading his novel. The other ornaments of the dormitory were in various stages of undress.

As Sheen appeared, a sudden hissing broke out from the farther corner of the room. Sheen flushed, and walked to his bed. The hissing increased in volume and richness.

"Shut up that noise," said Drummond, without looking up from his book.

The hissing diminished. Only two or three of the more reckless kept it up.

Drummond looked across the room at them.

"Stop that noise, and get into bed," he said quietly.

The hissing ceased. He went on with his book again.

Silence reigned in dormitory four.

VI

Albert Redivivus

By murdering in cold blood a large and respected family, and afterwards depositing their bodies in a reservoir, one may gain, we are told, much unpopularity in the neighbourhood of one's crime; while robbing a church will get one cordially disliked especially by the vicar. But, to be really an outcast, to feel that one has no friend in the world, one must break an important public-school commandment.

Sheen had always been something of a hermit. In his most sociable moments he had never had more than one or two friends; but he had never before known what it meant to be completely isolated. It was like living in a world of ghosts, or, rather, like being a ghost in a living world. That disagreeable experience of being looked through, as if one were invisible, comes to the average person, it may be half a dozen times in his life. Sheen had to put up with it a hundred times a day. People who were talking to one another stopped when he appeared and waited until he had passed on before beginning again. Altogether, he was made to feel that he had done for himself, that, as far as the life of the school was concerned, he did not exist.

There had been some talk, particularly in the senior day-room, of more active measures. It was thought that nothing less than a court-martial could meet the case. But the house prefects had been against it. Sheen was in the sixth, and, however monstrous and unspeakable might have been his acts, it would hardly do to treat him as if he were a junior. And the scheme had been definitely discouraged by Drummond, who had stated, without wrapping the gist of his remarks in elusive phrases, that in the event of a court-martial being held he would interview the president of the same and knock his head off. So Seymour's had fallen back on the punishment which from their earliest beginnings the public schools have meted out to their criminals. They had cut Sheen dead.

In a way Sheen benefited from this excommunication. Now that he could not even play fives, for want of an opponent, there was nothing left for him to do but work. Fortunately, he had an object. The Gotford would be coming on in a few weeks, and the more work he could do for it, the better. Though Stanning was the only one of his rivals whom he feared, and though *he* was known to be taking very little trouble over the matter, it was best to run as few risks as possible. Stanning was one of those people who produce great results in their work without seeming to do anything for them.

So Sheen shut himself up in his study and ground grimly away at his books, and for exercise went for cross-country walks. It was a monotonous kind of existence. For the space of a week the only Wrykinian who spoke a single word to him was Bruce, the son of the Conservative candidate for Wrykyn : and Bruce's conversation had been limited to two remarks. He had said, "You might play that again, will you?" and, later, "Thanks". He had come into the music-room while Sheen was practising one afternoon, and had sat down, without speaking, on a chair by the door. When Sheen had played for the second time the piece which had won his approval, Bruce thanked him and left the room. As the solitary break in the monotony of the week, Sheen remembered the incident rather vividly.

Since the great rout of Albert and his minions outside Cook's, things, as far as the seniors were concerned, had been quiet between school and town. Linton and Dunstable had gone to and from Cook's two days in succession without let or hindrance. It was generally believed that, owing to the unerring way in which he had put his head in front of Drummond's left on that memorable occasion, the scarlet-haired one was at present dry-docked for repairs. The story in the school—it had grown with the days—was that Drummond had laid the enemy out on the pavement with a sickening crash, and that he had still been there at, so to speak, the close of play. As a matter of fact, Albert was in excellent shape, and only an unfortunate previous engagement prevented him from ranging the streets near Cook's as before. Sir William Bruce was addressing a meeting in another part of the town, and Albert thought it his duty to be on hand to boo.

In the junior portion of the school the feud with the town was brisk. Mention has been made of a certain St Jude's, between which seat of learning and the fags of Dexter's and the School House there was a spirited vendetta.

Jackson, of Dexter's was one of the pillars of the movement. Jackson was

> a calm-brow'd lad,
> Yet mad, at moments, as a hatter,

and he derived a great deal of pleasure from warring against St Jude's. It helped him to enjoy his meals. He slept the better for it. After a little turn up with a Judy he was fuller of that spirit of manly fortitude and forbearance so necessary to those whom Fate brought frequently into contact with Mr Dexter. The Judies wore mortar-boards, and it was an enjoyable pastime sending these spinning into space during one of the usual *rencontres* in the High Street. From the fact that he and his friends were invariably outnumbered, there was a sporting element in these affairs, though occasionally this inferiority of numbers was the cause of his executing a scientific retreat with the enemy harassing his men up to the very edge of the town. This had happened on the last occasion. There had been casualties. No fewer than six house-caps had fallen into the enemy's hands, and he himself had been tripped up and rolled in a puddle.

He burned to avenge this disaster.

"Coming down to Cook's?" he said to his ally, Painter. It was just a week since the Sheen episode.

"All right," said Painter.

"Suppose we go by the High Street," suggested Jackson, casually.

"Then we'd better get a few more chaps," said Painter.

A few more chaps were collected, and the party, numbering eight, set off for the town. There were present such stalwarts as Borwick and Crowle, both of Dexter's, and Tomlin, of the School House, a useful man to have by you in an emergency. It was Tomlin who, on one occasion, attacked by two terrific champions of St Jude's in a narrow passage, had vanquished them both, and sent their mortarboards miles into the empyrean, so that they were never the same mortar-boards again, but wore ever after a bruised and draggled look.

The expedition passed down the High Street without adventure, until, by common consent, it stopped at the lofty wall which bounded the playground of St Jude's.

From the other side of the wall came sounds of revelry, shrill squealings and shoutings. The Judies were disporting themselves at one of their weird games. It was known that they played touch-last, and Scandal said that another of their favourite recreations was marbles. The juniors at Wrykyn believed that it was to hide these excesses from the gaze of the public that the playground wall had been made so high. Eye-witnesses, who had peeped through the door in the said wall, reported that what the Judies seemed to do mostly was to chase one another about the playground, shrieking at the top of their voices. But, they added, this was probably a mere ruse to divert suspicion. They had almost certainly got the marbles in their pockets all the time.

The expedition stopped, and looked itself in the face.

"How about buzzing something at them?" said Jackson earnestly.

"You can get oranges over the road," said Tomlin in his helpful way.

Jackson vanished into the shop indicated, and reappeared a few moments later with a brown paper bag.

"It seems a beastly waste," suggested the economical Painter.

"That's all right," said Jackson, "they're all bad. The man thought I was rotting him when I asked if he'd got

any bad oranges, but I got them at last. Give us a leg up,
some one."

Willing hands urged him to the top of the wall. He
drew out a green orange, and threw it.

There was a sudden silence on the other side of the wall.
Then a howl of wrath went up to the heavens. Jackson
rapidly emptied his bag.

"Got him!" he exclaimed, as the last orange sped on its
way. "Look out, they're coming!"

The expedition had begun to move off with quiet dignity,
when from the doorway in the wall there poured forth a
stream of mortar-boarded warriors, shrieking defiance. The
expedition advanced to meet them.

As usual, the Judies had the advantage in numbers, and,
filled to the brim with righteous indignation, they were
proceeding to make things uncommonly warm for the
invaders—Painter had lost his cap, and Tomlin three
waistcoat buttons—when the eye of Jackson, roving up and
down the street, was caught by a Seymour's cap. He was
about to shout for assistance when he perceived that the
newcomer was Sheen, and refrained. It was no use, he felt,
asking Sheen for help.

But just as Sheen arrived and the ranks of the expedition
were beginning to give way before the strenuous onslaught
of the Judies, the latter, almost with one accord, turned
and bolted into their playground again. Looking round,
Tomlin, that first of generals, saw the reason, and uttered a
warning.

A mutual foe had appeared. From a passage on the left
of the road there had debouched on to the field of action
Albert himself and two of his band.

The expedition flew without false shame. It is to be
doubted whether one of Albert's calibre would have
troubled to attack such small game, but it was the firm
opinion of the Wrykyn fags and the Judies that he and his
men were to be avoided.

The newcomers did not pursue them. They contented
themselves with shouting at them. One of the band threw
a stone.

Then they caught sight of Sheen.

Albert said, "Oo er!" and advanced at the double. His companions followed him.

Sheen watched them come, and backed against the wall. His heart was thumping furiously. He was in for it now, he felt. He had come down to the town with this very situation in his mind. A wild idea of doing something to restore his self-respect and his credit in the eyes of the house had driven him to the High Street. But now that the crisis had actually arrived, he would have given much to have been in his study again.

Albert was quite close now. Sheen could see the marks which had resulted from his interview with Drummond. With all his force Sheen hit out, and experienced a curious thrill as his fist went home. It was a poor blow from a scientific point of view, but Sheen's fives had given him muscle, and it checked Albert. That youth, however, recovered rapidly, and the next few moments passed in a whirl for Sheen. He received a stinging blow on his left ear, and another which deprived him of his whole stock of breath, and then he was on the ground, conscious only of a wish to stay there for ever.

VII

Almost involuntarily he staggered up to receive another blow which sent him down again.

"That'll do," said a voice.

Sheen got up, panting. Between him and his assailant stood a short, sturdy man in a tweed suit. He was waving Albert back, and Albert appeared to be dissatisfied. He was arguing hotly with the newcomer.

"Now, you go away," said that worthy, mildly, "just you go away."

Albert gave it as his opinion that the speaker would do well not to come interfering in what didn't concern him. What he wanted, asserted Albert, was a thick ear.

"Coming pushing yourself in," added Albert querulously.

"You go away," repeated the stranger. "You go away. I don't want to have trouble with you."

Albert's reply was to hit out with his left hand in the direction of the speaker's face. The stranger, without fuss, touched the back of Albert's wrist gently with the palm of his right hand, and Albert, turning round in a circle, ended the manoeuvre with his back towards his opponent. He faced round again irresolutely. The thing had surprised him.

"You go away," said the other, as if he were making the observation for the first time.

"It's Joe Bevan," said one of Albert's friends, excitedly.

Albert's jaw fell. His freckled face paled.

"You go away," repeated the man in the tweed suit, whose conversation seemed inclined to run in a groove.

This time Albert took the advice. His friends had already taken it.

"Thanks," said Sheen.

"Beware," said Mr Bevan oracularly, "of entrance to a

quarrel; but, being in, bear't that th' opposèd may beware of thee. Always counter back when you guard. When a man shows you his right like that, always push out your hand straight. The straight left rules the boxing world. Feeling better, sir?"

"Yes, thanks."

"He got that right in just on the spot. I was watching. When you see a man coming to hit you with his right like that, don't you draw back. Get on top of him. He can't hit you then."

That feeling of utter collapse, which is the immediate result of a blow in the parts about the waistcoat, was beginning to pass away, and Sheen now felt capable of taking an interest in sublunary matters once more. His ear smarted horribly, and when he put up a hand and felt it the pain was so great that he could barely refrain from uttering a cry. But, however physically battered he might be, he was feeling happier and more satisfied with himself than he had felt for years. He had been beaten, but he had fought his best, and not given in. Some portion of his self-respect came back to him as he reviewed the late encounter.

Mr Bevan regarded him approvingly

"He was too heavy for you," he said. "He's a good twelve stone, I make it. I should put you at ten stone—say ten stone three. Call it nine stone twelve in condition. But you've got pluck, sir."

Sheen opened his eyes at this surprising statement.

"Some I've met would have laid down after getting that first hit, but you got up again. That's the secret of fighting. Always keep going on. Never give in. You know what Shakespeare says about the one who first cries, 'Hold, enough!' Do you read Shakespeare, sir?"

"Yes," said Sheen.

"Ah, now *he* knew his business," said Mr Bevan enthusiastically. "*There* was ring-craft, as you may say. *He* wasn't a novice."

Sheen agreed that Shakespeare had written some good things in his time.

"That's what you want to remember. Always keep going

on, as the saying is. I was fighting Dick Roberts at the
National—an American, he was, from San Francisco. He
come at me with his right stretched out, and I think he's
going to hit me with it, when blessed if his left don't come
out instead, and, my Golly! it nearly knocked a passage
through me. Just where that fellow hit you, sir, he hit me.
It was just at the end of the round, and I went back to my
corner. Jim Blake was seconding me. 'What's this, Jim?' I
says, 'is the man mad, or what?' 'Why,' he says, 'he's left-
handed, that's what's the matter. Get on top of him.' 'Get
on top of him? I says. 'My Golly, I'll get on top of the roof
if he's going to hit me another of those.' But I kept on, and
got close to him, and he couldn't get in another of them,
and he give in after the seventh round."

"What competition was that?" asked Sheen.

Mr Bevan laughed. "It was a twenty-round contest, sir,
for seven-fifty aside and the Light Weight Championship
of the World."

Sheen looked at him in astonishment. He had always
imagined professional pugilists to be bullet-headed and
beetle-browed to a man. He was not prepared for one of
Mr Joe Bevan's description. For all the marks of his profession that he bore on his face, in the shape of lumps and
scars, he might have been a curate. His face looked tough,
and his eyes harboured always a curiously alert, questioning
expression, as if he were perpetually "sizing up" the person
he was addressing. But otherwise he was like other men. He
seemed also to have a pretty taste in Literature. This, combined with his strong and capable air, attracted Sheen.
Usually he was shy and ill at ease with strangers. Joe Bevan
he felt he had known all his life.

"Do you still fight?" he asked.

"No," said Mr Bevan, "I gave it up. A man finds he's
getting on, as the saying is, and it don't do to keep at it too
long. I teach and I train, but I don't fight now."

A sudden idea flashed across Sheen's mind. He was still
glowing with that pride which those who are accustomed to
work with their brains feel when they have gone honestly
through some labour of the hands. At that moment he felt

himself capable of fighting the world and beating it. The small point, that Albert had knocked him out of time in less than a minute, did not damp him at all. He had started on the right road. He had done something. He had stood up to his man till he could stand no longer. An unlimited vista of action stretched before him. He had tasted the pleasure of the fight, and he wanted more.

Why, he thought, should he not avail himself of Joe Bevan's services to help him put himself right in the eyes of the house? At the end of the term, shortly before the Public Schools' Competitions at Aldershot, inter-house boxing cups were competed for at Wrykyn. It would be a dramatic act of reparation to the house if he could win the Light-Weight cup for it. His imagination, jumping wide gaps, did not admit the possibility of his not being good enough to win it. In the scene which he conjured up in his mind he was an easy victor. After all, there was the greater part of the term to learn in, and he would have a Champion of the World to teach him.

Mr Bevan cut in on his reflections as if he had heard them by some process of wireless telegraphy.

"Now, look here, sir," he said, "you should let me give you a few lessons. You're plucky, but you don't know the game as yet. And boxing's a thing every one ought to know. Supposition is, you're crossing a field or going down a street with your sweetheart or your wife——"

Sheen was neither engaged nor married, but he let the point pass.

——"And up comes one of these hooligans, as they call 'em. What are you going to do if he starts his games? Why, nothing, if you can't box. You may be plucky, but you can't beat him. And if you beat him, you'll get half murdered yourself. What you want to do is to learn to box, and then what happens? Why, as soon as he sees you shaping, he says to himself, 'Hullo, this chap knows too much for me. I'm off,' and off he runs. Or supposition is, he comes for you. You don't mind. Not you. You give him one punch in the right place, and then you go off to your tea, leaving him lying there. He won't get up."

"I'd like to learn," said Sheen. "I should be awfully

obliged if you'd teach me. I wonder if you could make me
any good by the end of the term. The House Competitions
come off then."

"That all depends, sir. It comes easier to some than
others. If you know how to shoot your left out straight, that's
as good as six months' teaching. After that it's all ring-craft.
The straight left beats the world."

"Where shall I find you?"

"I'm training a young chap—eight stone seven, and he's
got to get down to eight stone four, for a bantam weight
match—at an inn up the river here. I daresay you know it,
sir. Or any one would tell you where it is. The 'Blue Boar,'
it's called. You come there any time you like to name, sir,
and you'll find me."

"I should like to come every day," said Sheen. "Would
that be too often?"

"Oftener the better, sir. You can't practise too much."

"Then I'll start next week. Thanks very much. By the
way, I shall have to go by boat, I suppose. It isn't far, is it?
I've not been up the river for some time, The School
generally goes down stream."

"It's not what you'd call far," said Bevan. "But it would
be easier for you to come by road."

"I haven't a bicycle."

"Wouldn't one of your friends lend you one?"

Sheen flushed.

"No, I'd better come by boat, I think. I'll turn up on
Tuesday at about five. Will that suit you?"

"Yes, sir. That will be a good time. Then I'll say good
bye, sir, for the present."

Sheen went back to his house in a different mood from the
one in which he had left it. He did not care now when the
other Seymourites looked through him.

In the passage he met Linton, and grinned pleasantly at
him.

"What the dickens was that man grinning at?" said Linton to himself. "I must have a smut or something on my face."

But a close inspection in the dormitory looking-glass
revealed no blemish on his handsome features.

VIII

A NAVAL BATTLE AND ITS CONSEQUENCES

What a go is life!

Let us examine the case of Jackson, of Dexter's. O'Hara, who had left Dexter's at the end of the summer term, had once complained to Clowes of the manner in which his house-master treated him, and Clowes had remarked in his melancholy way that it was nothing less than a breach of the law that Dexter should persist in leading a fellow a dog's life without a dog licence for him.

That was precisely how Jackson felt on the subject.

Things became definitely unbearable on the day after Sheen's interview with Mr Joe Bevan.

'Twas morn—to begin at the beginning—and Jackson sprang from his little cot to embark on the labours of the day. Unfortunately, he sprang ten minutes too late, and came down to breakfast about the time of the second slice of bread and marmalade. Result, a hundred lines. Proceeding to school, he had again fallen foul of his house-master—in whose form he was—over a matter of unprepared Livy. As a matter of fact, Jackson *had* prepared the Livy. Or, rather, he had not absolutely *prepare*d it; but he had meant to. But it was Mr Templar's preparation, and Mr Templar was short-sighted. Any one will understand, therefore, that it would have been simply chucking away the gifts of Providence if he had not gone on with the novel which he had been reading up till the last moment before prep-time, and had brought along with him accidentally, as it were. It was a book called *A Spoiler of Men*, by Richard Marsh, and there was a repulsive crime on nearly every page. It was Hot Stuff. Much better than Livy . . .

Lunch Score—Two hundred lines.

During lunch he had the misfortune to upset a glass of

water. Pure accident, of course, but there it *was*, don't you know, all over the table.

Mr Dexter had called him—

(*a*) clumsy;
(*b*) a pig;

and had given him

(1) Advice—"You had better be careful, Jackson".
(2) A present—"Two hundred lines, Jackson".

On the match being resumed at two o'clock, with four hundred lines on the score-sheet, he had played a fine, free game during afternoon school, and Mr Dexter, who objected to fine, free games—or, indeed, any games—during school hours, had increased the total to six hundred, when stumps were drawn for the day.

So on a bright sunny Saturday afternoon, when he should have been out in the field cheering the house-team on to victory against the School House, Jackson sat in the junior day-room at Dexter's copying out portions of Virgil, Æneid Two.

To him, later on in the afternoon, when he had finished half his task, entered Painter, with the news that Dexter's had taken thirty points off the School House just after half-time.

"Mopped them up," said the terse and epigrammatic Painter. "Made rings round them. Haven't you finished yet? Well, chuck it, and come out."

"What's on?" asked Jackson.

"We're going to have a boat race."

"Pile it on."

"We are, really. Fact. Some of these School House kids are awfully sick about the match, and challenged us. That chap Tomlin thinks he can row."

"He can't row for nuts," said Jackson. "He doesn't know which end of the oar to shove into the water. I've seen cats that could row better than Tomlin."

"That's what I told him. At least, I said he couldn't row for toffee, so he said all right, I bet I can lick you, and I said

I betted he couldn't, and he said all right, then, let's try, and then the other chaps wanted to join in, so we made an inter-house thing of it. And I want you to come and stroke us."

Jackson hesitated. Mr Dexter, setting the lines on Friday, had certainly said that they were to be shown up "tomorrow evening." He had said it very loud and clear. Still, in a case like this. . . . After all, by helping to beat the School House on the river he would be giving Dexter's a leg-up. And what more could the man want?

"Right ho," said Jackson.

Down at the School boat-house the enemy were already afloat when Painter and Jackson arrived.

"Buck up," cried the School House crew.

Dexter's embarked, five strong. There was room for two on each seat. Jackson shared the post of stroke with Painter. Crowle steered.

"Ready?" asked Tomlin from the other boat.

"Half a sec.," said Jackson. "What's the course?"

"Oh, don't you know *that* yet? Up to the town, round the island just below the bridge,—the island with the cro-quet ground on it, *you* know—and back again here. Ready?"

"In a jiffy. Look here, Crowle, remember about steering. You pull the right line if you want to go to the right and the other if you want to go to the left."

"All right," said the injured Crowle. "As if I didn't know that."

"Thought I'd mention it. It's your fault. Nobody could tell by looking at you that you knew anything except how to eat. Ready, you chaps?"

"When I say 'Three,' " said Tomlin.

It was a subject of heated discussion between the crews for weeks afterwards whether Dexter's boat did or did not go off at the word "Two." Opinions were divided on the topic. But it was certain that Jackson and his men led from the start. Pulling a good, splashing stroke which had drenched Crowle to the skin in the first thirty yards, Dexter's boat crept slowly ahead. By the time the island was reached, it led by a length. Encouraged by success, the leaders redoubled their already energetic efforts. Crowle sat in a shower-bath. He was even moved to speech about it.

"When you've finished," said Crowle.

Jackson, intent upon repartee, caught a crab, and the School House drew level again. The two boats passed the island abreast.

Just here occurred one of those unfortunate incidents. Both crews had quickened their stroke until the boats had practically been converted into submarines, and the rival coxswains were observing bitterly to space that this was jolly well the last time they ever let themselves in for this sort of thing, when round the island there hove in sight a flotilla of boats, directly in the path of the racers.

There were three of them, and not even the spray which played over them like a fountain could prevent Crowle from seeing that they were manned by Judies. Even on the river these outcasts wore their mortar-boards.

"Look out!" shrieked Crowle, pulling hard on his right line. "Stop rowing, you chaps. We shall be into them."

At the same moment the School House oarsmen ceased pulling. The two boats came to a halt a few yards from the enemy.

"What's up?" panted Jackson, crimson from his exertions. "Hullo, it's the Judies!"

Tomlin was parleying with the foe.

"Why the dickens can't you keep out of the way? Spoiling our race. Wait till we get ashore."

But the Judies, it seemed, were not prepared to wait even for that short space of time. A miscreant, larger than the common run of Judy, made a brief, but popular, address to his men.

"Splash them!" he said.

Instantly, amid shrieks of approval, oars began to strike the water, and the water began to fly over the Wrykyn boats, which were now surrounded. The latter were not slow to join battle with the same weapons. Homeric laughter came from the bridge above. The town bridge was a sort of loafers' club, to which the entrance fee was a screw of tobacco, and the subscription an occasional remark upon the weather. Here gathered together day by day that section of the populace which resented it when they "asked for employment, and only got work instead". From morn till eve they lounged against the balustrades, surveying nature, and hoping it would be kind enough to give them some excitement that day. An occasional dog-fight found in them an eager audience. No runaway horse ever bored them. A broken-down motor-car was meat and drink to them. They had an appetite for every spectacle.

When, therefore, the water began to fly from boat to boat, kind-hearted men fetched their friends from neighbouring public houses and craned with them over the parapet, observing the sport and commenting thereon. It was these comments that attracted Mr Dexter's attention. When, cycling across the bridge, he found the south side of it entirely congested, and heard raucous voices urging certain unseen "little 'uns" now to "go it" and anon to "vote for Pedder", his curiosity was aroused. He dismounted and pushed his way through the crowd until he got a clear view of what was happening below.

He was just in time to see the most stirring incident of the fight. The biggest of the Judy boats had been propelled by the current nearer and nearer to the Dexter Argo. No sooner was it within distance than Jackson, dropping his oar, grasped the side and pulled it towards him. The two boats crashed together and rocked violently as the crews rose from their seats and grappled with one another. A hurricane of laughter and applause went up from the crowd upon the bridge.

The next moment both boats were bottom upwards and drifting sluggishly down towards the island, while the crews swam like rats for the other boats.

Every Wrykinian had to learn to swim before he was allowed on the river; so that the peril of Jackson and his crew was not extreme : and it was soon speedily evident that swimming was also part of the Judy curriculum, for the shipwrecked ones were soon climbing drippingly on board the surviving ships, where they sat and made puddles, and shrieked defiance at their antagonists.

This was accepted by both sides as the end of the fight, and the combatants parted without further hostilities, each fleet believing that the victory was with them.

And Mr Dexter, mounting his bicycle again, rode home to tell the headmaster.

That evening, after preparation, the headmaster held a reception. Among distinguished visitors were Jackson, Painter, Tomlin, Crowle, and six others.

On the Monday morning the headmaster issued a manifesto to the school after prayers. He had, he said, for some time entertained the idea of placing the town out of bounds. He would do so now. No boy, unless he was a prefect, would be allowed till further notice to cross the town bridge. As regarded the river, for the future boating Wrykinians must confine their attentions to the lower river. Nobody must take a boat up-stream. The school boatman would have strict orders to see that this rule was rigidly enforced. Any breach of these bounds would, he concluded, be punished with the utmost severity.

The headmaster of Wrykyn was not a hasty man. He thought before he put his foot down. But when he did, he put it down heavily.

Sheen heard the ultimatum with dismay. He was a law-abiding person, and here he was, faced with a dilemma that made it necessary for him to choose between breaking school rules of the most important kind, or pulling down all the castles he had built in the air before the mortar had had time to harden between their stones.

He wished he could talk it over with somebody. But he had nobody with whom he could talk over anything. He must think it out for himself.

He spent the rest of the day thinking it out, and by nightfall he had come to his decision.

Even at the expense of breaking bounds and the risk of being caught at it, he must keep his appointment with Joe Bevan. It would mean going to the town landing-stage for a boat, thereby breaking bounds twice over.

But it would have to be done.

IX

SHEEN BEGINS HIS EDUCATION

The "Blue Boar" was a picturesque inn, standing on the bank of the river Severn. It was much frequented in the summer by fishermen, who spent their days in punts and their evenings in the old oak parlour, where a picture in boxing costume of Mr Joe Bevan, whose brother was the landlord of the inn, gazed austerely down on them, as if he disapproved of the lamentable want of truth displayed by the majority of their number. Artists also congregated there to paint the ivy-covered porch. At the back of the house were bedrooms, to which the fishermen would make their way in the small hours of a summer morning, arguing to the last as they stumbled upstairs. One of these bedrooms, larger than the others, had been converted into a gymnasium for the use of mine host's brother. Thither he brought pugilistic aspirants who wished to be trained for various contests, and it was the boast of the "Blue Boar" that it had never turned out a loser. A reputation of this kind is a valuable asset to an inn, and the boxing world thought highly of it, in spite of the fact that it was off the beaten track. Certainly the luck of the "Blue Boar" had been surprising.

Sheen pulled steadily up stream on the appointed day, and after half an hour's work found himself opposite the little landing-stage at the foot of the inn lawn.

His journey had not been free from adventure. On his way to the town he had almost run into Mr Templar, and but for the lucky accident of that gentleman's short sight must have been discovered. He had reached the landing-stage in safety, but he had not felt comfortable until he was well out of sight of the town. It was fortunate for him in the present case that he was being left so severely alone by the school. It was an advantage that nobody took the least interest in his goings and comings.

Having moored his boat and proceeded to the inn, he was directed upstairs by the landlord, who was an enlarged and coloured edition of his brother. From the other side of the gymnasium door came an unceasing and mysterious shuffling sound.

He tapped at the door and went in.

He found himself in a large, airy room, lit by two windows and a broad skylight. The floor was covered with linoleum. But it was the furniture that first attracted his attention. In a farther corner of the room was a circular wooden ceiling, supported by four narrow pillars, From the centre of this hung a ball, about the size of an ordinary football. To the left, suspended from a beam, was an enormous leather bolster. On the floor, underneath a table bearing several pairs of boxing-gloves, a skipping-rope, and some wooden dumb-bells, was something that looked like a dozen Association footballs rolled into one. All the rest of the room, a space some few yards square, was bare of furniture. In this space a small sweater-clad youth, with a head of light hair cropped very short, was darting about and ducking and hitting out with both hands at nothing, with such a serious, earnest expression on his face that Sheen could not help smiling. On a chair by one of the windows Mr Joe Bevan was sitting, with a watch in his hand.

As Sheen entered the room the earnest young man made a sudden dash at him. The next moment he seemed to be in a sort of heavy shower of fists. They whizzed past his ear, flashed up from below within an inch of his nose, and tapped him caressingly on the waistcoat. Just as the shower was at its heaviest his assailant darted away again, sidestepped an imaginary blow, ducked another, and came at him once more. None of the blows struck him, but it was with more than a little pleasure that he heard Joe Bevan call "Time!" and saw the active young gentleman sink panting into a seat.

"You and your games, Francis!" said Joe Bevan, reproachfully. "This is a young gentleman from the college come for tuition."

"Gentleman—won't mind—little joke—take it in spirit which is—meant," said Francis, jerkily.

Sheen hastened to assure him that he had not been offended.

"You take your two minutes, Francis," said Mr Bevan, "and then have a turn with the ball. Come this way, Mr—"

"Sheen."

"Come this way, Mr Sheen, and I'll show you where to put on your things."

Sheen had brought his football clothes with him. He had not put them on for a year.

"That's the lad I was speaking of. Getting on prime, he is. Fit to fight for his life, as the saying is."

"What was he doing when I came in?"

"Oh, he always has three rounds like that every day. It teaches you to get about quick. You try it when you get back, Mr. Sheen. Fancy you're fighting me."

"Are you sure I'm not interrupting you in the middle of your work?" asked Sheen.

"Not at all, sir, not at all. I just have to rub him down, and give him his shower-bath, and then he's finished for the day."

Having donned his football clothes and returned to the gymnasium, Sheen found Francis in a chair, having his left leg vigorously rubbed by Mr Bevan.

"You fon' of dargs?" inquired Francis affably, looking up as he came in.

Sheen replied that he was, and, indeed, was possessed of one. The admission stimulated Francis, whose right leg was now under treatment, to a flood of conversation. He, it appeared, had always been one for dargs. Owned two. Answering to the names of Tim and Tom. Beggars for rats, yes. And plucked 'uns? Well—he would like to see, would Francis, a dog that Tim or Tom would not stand up to. Clever, too. Why once—

Joe Bevan cut his soliloquy short at this point by leading him off to another room for his shower-bath; but before he went he expressed a desire to talk further with Sheen on the subject of dogs, and, learning that Sheen would be there every day, said he was glad to hear it. He added that for a brother dog-lover he did not mind stretching a point, so that, if ever Sheen wanted a couple of rounds any day, he, Francis, would see that he got them. This offer, it may be mentioned, Sheen accepted with gratitude, and the extra practice he acquired thereby was subsequently of the utmost use to him. Francis, as a boxer, excelled in what is known in pugilistic circles as shiftiness. That is to say, he had a number of ingenious ways of escaping out of tight corners; and these he taught Sheen, much to the latter's profit.

But this was later, when the Wrykinian had passed those preliminary stages on which he was now to embark.

The art of teaching boxing really well is a gift, and it is given to but a few. It is largely a matter of personal magnetism, and, above all, sympathy. A man may be a fine boxer himself, up to every move of the game, and a champion of champions, but for all that he may not be a good teacher. If he has not the sympathy necessary for the appreciation of the difficulties experienced by the beginner, he cannot produce good results. A boxing instructor needs three qualities —skill, sympathy, and enthusiasm. Joe Bevan had all three, particularly enthusiasm. His heart was in his work, and he carried Sheen with him. "Beautiful, sir, beautiful," he kept saying, as he guarded the blows; and Sheen, though too clever to be wholly deceived by the praise, for he knew perfectly well that his efforts up to the present had been anything but beautiful, was nevertheless encouraged, and put all he knew into his hits. Occasionally Joe Bevan would push out his left glove. Then, if Sheen's guard was in the proper place and the push did not reach its destination, Joe would mutter a word of praise. If Sheen dropped his right hand, so that he failed to stop the blow, Bevan would observe, "Keep that guard up, sir!" with almost a pained intonation, as if he had been disappointed in a friend.

The constant repetition of this maxim gradually drove it into Sheen's head, so that towards the end of the lesson he no longer lowered his right hand when he led with his left; and he felt the gentle pressure of Joe Bevan's glove less frequently. At no stage of a pupil's education did Joe Bevan hit him really hard, and in the first few lessons he could scarcely be said to hit him at all. He merely rested his glove against the pupil's face. On the other hand, he was urgent in imploring the pupil to hit *him* as hard as he could.

"Don't be too kind, sir," he would chant, "*I* don't mind being hit. Let me have it. Don't flap. Put it in with some weight behind it." He was also fond of mentioning that extract from Polonius' speech to Laertes, which he had quoted to Sheen on their first meeting.

Sheen finished his first lesson, feeling hotter than he had ever felt in his life.

"Hullo, sir, you're out of condition," commented Mr Bevan. "Have a bit of a rest."

Once more Sheen had learnt the lesson of his weakness. He could hardly realise that he had only begun to despise himself in the last fortnight. Before then, he had been, on the whole, satisfied with himself. He was brilliant at work, and would certainly get a scholarship at Oxford or Cambridge when the time came; and he had specialised in work to the exclusion of games. It is bad to specialise in games to the exclusion of work, but of the two courses the latter is probably the less injurious. One gains at least health by it.

But Sheen now understood thoroughly, what he ought to have learned from his study of the Classics, that the happy mean was the thing at which to strive. And for the future he meant to aim at it. He would get the Gotford, if he could, but also would he win the house boxing at his weight.

After he had rested he discovered the use of the big ball beneath the table. It was soft, but solid and heavy. By throwing this—the medicine-ball, as they call it in the profession—at Joe Bevan, and catching it, Sheen made himself very hot again, and did the muscles of his shoulders a great deal of good.

"That'll do for today, then, sir." said Joe Bevan. "Have a

good rub down tonight, or you'll find yourself very stiff in the morning."

"Well, do you think I shall be any good?" asked Sheen.

"You'll do fine, sir. But remember what Shakespeare says."

"About vaulting ambition?"

"No, sir, no. I meant what Hamlet says to the players. 'Nor do not saw the air too much, with your hand, thus, but use all gently.' That's what you've got to remember in boxing, sir. Take it easy. Easy and cool does it, and the straight left beats the world."

Sheen paddled quietly back to the town with the stream, pondering over this advice. He felt that he had advanced another step. He was not foolish enough to believe that he knew anything about boxing as yet, but he felt that it would not be long before he did.

X

SHEEN'S PROGRESS

Sheen improved. He took to boxing as he had taken to fives. He found that his fives helped him. He could get about on his feet quickly, and his eye was trained to rapid work.

His second lesson was not encouraging. He found that he had learned just enough to make him stiff and awkward, and no more. But he kept on, and by the end of the first week Joe Bevan declared definitely that he would do, that he had the root of the matter in him, and now required only practice.

"I wish you could see like I can how you're improving," he said at the end of the sixth lesson, as they were resting after five minutes' exercise with the medicine-ball. "I get four blows in on some of the gentlemen I teach to one what I get in on you. But it's like riding. When you can trot, you look forward to when you can gallop. And when you can gallop, you can't see yourself getting on any further. But you're improving all the time."

"But I can't gallop yet," said Sheen.

"Well, no, not gallop exactly, but you've only had six lessons. Why, in another six weeks, if you come regular, you won't know yourself. You'll be making some of the young gentlemen at the college wish they had never been born. You'll make babies of them, that's what you'll do."

"I'll bet I couldn't, if I'd learnt with some one else," said Sheen, sincerely. "I don't believe I should have learnt a thing if I'd gone to the school instructor."

"Who is your school instructor, sir?"

"A man named Jenkins. He used to be in the army."

"Well, there, you see, that's what it is. I know old George Jenkins. He used to be a pretty good boxer in his time, but there! boxing's a thing, like everything else, that moves with the times. We used to go about in iron trucks. Now we go in motor-cars. Just the same with boxing. What you're learning now is the sort of boxing that wins championship fights nowadays. Old George, well, he teaches you how to put your left out, but, my Golly, he doesn't know any tricks. He hasn't studied it same as I have. It's the ring-craft that wins battles. Now sir, if you're ready."

They put on the gloves again. When the round was over, Mr Bevan had further comments to make.

"You don't hit hard enough, sir," he said. "Don't flap. Let it come straight out with some weight behind it. You want to be earnest in the ring. The other man's going to do his best to hurt you, and you've got to stop him. One good punch is worth twenty taps. You hit him. And when you've hit him, don't you go back; you hit him again. They'll only give you three rounds in any competition you go in for, so you want to do the work you can while you're at it."

As the days went by, Sheen began to imbibe some of Joe Bevan's rugged philosophy of life. He began to understand that the world is a place where every man has to look after himself, and that it is the stronger hand that wins. That sentence from *Hamlet* which Joe Bevan was so fond of quoting practically summed up the whole duty of man—and boy too. One should not seek quarrels, but, "being in," one should do one's best to ensure that one's opponent thought twice in future before seeking them. These afternoons at the "Blue Boar" were gradually giving Sheen what he had never before possessed—self-confidence. He was beginning to find that he was capable of something after all, that in an emergency he would be able to keep his end up. The feeling added a zest to all that he did. His work in school improved. He looked at the Gotford no longer as a prize which he would have to struggle to win. He felt that his rivals would have to struggle to win it from him.

After his twelfth lesson, when he had learned the ground-work of the art, and had begun to develop a style of his own, like some nervous batsman at cricket who does not show his true form till he has been at the wickets for several overs, the dog-loving Francis gave him a trial. This was a

very different affair from his spars with Joe Bevan. Frank
Hunt was one of the cleverest boxers at his weight in England, but he had not Joe Bevan's gift of hitting gently. He
probably imagined that he was merely tapping, and certainly his blows were not to be compared with those he
delivered in the exercise of his professional duties; but,
nevertheless, Sheen had never felt anything so painful before, not even in his passage of arms with Albert. He came
out of the encounter with a swollen lip and a feeling that
one of his ribs was broken, and he had not had the pleasure
of landing a single blow upon his slippery antagonist, who
flowed about the room like quicksilver. But he had not
flinched, and the statement of Francis, as they shook hands,
that he had "done varry well," was as balm. Boxing is one
of the few sports where the loser can feel the same thrill of
triumph as the winner. There is no satisfaction equal to that
which comes when one has forced oneself to go through an
ordeal from which one would have liked to have escaped.

"Capital, sir, capital," said Joe Bevan. "I wanted to see
whether you would lay down or not when you began to get
a few punches. You did capitally, Mr Sheen."

"I didn't hit him much," said Sheen with a laugh.

"Never mind, sir, you got hit, which was just as good.
Some of the gentlemen I've taught wouldn't have taken half
that. They're all right when they're on top and winning, and
to see them shape you'd say to yourself, By George, here's a
champion. But let 'em get a punch or two, and hullo! says
you, what's this? They don't like it. They lay down. But you
kept on. There's one thing, though, you want to keep that
guard up when you duck. You slip him that way once. Very
well. Next time he's waiting for you. He doesn't hit straight.
He hooks you, and you don't want many of those."

Sheen enjoyed his surreptitious visits to the "Blue Boar."
Twice he escaped being caught in the most sensational way;
and once Mr Spence, who looked after the Wrykyn cricket
and gymnasium, and played everything equally well, nearly
caused complications by inviting Sheen to play fives with
him after school. Fortunately the Gotford afforded an
excellent excuse. As the time for the examination drew near,

those who had entered for it were accustomed to become hermits to a great extent, and to retire after school to work in their studies.

"You mustn't overdo it, Sheen," said Mr Spence. "You ought to get some exercise."

"Oh, I do, sir," said Sheen. "I still play fives, but I play before breakfast now."

He had had one or two games with Harrington of the School House, who did not care particularly whom he played with so long as his opponent was a useful man. Sheen being one of the few players in the school who were up to his form, Harrington ignored the cloud under which Sheen rested. When they met in the world outside the fives-courts Harrington was polite, but made no overtures of friendship. That, it may be mentioned, was the attitude of every one who did not actually cut Sheen. The exception was Jack Bruce, who had constituted himself audience to Sheen, when the latter was practising the piano, on two further occasions. But then Bruce was so silent by nature that for all practical purposes he might just as well have cut Sheen like the others.

"We might have a game before breakfast some time, then," said Mr Spence.

He had noticed, being a master who did notice things, that Sheen appeared to have few friends, and had made up his mind that he would try and bring him out a little. Of the real facts of the case, he knew of course, nothing.

"I should like to, sir," said Sheen.

"Next Wednesday?"

"All right, sir."

"I'll be there at seven. If you're before me, you might get the second court, will you?"

The second court from the end nearest the boarding-house was the best of the half-dozen fives-courts at Wrykyn. After school sometimes you would see fags racing across the gravel to appropriate it for their masters. The rule was that whoever first pinned to the door a piece of paper with his name on it was the legal owner of the court—and it was a stirring sight to see a dozen fags fighting to get at the door.

But before breakfast the court might be had with less trouble.

Meanwhile, Sheen paid his daily visits to the "Blue Boar," losing flesh and gaining toughness with every lesson. The more he saw of Joe Bevan the more he liked him, and appreciated his strong, simple outlook on life. Shakespeare was a great bond between them. Sheen had always been a student of the Bard, and he and Joe would sit on the little verandah of the inn, looking over the river, until it was time for him to row back to the town, quoting passages at one another. Joe Bevan's knowledge of the plays, especially the tragedies, was wide, and at first inexplicable to Sheen. It was strange to hear him declaiming long speeches from *Macbeth* or *Hamlet*, and to think that he was by profession a pugilist. One evening he explained his curious erudition. In his youth, before he took to the ring in earnest, he had travelled with a Shakespearean repertory company. "I never played a star part," he confessed, "but I used to come on in the Battle of Bosworth and in Macbeth's castle and what not. I've been First Citizen sometimes. I was the carpenter in *Julius Cæsar*. That was my biggest part. 'Truly sir, in respect of a fine workman, I am but, as you would say, a cobbler.' But somehow the stage—well . . . *you* know what it is, sir. Leeds one week, Manchester the next, Brighton the week after, and travelling all Sunday. It wasn't quiet enough for me."

The idea of becoming a professional pugilist for the sake of peace and quiet tickled Sheen. "But I've always read Shakespeare ever since then," continued Mr Bevan, "and I always shall read him."

It was on the next day that Mr Bevan made a suggestion which drew confidences from Sheen, in his turn.

"What you want now, sir," he said, "is to practise on someone of about your own form, as the saying is. Isn't there some gentleman friend of yours at the college who would come here with you?"

They were sitting on the verandah when he asked this question. It was growing dusk, and the evening seemed to invite confidences. Sheen, looking out across the river and avoiding his friend's glance, explained just what it was that made it so difficult for him to produce a gentleman friend at that particular time. He could feel Mr Bevan's eye upon him, but he went through with it till the thing was told—boldly, and with no attempt to smooth over any of the unpleasant points.

"Never you mind, sir," said Mr Bevan consolingly, as he finished. "We all lose our heads sometimes. I've seen the way you stand up to Francis, and I'll eat—I'll eat the medicine-ball if you're not as plucky as anyone. It's simply a question of keeping your head. You wouldn't do a thing like that again, not you. Don't you worry yourself, sir. We're all alike when we get bustled. We don't know what we're doing, and by the time we've put our hands up and got into shape, why, it's all over, and there you are. Don't you worry yourself, sir."

"You're an awfully good sort, Joe," said Sheen gratefully.

XI

A SMALL INCIDENT

Failing a gentleman friend, Mr Bevan was obliged to do what he could by means of local talent. On Sheen's next visit he was introduced to a burly youth of his own age, very taciturn, and apparently ferocious. He, it seemed, was the knife and boot boy at the "Blue Boar", "did a bit" with the gloves, and was willing to spar with Sheen provided Mr Bevan made it all right with the guv'nor; saw, that is so say, that he did not get into trouble for passing in unprofessional frivolity moments which should have been sacred to knives and boots. These terms having been agreed to, he put on the gloves.

For the first time since he had begun his lessons, Sheen experienced an attack of his old shyness and dislike of hurting other people's feelings. He could not resist the thought that he had no grudge against the warden of the knives and boots. He hardly liked to hit him.

The other, however, did not share this prejudice. He rushed at Sheen with such determination, that almost the first warning the latter had that the contest had begun was the collision of the back of his head with the wall. Out in the middle of the room he did better, and was beginning to hold his own, in spite of a rousing thump on his left eye, when Joe Bevan called "Time!" A second round went off in much the same way. His guard was more often in the right place, and his leads less wild. At the conclusion of the round, pressure of business forced his opponent to depart, and Sheen wound up his lesson with a couple of minutes at the punching-ball. On the whole, he was pleased with his first spar with someone who was really doing his best and trying to hurt him. With Joe Bevan and Francis there was always the feeling that they were playing down to him. Joe Bevan's gentle taps, in particular, were a little humiliating. But with his late opponent all had been serious. It had been a real test, and he had come through it very fairly. On the whole, he had taken more than he had given —his eye would look curious tomorrow—but already he had thought out a way of foiling the burly youth's rushes. Next time he would really show his true form.

The morrow, on which Sheen expected his eye to look curious, was the day he had promised to play fives with Mr Spence. He hoped that at the early hour at which they had arranged to play it would not have reached its worst stage; but when he looked in the glass at a quarter to seven, he beheld a small ridge of purple beneath it. It was not large, nor did it interfere with his sight, but it was very visible. Mr Spence, however, was a sportsman, and had boxed himself in his time, so there was a chance that nothing would be said.

It was a raw, drizzly morning. There would probably be few fives-players before breakfast, and the capture of the second court should be easy. So it turned out. Nobody was about when Sheen arrived. He pinned his slip of paper to the door, and, after waiting for a short while for Mr Spence and finding the process chilly, went for a trot round the gymnasium to pass the time.

Mr Spence had not arrived during his absence, but somebody else had. At the door of the second court, gleaming in first-fifteen blazer, sweater, stockings, and honour-cap, stood Attell.

Sheen looked at Attell, and Attell looked through Sheen.

It was curious, thought Sheen, that Attell should be standing in the very doorway of court two. It seemed to suggest that he claimed some sort of ownership. On the other hand, there was his, Sheen's, paper on the . . . His eye happened to light on the cement flooring in front of the court. There was a crumpled ball of paper there.

When he had started for his run, there had been no such ball of paper.

Sheen picked it up and straightened it out. On it was written "R. D. Sheen".

He looked up quickly. In addition to the far-away look, Attell's face now wore a faint smile, as if he had seen something rather funny on the horizon. But he spake no word.

A curiously calm and contented feeling came upon Sheen. Here was something definite at last. He could do nothing, however much he might resent it, when fellows passed him by as if he did not exist; but when it came to removing his landmark . . .

"Would you mind shifting a bit?" he said very politely. "I want to pin my paper on the door again. It seems to have fallen down."

Attell's gaze shifted slowly from the horizon and gradually embraced Sheen.

"I've got this court," he said.

"I think not," said Sheen silkily. "I was here at ten to seven, and there was no paper on the door then. So I put mine up. If you move a little, I'll put it up again."

"Go and find another court, if you want to play," said Attell, "and if you've got anybody to play with," he added with a sneer. "This is mine."

"I think not," said Sheen.

Attell resumed his inspection of the horizon.

"Attell," said Sheen.

Attell did not answer.

Sheen pushed him gently out of the way, and tore down the paper from the door.

Their eyes met. Attell, after a moment's pause, came forward, half-menacing, half irresolute; and as he came Sheen hit him under the chin in the manner recommended by Mr Bevan.

"When you upper-cut," Mr Bevan was wont to say, "don't make it a swing. Just a half-arm jolt's all you want."

It was certainly all Attell wanted. He was more than surprised. He was petrified. The sudden shock of the blow, coming as it did from so unexpected a quarter, deprived him of speech : which was, perhaps, fortunate for him, for what he would have said would hardly have commended itself to Mr Spence, who came up at this moment.

"Well, Sheen," said Mr Spence, "here you are. I hope

I haven't kept you waiting. What a morning! You've got the court, I hope?"

"Yes, sir," said Sheen.

He wondered if the master had seen the little episode which had taken place immediately before his arrival. Then he remembered that it had happened inside the court. It must have been over by the time Mr Spence had come upon the scene.

"Are you waiting for somebody, Attell?" asked Mr Spence. "Stanning? He will be here directly. I passed him on the way."

Attell left the court, and they began their game.

"You've hurt your eye, Sheen," said Mr Spence, at the end of the first game. "How did that happen?"

"Boxing, sir," said Sheen.

"Oh," replied Mr Spence, and to Sheen's relief he did not pursue his inquiries.

Attell had wandered out across the gravel to meet Stanning.

"Got that court?" inquired Stanning.

"No."

"You idiot, why on earth didn't you? It's the only court worth playing in. Who's got it?"

"Sheen."

"Sheen !"Stanning stopped dead. "Do you mean to say you let a fool like Sheen take it from you! Why didn't you turn him out?"

"I couldn't," said Attell. "I was just going to when Spence came up. He's playing Sheen this morning. I couldn't very well bag the court when a master wanted it."

"I suppose not," said Stanning. "What did Sheen say when you told him you wanted the court?"

This was getting near a phase of the subject which Attell was not eager to discuss.

"Oh, he didn't say much," he said.

"Did you do anything?" persisted Stanning.

Attell suddenly remembered having noticed that Sheen was wearing a black eye. This was obviously a thing to be turned to account.

"I hit him in the eye," he said. "I'll bet it's coloured by school-time."

And sure enough, when school-time arrived, there was Sheen with his face in the condition described, and Stanning hastened to spread abroad this sequel to the story of Sheen's failings in the town battle. By the end of preparation it had got about the school that Sheen had cheeked Attell, that Attell had hit Sheen, and that Sheen had been afraid to hit him back. At the precise moment when Sheen was in the middle of a warm two-minute round with Francis at the "Blue Boar," an indignation meeting was being held in the senior day-room at Seymour's to discuss this latest disgrace to the house.

"This is getting a bit too thick," was the general opinion. Moreover, it was universally agreed that something ought to be done. The feeling in the house against Sheen had been stirred to a dangerous pitch by this last episode. Seymour's thought more of their reputation than any house in the school. For years past the house had led on the cricket and football field and off it. Sometimes other houses would actually win one of the cups, but, when this happened, Seymour's was always their most dangerous rival. Other houses had their ups and downs, were very good one year and very bad the next; but Seymour's had always managed to maintain a steady level of excellence. It always had a man or two in the School eleven and fifteen, generally supplied one of the School Racquets pair for Queen's Club in the Easter vac., and when this did not happen always had one of two of the Gym. Six or Shooting Eight, or a few men who had won scholarships at the 'Varsities. The pride of a house is almost keener than the pride of a school. From the first minute he entered the house a new boy was made to feel that, in coming to Seymour's, he had accepted a responsibility that his reputation was not his own, but belonged to the house. If he did well, the glory would be Seymour's glory. If he did badly, he would be sinning against the house.

This second story about Sheen, therefore, stirred Seymour's to the extent of giving the house a resemblance to a hornet's nest into which a stone had been hurled. After school that day the house literally hummed. The noise of the two day-rooms talking it over could be heard in the road outside. The only bar that stood between the outraged Seymourites and Sheen was Drummond. As had happened before, Drummond resolutely refused to allow anything in the shape of an active protest, and no argument would draw him from this unreasonable attitude, though why it was that he had taken it up he himself could not have said. Perhaps it was that rooted hatred a boxer instinctively acquires of anything in the shape of unfair play that influenced him. He revolted against the idea of a whole house banding together against one of its members.

So even this fresh provocation did not result in any active interference with Sheen; but it was decided that he must be cut even more thoroughly than before.

And about the time when this was resolved, Sheen was receiving the congratulations of Francis on having positively landed a blow upon him. It was an event which marked an epoch in his career.

XII

DUNSTABLE AND LINTON GO UP THE RIVER

There are some proud, spirited natures which resent rules and laws on principle as attempts to interfere with the rights of the citizen. As the Duchess in the play said of her son, who had had unpleasantness with the authorities at Eton because they had been trying to teach him things, "Silwood is a sweet boy, but he will not stand the bearing-rein". Dunstable was also a sweet boy, but he, too, objected to the bearing-rein. And Linton was a sweet boy, and he had similar prejudices. And this placing of the town out of bounds struck both of them simultaneously as a distinct attempt on the part of the headmaster to apply the bearing-rein.

"It's all very well to put it out of bounds for the kids," said Dunstable, firmly, "but when it comes to Us—why, I never heard of such a thing."

Linton gave it as his opinion that such conduct was quite in a class of its own as regarded cool cheek.

"It fairly sneaks," said Linton, with forced calm, "the Garibaldi."

"Kids," proceeded Dunstable, judicially, "are idiots, and can't be expected to behave themselves down town. Put the show out of bounds to them if you like. But We—"

"We!" echoed Linton.

"The fact is," said Dunstable, "it's a beastly nuisance, but we shall have to go down town and up the river just to assert ourselves. We can't have the thin end of the wedge coming and spoiling our liberties. We may as well chuck life altogether if we aren't able to go to the town whenever we like."

"And Albert will be pining away," added Linton.

"Hullo, young gentlemen," said the town boatman, when they presented themselves to him, "what can I do for you?"

"I know it seems strange," said Dunstable, "but we want a boat. We are the Down-trodden British Schoolboys' League for Demanding Liberty and seeing that We Get It. Have you a boat?"

The man said he believed he had a boat. In fact, now that he came to think of it, he rather fancied he had one or two. He proceeded to get one ready, and the two martyrs to the cause stepped in.

Dunstable settled himself in the stern, and collected the rudder-lines.

"Hullo," said Linton, "aren't you going to row?"

"It may be only my foolish fancy," replied Dunstable, "but I rather think you're going to do that. I'll steer."

"Beastly slacker," said Linton. "Anyhow, how far are we going? I'm not going to pull all night."

"If you row for about half an hour without exerting yourself—and I can trust you not to do that—and then look to your left, you'll see a certain hostelry, if it hasn't moved since I was last there. It's called the 'Blue Boar'. We will have tea there, and then I'll pull gently back, and that will end the programme."

"Except being caught in the town by half the masters," said Linton. "Still, I'm not grumbling. This had to be done. Ready?"

"Not just yet," said Dunstable, looking past Linton and up the landing-stage. "Wait just one second. Here are some friends of ours."

Linton looked over his shoulder.

"Albert!" he cried.

"And the blighter in the bowler who struck me divers blows in sundry places. Ah, they've sighted us."

"What are you going to do?" We can't have another scrap with them."

"Far from it," said Dunstable gently. "Hullo, Albert.

And my friend in the moth-eaten bowler! This is well met."

"You come out here," said Albert, pausing on the brink.

"Why?" asked Dunstable.

"You see what you'll get."

"But we don't want to see what we'll get. You've got such a narrow mind, Albert—may I call you Bertie? You seem to think that nobody has any pleasures except vulgar brawls. We are going to row up river, and think beautiful thoughts."

Albert was measuring with his eye the distance between the boat and landing-stage. It was not far. A sudden spring. . . .

"If you want a fight, go up to the school and ask for Mr Drummond. He's the gentlemen who sent you to hospital last time. Any time you're passing, I'm sure he'd—"

Albert leaped.

But Linton had had him under observation, and, as he sprung, pushed vigorously with his oar. The gap between boat and shore widened in an instant, and Albert, failing to obtain a foothold on the boat, fell back, with a splash that sent a cascade over his friend and the boatman, into three feet of muddy water. By the time he had scrambled out, his enemies were moving pensively up-stream.

The boatman was annoyed.

"Makin' me wet and spoilin' my paint—what yer mean by it?"

"Me and my friend here we want a boat," said Albert, ignoring the main issue.

"Want a boat! Then you'll not get a boat. Spoil my cushions, too, would you? What next, I wonder! You go to Smith and ask *him* for a boat. Perhaps he ain't so particular about having his cushions—"

"Orl right," said Albert, "*orl* right."

Mr Smith proved more complaisant, and a quarter of an hour after Dunstable and Linton had disappeared, Albert and his friend were on the water. Moist outside, Albert burned with a desire for Revenge. He meant to follow his men till he found them. It almost seemed as if there would be a repetition of the naval battle which had caused the town to be put out of bounds. Albert was a quick-tempered youth, and he had swallowed fully a pint of Severn water.

Dunstable and Linton sat for some time in the oak parlour of the "Blue Boar". It was late when they went out. As they reached the water's edge Linton uttered a cry of consternation.

"What's up?" asked Dunstable. "I wish you wouldn't do that so suddenly. It gives me a start. Do you feel bad?"

"Great Scott! it's gone."

"The pain?"

"Our boat. I tied it up to this post."

"You can't have done. What's that boat over there! That looks like ours."

"No, it isn't. That was there when we came. I noticed it. I tied ours up here, to this post."

"This is a shade awkward," said Dunstable thoughfully. "You must have tied it up jolly rottenly. It must have slipped away and gone down-stream. This is where we find ourselves in the cart. Right among the ribstons, by Jove. I feel like that Frenchman in the story, who lost his glasses just as he got to the top of the mountain, and missed the view. Altogezzer I do not vish I 'ad kom."

"I'm certain I tied it up all right. And—why, look! here's the rope still on the pole, just as I left it."

For the first time Dunstable seemed interested.

"This is getting mysterious. Did we hire a rowing-boat or a submarine? There's something on the end of this rope. Give it a tug, and see. There, didn't you feel it?"

"I do believe," said Linton in an awed voice, "the thing's sunk."

They pulled at the rope together. The waters heaved and broke, and up came the nose of the boat, to sink back with a splash as they loosened their hold.

"There are more things in Heaven and Earth—" said Dunstable, wiping his hands. "If you ask me, I should say an enemy hath done this. A boat doesn't sink of its own accord."

"Albert!" said Linton. "The blackguard must have followed us up and done it while we were at tea."

"That's about it," said Dunstable. "And now—how about getting home?"

"I suppose we'd better walk. We shall be hours late for lock-up."

"You," said Dunstable, "may walk if you are fond of exercise and aren't in a hurry. Personally, I'm going back by river."

"But—"

"That looks a good enough boat over there. Anyhow, we must make it do. One mustn't be particular for once."

"But it belongs—what will the other fellow do?"

"I can't help *his* troubles," said Dunstable mildly, "having enough of my own. Coming?"

It was about ten minutes later that Sheen, approaching the waterside in quest of his boat, found no boat there. The time was a quarter to six, and lock-up was at six-thirty.

XIII

Deus Ex Machina

It did not occur to Sheen immediately that his boat had actually gone. The full beauty of the situation was some moments in coming home to him. At first he merely thought that somebody had moved it to another part of the bank, as the authorities at the inn had done once or twice in the past, to make room for the boats of fresh visitors. Walking along the lawn in search of it, he came upon the stake to which Dunstable's submerged craft was attached. He gave the rope a tentative pull, and was surprised to find that there was a heavy drag on the end of it.

Then suddenly the truth flashed across him. "Heavens!" he cried, "it's sunk."

Joe Bevan and other allies lent their aid to the pulling. The lost boat came out of the river like some huge fish, and finally rested on the bank, oozing water and drenching the grass in all directions.

Joe Bevan stooped down, and examined it in the dim light.

"What's happened here, sir," he said, "is that there's a plank gone from the bottom. Smashed clean out, it is. Not started it isn't. Smashed clean out. That's what it is. Some one must have been here and done it."

Sheen looked at the boat, and saw that he was right. A plank in the middle had been splintered. It looked as if somebody had driven some heavy instrument into it. As a matter of fact, Albert had effected the job with the butt-end of an oar.

The damage was not ruinous. A carpenter could put the thing right at no great expense. But it would take time. And meanwhile the minutes were flying, and lock-up was now little more than half an hour away.

"What'll you do, sir?" asked Bevan.

That was just what Sheen was asking himself. What could he do? The road to the school twisted and turned to such an extent that, though the distance from the "Blue Boar" to Seymour's was only a couple of miles as the crow flies, he would have to cover double that distance unless he took a short cut across the fields. And if he took a short cut in the dark he was certain to lose himself. It was a choice of evils. The "Blue Boar" possessed but one horse and trap, and he had seen that driven away to the station in charge of a fisherman's luggage half an hour before.

"I shall have to walk," he said.

"It's a long way. You'll be late, won't you?" said Mr Bevan.

"It can't be helped. I suppose I shall. I wonder who smashed that boat," he added after a pause.

Passing through the inn on his way to the road, he made inquiries. It appeared that two young gentlemen from the school had been there to tea. They had arrived in a boat and gone away in a boat. Nobody else had come into the inn. Suspicion obviously rested upon them.

"Do you remember anything about them?" asked Sheen.

Further details came out. One of the pair had worn a cap like Sheen's. The other's headgear, minutely described, showed him that its owner was a member of the school second eleven.

Sheen pursued the inquiry. He would be so late in any case that a minute or so more or less would make no material difference; and he was very anxious to find out, if possible, who it was that had placed him in this difficulty. He knew that he was unpopular in the school, but he had not looked for this sort of thing.

Then somebody suddenly remembered having heard one of the pair address the other by name.

"What name?" asked Sheen.

His informant was not sure. Would it be Lindon?

"Linton," said Sheen.

That was it.

Sheen thanked him and departed, still puzzled. Linton, as

he knew him, was not the sort of fellow to do a thing like that. And the other, the second eleven man, must be Dunstable. They were always about together. He did not know much about Dunstable, but he could hardly believe that this sort of thing was his form either. Well, he would have to think of that later. He must concentrate himself now on covering the distance to the school in the minimum of time. He looked at his watch. Twenty minutes more. If he hurried, he might not be so very late. He wished that somebody would come by in a cart, and give him a lift.

He stopped and listened. No sound of horse's hoof broke the silence. He walked on again.

Then, faint at first, but growing stronger every instant, there came from some point in the road far behind him a steady droning sound. He almost shouted with joy. A motor! Even now he might do it.

But could he stop it? Would the motorist pay any attention to him, or would he flash past and leave him in the dust? From the rate at which the drone increased the car seemed to be travelling at a rare speed.

He moved to one side of the road, and waited. He could see the lights now, flying towards him.

Then, as the car hummed past, he recognised its driver, and put all he knew into a shout.

"Bruce!" he cried.

For a moment it seemed as if he had not been heard. The driver paid not the smallest attention, as far as he could see. He looked neither to the left nor to right. Then the car slowed down, and, backing, came slowly to where he stood.

"Hullo," said the driver, "who's that?"

Jack Bruce was alone in the car, muffled to the eyes in an overcoat. It was more by his general appearance than his face that Sheen had recognised him.

"It's me, Sheen. I say, Bruce, I wish you'd give me a lift to Seymour's, will you?"

There was never any waste of words about Jack Bruce. Of all the six hundred and thirty-four boys at Wrykyn he was probably the only one whose next remark in such circumstances would not have been a question. Bruce seldom asked questions—never, if they wasted time.

"Hop in," he said.

Sheen consulted his watch again.

"Lock-up's in a quarter of an hour," he said, "but they give us ten minutes' grace. That allows us plenty of time, doesn't it?"

"Do it in seven minutes, if you like."

"Don't hurry," said Sheen. "I've never been in a motor before, and I don't want to cut the experience short. It's awfully good of you to give me a lift."

"That's all right," said Bruce.

"Were you going anywhere? Am I taking you out of your way?"

"No. I was just trying the car. It's a new one. The pater's just got it."

"Do you do much of this?" said Sheen.

"Good bit. I'm going in for the motor business when I leave school."

"So all this is training?"

"That's it."

There was a pause.

"You seemed to be going at a good pace just now," said Sheen.

"About thirty miles an hour. She can move all right."

"That's faster than you're allowed to go, isn't it?"

"Yes."

"You've never been caught, have you?"

"Not yet. I want to see how much pace I can get out of her, because she'll be useful when the election really comes on. Bringing voters to the poll, you know. That's why the pater bought this new car. It's a beauty. His other's only a little runabout."

"Doesn't your father mind your motoring?"

"Likes it," said Jack Bruce.

It seemed to Sheen that it was about time that he volunteered some information about himself, instead of plying his companion with questions. It was pleasant talking to a Wrykinian again; and Jack Bruce had apparently either not heard of the Albert incident, or else he was not influenced by it in any way.

"You've got me out of an awful hole, Bruce," he began.

"That's all right. Been out for a walk?"

"I'd been to the 'Blue Boar'. "

"Oh!" said Bruce. He did not seem to wish to know why Sheen had been there.

Sheen proceeded to explain.

"I suppose you've heard all about me," he said uncomfortably. "About the town, you know. That fight. Not joining in."

"Heard something about it," said Bruce.

"I went down town again after that," said Sheen, "and met the same fellows who were fighting Linton and the others. They came for me, and I was getting awfully mauled when Joe Bevan turned up."

"Oh, is Joe back again?"

"Do you know him?" asked Sheen in surprise.

"Oh yes. I used to go to the 'Blue Boar' to learn boxing from him all last summer holidays."

"Did you really? Why, that's what I'm doing now."

"Good man," said Bruce.

"Isn't he a splendid teacher?"

"Ripping."

"But I didnt know you boxed, Bruce. You never went in for any of the School competitions."

"I'm rather a rotten weight. Ten six. Too heavy for the Light-Weights and not heavy enough for the Middles. Besides, the competitions here are really inter-house. They don't want day-boys going in for them. Are you going to box for Seymour's?"

"That's what I want to do. You see, it would be rather a score, wouldn't it? After what's happened, you know."

"I suppose it would."

"I should like to do something. It's not very pleasant," he added, with a forced laugh, "being considered a disgrace to the house, and cut by everyone."

"Suppose not."

"The difficulty is Drummond. You see, we are both the

same weight, and he's much better than I am. I'm hoping that he'll go in for the Middles and let me take the Light-Weights. There's nobody he couldn't beat in the Middles, though he would be giving away a stone."

"Have you asked him?"

"Not yet. I want to keep it dark that I'm learning to box, just at present."

"Spring it on them suddenly?"

"Yes. Of course, I can't let it get about that I go to Joe Bevan, because I have to break bounds every time I do it."

"The upper river's out of bounds now for boarders, isn't it?"

"Yes."

Jack Bruce sat in silence for a while, his gaze concentrated on the road in front of him.

"Why go by river at all?" he said at last. "If you like, I'll run you to the 'Blue Boar' in the motor every day."

"Oh, I say, that's awfully decent of you," said Sheen.

"I should like to see old Joe again. I think I'll come and spar, too. If you're learning, what you want more than anything is somebody your own size to box with."

"That's just what Joe was saying. Will you really? I should be awfully glad if you would. Boxing with Joe is all right, but you feel all the time he's fooling with you. I should like to try how I got on with somebody else."

"You'd better meet me here, then, as soon after school as you can."

As he spoke, the car stopped.

"Where are we?" asked Sheen.

"Just at the corner of the road behind the houses."

"Oh, I know. Hullo, there goes the lock-up bell. I shall do it comfortably."

He jumped down.

"I say, Bruce," he said, "I really am most awfully obliged for the lift. Something went wrong with my boat, and I couldn't get back in it. I should have been frightfully in the cart if you hadn't come by."

"That's all right," said Jack Bruce. "I say, Sheen!"

"Hullo?"

"Are you going to practise in the music-room after morning school tomorrow?"

"Yes. Why?"

"I think I'll turn up."

"I wish you would."

"What's that thing that goes like this? I forget most of it. He whistled a few bars.

"That's a thing of Greig's," said Sheen.

"You might play it tomorrow," said Bruce.

"Rather. Of course I will."

"Thanks," said Jack Bruce. "Good night."

He turned the car, and vanished down the road. From the sound Sheen judged that he was once more travelling at a higher rate of speed than the local police would have approved.

XIV

A Skirmish

Upon consideration Sheen determined to see Linton about that small matter of the boat without delay. After prayers that night he went to his study.

"Can I speak to you for a minute, Linton?" he said.

Linton was surprised. He disapproved of this intrusion. When a fellow is being cut by the house, he ought, by all the laws of school etiquette, to behave as such, and not speak till he is spoken to.

"What do you want?" asked Linton.

"I shan't keep you long. Do you think you could put away that book for a minute, and listen?"

Linton hesitated, then shut the book.

"Hurry up, then," he said.

"I was going to," said Sheen. "I simply came in to tell you that I know perfectly well who sunk my boat this afternoon."

He felt at once that he had now got Linton's undivided attention.

"Your boat!" said Linton. "You don't mean to say that was yours! What on earth were you doing at the place?"

"I don't think that's any business of yours, is it, Linton?"

"How did you get back?"

"I don't think that's any business of yours, either. I daresay you're disappointed, but I did manage to get back. In time for lock-up, too."

"But I don't understand. Do you mean to say that that was your boat we took?"

"Sunk," corrected Sheen.

"Don't be a fool, Sheen. What the dickens should we want to sink your boat for? What happened was this. Albert

—you remember Albert?—followed us up to the inn, and smashed our boat while we were having tea. When we got out and found it sunk, we bagged the only other one we could see. We hadn't a notion it was yours. We thought it belonged to some fisherman chap."

"Then you didn't sink my boat?"

"Of course we didn't. What do you take us for?"

"Sorry," said Sheen. "I thought it was a queer thing for you to have done. I'm glad it wasn't you. Good night."

"But look here," said Linton, "don't go. It must have landed you in a frightful hole, didn't it?"

"A little. But it doesn't matter. Good night."

"But half a second, Sheen—"

Sheen had disappeared.

Linton sat on till lights were turned off, ruminating. He had a very tender conscience where other members of the school were concerned, though it was tougher as regarded masters; and he was full of remorse at the thought of how nearly he had got Sheen into trouble by borrowing his boat that afternoon. It seemed to him that it was his duty to make it up to him in some way.

It was characteristic of Linton that the episode did not, in any way, alter his attitude towards Sheen. Another boy in a similar position might have become effusively friendly. Linton looked on the affair in a calm, judicial spirit. He had done Sheen a bad turn, but that was no reason why he should fling himself on his neck and swear eternal friendship. His demeanour on the occasions when they came in contact with each other remained the same. He did not speak to him, and he did not seem to see him. But all the while he was remembering that somehow or other he must do him a good turn of some sort, by way of levelling things up again. When that good turn had been done, he might dismiss him from his thoughts altogether.

Sheen, for his part, made no attempt to trade on the matter of the boat. He seemed as little anxious to be friendly with Linton as Linton was to be friendly with him. For this Linton was grateful, and continued to keep his eyes open in the hope of finding some opportunity of squaring up matters between them.

His chance was not long in coming. The feeling in the house against Sheen, caused by the story of his encounter with Attell, had not diminished. Stanning had fostered it in various little ways. It was not difficult. When a house of the standing in the school which Seymour's possessed exhibits a weak spot, the rest of the school do not require a great deal of encouragement to go on prodding that weak spot. In short, the school rotted Seymour's about Sheen, and Seymour's raged impotently. Fags of other houses expended much crude satire on Seymour's fags, and even the seniors of the house came in for their share of the baiting. Most of the houses at Wrykyn were jealous of Seymour's, and this struck them as an admirable opportunity of getting something of their own back.

One afternoon, not long after Sheen's conversation with Linton, Stanning came into Seymour's senior day-room and sat down on the table. The senior day-room objected to members of other houses coming and sitting on their table as if they had bought that rickety piece of furniture; but Stanning's reputation as a bruiser kept their resentment within bounds.

"Hullo, you chaps," said Stanning.

The members of the senior day-room made no reply, but continued, as Mr Kipling has it, to persecute their vocations. Most of them were brewing. They went on brewing with the earnest concentration of *chefs*.

"You're a cheery lot," said Stanning. "But I don't wonder you've got the hump. I should be a bit sick if we'd got a skunk like that in our house. Heard the latest?"

Some lunatic said, "No. What?" thereby delivering the day-room bound into the hands of the enemy.

"Sheen's apologised to Attell."

There was a sensation in the senior day-room, as Stanning had expected. He knew his men. He was perfectly aware that any story which centred round Sheen's cowardice would be believed by them, so he had not troubled to invent a lie which it would be difficult to disprove. He knew that in the present state of feeling in the house Sheen would not be given a hearing.

"No!" shouted the senior day-room.

This was the last straw. The fellow seemed to go out of his way to lower the prestige of the house.

"Fact," said Stanning. "I thought you knew."

He continued to sit on the table, swinging his legs, while the full horror of his story sunk into the senior day-room mind.

"I wonder you don't do something about it. Why don't you touch him up? He's not a prefect."

But they were not prepared to go to that length. The senior day-room had a great respect both for Drummond's word and his skill with his hands. He had said he would slay any one who touched Sheen, and they were of opinion that he would do it.

"He isn't in," said one of the brewers, looking up from his toasting-fork. "His study door was open when I passed."

"I say, why not rag his study?" suggested another thickly, through a mouthful of toast.

Stanning smiled.

"Good idea," he said.

It struck him that some small upheaval of Sheen's study furniture, coupled with the burning of one or two books, might check to some extent that student's work for the Gotford. And if Sheen could be stopped working for the Gotford, he, Stanning, would romp home. In the matter of brilliance there was no comparison between them. It was Sheen's painful habit of work which made him dangerous.

Linton had been listening to this conversation in silence. He had come to the senior day-room to borrow a book. He now slipped out, and made his way to Drummond's study.

Drummond was in. Linton proceeded to business.

"I say, Drummond."

"Hullo?"

"That man Stanning has come in. He's getting the senior day-room to rag Sheen's study."

"What!"

Linton repeated his statement.

"Does the man think he owns the house?" said Drummond. "Where is he?"

"Coming up now. I hear them. What are you going to do? Stop them?"

"What do you think? Of course I am. I'm not going to have any of Appleby's crew coming into Seymour's and ragging studies."

"This ought to be worth seeing," said Linton. "Look on me as 'Charles, his friend'. I'll help if you want me, but it's your scene."

Drummond opened his door just as Stanning and his myrmidons were passing it.

"Hullo, Stanning," he said.

Stanning turned. The punitive expedition stopped.

"Do you want anything?" inquired Drummond politely.

The members of the senior day-room who were with Stanning rallied round, silent and interested. This dramatic situation appealed to them. They had a passion for rows, and this looked distinctly promising.

There was a pause. Stanning looked carefully at Drummond. Drummond looked carefully at Stanning.

"I was going to see Sheen," said Stanning at length.

"He isn't in."

"Oh!"

Another pause.

"Was it anything special?" inquired Drummond pleasantly.

The expedition edged a little forward.

"No. Oh, no. Nothing special," said Stanning.

The expedition looked disappointed.

"Any message I can give him?" asked Drummond.

"No, thanks," said Stanning.

"Sure?"

"Quite, thanks."

"I don't think it's worth while your waiting. He may not be in for some time."

"No, perhaps not. Thanks. So long."

"So long."

Stanning turned on his heel, and walked away down the

passage. Drummond went back into his study, and shut the door.

The expedition, deprived of its commander-in-chief, paused irresolutely outside. Then it followed its leader's example.

There was peace in the passage.

XV

The Rout at Ripton

On the Saturday following this episode, the first fifteen travelled to Ripton to play the return match with that school on its own ground. Of the two Ripton matches, the one played at Wrykyn was always the big event of the football year; but the other came next in importance, and the telegram which was despatched to the school shop at the close of the game was always awaited with anxiety. This year Wrykyn looked forward to the return match with a certain amount of apathy, due partly to the fact that the school was in a slack, unpatriotic state, and partly to the hammering the team had received in the previous term, when the Ripton centre three-quarters had run through and scored with monotonous regularity. "We're bound to get sat on," was the general verdict of the school.

Allardyce, while thoroughly agreeing with this opinion, did his best to conceal the fact from the rest of the team. He had certainly done his duty by them. Every day for the past fortnight the forwards and outsides had turned out to run and pass, and on the Saturdays there had been matches with Corpus, Oxford, and the Cambridge Old Wrykinians. In both games the school had been beaten. In fact, it seemed as if they could only perform really well when they had no opponents. To see the three-quarters racing down the field (at practice) and scoring innumerable (imaginary) tries, one was apt to be misled into considering them a fine quartette. But when there was a match, all the beautiful dash and precision of the passing faded away, and the last thing they did was to run straight. Barry was the only one of the four who played the game properly.

But, as regarded condition, there was nothing wrong with

the team. Even Trevor could not have made them train harder; and Allardyce in his more sanguine moments had a shadowy hope that the Ripton score might, with care, be kept in the teens.

Barry had bought a *Sportsman* at the station, and he unfolded it as the train began to move. Searching the left-hand column of the middle page, as we all do when we buy the *Sportsman* on Saturday—to see how our names look in print, and what sort of a team the enemy has got—he made a remarkable discovery. At the same moment Drummond, on the other side of the carriage, did the same.

"I say," he said, "they must have had a big clear-out at Ripton. Have you seen the team they've got out today?"

"I was just looking at it," said Barry.

"What's up with it? inquired Allardyce. "Let's have a look."

"They've only got about half their proper team. They've got a different back—Grey isn't playing."

"Both their centres are, though," said Drummond.

"More fun for us, Drum., old chap," said Attell. "I'm going home again. Stop the train."

Drummond said nothing. He hated Attell most when he tried to be facetious.

"Dunn isn't playing, nor is Waite," said Barry, "so they haven't got either of their proper halves. I say, we might have a chance of doing something today."

"Of course we shall," said Allardyce. "You've only got to buck up and we've got them on toast."

The atmosphere in the carriage became charged with optimism. It seemed a simple thing to defeat a side which was practically a Ripton "A" team. The centre three-quarters were there still, it was true, but Allardyce and Drummond ought to be able to prevent the halves ever getting the ball out to them. The team looked on those two unknown halves as timid novices, who would lose their heads at the kick-off. As a matter of fact, the system of football teaching at Ripton was so perfect, and the keenness so great, that the second fifteen was nearly as good as the first every year. But the Wrykyn team did not know this, with the exception of Allardyce, who kept his knowledge to himself; and they arrived at Ripton jaunty and confident.

Keith, the Ripton captain, who was one of the centre three-quarters who had made so many holes in the Wrykyn defence in the previous term, met the team at the station, and walked up to the school with them, carrying Allardyce's bag.

"You seem to have lost a good many men at Christmas," said Allardyce. "We were reading the *Sportsman* in the train. Apparently, you've only got ten of your last term's lot. Have they all left?"

The Ripton captain grinned ruefully.

"Not much," he replied. "They're all here. All except Dunn. You remember Dunn? Little thick-set chap who played half. He always had his hair quite tidy and parted exactly in the middle all through the game."

"Oh, yes, I remember Dunn. What's he doing now?"

"Gone to Coopers Hill. Rot, his not going to the Varsity. He'd have walked into his blue."

Allardyce agreed. He had marked Dunn in the match of the previous term, and that immaculate sportsman had made things not a little warm for him.

"Where are all the others, then?" he asked. "Where's that other half of yours? And the rest of the forwards?"

"Mumps," said Keith.

"What!"

"It's a fact. Rot, isn't it? We've had a regular bout of it. Twenty fellows got it altogether. Naturally, four of those were in the team. That's the way things happen. I only wonder the whole scrum didn't have it."

"What beastly luck," said Allardyce. "We had measles like that a couple of years ago in the summer term, and had to play the Incogs and Zingari with a sort of second eleven. We got mopped."

"That's what we shall get this afternoon, I'm afraid," said Keith.

"Oh, no," said Allardyce. "Of course you won't."

And, as events turned out, that was one of the truest remarks he had ever made in his life.

One of the drawbacks to playing Ripton on its own ground was the crowd. Another was the fact that one generally got beaten. But your sportsman can put up with defeat. What he does not like is a crowd that regards him as a subtle blend of incompetent idiot and malicious scoundrel, and says so very loud and clear. It was not, of course, the school that did this. They spent their time blushing for the shouters. It was the patriotic inhabitants of Ripton town who made the school wish that they could be saved from their friends. The football ground at Ripton was at the edge of the school fields, separated from the road by narrow iron railings; and along these railings the choicest spirits of the town would line up, and smoke and yell, and spit and yell again. As Wordsworth wrote, "There are two voices". They were on something like the following lines.

Inside the railings: "Sch-oo-oo-oo-oo-l! Buck up Sch-oo-oo-oo-oo-l!! Get it OUT, Schoo-oo-oo-oo-l!!!"

Outside the railings: "Gow it, Ripton! That's the way, Ripton! Twist his good-old-English-adjectived neck, Ripton! Sit on his forcibly described head, Ripton! Gow it, Ripton! Haw, Haw, Haw! They ain't no use, RIPTON! Kick 'im in the eye, RIPTON! Haw, Haw, Haw!

The bursts of merriment signalised the violent downfall of some dangerous opponent.

The school loathed these humble supporters, and occasionally fastidious juniors would go the length of throwing chunks of mud at them through the railings. But nothing discouraged them or abated their fervid desire to see the school win. Every year they seemed to increase in zeal, and they were always in great form at the Wrykyn match.

It would be charitable to ascribe to this reason the gruesome happenings of that afternoon. They needed some explaining away.

Allardyce won the toss, and chose to start downhill, with the wind in his favour. It is always best to get these advan-

tages at the beginning of the game. If one starts against
the wind, it usually changes ends at half-time. Amidst a
roar from both touch-lines and a volley of howls from the
road, a Ripton forward kicked off. The ball flew in the
direction of Stanning, on the right wing. A storm of laughter
arose from the road as he dropped it. The first scrum was
formed on the Wrykyn twenty-five line.

The Ripton forwards got the ball, and heeled with their
usual neatness. The Ripton half who was taking the scrum
gathered it cleanly, and passed to his colleague. He was a
sturdy youth with a dark, rather forbidding face, in which
the acute observer might have read signs of the savage. He
was of the breed which is vaguely described at public schools
as "nigger", a term covering every variety of shade from
ebony to light lemon. As a matter of fact he was a half-caste,
sent home to England to be educated. Drummond recognised him as he dived forward to tackle him. The last place
where they had met had been the roped ring at Aldershot.
It was his opponent in the final of the Feathers.

He reached him as he swerved, and they fell together.
The ball bounded forward.

"Hullo, Peteiro," he said. "Thought you'd left."

The other grinned recognition.

"Hullo, Drummond."

"Going up to Aldershot this year?"

"Yes. Light-Weight."

"So am I."

The scrum had formed by now, and further conversation
was impossible. Drummond looked a little thoughtful as he
put the ball in. He had been told that Peteiro was leaving
Ripton at Christmas. It was a nuisance his being still at
school. Drummond was not afraid of him—he would have
fought a champion of the world if the school had expected
him to—but he could not help remembering that it was only
by the very narrowest margin, and after a terrific three
rounds, that he had beaten him in the Feathers the year
before. It would be too awful for words if the decision were
to be reversed in the coming competition.

But he was not allowed much leisure for pondering on

the future. The present was too full of incident and excitement. The withdrawal of the four invalids and the departure of Dunn had not reduced the Ripton team to that wreck of its former self which the Wrykyn fifteen had looked for. On the contrary, their play seemed, if anything, a shade better than it had been in the former match. There was all the old aggressiveness, and Peteiro and his partner, so far from being timid novices and losing their heads, eclipsed the exhibition given at Wrykyn by Waite and Dunn. Play had only been in progress six minutes when Keith, taking a pass on the twenty-five line, slipped past Attell, ran round the back, and scored between the posts. Three minutes later the other Ripton centre scored. At the end of twenty minutes the Wrykyn line had been crossed five times, and each of the tries had been converted.

"*Can't* you fellows get that ball in the scrum?" demanded Allardyce plaintively, as the team began for the fifth time the old familiar walk to the half-way line. "Pack tight, and get the first shove."

The result of this address was to increase the Ripton lead by four points. In his anxiety to get the ball, one of the Wrykyn forwards started heeling before it was in, and the referee promptly gave a free kick to Ripton for "foot up". As this event took place within easy reach of the Wrykyn goal, and immediately in front of the same, Keith had no difficulty in bringing off the penalty.

By half-time the crowd in the road, hoarse with laughter, had exhausted all their adjectives and were repeating themselves. The Ripton score was six goals, a penalty goal, and two tries to *nil*, and the Wrykyn team was a demoralised rabble.

The fact that the rate of scoring slackened somewhat after the interval may be attributed to the disinclination of the Riptonians to exert themselves unduly. They ceased playing in the stern and scientific spirit in which they had started; and, instead of adhering to an orthodox game, began to enjoy themselves. The forwards no longer heeled like a machine. They broke through ambitiously, and tried to score on their own account. When the outsides got as far as the back, they did not pass. They tried to drop goals. In this way only twenty-two points were scored after half-time. Allardyce and Drummond battled on nobly, but with their pack hopelessly outclassed it was impossible for them to do anything of material use. Barry, on the wing, tackled his man whenever the latter got the ball, but, as a rule, the centres did not pass, but attacked by themselves. At last, by way of a fitting conclusion to the rout, the Ripton back, catching a high punt, ran instead of kicking, and, to the huge delight of the town contingent, scored. With this incident the visiting team drained the last dregs of the bitter cup. Humiliation could go no further. Almost immediately afterwards the referee blew his whistle for "No side".

"Three cheers for Wrykyn," said Keith.

To the fifteen victims it sounded ironical.

XVI

Drummond Goes Into Retirement

The return journey of a school team after a crushing defeat in a foreign match is never a very exhilarating business. Those members of the side who have not yet received their colours are wondering which of them is to be sacrificed to popular indignation and "chucked": the rest, who have managed to get their caps, are feeling that even now two-thirds of the school will be saying that they are not worth a place in the third fifteen; while the captain, brooding apart, is becoming soured at the thought that Posterity will forget what little good he may have done, and remember only that it was in his year that the school got so many points taken off them by So-and-So. Conversation does not ripple and sparkle during these home-comings. The Wrykyn team made the journey in almost unbroken silence. They were all stiff and sore, and their feelings were such as to unfit them for talking to people.

The school took the thing very philosophically—a bad sign. When a school is in a healthy, normal condition, it should be stirred up by a bad defeat by another school, like a disturbed wasps' nest. Wrykyn made one or two remarks about people who could not play footer for toffee, and then let the thing drop.

Sheen was too busy with his work and his boxing to have much leisure for mourning over this latest example of the present inefficiency of the school. The examination for the Gotford was to come off in two days, and the inter-house boxing was fixed for the following Wednesday. In five days, therefore, he would get his chance of retrieving his lost place in the school. He was certain that he could, at any rate make a very good show against anyone in the school, even Drummond. Joe Bevan was delighted with his progress, and quoted Shakespeare volubly in his admiration. Jack Bruce and Francis added their tribute, and the knife and boot boy paid him the neatest compliment of all by refusing point-blank to have any more dealings with him whatsoever. His professional duties, explained the knife and boot boy, did not include being punched in the heye by blokes, and he did not intend to be put upon.

"You'll do all right," said Jack Bruce, as they were motoring home, "if they'll let you go in for it all. But how do you know they will? Have they chosen the men yet?"

"Not yet. They don't do it till the day before. But there won't be any difficulty about that. Drummond will let me have a shot if he thinks I'm good enough."

"Oh, you're good enough," said Bruce.

And when, on Monday evening, Francis, on receipt of no fewer than four blows in a single round—a record, shook him by the hand and said that if ever he happened to want a leetle darg that was a perfect bag of tricks and had got a pedigree, mind you, he, Francis, would be proud to supply that animal, Sheen felt that the moment had come to approach Drummond on the subject of the house boxing. It would be a little awkward at first, and conversation would probably run somewhat stiffly; but all would be well once he had explained himself.

But things had been happening in his absence which complicated the situation. Allardyce was having tea with Drummond, who had been stopping in with a sore throat. He had come principally to make arrangements for the match between his house and Seymour's in the semi-final round of the competition.

"You're looking bad," he said, taking a seat.

"I'm feeling bad," said Drummond. For the past few days he had been very much out of sorts. He put it down to a chill caught after the Ripton match. He had never mustered up sufficient courage to sponge himself with cold water after soaking in a hot bath, and he occasionally suffered for it.

"What's up?" inquired Allardyce.

"Oh, I don't know. Sort of beastly feeling. Sore throat. Nothing much. Only it makes you feel rather rotten."

Allardyce looked interested.

"I say," he said, "it looks as if—I wonder. I hope you haven't."

"What?"

"Mumps. It sounds jolly like it."

"Mumps! Of course I've not. Why should I?"

Allardyce produced a letter from his pocket. "I got this from Keith, the Ripton captain, this morning. You know they've had a lot of the thing there. Oh, didn't you? That was why they had such a bad team out."

"Bad team!" murmured Drummond.

"Well, I mean not their best team. They had four of their men down with mumps. Here's what Keith says. Listen. Bit about hoping we got back all right, and so on, first. Then he says—here it is, 'Another of our fellows has got the mumps. One of the forwards; rather a long man who was good out of touch. He developed it a couple of days after the match. It's lucky that all our card games are over. We beat John's, Oxford, last Wednesday, and that finished the card. But it'll rather rot up the House matches. We should have walked the cup, but there's no knowing what will happen now. I hope none of your lot caught the mumps from Browning during the game. It's quite likely, of course. Browning ought not to have been playing, but I had no notion that there was anything wrong with him. He never said he felt bad.' You've got it, Drummond. That's what's the matter with you."

"Oh, rot," said Drummond. "It's only a chill."

But the school doctor, who had looked in at the house to dose a small Seymourite who had indulged too heartily in the pleasures of the table, had other views, and before lock-up Drummond was hurried off to the infirmary.

Sheen went to Drummond's study after preparation had begun, and was surprised to find him out. Not being on speaking terms with a single member of the house, he was always out-of-date as regarded items of school news. As a rule he had to wait until Jack Bruce told him before learning of any occurrence of interest. He had no notion that mumps was the cause of Drummond's absence, and he sat

and waited patiently for him in his study till the bell rang
for prayers. The only possible explanation that occurred to
him was that Drummond was in somebody else's study, and
he could not put his theory to the test by going and looking.
It was only when Drummond did not put in an appearance
at prayers that Sheen began to suspect that something might
have happened.

It was maddening not to be able to make inquiries. He
had almost decided to go and ask Linton, and risk whatever
might be the consequences of such a step, when he remembered that the matron must know. He went to her, and was
told that Drummond was in the infirmary.

He could not help seeing that this made his position a
great deal more difficult. In ten minutes he could have explained matters to Drummond if he had found him in his
study. But it would be a more difficult task to put the thing
clearly in a letter.

Meanwhile, it was bed-time, and he soon found his hands
too full with his dormitory to enable him to think out the
phrasing of that letter. The dormitory, which was recruited
entirely from the junior day-room, had heard of Drummond's departure with rejoicings. They liked Drummond,
but he was a good deal too fond of the iron hand for their
tastes. A night with Sheen in charge should prove a welcome
change.

A deafening uproar was going on when Sheen arrived,
and as he came into the room somebody turned the gas out.
He found some matches on the chest of drawers, and lit it
again just in time to see a sportive youth tearing the clothes
off his bed and piling them on the floor. A month before
he would not have known how to grapple with such a
situation, but his evenings with Joe Bevan had given him
the habit of making up his mind and acting rapidly. Drummond was wont to keep a swagger-stick by his bedside for
the better observance of law and order. Sheen possessed
himself of this swagger-stick, and reasoned with the sportive
youth. The rest of the dormitory looked on in interested
silence. It was a critical moment, and on his handling of it
depended Sheen's victory or defeat. If he did not keep his

head he was lost. A domitory is merciless to a prefect whose weakness they have discovered.

Sheen kept his head. In a quiet, pleasant voice, fingering the swagger-stick, as he spoke, in an absent manner, he requested his young friend to re-make the bed—rapidly and completely. For the space of five minutes no sound broke the silence except the rustle of sheets and blankets. At the end of that period the bed looked as good as new.

"Thanks," said Sheen gratefully. "That's very kind of you."

He turned to the rest of the dormitory.

"Don't let me detain you," he said politely. "Get into bed as soon as you like."

The dormitory got into bed sooner than they liked. For some reason the colossal rag they had planned had fizzled out. They were thoughtful as they crept between the sheets. Could these things be?

After much deliberation Sheen sent his letter to Drummond on the following day. It was not a long letter, but it was carefully worded. It explained that he had taken up boxing of late, and ended with a request that he might be allowed to act as Drummond's understudy in the House competitions.

It was late that evening when the infirmary attendant came over with the answer.

Like the original letter, the answer was brief.

"Dear Sheen," wrote Drummond, "thanks for the offer. I am afraid I can't accept it. We must have the best man. Linton is going to box for the House in the Light-Weights."

XVII

Seymour's One Success

This polite epistle, it may be mentioned, was a revised version of the one which Drummond originally wrote in reply to Sheen's request. His first impulse had been to answer in the four brief words, "Don't be a fool"; for Sheen's letter had struck him as nothing more than a contemptible piece of posing, and he had all the hatred for poses which is a characteristic of the plain and straightforward type of mind. It seemed to him that Sheen, as he expressed it to himself, was trying to "do the boy hero". In the school library, which had been stocked during the dark ages, when that type of story was popular, there were numerous school stories in which the hero retrieved a rocky reputation by thrashing the bully, displaying in the encounter an intuitive but overwhelming skill with his fists. Drummond could not help feeling that Sheen must have been reading one of these stories. It was all very fine and noble of him to want to show that he was No Coward After All, like Leo Cholmondeley or whatever his beastly name was, in *The Lads of St. Ethelberta's* or some such piffling book; but, thought Drummond in his cold, practical way, what about the house? If Sheen thought that Seymour's was going to chuck away all chance of winning one of the inter-house events, simply in order to give him an opportunity of doing the Young Hero, the sooner he got rid of that sort of idea, the better. If he wanted to do the Leo Cholmondeley business, let him go and chuck a kid into the river, and jump in and save him. But he wasn't going to have the house let in for twenty Sheens.

Such were the meditations of Drummond when the infirmary attendant brought Sheen's letter to him; and he seized pencil and paper and wrote, "Don't be a fool". But pity succeeded contempt, and he tore up the writing. After all, however much he had deserved it, the man had had a bad time. It was no use jumping on him. And at one time they had been pals. Might as well do the thing politely.

All of which reflections would have been prevented had Sheen thought of mentioning the simple fact that it was Joe Bevan who had given him the lessons to which he referred in his letter. But he had decided not to do so, wishing to avoid long explanations. And there was, he felt, a chance that the letter might come into other hands than those of Drummond. So he had preserved silence on that point, thereby wrecking his entire scheme.

It struck him that he might go to Linton, explain his position, and ask him to withdraw in his favour, but there were difficulties in the way of that course. There is a great deal of red tape about the athletic arrangements of a house at a public school. When once an order has gone forth, it is difficult to get it repealed. Linton had been chosen to represent the house in the Light-Weights, and he would carry out orders. Only illness would prevent him appearing in the ring.

Sheen made up his mind not to try to take his place, and went through the days a victim to gloom, which was caused by other things besides his disappointment respecting the boxing competition. The Gotford examination was over now, and he was not satisfied with his performance. Though he did not know it, his dissatisfaction was due principally to the fact that, owing to his isolation, he had been unable to compare notes after the examinations with the others. Doing an examination without comparing notes subsequently with one's rivals, is like playing golf against a bogey. The imaginary rival against whom one pits oneself never makes a mistake. Our own "howlers" stand out in all their horrid nakedness; but we do not realise that our rivals have probably made others far worse. In this way Sheen plumbed the depths of depression. The Gotford was a purely Classical examination, with the exception of one paper, a General Knowledge paper; and it was in this that Sheen fancied he had failed so miserably. His Greek and Latin verse were always good; his prose, he felt, was not altogether beyond the pale; but in the General Knowledge paper he had come down heavily. As a matter of fact, if he had only known, the paper was an exceptionally hard one, and there was not a single candidate for the scholarship who felt satisfied with his treatment of it. It was to questions ten, eleven, and thirteen of this paper that Cardew, of the School House, who had entered for the scholarship for the sole reason that competitors got excused two clear days of ordinary school-work, wrote the following answer :

See "Encylopædia Britannica," *Times* edition.

If they really wanted to know, he said subsequently, that was the authority to go to. He himself would probably misinform them altogether.

In addition to the Gotford and the House Boxing, the House Fives now came on, and the authorities of Seymour's were in no small perplexity. They met together in Rigby's study to discuss the matter. Their difficulty was this. There was only one inmate of Seymour's who had a chance of carrying off the House Fives Cup. And that was Sheen. The house was asking itself what was to be done about it.

"You see," said Rigby, "you can look at it in two ways, whichever you like. We ought certainly to send in our best man for the pot, whatever sort of chap he is. But then, come to think of it, Sheen can't very well be said to belong to the house at all. When a man's been cut dead during the whole term, he can't be looked on as one of the house very well. See what I mean?"

"Of course he can't," said Mill, who was second in command at Seymour's. Mill's attitude towards his fellow men was one of incessant hostility. He seemed to bear a grudge against the entire race.

Rigby resumed. He was a pacific person, and hated anything resembling rows in the house. He had been sorry for Sheen, and would have been glad to give him a chance of setting himself on his legs again.

"You see." he said, "this is what I mean. We either recognise Sheen's existence or we don't. Follow? We can't get him to win this Cup for us, and then, when he has done it, go on cutting him and treating him as if he didn't belong to the house at all. I know he let the house down awfully badly in that business, but still, if he lifts the Fives Cup, that'll square the thing. If he does anything to give the house a leg-up, he must be treated as if he'd never let it down at all."

"Of course," said Barry. "I vote we send him in for the Fives."

"What rot!" said Mill. "It isn't as if none of the rest of us played fives."

"We aren't as good as Sheen," said Barry.

"I don't care. I call it rot letting a chap like him represent the house at anything. If he were the best fives-player in the world I wouldn't let him play for the house."

Rigby was impressed by his vehemence. He hesitated.

"After all, Barry," he said, "I don't know. Perhaps it might—you see, he did—well, I really think we'd better have somebody else. The house has got its knife into Sheen too much just at present to want him as a representative. There'd only be sickness, don't you think? Who else is there?"

So it came about that Menzies was chosen to uphold the house in the Fives Courts. Sheen was not surprised. But it was not pleasant. He was certainly having bad luck in his attempts to do something for the house. Perhaps if he won the Gotford they might show a little enthusiasm. The Gotford always caused a good deal of interest in the school. It was the best thing of its kind in existence at Wrykyn, and even the most abandoned loafers liked to feel that their house had won it. It was just possible, thought Sheen, that a brilliant win might change the feelings of Seymour's towards him. He did not care for the applause of the multitude more than a boy should, but he preferred it very decidedly to the cut direct.

Things went badly for Seymour's. Never in the history of the house, or, at any rate, in the comparatively recent history of the house, had there been such a slump in athletic trophies. To begin with, they were soundly beaten in the semi-final for the House football cup by Allardyce's lot. With Drummond away, there was none to mark the captain of the School team at half, and Allardyce had raced through in a manner that must have compensated him to a certain extent for the poor time he had had in first fifteen matches. The game had ended in a Seymourite defeat by nineteen points to five.

Nor had the Boxing left the house in a better position. Linton fought pluckily in the Light-Weights, but went down before Stanning, after beating a representative of Templar's. Mill did not show up well in the Heavy-Weights, and was defeated in his first bout. Seymour's were reduced to telling themselves how different it all would have been if Drummond had been there.

Sheen watched the Light-Weight contests, and nearly danced with irritation. He felt that he could have eaten Stanning. The man was quick with his left, but he couldn't *box*. He hadn't a notion of side-stepping, and the upper-cut appeared to be entirely outside his range. He would like to see him tackle Francis.

Sheen thought bitterly of Drummond. Why on earth couldn't he have given him a chance. It was maddening.

The Fives carried on the story. Menzies was swamped by a Day's man. He might just as well have stayed away altogether. The star of Seymour's was very low on the horizon.

And then the house scored its one success. The headmaster announced it in the Hall after prayers in his dry, unemotional way.

"I have received the list of marks," he said, "from the examiners for the Gotford Scholarship." He paused. Sheen felt a sudden calm triumph flood over him. Somehow, intuitively, he knew that he had won. He waited without excitement for the next words.

"Out of a possible thousand marks, Sheen, who wins the scholarship, obtained seven hundred and one, Stanning six hundred and four, Wilson . . ."

Sheen walked out of the Hall in the unique position of a Gotford winner with only one friend to congratulate him.

Jack Bruce was the one. The other six hundred and thirty-three members of the school made no demonstration.

There was a pleasant custom at Seymour's of applauding at tea any Seymourite who had won distinction, and so shed a reflected glory on the house. The head of the house would observe, "Well played, So-and-So!" and the rest of the house would express their emotion in the way that seemed best to them, to the subsequent exultation of the local crockery merchant, who had generally to supply at least a dozen fresh cups and plates to the house after one of these occasions. When it was for getting his first eleven or first fifteen cap that the lucky man was being cheered, the total of breakages sometimes ran into the twenties.

Rigby, good, easy man, was a little doubtful as to what course to pursue in the circumstances. Should he give the signal? After all, the fellow *had* won the Gotford. It was a score for the house, and they wanted all the scores they could get in these lean years. Perhaps, then, he had better.

"Well played, Sheen," said he.

There was a dead silence. A giggle from the fags' table showed that the comedy of the situation was not lost on the young mind.

The head of the house looked troubled. This was awfully awkward.

"Well played, Sheen," he said again.

"Don't mention it, Rigby," said the winner of the Gotford politely, looking up from his plate.

XVIII

Mr Bevan Makes a Suggestion

When one has been working hard with a single end in view, the arrival and departure of the supreme moment is apt to leave a feeling of emptiness, as if life had been drained of all its interest, and left nothing sufficiently exciting to make it worth doing. Horatius, as he followed his plough on a warm day over the corn land which his gratified country bestowed on him for his masterly handling of the traffic on the bridge, must sometimes have felt it was a little tame. The feeling is far more acute when one has been unexpectedly baulked in one's desire for action. Sheen, for the first few days after he received Drummond's brief note, felt that it was useless for him to try to do anything. The Fates were against him. In stories, as Mr Anstey has pointed out, the hero is never long without his chance of retrieving his reputation. A mad bull comes into the school grounds, and he alone (the hero, not the bull) is calm. Or there is a fire, and whose is that pale and gesticulating form at the upper window? The bully's, of course. And who is that climbing nimbly up the Virginia creeper? Why, the hero. Who else? Three hearty cheers for the plucky hero.

But in real life opportunities of distinguishing oneself are less frequent.

Sheen continued his visits to the "Blue Boar", but more because he shrank from telling Joe Bevan that all his trouble had been for nothing, than because he had any definite object in view. It was bitter to listen to the eulogies of the pugilist, when all the while he knew that, as far as any immediate results were concerned, it did not really matter whether he boxed well or feebly. Some day, perhaps, as Mr Bevan was fond of pointing out when he approached the subject of disadvantages of boxing, he might meet a hooligan when he was crossing a field with his sister; but he found that but small consolation. He was in the position of one who wants a small sum of ready money, and is told that, in a few years, he may come into a fortune. By the time he got a chance of proving himself a man with his hands, he would be an Old Wrykinian. He was leaving at the end of the summer term.

Jack Bruce was sympathetic, and talked more freely than was his wont.

"I can't understand it," he said. "Drummond always seemed a good sort. I should have thought he would have sent you in for the house like a shot. Are you sure you put it plainly in your letter? What did you say?"

Sheen repeated the main points of his letter.

"Did you tell him who had been teaching you?"

"No. I just said I'd been boxing lately."

"Pity," said Jack Bruce. "If you'd mentioned that it was Joe who'd been training you, he would probably have been much more for it. You see, he couldn't know whether you were any good or not from your letter. But if you'd told him that Joe Bevan and Hunt both thought you good, he'd have seen there was something in it."

"It never occurred to me. Like a fool, I was counting on the thing so much that it didn't strike me there would be any real difficulty in getting him to see my point. Especially when he got mumps and couldn't go in himself. Well, it can't be helped now."

And the conversation turned to the prospects of Jack Bruce's father in the forthcoming election, the polling for which had just begun.

"I'm busy now," said Bruce. "I'm not sure that I shall be able to do much sparring with you for a bit."

"My dear chap, don't let me—"

"Oh, it's all right, really. Taking you to the 'Blue Boar' doesn't land me out of my way at all. Most of the work lies round in this direction. I call at cottages, and lug oldest inhabitants to the poll. It's rare sport."

"Does your pater know?"

"Oh, yes. He rots me about it like anything, but, all the

same, I believe he's really rather bucked because I've roped in quite a dozen voters who wouldn't have stirred a yard if I hadn't turned up. That's where we're scoring. Pedder hasn't got a car yet, and these old rotters round here aren't going to move out of their chairs to go for a ride in an ordinary cart. But they chuck away their crutches and hop into a motor like one o'clock."

"It must be rather a rag," said Sheen.

The car drew up at the door of the "Blue Boar". Sheen got out and ran upstairs to the gymnasium. Joe Bevan was sparring a round with Francis. He watched them while he changed, but without the enthusiasm of which he had been conscious on previous occasions. The solid cleverness of Joe Bevan, and the quickness and cunning of the bantam-weight, were as much in evidence as before, but somehow the glamour and romance which had surrounded them were gone. He no longer watched eagerly to pick up the slightest hint from these experts. He felt no more interest than he would have felt in watching a game of lawn tennis. He *had* been keen. Since his disappointment with regard to the House Boxing he had become indifferent.

Joe Bevan noticed this before he had been boxing with him a minute.

"Hullo, sir," he said, "what's this? Tired today? Not feeling well? You aren't boxing like yourself, not at all you aren't. There's no weight behind 'em. You're tapping. What's the matter with your feet, too? You aren't getting about as quickly as I should like to see. What have you been doing to yourself?"

"Nothing that I know of," said Sheen. "I'm sorry I'm so rotten. Let's have another try."

The second try proved as unsatisfactory as the first. He was listless, and his leads and counters lacked conviction.

Joe Bevan, who identified himself with his pupils with that thoroughness which is the hall-mark of the first-class boxing instructor, looked so pained at his sudden loss of form, that Sheen could not resist the temptation to confide in him. After all, he must tell him some time.

"The fact is," he said, as they sat on the balcony

overlooking the river, waiting for Jack Bruce to return with his car, "I've had a bit of a sickener."

"I thought you'd got sick of it," said Mr Bevan. "Well, have a bit of a rest."

"I don't mean that I'm tired of boxing," Sheen hastened to explain. "After all the trouble you've taken with me, it would be a bit thick if I chucked it just as I was beginning to get on. It isn't that. But you know how keen I was on boxing for the house?"

Joe Bevan nodded.

"Did you get beat?"

"They wouldn't let me go in," said Sheen.

"But, bless me! you'd have made babies of them. What was the instructor doing? Couldn't he see that you were good?"

"I didn't get a chance of showing what I could do." He explained the difficulties of the situation.

Mr Bevan nodded his head thoughtfully.

"So naturally," concluded Sheen, "the thing has put me out a bit. It's beastly having nothing to work for. I'm at a loose end. Up till now, I've always had the thought of the House Competition to keep me going. But now—well, you see how it is. It's like running to catch a train, and then finding suddenly that you've got plenty of time. There doesn't seem any point in going on running."

"Why not Aldershot, sir? said Mr Bevan.

"What!" cried Sheen.

The absolute novelty of the idea, and the gorgeous possibilities of it, made him tingle from head to foot. Aldershot! Why hadn't he thought of it before! The House Competition suddenly lost its importance in his eyes. It was a trivial affair, after all, compared with Aldershot, that Mecca of the public-school boxer.

Then the glow began to fade. Doubts crept in. He might have learned a good deal from Joe Bevan, but had he learned enough to be able to hold his own with the best boxers of all the public schools in the country? And if he had the skill to win, had he the heart? Joe Bevan had said that he would not disgrace himself again, and he felt that the chances were against his doing so, but there was the terrible possibility. He had stood up to Francis and the others, and he had taken their blows without flinching; but in these encounters there was always at the back of his mind the comforting feeling that there was a limit to the amount of punishment he would receive. If Francis happened to drive him into a corner where he could neither attack, nor defend himself against attack, he did not use his advantage to the full. He indicated rather than used it. A couple of blows, and he moved out into the open again. But in the Public Schools Competition at Aldershot there would be no quarter. There would be nothing but deadly earnest. If he allowed himself to be manoeuvred into an awkward position, only his own skill, or the call of time, could extricate him from it.

In a word, at the "Blue Boar" he sparred. At Aldershot he would have to fight. Was he capable of fighting?

Then there was another difficulty. How was he to get himself appointed as the Wrykyn light-weight representative? Now that Drummond was unable to box, Stanning would go down, as the winner of the School Competition. These things were worked by an automatic process. Sheen felt that he could beat Stanning, but he had no means of publishing this fact to the school. He could not challenge him to a trial of skill. That sort of thing was not done.

He explained this to Joe Bevan.

"Well, it's a pity," said Joe regretfully. "It's a pity."

At this moment Jack Bruce appeared.

"What's a pity, Joe?" he asked.

"Jo wants me to go to Aldershot as a light-weight," explained Sheen, "and I was just saying that I couldn't, because of Stanning."

"What about Stanning?"

"He won the School Competition, you see, so they're bound to send him down."

"Half a minute," said Jack Bruce. "I never thought of Aldershot for you before. It's a jolly good idea. I believe you'd have a chance. And it's all right about Stanning. He's not going down. Haven't you heard?"

"I don't hear anything. Why isn't he going down?"

"He's knocked up one of his wrists. So he says."

"How do you mean—so he says?" asked Sheen.

"I believe he funks it."

"Why? What makes you think that?"

"Oh, I don't know. It's only my opinion. Still, it's a little queer. Stanning says he crocked his left wrist in the final of the House Competition."

"Well, what's wrong with that? Why shouldn't he have done so?"

Sheen objected strongly to Stanning, but he had the elements of justice in him, and he was not going to condemn him on insufficient evidence, particularly of a crime of which he himself had been guilty.

"Of course he may have done," said Bruce. "But it's a bit fishy that he should have been playing fives all right two days running just after the competition."

"He might have crocked himself then."

"Then why didn't he say so?"

A question which Sheen found himself unable to answer.

"Then there's nothing to prevent you fighting, sir," said Joe Bevan, who had been listening attentively to the conversation.

"Do you really think I've got a chance?"

"I do, sir."

"Of course you have," said Jack Bruce. "You're quite as good as Drummond was, last time I saw him box."

"Then I'll have a shot at it," said Sheen.

"Good for you, sir," cried Joe Bevan.

"Though it'll be a bit of a job getting leave," said Sheen. "How would you start about it, Bruce?"

"You'd better ask Spence. He's the man to go to."

"That's all right. I'm rather a pal of Spence's."

"Ask him tonight after prep.," suggested Bruce.

"And then you can come here regular," said Joe Bevan, "and we'll train you till you're that fit you could eat bricks, and you'll make babies of them up at Aldershot."

XIX

Paving the Way

Bruce had been perfectly correct in his suspicions. Stanning's
wrist was no more sprained than his ankle. The advisability
of manufacturing an injury had come home to him very
vividly on the Saturday morning following the Ripton
match, when he had read the brief report of that painful
episode in that week's number of the *Field* in the school
library. In the list of the Ripton team appeared the name
R. Peteiro. He had heard a great deal about the dusky
Riptonian when Drummond had beaten him in the Feather-
Weights the year before. Drummond had returned from
Aldershot on that occasion cheerful, but in an extremely
battered condition. His appearance as he limped about the
field on Sports Day had been heroic, and, in addition, a fine
advertisment for the punishing powers of the Ripton
champion. It is true that at least one of his injuries had
been the work of a Pauline whom he had met in the opening
bout; but the great majority were presents from Ripton, and
Drummond had described the dusky one, in no uncertain
terms, as a holy terror.

These things had sunk into Stanning's mind. It had been
generally understood at Wrykyn that Peteiro had left school
at Christmas. When Stanning, through his study of the
Field, discovered that the redoubtable boxer had been one
of the team against which he had played at Ripton, and
realised that, owing to Drummond's illness, it would fall to
him, if he won the House Competition, to meet this man of
wrath at Aldershot, he resolved on the instant that the most
persuasive of wild horses should not draw him to that military centre on the day of the Public Schools Competition.
The difficulty was that he particularly wished to win the
House Cup. Then it occurred to him that he could combine

the two things—win the competition and get injured while doing so.

Accordingly, two days after the House Boxing he was observed to issue from Appleby's with his left arm slung in a first fifteen scarf. He was too astute to injure his right wrist. What happens to one's left wrist at school is one's own private business. When one injures one's right arm, and so incapacitates oneself for form work, the authorities begin to make awkward investigations.

Mr Spence, who looked after the school's efforts to win medals at Aldershot, was the most disappointed person in the place. He was an enthusiastic boxer—he had represented Cambridge in the Middle-Weights in his day—and with no small trouble had succeeded in making boxing a going concern at Wrykyn. Years of failure had ended, the Easter before, in a huge triumph, when O'Hara, of Dexter's and Drummond had won silver medals, and Moriarty, of Dexter's, a bronze. If only somebody could win a medal this year, the tradition would be established, and would not soon die out. Unfortunately, there was not a great deal of boxing talent in the school just now. The rule that the winner at his weight in the House Competitions should represent the school at Aldershot only applied if the winner were fairly proficient. Mr Spence exercised his discretion. It was no use sending down novices to be massacred. This year Drummond and Stanning were the only Wrykinians up to Aldershot form. Drummond would have been almost a certainty for a silver medal, and Stanning would probably have been a runner-up. And here they were, both injured; Wrykyn would not have a single representative at the Queen's Avenue Gymnasium. It would be a set-back to the cult of boxing at the school.

Mr Spence was pondering over this unfortunate state of things when Sheen was shown in.

"Can I speak to you for a minute, sir?" said Sheen.

"Certainly, Sheen. Take one of those cig—I mean, sit down. What is it?"

Sheen had decided how to open the interview before knocking at the door. He came to the point at once.

"Do you think I could go down to Aldershot, sir?" he asked.

Mr Spence looked surprised.

"Go down? You mean—? Do you want to watch the competition? Really, I don't know if the headmaster—"

"I mean, can I box?"

Mr Spence's look of surprise became more marked.

"Box?" he said. "But surely—I didn't know you were a boxer, Sheen."

"I've only taken it up lately."

"But you didn't enter for the House Competitions, did you? What weight are you?"

"Just under ten stone."

"A light-weight. Why, Linton boxed for your house in the Light-Weights surely?"

"Yes sir. They wouldn't let me go in."

"You hurt yourself?"

"No, sir."

"Then why wouldn't they let you go in?"

"Drummond thought Linton was better. He didn't know I boxed."

"But—this is very curious. I don't understand it at all. You see, if you were not up to House form, you would hardly— At Aldershot, you see, you would meet the best boxers of all the public schools."

"Yes, sir."

There was a pause.

"It was like this, sir," said Sheen nervously. "At the beginning of the term there was a bit of a row down in the town, and I got mixed up in it. And I didn't—I was afraid to join in. I funked it."

Mr Spence nodded. He was deeply interested now. The office of confessor is always interesting.

"Go on, Sheen. What happened then?"

"I was cut by everybody. The fellows thought I had let the house down, and it got about, and the other houses scored off them, so I had rather a rotten time."

Here it occurred to him that he was telling his story

without that attention to polite phraseology which a master expects from a boy, so he amended the last sentence.

"I didn't have a very pleasant time, sir," was his correction.

"Well?" said Mr Spence.

"So I was a bit sick," continued Sheen, relapsing once more into the vernacular, "and I wanted to do something to put things right again, and I met—anyhow, I took up boxing. I wanted to box for the house, if I was good enough. I practised every day, and stuck to it, and after a bit I did become pretty good."

"Well?"

"Then Drummond got mumps, and I wrote to him asking if I might represent the house instead of him, and I suppose he didn't believe I was any good. At any rate, he wouldn't let me go in. Then Joe—a man who knows something about boxing—suggested I should go down to Aldershot."

"Joe?" said Mr Spence inquiringly.

Sheen had let the name slip out unintentionally, but it was too late now to recall it.

"Joe Bevan, sir," he said. "He used to be champion of England, light-weight."

"Joe Bevan!" cried Mr Spence. "Really? Why, he trained me when I boxed for Cambridge. He's one of the best of fellows. I've never seen any one who took such trouble with his man. I wish we could get him here. So it was Joe who suggested that you should go down to Aldershot? Well, he ought to know. Did he say you would have a good chance?"

"Yes, sir."

"My position is this, you see, Sheen. There is nothing I should like more than to see the school represented at Aldershot. But I cannot let anyone go down, irrespective of his abilities. Aldershot is not child's play. And in the Light-Weights you get the hardest fighting of all. It wouldn't do for me to let you go down if you are not up to the proper form. You would be half killed."

"I should like to have a shot, sir," said Sheen.

"Then this year, as you probably know, Ripton are

sending down Peteiro for the Light-Weights. He was the
fellow whom Drummond only just beat last year. And you
saw the state in which Drummond came back. If Drummond could hardly hold him, what would you do?"

"I believe I could beat Drummond, sir," said Sheen.

Mr Spence's eyes opened wider. Here were brave words.
This youth evidently meant business. The thing puzzled
him. On the one hand, Sheen had been cut by his house
for cowardice. On the other, Joe Bevan, who of all men was
best able to judge, had told him that he was good enough to
box at Aldershot.

"Let me think it over, Sheen," he said. "This is a matter
which I cannot decide in a moment. I will tell you tomorrow
what I think about it."

"I hope you will let me go down, sir," said Sheen. "It's
my one chance."

"Yes, yes, I see that, I see that," said Mr Spence, "but
all the same—well, I will think it over."

All the rest of that evening he pondered over the matter,
deeply perplexed. It would be nothing less than cruel to let
Sheen enter the ring at Aldershot if he were incompetent.
Boxing in the Public Schools Boxing Competition is not
a pastime for the incompetent. But he wished very much
that Wrykyn should be represented, and also he sympathised
with Sheen's eagerness to wipe out the stain on his honour,
and the honour of the house. But, like Drummond, he could
not help harbouring a suspicion that this was a pose. He felt
that Sheen was intoxicated by his imagination. Every one
likes to picture himself doing dashing things in the limelight,
with an appreciative multitude to applaud. Would this
mood stand the test of action?

Against this there was the evidence of Joe Bevan. Joe had
said that Sheen was worthy to fight for his school, and Joe
knew.

Mr Spence went to bed still in a state of doubt.

Next morning he hit upon a solution of the difficulty.
Wandering in the grounds before school, he came upon
O'Hara, who, as has been stated before, had won the Light-
Weights at Aldershot in the previous year. He had come to

Wrykyn for the Sports. Here was the man to help him. O'Hara should put on the gloves with Sheen and report.

"I'm in rather a difficulty, O'Hara," he said, "and you can help me."

"What's that?" inquired O'Hara.

"You know both our light-weights are on the sick list? I had just resigned myself to going down to Aldershot without any one to box, when a boy in Seymour's volunteered for the vacant place. I don't know if you knew him at school? Sheen. Do you remember him?"

"Sheen?" cried O'Hara in amazement. "Not *Sheen*!"...

His recollections of Sheen were not conducive to a picture of him as a public-school boxer.

"Yes. I had never heard of him as a boxer. Still, he seems very anxious to go down, and he certainly has one remarkable testimonial, and as there's no one else—"

"And what shall I do?" asked O'Hara.

"I want you, if you will, to give him a trial in the dinner-hour. Just see if he's any good at all. If he isn't, of course, don't hit him about a great deal. But if he shows signs of being a useful man, extend him. See what he can do."

"Very well, sir," said O'Hara.

"And you might look in at my house at tea-time, if you have nothing better to do, and tell me what you think of him."

At five o'clock, when he entered Mr Spence's study, O'Hara's face wore the awe-struck look of one who had seen visions.

"Well?" said Mr Spence. "Did you find him any good?"

"Good?" said O'Hara. "He'll beat them all. He's a a champion. There's no stopping him."

"What an extraordinary thing! said Mr Spence.

XX

Sheen Goes to Aldershot

At Sheen's request Mr Spence made no announcement of the fact that Wrykyn would be represented in the Light-Weights. It would be time enough, Sheen felt, for the School to know that he was a boxer when he had been down and shown what he could do. His appearance in his new role would be the most surprising thing that had happened in the place for years, and it would be a painful anti-climax if, after all the excitement which would be caused by the discovery that he could use his hands, he were to be defeated in his first bout. Whereas, if he happened to win, the announcement of his victory would be all the more impressive, coming unexpectedly. To himself he did not admit the possibility of defeat. He had braced himself up for the ordeal, and he refused to acknowledge to himself that he might not come out of it well. Besides, Joe Bevan continued to express hopeful opinions.

"Just you keep your head, sir." he said, "and you'll win. Lots of these gentlemen, they're champions when they're practising, and you'd think nothing wouldn't stop them when they get into the ring. But they get wild directly they begin, and forget everything they've been taught, and where are they then? Why, on the floor, waiting for the referee to count them out."

This picture might have encouraged Sheen more if he had not reflected that he was just as likely to fall into this error as were his opponents.

"What you want to remember is to keep that guard up. Nothing can beat that. And push out your left straight. The straight left rules the boxing world. And be earnest about it. Be as friendly as you like afterwards, but while you're in the ring say to yourself, 'Well, it's you or me', and don't be too kind."

"I wish you could come down to second me, Joe," said Sheen.

"I'll have a jolly good try, sir," said Joe Bevan. "Let me see. You'll be going down the night before—I can't come down then, but I'll try and manage it by an early train on the day."

"How about Francis?"

"Oh, Francis can look after himself for one day. He's not the sort of boy to run wild if he's left alone for a few hours."

"Then you think you can manage it?"

"Yes, sir. If I'm not there for your first fight, I shall come in time to second you in the final."

"If I get there," said Sheen.

"Good seconding's half the battle. These soldiers they give you at Aldershot—well, they don't know the business, as the saying is. They don't look after their man, not like I could. I saw young what's-his-name, of Rugby—Stevens: he was beaten in the final by a gentleman from Harrow—I saw him fight there a couple of years ago. After the first round he was leading—not by much, but still, he was a point or two ahead. Well! He went to his corner and his seconds sent him up for the next round in the same state he'd got there in. They hadn't done a thing to him. Why, if I'd been in his corner I'd have taken him and sponged him and sent him up again as fresh as he could be. You must have a good second if you're to win. When you're all on top of your man, I don't say. But you get a young gentleman of your own class, just about as quick and strong as you are, and then you'll know where the seconding comes in."

"Then, for goodness' sake, don't make any mistake about coming down," said Sheen.

"I'll be there, sir," said Joe Bevan.

The Queen's Avenue Gymnasium at Aldershot is a roomy place, but it is always crowded on the Public Schools' Day. Sisters and cousins and aunts of competitors flock there to see Tommy or Bobby perform, under the impression, it is to be supposed, that he is about to take part in a pleasant frolic, a sort of merry parlour game. What their opinion is after he emerges from a warm three rounds is not known. Then there are soldiers in scores. Their views on boxing as a sport are crisp and easily defined. What they want is Gore. Others of the spectators are Old Boys, come to see how the school can behave in an emergency, and to find out whether there are still experts like Jones, who won the Middles in '96 or Robinson, who was runner-up in the Feathers in the same year; or whether, as they have darkly suspected for some time, the school has Gone To The Dogs Since They Left.

The usual crowd was gathered in the seats round the ring when Sheen came out of the dressing-room and sat down in an obscure corner at the end of the barrier which divides the gymnasium into two parts on these occasions. He felt very lonely. Mr Spence and the school instructor were watching the gymnastics, which had just started upon their lengthy course. The Wrykyn pair were not expected to figure high on the list this year. He could have joined Mr Spence, but, at the moment, he felt disinclined for conversation. If he had been a more enthusiastic cricketer, he would have recognised the feeling as that which attacks a batsman before he goes to the wicket. It is not precisely funk. It is rather a desire to accelerate the flight of Time, and get to business quickly. All things come to him who waits, and among them is that unpleasant sensation of a cold hand upon the portion of the body which lies behind the third waistcoat button.

The boxing had begun with a bout between two feather-weights, both obviously suffering from stage-fright. They were fighting in a scrambling and unscientific manner, which bore out Mr Bevan's statements on the subject of losing one's head. Sheen felt that both were capable of better things. In the second and third rounds this proved to be the case and the contest came to an end amidst applause.

The next pair were light-weights, and Sheen settled himself to watch more attentively. From these he would gather some indication of what he might expect to find when he entered the ring. He would not have to fight for some time yet. In the drawing for numbers, which had taken place in the dressing-room, he had picked a three. There would be another light-weight battle before he was called upon. His opponent was a Tonbridgian, who, from the glimpse Sheen caught of him, seemed muscular. But he (Sheen) had the advantage in reach, and built on that.

After opening tamely, the light-weight bout had become vigorous in the second round, and both men had apparently forgotten that their right arms had been given them by Nature for the purpose of guarding. They were going at it in hurricane fashion all over the ring. Sheen was horrified to feel symptoms of a return of that old sensation of panic which had caused him, on that dark day early in the term, to flee Albert and his wicked works. He set his teeth, and fought it down. And after a bad minute he was able to argue himself into a proper frame of mind again. After all, that sort of thing looked much worse than it really was. Half those blows, which seemed as if they must do tremendous damage, were probably hardly felt by their recipient. He told himself that Francis, and even the knife-and-boot boy, hit fully as hard, or harder, and he had never minded them. At the end of the contest he was once more looking forward to his entrance to the ring with proper fortitude.

The fighting was going briskly forward now, sometimes good, sometimes moderate, but always earnest, and he found himself contemplating, without undue excitement, the fact that at the end of the bout which had just begun, between middle-weights from St Paul's and Wellington, it would be his turn to perform. As luck would have it, he had not so long to wait as he had expected, for the Pauline, taking the lead after the first few exchanges, out-fought his man so completely that the referee stopped the contest in the second round. Sheen got up from his corner and went to the dressing-room. The Tonbridgian was already there. He took off his coat. Somebody crammed his hands into the gloves and from that moment the last trace of nervousness left him. He trembled with the excitement of the thing, and hoped sincerely that no one would notice it, and think that he was afraid.

Then, amidst a clapping of hands which sounded faint

and far-off, he followed his opponent to the ring, and ducked under the ropes.

The referee consulted a paper which he held, and announced the names.

"R. D. Sheen, Wrykyn College."

Sheen wriggled his fingers right into the gloves, and thought of Joe Bevan. What had Joe said? Keep that guard up. The straight left. Keep that guard—the straight left. Keep that—

"A. W. Bird, Tonbridge School."

There was a fresh outburst of applause. The Tonbridgian had shown up well in the competition of the previous year, and the crowd welcomed him as an old friend.

Keep that guard up—straight left. Straight left—guard up.

"Seconds out of the ring."

Guard up. Not too high. Straight left. It beats the world. What an age that man was calling Time. Guard up. Straight—

"Time," said the referee.

Sheen, filled with a great calm, walked out of his corner and shook hands with his opponent.

XXI

A Good Start

It was all over in half a minute.

The Tonbridgian was a two-handed fighter of the rushing type almost immediately after he had shaken hands. Sheen found himself against the ropes, blinking from a heavy hit between the eyes. Through the mist he saw his opponent sparring up to him, and as he hit he side-stepped. The next moment he was out in the middle again, with his man pressing him hard. There was a quick rally, and then Sheen swung his right at a venture. The blow had no conscious aim. It was purely speculative. But it succeeded. The Tonbridgian fell with a thud.

Sheen drew back. The thing seemed pathetic. He had braced himself up for a long fight, and it had ended in half a minute. His sensations were mixed. The fighting half of him was praying that his man would get up and start again. The prudent half realised that it was best that he should stay down. He had other fights before him before he could call that silver medal his own, and this would give him an invaluable start in the race. His rivals had all had to battle hard in their opening bouts.

The Tonbridgian's rigidity had given place to spasmodic efforts to rise. He got on one knee, and his gloved hand roamed feebly about in search of a hold. It was plain that he had shot his bolt. The referee signed to his seconds, who ducked into the ring and carried him to his corner. Sheen walked back to his own corner, and sat down. Presently the referee called out his name as the winner, and he went across the ring and shook hands with his opponent, who was now himself again.

He overheard snatches of conversation as he made his way through the crowd to the dressing-room.

"Useful boxer, that Wrykyn boy."

"Shortest fight I've seen here since Hopley won the Heavy-Weights."

"Fluke, do you think?"

"Don't know. Came to the same thing in the end, any-how. Caught him fair."

"Hard luck on that Tonbridge man. He's a good boxer, really. Did well here last year."

Then an outburst of hand-claps drowned the speakers' voices. A swarthy youth with the Ripton pink and green on his vest had pushed past him and was entering the ring. As he entered the dressing-room he heard the referee announcing the names. So that was the famous Peteiro! Sheen admitted to himself that he looked tough, and hurried into his coat and out of the dressing-room again so as to be in time to see how the Ripton terror shaped.

It was plainly not a one-sided encounter. Peteiro's opponent hailed from St Paul's, a school that has a habit of turning out boxers. At the end of the first round it seemed that honours were even. The great Peteiro had taken as much as he had given, and once had been uncompromisingly floored by the Pauline's left. But in the second round he began to gain points. For a boy of his weight he had a terrific hit with the right, and three applications of this to the ribs early in the round took much of the sting out of the Pauline's blows. He fought on with undiminished pluck, but the Riptonian was too strong for him, and the third round was a rout. To quote the *Sportsman* of the following day, "Peteiro crowded in a lot of work with both hands, and scored a popular victory".

Sheen looked thoughtful at the conclusion of the fight. There was no doubt that Drummond's antagonist of the previous year was formidable. Yet Sheen believed himself to be the cleverer of the two. At any rate, Peteiro had given no signs of possessing much cunning. To all appearances he was a tough, go-ahead fighter, with a right which would drill a hole in a steel plate. Had he sufficient skill to baffle his (Sheen's) strong tactics? If only Joe Bevan would come! With Joe in his corner to direct him, he would feel safe.

But of Joe up to the present there were no signs.

Mr Spence came and sat down beside him.

"Well, Sheen," he said, "so you won your first fight. Keep it up."

"I'll try, sir," said Sheen.

"What do you think of Peteiro?"

"I was just wondering, sir. He hits very hard."

"Very hard indeed."

"But he doesn't look as if he was very clever."

"Not a bit. Just a plain slogger. That's all. That's why Drummond beat him last year in the Feather-Weights. In strength there was no comparison, but Drummond was just too clever for him. You will be the same, Sheen."

"I hope so, sir," said Sheen.

After lunch the second act of the performance began. Sheen had to meet a boxer from Harrow who had drawn a bye in the first round of the competition. This proved a harder fight than his first encounter, but by virtue of a stout heart and a straight left he came through it successfully, and there was no doubt as to what the decision would be. Both judges voted for him.

Peteiro demolished a Radleian in his next fight.

By the middle of the afternoon there were three light-weights in the running— Sheen, Peteiro, and a boy from Clifton. Sheen drew the bye, and sparred in an outer room with a soldier, who was inclined to take the thing easily. Sheen, with the thought of the final in his mind, was only too ready to oblige him. They sparred an innocuous three rounds, and the man of war was kind enough to whisper in his ear as they left the room that he hoped he would win the final, and that he himself had a matter of one-and-sixpence with Old Spud Smith on his success.

"For I'm a man," said the amiable warrior confidentially,

"as knows Class when he sees it. You're Class, sir, that's what you are."

This, taken in conjunction with the fact that if the worst came to the worst he had, at any rate, won a medal by having got into the final, cheered Sheen. If only Joe Bevan had appeared he would have been perfectly contented.

But there were no signs of Joe.

A Good Finish

Final, Light-Weights," shouted the referee.

A murmur of interest from the ring-side chairs.

"R. D. Sheen, Wrykyn College."

Sheen got his full measure of applause this time. His victories in the preliminary bouts had won him favour with the spectators.

"J. Peteiro, Ripton School."

"Go it, Ripton!" cried a voice from near the door. The referee frowned in the direction of this audacious partisan, and expressed a hope that the audience would kindly refrain from comment during the rounds.

Then he turned to the ring again, and announced the names a second time.

"Sheen—Peteiro."

The Ripton man was sitting with a hand on each knee, listening to the advice of his school instructor, who had thrust head and shoulders through the ropes, and was busy impressing some point upon him. Sheen found himself noticing the most trivial things with extraordinary clearness. In the front row of the spectators sat a man with a parti-coloured tie. He wondered idly what tie it was. It was rather like one worn by members of Templar's house at Wrykyn. Why were the ropes of the ring red? He rather liked the colour. There was a man lighting a pipe. Would he blow out the match or extinguish it with a wave of the hand? What a beast Peteiro looked. He really was a nigger. He must look out for that right of his. The straight left. Push it out. Straight left ruled the boxing world. Where was Joe? He must have missed the train. Or perhaps he hadn't been able to get away. Why did he want to yawn, he wondered.

"Time!"

The Ripton man became suddenly active. He almost ran across the ring. A brief handshake, and he had penned Sheen up in his corner before he had time to leave it. It was evident what advice his instructor had been giving him. He meant to force the pace from the start.

The suddenness of it threw Sheen momentarily off his balance. He seemed to be in a whirl of blows. A sharp shock from behind. He had run up against the post. Despite everything, he remembered to keep his guard up, and stopped a lashing hit from his antagonist's left. But he was too late to keep out his right. In it came, full on the weakest spot on his left side. The pain of it caused him to double up for an instant, and as he did so his opponent upper-cut him. There was no rest for him. Nothing that he had ever experienced with the gloves on approached this. If only he could get out of this corner.

Then, almost unconsciously, he recalled Joe Bevan's advice.

"If a man's got you in a corner," Joe had said, "fall on him."

Peteiro made another savage swing. Sheen dodged it and hurled himself forward.

"Break away," said a dispassionate official voice.

Sheen broke away, but now he was out of the corner with the whole good, open ring to manoeuvre in.

He could just see the Ripton instructor signalling violently to his opponent, and, in reply to the signals, Peteiro came on again with another fierce rush.

But Sheen in the open was a different person from Sheen cooped up in a corner. Francis Hunt had taught him to use his feet. He side-stepped, and, turning quickly, found his man staggering past him, over-balanced by the force of his wasted blow. And now it was Sheen who attacked, and Peteiro who tried to escape. Two swift hits he got in before his opponent could face round, and another as he turned and rushed. Then for a while the battle raged without science all over the ring. Gradually, with a cold feeling of dismay, Sheen realised that his strength was going. The pace was too hot. He could not keep it up. His left counters were losing their force. Now he was merely pushing his glove into the Ripton man's face. It was not enough. The other was getting to close quarters, and that right of his seemed stronger than ever.

He was against the ropes now, gasping for breath, and Peteiro's right was thudding against his ribs. It could not last. He gathered all his strength and put it into a straight left. It took the Ripton man in the throat, and drove him back a step. He came on again. Again Sheen stopped him.

It was his last effort. He could do no more. Everything seemed black to him. He leaned against the ropes and drank in the air in great gulps.

"Time!" said the referee.

The word was lost in the shouts that rose from the packed seats.

Sheen tottered to his corner and sat down.

"Keep it up, sir, keep it up," said a voice. "Bear't that the opposèd may beware of thee. Don't forget the guard. And the straight left beats the world."

It was Joe—at the eleventh hour.

With a delicious feeling of content Sheen leaned back in his chair. It would be all right now. He felt that the matter had been taken out of his hands. A more experienced brain than his would look after the generalship of the fight.

As the moments of the half-minute's rest slid away he discovered the truth of Joe's remarks on the value of a good second. In his other fights the flapping of the towel had hardly stirred the hair on his forehead. Joe's energetic arms set a perfect gale blowing. The cool air revived him. He opened his mouth and drank it in. A spongeful of cold water completed the cure. Long before the call of Time he was ready for the next round.

"Keep away from him, sir," said Joe, "and score with that left of yours. Don't try the right yet. Keep it for guarding. Box clever. Don't let him corner you. Slip him when he rushes. Cool and steady does it. Don't aim at his face too much. Go down below. That's the *de*-partment. And use your feet. Get about quick, and you'll find he don't like that.

Hullo, says he, I can't touch him. Then, when he's tired, go in."

The pupil nodded with closed eyes.

While these words of wisdom were proceeding from the mouth of Mr Bevan, another conversation was taking place which would have interested Sheen if he could have heard it. Mr Spence and the school instructor were watching the final from the seats under the side windows.

"It's extraordinary," said Mr Spence. "The boy's wonderfully good for the short time he has been learning. You ought to be proud of your pupil."

"Sir?"

"I was saying that Sheen does you credit."

"Not me, sir."

"What! He told me he had been taking lessons. Didn't you teach him?"

"Never set eyes on him, till this moment. Wish I had, sir. He's the sort of pupil I could wish for."

Mr Spence bent forward and scanned the features of the man who was attending the Wrykinian.

"Why," he said, "surely that's Bevan—Joe Bevan! I knew him at Cambridge."

"Yes, sir, that's Bevan," replied the instructor. "He teaches boxing at Wrykyn now, sir."

"At Wrykyn—where?"

"Up the river—at the 'Blue Boar', sir," said the instructor, quite innocently—for it did not occur to him that this simple little bit of information was just so much incriminating evidence against Sheen.

Mr Spence said nothing, but he opened his eyes very wide. Recalling his recent conversation with Sheen, he remembered that the boy had told him he had been taking lessons, and also that Joe Bevan, the ex-pugilist, had expressed a high opinion of his work. Mr Spence had imagined that Bevan had been a chance spectator of the boy's skill; but it would now seem that Bevan himself had taught Sheen. This matter, decided Mr Spence, must be looked into, for it was palpable that Sheen had broken bounds in order to attend Bevan's boxing-saloon up the river.

For the present, however, Mr Spence was content to say nothing.

Sheen came up for the second round fresh and confident. His head was clear, and his breath no longer came in gasps. There was to be no rallying this time. He had had the worst of the first round, and meant to make up his lost points.

Peteiro, losing no time, dashed in. Sheen met him with a left in the face, and gave way a foot. Again Peteiro rushed, and again he was stopped. As he bored in for the third time Sheen slipped him. The Ripton man paused, and dropped his guard for a moment.

Sheen's left shot out once more, and found its mark. Peteiro swung his right viciously, but without effect. Another swift counter added one more point to Sheen's score.

Sheen nearly chuckled. It was all so beautifully simple. What a fool he had been to mix it up in the first round. If he only kept his head and stuck to out-fighting he could win with ease. The man couldn't box. He was nothing more than a slogger. Here he came, as usual, with the old familiar rush. Out went his left. But it missed its billet. Peteiro had checked his rush after the first movement, and now he came in with both hands. It was the first time during the round that he had got to close quarters, and he made the most of it. Sheen's blows were as frequent, but his were harder. He drove at the body, right and left; and once again the call of Time extricated Sheen from an awkward position. As far as points were concerned he had had the best of the round, but he was very sore and bruised. His left side was one dull ache.

"Keep away from him, sir," said Joe Bevan. "You were ahead on that round. Keep away all the time unless he gets tired. But if you see me signalling, then go in all you can and have a fight."

There was a suspicion of weariness about the look of the Ripton champion as he shook hands for the last round. He was beginning to feel the effects of his hurricane fighting in the opening rounds. He began quietly, sparring for an opening. Sheen led with his left. Peteiro was too late with his guard. Sheen tried again—a double lead. His opponent guarded the first blow, but the second went home heavily on the body, and he gave way a step.

Then from the corner of his eye Sheen saw Bevan gesticulating wildly, so, taking his life in his hands, he abandoned his waiting game, dropped his guard, and dashed in to fight. Peteiro met him doggedly. For a few moments the exchanges were even. Then suddenly the Riptonian's blows began to weaken. He got home his right on the head, and Sheen hardly felt it. And in a flash there came to him the glorious certainty that the game was his.

He was winning—winning—winning.

"That's enough," said the referee.

The Ripton man was leaning against the ropes, utterly spent, at almost the same spot where Sheen had leaned at the end of the first round. The last attack had finished him. His seconds helped him to his corner.

The referee waved his hand.

"Sheen wins," he said.

And that was the greatest moment of his life.

XXIII

A Surprise for Seymour's

Seymour's house took in one copy of the *Sportsman* daily. On the morning after the Aldershot competition Linton met the paper-boy at the door on his return from the fives courts, where he had been playing a couple of before-breakfast games with Dunstable. He relieved him of the house copy, and opened it to see how the Wrykyn pair had performed in the gymnastics. He did not expect anything great, having a rooted contempt for both experts, who were small and, except in the gymnasium, obscure. Indeed, he had gone so far on the previous day as to express a hope that Biddle, the more despicable of the two, would fall off the horizontal bar and break his neck. Still he might as well see where they had come out. After all, with all their faults, they were human beings like himself, and Wrykinians.

The competition was reported in the Boxing column. The first thing that caught his eye was the name of the school among the headlines. "Honours", said the headline, "for St Paul's, Harrow, and Wrykyn".

"Hullo," said Linton, "what's all this?"

Then the thing came on him with nothing to soften the shock. He had folded the paper, and the last words on the half uppermost were, *"Final. Sheen beat Peteiro"*.

Linton had often read novels in which some important document "swam before the eyes" of the hero or the heroine; but he had never understood the full meaning of the phrase until he read those words, "Sheen beat Peteiro".

There was no mistake about it. There the thing was. It was impossible for the *Sportsman* to have been hoaxed. No, the incredible, outrageous fact must be faced. Sheen had been down to Aldershot and won a silver medal! Sheen!

Sheen!! Sheen who had—who was—well, who, in a word, was SHEEN!!!

Linton read on like one in a dream.

"The Light-Weights fell," said the writer, "to a newcomer Sheen, of Wrykyn" (Sheen!), "a clever youngster with a strong defence and a beautiful straight left, doubtless the result of tuition from the middle-weight ex-champion, Joe Bevan, who was in his corner for the final bout. None of his opponents gave him much trouble except Peteiro of Ripton, whom he met in the final. A very game and determined fight was seen when these two met, but Sheen's skill and condition discounted the rushing tactics of his adversary, and in the last minute of the third round the referee stopped the encounter." (Game and determined! Sheen!!) "Sympathy was freely expressed for Peteiro, who has thus been runner-up two years in succession. He, however, met a better man, and paid the penalty. The admirable pluck with which Sheen bore his punishment and gradually wore his man down made his victory the most popular of the day's programme."

Well!

Details of the fighting described Sheen as "cutting out the work", "popping in several nice lefts", "swinging his right for the point", and executing numerous other incredible manoeuvres.

Sheen!

You caught the name correctly? SHEEN, I'll trouble you.

Linton stared blankly across the school grounds. Then he burst into a sudden yell of laughter.

On that very morning the senior day-room was going to court-martial Sheen for disgracing the house. The resolution had been passed on the previous afternoon, probably just as he was putting the finishing touches to the "most popular victory of the day's programme". "This," said Linton, "is rich."

He grubbed a little hole in one of Mr Seymour's flower-beds, and laid the *Sportsman* to rest in it. The news would be about the school at nine o'clock, but if he could keep it from the senior day-room till the brief interval between breakfast and school, all would be well, and he would have the pure pleasure of seeing that backbone of the house make a complete ass of itself. A thought struck him. He unearthed the *Sportsman*, and put it in his pocket.

He strolled into the senior day-room after breakfast.

"Any one seen the *Sporter* this morning?" he inquired.

No one had seen it.

"The thing hasn't come," said some one.

"Good!" said Linton to himself.

At this point Stanning strolled into the room. "I'm a witness," he said, in answer to Linton's look of inquiry. "We're doing this thing in style. I depose that I saw the prisoner cutting off on the—whatever day it was, when he ought to have been saving our lives from the fury of the mob. Hadn't somebody better bring the prisoner into the dock?"

"I'll go," said Linton promptly. "I may be a little time, but don't get worried. I'll bring him all right."

He went upstairs to Sheen's study, feeling like an *impresario* about to produce a new play which is sure to create a sensation.

Sheen was in. There was a ridge of purple under his left eye, but he was otherwise intact.

" 'Gratulate you, Sheen," said Linton.

For an instant Sheen hesitated. He had rehearsed this kind of scene in his mind, and sometimes he saw himself playing a genial, forgiving, let's-say-no-more-about-it-we-all-make-mistakes-but-in-future! role, sometimes being cold haughty, and distant, and repelling friendly advances with icy disdain. If anybody but Linton had been the first to congratulate him he might have decided on this second line of action. But he liked Linton, and wanted to be friendly with him.

"Thanks," he said.

Linton sat down on the table and burst into a torrent of speech.

"You *are* a man! What did you want to do it for? Where the dickens did you learn to box? And why on earth, if you can win silver medals at Aldershot, didn't you box for the house and smash up that sidey ass Stanning? I say, look here, I suppose we haven't been making idiots of ourselves all the time, have we?"

"I shouldn't wonder," said Sheen. "How?"

"I mean, you did— What I mean to say is— Oh, hang it, *you* know! You did cut off when we had that row in the town, didn't you?"

"Yes," said Sheen, "I did."

With that medal in his pocket it cost him no effort to make the confession.

"I'm glad of that. I mean, I'm glad we haven't been such fools as we might have been. You see, we only had Stannings word to go on."

Sheen started.

"Stanning!" he said. "What do you mean?"

"He was the chap who started the story. Didn't you know? He told everybody."

"I thought it was Drummond," said Sheen blankly. "You remember meeting me outside his study the day after? I thought he told you then."

"Drummond! Not a bit of it. He swore you hadn't been with him at all. He was as sick as anything when I said I thought I'd seen you with him."

"I—" Sheen stopped. "I wish I'd known," he concluded. Then, after a pause, "So it was Stanning!"

"Yes,—conceited beast. Oh. I say."

"Um?"

"I see it all now. Joe Bevan taught you to box."

"Yes."

"Then that's how you came to be at the 'Blue Boar' that day. He's the Bevan who runs it."

"That's his brother. He's got a gymnasium up at the top. I used to go there every day."

"But I say, Great Scott, what are you going to do about that?"

"How do you mean?"

"Why, Spence is sure to ask you who taught you to box. He must know you didn't learn with the instructor. Then it'll all come out, and you'll get dropped on for going up the river and going to the pub."

"Perhaps he won't ask," said Sheen.

"Hope not. Oh, by the way—"

"What's up?"

"Just remembered what I came up for. It's an awful rag. The senior day-room are going to court-martial you."

"Court-martial me!"

"For funking. They don't know about Aldershot, not a word. I bagged the *Sportsman* early, and hid it. They are going to get the surprise of their lifetime. I said I'd come up and fetch you."

"I shan't go." said Sheen.

Linton looked alarmed.

"Oh, but I say, you must. Don't spoil the thing. Can't you see what a rag it'll be?"

"I'm not going to sweat downstairs for the benefit of the senior day-room."

"I say," said Linton, "Stanning's there."

"What!"

"He's a witness," said Linton, grinning.

Sheen got up.

"Come on," he said.

Linton came on.

Down in the senior day-room the court was patiently awaiting the prisoner. Eager anticipation was stamped on its expressive features.

"Beastly time he is," said Clayton. Clayton was acting as president.

"We shall have to buck up," said Stanning. "Hullo, here he is at last. Come in, Linton."

"I was going to," said Linton, "but thanks all the same. Come along, Sheen."

"Shut that door, Linton," said Stanning from his seat on the table.

"All right, Stanning," said Linton. "Anything to oblige. Shall I bring up a chair for you to rest your feet on?"

"Forge ahead, Clayton," said Stanning to the president.

The president opened the court-martial in unofficial phraseology.

"Look here, Sheen," he said, "we've come to the conclusion that this has got a bit too thick."

"You mustn't talk in that chatty way, Clayton," interrupted Linton. " 'Prisoner at the bar's' the right expression to use. Why don't you let somebody else have a look in? You're the rottenest president of a court-martial I ever saw."

"Don't rag, Linton," said Clayton, with an austere frown. "This is serious."

"Glad you told me," said Linton. "Go on."

"Can't you sit down, Linton!" said Stanning.

"I was only waiting for leave. Thanks. You were saying something, Clayton. It sounded pretty average rot, but you'd better unburden your soul."

The president resumed.

"We want to know if you've anything to say—"

"You don't give him a chance," said Linton. "You bag the conversation so."

"—about disgracing the house."

"By getting the Gotford, you know, Sheen," explained Linton. "Clayton thinks that work's a bad habit, and ought to be discouraged."

Clayton glared, and looked at Stanning. He was not equal to the task of tackling Linton himself.

Stanning interposed.

"Don't rot, Linton. We haven't much time as it is."

"Sorry," said Linton.

"You've let the house down awfully," said Clayton.

"Yes?" said Sheen.

Linton took the paper out of his pocket, and smoothed it out.

"Seen the *Sporter*?" he asked casually. His neighbour grabbed at it.

"I thought it hadn't come," he said.

"Good account of Aldershot," said Linton.

He leaned back in his chair as two or three of the senior day-room collected round the *Sportsman*.

"Hullo! We won the gym.!"

"Rot! Let's have a look!"

This tremendous announcement quite eclipsed the court-martial as an object of popular interest. The senior day-room surged round the holder of the paper.

"Give us a chance," he protested.

"We can't have. Where is it? Biddle and Smith are simply hopeless. How the dickens can they have got the shield?"

"What a goat you are!" said a voice reproachfully to the possessor of the paper. "Look at this. It says Cheltenham got it. And here we are—seventeenth. Fat lot of shield we've won."

"Then what the deuce does this mean? 'Honours for St Paul's, Harrow, and Wrykyn'."

"Perhaps it refers to the boxing," suggested Linton.

"But we didn't send any one up. Look here. Harrow won the Heavies. St Paul's got the Middles. *Hullo!*"

"Great Scott!" said the senior day-room.

There was a blank silence. Linton whistled softly to himself.

The gaze of the senior day-room was concentrated on that ridge of purple beneath Sheen's left eye.

Clayton was the first to speak. For some time he had been waiting for sufficient silence to enable him to proceed with his presidential duties. He addressed himself to Sheen.

"Look here, Sheen," he said, "we want to know what you've got to say for yourself. You go disgracing the house—"

The stunned senior day-room were roused to speech.

"Oh, chuck it, Clayton."

"Don't be a fool, Clayton."

"Silly idiot!"

Clayton looked round in pained surprise at this sudden withdrawal of popular support.

"You'd better be polite to Sheen," said Linton; "he won the Light-Weights at Aldershot yesterday."

The silence once more became strained

"Well," said Sheen, "weren't you going to court-martial

me, or something? Clayton, weren't you saying something?"

Clayton started. He had not yet grasped the situation entirely; but he realised dimly that by some miracle Sheen had turned in an instant into a most formidable person.

"Er—no," he said. "No, nothing."

"The thing seems to have fallen through, Sheen," said Linton. "Great pity. Started so well, too. Clayton always makes a mess of things."

"Then I'd just like to say one thing," said Sheen.

Respectful attention from the senior day-room.

"I only want to know why you can't manage things of this sort by yourselves, without dragging in men from other houses."

"Especially men like Stanning," said Linton. "The same thing occurred to me. It's lucky Drummond wasn't here. Remember the last time, you chaps?"

The chaps did. Stanning became an object of critical interest. After all, who *was* Stanning? What right had he to come and sit on tables in Seymour's and interfere with the affairs of the house?

The allusion to "last time" was lost upon Sheen, but he saw that it had not improved Stanning's position with the spectators.

He opened the door.

"Good bye, Stanning," he said.

"If I hadn't hurt my wrist—" Stanning began.

"Hurt your wrist!" said Sheen. "You got a bad attack of Peteiro. That was what was the matter with you."

"You think that every one's a funk like yourself," said Stanning.

"Pity they aren't," said Linton; "we should do rather well down at Aldershot. And he wasn't such a terror after all, Sheen, was he? You beat him in two and a half rounds, didn't you? Think what Stanning might have done if only he hadn't sprained his poor wrist just in time.

"Look here, Linton—"

"Some are born with sprained wrists," continued the speaker, "some achieve sprained wrists—like Stanning—"

Stanning took a step towards him.

"Don't forget you've a sprained wrist," said Linton.

"Come on, Stanning," said Sheen, who was still holding the door open, "you'll be much more comfortable in your own house. I'll show you out."

"I suppose," said Stanning in the passage, "you think you've scored off me."

"That," said Sheen pleasantly, "is rather the idea. Good bye."

XXIV

Bruce Explains

Mr Spence was a master with a great deal of sympathy and a highly developed sense of duty. It was the combination of these two qualities which made it so difficult for him to determine on a suitable course of action in relation to Sheen's out-of-bounds exploits. As a private individual he had nothing but admiration for the sporting way in which Sheen had fought his up-hill fight. He felt that he himself in similar circumstances would have broken any number of school rules. But, as a master, it was his duty, he considered, to report him. If a master ignored a breach of rules in one case, with which he happened to sympathise, he would in common fairness be compelled to overlook a similar breach of rules in other cases, even if he did not sympathise with them. In which event he would be of small use as a master.

On the other hand, Sheen's case was so exceptional that he might very well compromise to a certain extent between the claims of sympathy and those of duty. If he were to go to the headmaster and state baldly that Sheen had been in the habit for the last half-term of visiting an up-river public-house, the headmaster would get an entirely wrong idea of the matter, and suspect all sorts of things which had no existence in fact. When a boy is accused of frequenting a public-house, the head-magisterial mind leaps naturally to Stale Fumes and the Drunken Stagger.

So Mr Spence decided on a compromise. He sent for Sheen, and having congratulated him warmly on his victory in the Light-Weights, proceeded as follows :

"You have given me to understand, Sheen, that you were taught boxing by Bevan?"

"Yes, sir."

"At the 'Blue Boar'?"

"Yes, sir."

"This puts me in a rather difficult position, Sheen. Much as I dislike doing it, I am afraid I shall have to report this matter to the headmaster."

Sheen said he supposed so. He saw Mr Spence's point.

"But I shall not mention the 'Blue Boar'. If I did, the headmaster might get quite the wrong impression. He would not understand all the circumstances. So I shall simply mention that you broke bounds by going up the river. I shall tell him the whole story, you understand, and it's quite possible that you will hear no more of the affair. I'm sure I hope so. But you understand my position?"

"Yes, sir."

"That's all, then, Sheen. Oh, by the way, you wouldn't care for a game of fives before breakfast tomorrow, I suppose?"

"I should like it, sir."

"Not too stiff?"

"No, sir."

"Very well, then. I'll be there by a quarter-past seven."

Jack Bruce was waiting to see the headmaster in his study at the end of afternoon school.

"Well, Bruce," said the headmaster, coming into the room and laying down some books on the table, "do you want to speak to me? Will you give your father my congratulations on his victory. I shall be writing to him tonight. I see from the paper that the polling was very even. Apparently one or two voters arrived at the last moment and turned the scale."

"Yes, sir."

"It is a most gratifying result. I am sure that, apart from our political views, we should all have been disappointed if your father had not won. Please congratulate him sincerely."

"Yes, sir."

"Well, Bruce, and what was it that you wished to see me about?"

Bruce was about to reply when the door opened, and Mr Spence came in.

"One moment, Bruce," said the headmaster. "Yes, Spence?"

Mr Spence made his report clearly and concisely. Bruce listened with interest. He thought it hardly playing the game for the gymnasium master to hand Sheen over to be executed at the very moment when the school was shaking hands with itself over the one decent thing that had been done for it in the course of the athletic year; but he told himself philosophically that he supposed masters had to do these things. Then he noticed with some surprise that Mr Spence was putting the matter in a very favourable light for the accused. He was avoiding with some care any mention of the "Blue Boar". When he had occasion to refer to the scene of Sheen's training, he mentioned it vaguely as a house.

"This man Bevan, who is an excellent fellow and a personal friend of my own, has a house some way up the river."

Of course a public-house *is* a house.

"Up the river," said the headmaster meditatively.

It seemed that that was all that was wrong. The prosecution centred round that point, and no other. Jack Bruce, as he listened, saw his way of coping with the situation.

"Thank you, Spence," said the headmaster at the conclusion of the narrative. "I quite understand that Sheen's conduct was very excusable. But—I distinctly said—I placed the upper river out of bounds . . . Well, I will see Sheen, and speak to him. I will speak to him."

Mr Spence left the room.

"Please sir—" said Jack Bruce.

"Ah, Bruce. I am afraid I have kept you some little time. Yes?

"I couldn't help hearing what Mr Spence was saying to you about Sheen, sir. I don't think he knows quite what really happened."

"You mean—?"

"Sheen went there by road. I used to take him in my motor."

"Your—! What did you say, Bruce?"

"My motor-car, sir. That's to say, my father's. We used to go together every day."

"I am glad to hear it. I am glad. Then I need say nothing to Sheen after all. I am glad . . . But—er—Bruce," proceeded the headmaster after a pause.

"Yes, sir?"

"Do you—are you in the habit of driving a motor-car frequently?"

"Every day, sir. You see, I am going to take up motors when I leave school, so it's all education."

The headmaster was silent. To him the word "Education" meant Classics. There was a Modern side at Wrykyn, and an Engineering side, and also a Science side; but in his heart he recognised but one Education—the Classics. Nothing that he had heard, nothing that he had read in the papers and the monthly reviews had brought home to him the spirit of the age and the fact that Things were not as they used to be so clearly as this one remark of Jack Bruce's. For here was Bruce admitting that in his spare time he drove motors. And, stranger still, that he did it not as a wild frolic but seriously, with a view to his future career.

"The old order changeth," thought the headmaster a little sadly.

Then he brought himself back from his mental plunge into the future.

"Well, well, Bruce," he said, "we need not discuss the merits and demerits of driving motor-cars, need we? What did you wish to see me about?"

"I came to ask if I might get off morning school tomorrow, sir. Those voters who got to the poll just in time and settled the election—I brought them down in the car. And the policeman—he's a Radical, and voted for Pedder—Mr Pedder—has sworn—says I was exceeding the speed-limit."

The headmaster pressed a hand to his forehead, and his mind swam into the future.

"Well, Bruce?" he said at length, in the voice of one whom nothing can surprise now.

"He says I was going twenty-eight miles an hour. And if I can get to the Court tomorrow morning I can prove that I wasn't. I brought them to the poll in the little runabout."

"And the —er—little runabout," said the headmaster, "does not travel at twenty-eight miles an hour?"

"No, sir. It can't go more than twenty at the outside."

"Very well, Bruce, you need not come to school tomorrow morning."

"Thank you, sir."

The headmaster stood thinking . . . The new order . . .

"Bruce," he said.

"Yes, sir?"

"Tell me, do I look very old?"

Bruce stared.

"Do I look three hundred years old?"

"No, sir," said Bruce, with the stolid wariness of the boy who fears that a master is subtly chaffing him.

"I feel more, Bruce," said the headmaster, with a smile. "I feel more. You will remember to congratulate your father for me, won't you?"

Outside the door Jack Bruce paused in deep reflection. "Rum!" he said to himself. "Jolly rum!"

On the senior gravel he met Sheen.

"Hullo, Sheen," he said, "what are you going to do?"

"Drummond wants me to tea with him in the infirmary."

"It's all right, then?"

"Yes. I got a note from him during afternoon school. You coming?"

"All right. I say, Sheen, the Old Man's rather rum sometimes, isn't he?"

"What's he been doing now?"

"Oh—nothing. How do you feel after Aldershot? Tell us all about it. I've not heard a word yet."